POLDARK

The Complete Scripts

Series 2

DEBBIE HORSFIELD

MACMILLAN

First published 2016 by Macmillan
an imprint of Pan Macmillan
20 New Wharf Road, London N1 9RR
Associated companies throughout the world
www.panmacmillan.com

ISBN 978-1-5098-1467-1

1 3 5 7 9 8 6 4 2

A CIP catalogue record for this book is available from the British Library.

Typeset by Ellipsis Digital Limited, Glasgow
Printed and bound by CPI Group (UK) Ltd, Croydon, CR0 4YY

Visit www.panmacmillan.com to read more about all our books
and to buy them. You will also find features, author interviews and
news of any author events, and you can sign up for e-newsletters
so that you're always first to hear about our new releases.

POLDARK

The Complete Scripts
Series 2

Foreword

The terrific response to series one of *Poldark* was something which took all of us by surprise and everyone involved in the production is hugely grateful for the continued enthusiasm and support of our fans in the run-up to series two. In the intervening period, I was fortunate enough to be invited to various literary festivals where I had the pleasure of meeting many fans of the show. One of the most pleasing aspects of the show's success has been the way in which it has introduced so many people to Winston Graham's glorious books. However, I also met a great many fans who were keen to understand much more about the production process of the series and also my own journey as a writer in both adapting the material and seeing the scripts brought to the screen. Therefore, with this second collection, we have decided to take a slightly different approach, and one which highlights the many changes which take place between writing, shooting and then editing the show. One example in the first episode shows how the number of days over which the story is told changed during the shoot and again in the edit.

Television production is a far more collaborative process than the writing of a novel as it involves so many more people, all wonderfully talented in their own right and each with their own specific role. Each stage of production requires an incredible amount of work from all involved, with the script continuing to evolve throughout that process. A screenplay is as much a working document as it is a piece of literature and I hope that this latest collection shows how much that can evolve.

Poldark is an epic world, populated with a wealth of characters and stories. Adapting this to series television often means that some elements and details are lost or moved, whilst others grow into something new. This is also how each stage of the scripting progresses. The script really has three lives: the development stage, where we find our stories and begin to hone them; the shooting stage, where the script is often adapted and finessed, based on the demands of locations, time and money; and finally in the edit, where we finalize the script and restructure around those organic changes that have occurred throughout the process.

The scripts in this volume represent the final shooting scripts and the culmination of their evolution through development and production, embodying the responses to various creative decisions and production hurdles. The versions seen on screen reveal the last stage in the progression of each episode, one where the fine tuning no longer happens on the page, and you will be able to see for yourself where the edit changed them again!

DEBBIE HORSFIELD

POLDARK

The Complete Scripts
Series 2

A LIST OF TV SCRIPT ABBREVIATIONS

CU	*close up*
EXT	*exterior*
GV	*general views*
INT	*interior*
OS	*off screen*
POV	*point of view*
VO	*voice-over*

Episode 1

1: EXT. CLIFF-TOP PATHWAY – DAY 1

Spectacular panoramic views of Cornish coastline. We pick out a distant figure who is being marched along a cliff-top path by a sergeant and a group of soldiers. As we get closer we see that the prisoner is Ross. A rumble of distant thunder. Dark storm clouds are gathering on the horizon.

CUT TO:

2: EXT. OPEN COUNTRYSIDE – DAY 1

Demelza walks home, tearful, not yet knowing if Ross is lost to her for ever.

CUT TO:

3: INT. PANELLED ROOM – DAY 1

A court has been hastily convened. Two magistrates, clearly called at short notice, are hastily pulling on their robes, muttering to each other: 'Utter waste of time', 'Of course he'll be released', 'A man of his standing?', 'Recently bereaved?' Ross glances at the two magistrates. They both nod sympathetically. He bows his acknowledgement. Things are looking up. Until the presiding magistrate comes in: it's the Reverend Dr Halse. Ross's face falls.

CUT TO:

4: INT. PANELLED ROOM – DAY 1

The Reverend Dr Halse eyeballs Ross. He can't believe his luck!

REVEREND DR HALSE It is alleged that you roused the neighbourhood and led a bloodthirsty mob down to the beach.

ROSS Incorrect.

REVEREND DR HALSE Which part?

ROSS They were not thirsty for blood. They were starving for food.

REVEREND DR HALSE Did you direct them to the shipwreck?

ROSS They needed no directing. They knew the way as well as I.

REVEREND DR HALSE Did you encourage the riot which broke out on the beach?

ROSS I did not consider it a riot.

REVEREND DR HALSE Do you approve of plunder and lawlessness?

ROSS Do you approve of whole families being without sufficient food to keep them alive?

REVEREND DR HALSE What part did you play in the death of Matthew Sanson?

ROSS Regrettably none whatsoever.

The two sympathetic magistrates look at Ross in despair at this comment. Reverend Dr Halse seems delighted that Ross is condemned out of his own mouth.

REVEREND DR HALSE Enough of this insolence. Ross Vennor Poldark, I am committing you for trial at the Bodmin assizes. Bail will be set at one hundred pounds.

A glance between Ross and the two sympathetic magistrates. A sugges-
tion that they themselves will provide the bail money. A nod of
acknowledgement from Ross – which is not seen by Halse.

REVEREND DR HALSE *(cont'd)* May God have mercy upon
you – for I most assuredly would not.

5: INT. NAMPARA HOUSE, ROSS & DEMELZA'S BEDROOM – NIGHT 1

Silence. Demelza alone, scared, wondering where Ross is. Outside the
screech of an owl. Her eye is drawn to Julia's empty crib. She takes a
rose from a vase, breaks it into petals, scatters the petals across Julia's
crib. Downstairs a door slams, then the sound of footsteps running
upstairs. Ross comes in. He looks exhausted. Demelza runs into his
arms.

DEMELZA They let you go! I knew they would! Did they dismiss all the charges?

ROSS Not quite. *(trying to be matter-of-fact)* I'm to be tried by
Justice Lister – at the Bodmin assizes – in five days' time. I
must present myself at the jail the night before—

DEMELZA *(aghast)* Like – a proper trial? 'Fore judge and
jury? But if you're found guilty—? Ross, you could hang! Dear
God, how has it come to this?

ROSS George? *(then, trying to downplay it)* The entire thing is a
nonsense. I'll be back before you know I've gone!

DEMELZA I'll come with you—

ROSS No, wait for me here. God knows, you've had enough
to endure of late.

Involuntarily they both glance at Julia's empty crib. Demelza reaches
for his hand.

CUT TO:

6: EXT. AUTUMN MONTAGE – DAY

Time passing. Autumn leaves; berries on hedgerows; apples ripening; cobwebs hung with dew on misty morning, etc.

CUT TO:

7: EXT. HENDRAWNA BEACH – DAY 2

Ross and Demelza walk along the beach in the direction of the mine. A distant rumble of thunder is heard.

ROSS There's a storm coming.

DEMELZA Julia's afeared o' thunder. *(then, correcting herself)* I keep thinkin' she's still here – that if I jus' call her name—

Her eyes fill with tears. Ross brushes them away gently. She smiles gratefully.

DEMELZA *(cont'd)* I'll be better – by an' by.

ROSS That's what I tell myself – every day. And every day I fail.

A look between them. Julia's death is still raw for both of them. Then:

DEMELZA We must think o' th' trial.

ROSS Must we?

DEMELZA 'Tis no little thing, Ross. 'Tis a proper trial – not just a magistrate. You must answer to a judge and jury. An' if you're found guilty—

ROSS They cannot hang me! I've too much to do!

DEMELZA But truly, Ross—

ROSS Truly, Demelza, I decline to be distracted by matters beyond my control! Give me leave to attend on something I *can* influence.

And up ahead looms Wheal Leisure.

CUT TO:

8: EXT. WHEAL LEISURE – DAY 2

Ross and Demelza are greeted by Zacky. Paul and other miners are waiting for the shift to commence. Women and Beth Daniel are processing ore. Dwight is treating a line of patients. Ross is already heading for the mine entrance.

ROSS (*to Paul & co.*) Gentlemen? What are we waiting for? I leave for Bodmin in three days!

ZACKY An' no doubt ye aim to strike a new lode before ye go?

ROSS Three at least! So let's get down there!

He greets Paul and the other miners and they all head for the mine entrance. Zacky shakes his head and smiles at Demelza.

ZACKY New lode? He'll be lucky!

DEMELZA He don' believe in luck.

ZACKY Or facing facts? The old Trebartha lode's near petered out – but he won't have it.

DEMELZA No more 'n he will this trial! To hear him, you'd think he was headin' f' Michaelmas Fair!

A moment of understanding and commiseration between them. Then Zacky heads for the mine and Dwight, who has just finished with his patients, arrives.

DWIGHT He cannot just bury his head.

DEMELZA Will you tell him? 'Tis almost upon him and how will he defend himself? Who will speak for him?

DWIGHT I will.

DEMELZA *(heartened)* You will?

DWIGHT But there must be others. And plenty of them. The Crown will already have assembled its case.

DEMELZA An' no doubt there'll be plenty who'll be glad t' help it.

CUT TO:

9: EXT. WARLEGGAN HOUSE – DAY 2

George is shaking hands with Tankard.

GEORGE Can I rely on you, Tankard?

TANKARD Always happy to be of service.

Tankard now departs. Cary comes up behind George.

CARY Why is our attorney here?

GEORGE My attorney. He's been assisting the Crown to 'strengthen its case'.

CARY Wrecking? Riot? Attacking a customs official? Are these not enough?

GEORGE I wanted Murder.

CARY And I told you that charge would not stick.

George seems frustrated to hear this.

CARY *(cont'd)* Cousin Matthew was dead before he was washed ashore. Poldark merely found him—

GEORGE And left him lifeless on the strand—

CARY Which is not a crime—

GEORGE But it is a personal affront to this family. And one which I intend to make him regret.

CUT TO:

10: INT. WHEAL LEISURE, TUNNEL – DAY 2

Ross is hard at work. Zacky and Paul, both stripped to the waist, are working beside him. Zacky and Paul exchange a glance. The suggestion is that both fear Ross is flogging a dead horse but neither wants to be the one to pour cold water on his efforts.

CUT TO:

11: INT. TRENWITH HOUSE, GREAT HALL – DAY 2

Aunt Agatha and Elizabeth are having supper. Francis is pacing.

FRANCIS He should never have been charged. This is Cornwall! He's a gentleman – and a Poldark!

AUNT AGATHA And his own worst enemy?

Elizabeth and Francis exchange a glance. They can't deny the truth of what she's said.

FRANCIS I would speak to him, but he avoids me—

ELIZABETH He avoids us all. Since they lost Julia—

FRANCIS Something must be done or he'll walk his head into the noose.

AUNT AGATHA Or that new contraption they have in France?

She brings her knife down sharply on a fig. Elizabeth flinches.

FRANCIS If he's a sensible man, he'll seek assistance – have words in the ears of those that matter.

ELIZABETH The Boscowans—?

FRANCIS St Aubyns.

ELIZABETH Warleggans?

FRANCIS When their cousin died in the wreck? George is very likely *behind* the accusations.

ELIZABETH But he could exert influence – if he chose?

FRANCIS His reach extends everywhere. It may even reach Parliament if he succeeds in getting his protégé elected. But why would he throw his might behind Ross?

ELIZABETH You're right. Why would he?

But clearly this has given her pause for thought. Could she herself bring some influence to bear?

CUT TO:

12: INT. NAMPARA HOUSE, PARLOUR – DUSK 2

Ross is having supper. Demelza brings ale to the table and joins him. He's tucking in heartily, as if he hadn't a care in the world.

ROSS Pascoe's asked to see me. And the Wheal Leisure shareholders. They worry excessively.

DEMELZA An' Dwight? Zacky? Henshawe? Do *they* 'worry excessively' too?

Ross attacks his supper and doesn't reply.

DEMELZA *(cont'd)* Surely, Ross, if the Crown be arranging its case, ought you not to do the same? Speak to people? Get them on your side?

ROSS *(amused)* Stoop to bribery and flattery?

DEMELZA Is that not how it works?

ROSS It's not how I work.

DEMELZA Oh, 'tis against your principles? *(Ross shrugs.)* Nay, Ross, 'tis against your *pride*!

Ross doesn't argue. He tucks into another mouthful of supper.

ROSS This stew is excellent!

CUT TO:

13: INT. SAWLE KIDDLEY – NIGHT 2

Prudie picks at some unappetizing stew while Jud stares balefully into his mug of ale.

PRUDIE I'd miss Nampara.

JUD Cap'n Ross'll miss *me*.

PRUDIE An' tha's why he say he'll beat 'ee senseless if ever 'ee darken 'is door agin?

JUD Best thing I ever done – quittin' 'is service!

PRUDIE '*Quit*', ye black worm? 'Ee'd still be stuffin' yer guts with 'is vittles if 'ee 'adn't ope'd yer g'eat trap once too often!

She whacks him over the head.

CUT TO:

14: EXT. NAMPARA HOUSE, COURTYARD – DAY 3

Ross is on horseback, ready to depart. Demelza hands him his travelling bags.

ROSS I'll not be long. I can only take so much of Pascoe's fretting!

DEMELZA You'll not forget what I said? *(beat)* If help is offered—?

Ross smiles dismissively, spurs his horse and rides off. Demelza remains, frustrated.

CUT TO:

15: EXT. MARKET PLACE, TRURO – DAY 3

Ross rides into town. Market day is busy and bustling. Rows of stalls and sellers – pilchards, fish, trinkets, herbal remedies, sweetmeats, nosegays, etc. Children laugh raucously at a Punch and Judy show where Punch is being led towards a guillotine. All society is here, from the poorest to the wealthiest. All this is noted by Ross. What he fails to notice, however, is Elizabeth. Wandering through the stalls, pausing occasionally to inspect a ribbon or a trinket or a nosegay or to look at the Punch and Judy show (which makes her shudder with distaste), suddenly she spots Ross. She pulls back so as not to be seen. Ross rides on. Elizabeth dallies, as if she's stalling for time, waiting for something to happen. And presently it does.

GEORGE'S VOICE Elizabeth!

Elizabeth turns to see George hurrying towards her. He sees the Punch and Judy show.

GEORGE A pretty spectacle, is it not? *(then)* Are you alone?

ELIZABETH I was about to return to Trenwith.

GEORGE Would you consider a small delay?

He offers his arm. Elizabeth accepts. He has no idea this is exactly what she'd planned.

CUT TO:

16: EXT. MARKET PLACE, TRURO – DAY 3

Ross strides along the street on his way to the shareholders' meeting. An open carriage passes, containing Unwin Trevaunance, who is wearing an election cockade, accompanied by a pretty, well-dressed young woman, carrying a fat, pampered pug. This is Caroline Penvenen.

(NB The two parties do not meet face to face but remain at a distance – in other words, no formal introductions are necessary.)

UNWIN Captain Poldark!

ROSS *(bows in acknowledgement)* Mr Trevaunance. How goes your campaign?

UNWIN Better than yours, I imagine!

He roars with laughter as the carriage passes by. The girl turns round and gives Ross an arch smile. Ross nods politely, and keeps walking.

CAROLINE Who was that?

UNWIN No one of any use to my campaign.

Nevertheless, Caroline looks intrigued.

CUT TO:

17: INT. RED LION, MEETING ROOM – DAY 3

Ross and Henshawe address Horace Treneglos, Aukitt, Renfrew and four others.

HENSHAWE Gentlemen, welcome to the Wheal Leisure shareholders' meeting.

AUKITT *(to Horace Treneglos)* Damned irregular! Called at such short notice?

HENSHAWE As you know, Captain Poldark's presence is shortly required elsewhere—

Looks are exchanged between Aukitt and Horace Treneglos. Ross is in high spirits – and in total denial about his imminent trial.

ROSS But in the meantime – copper prices remain low. To counter that we have three shifts working day and night, extracting every last crumb of ore – *and* on the hunt for fresh lodes. I myself work six days in seven—

HORACE TRENEGLOS Your wife must be delighted!

ROSS *(laughs)* My wife is a miner's daughter.

HORACE TRENEGLOS And the trial? How will that affect things?

ROSS Not at all. I'll be there and back in a day.

An awkward silence. Looks of disbelief are exchanged between the shareholders.

HORACE TRENEGLOS I admire your optimism!

CUT TO:

18: EXT. TRURO HARBOUR – DAY 3

Elizabeth and George are strolling along the harbour.

ELIZABETH I hear you're backing Unwin Trevaunance in the election?

GEORGE I've given him my endorsement – for what that's worth!

ELIZABETH Surely a great deal, since your influence is considerable.

George nods in acknowledgement.

ELIZABETH *(cont'd) (teasing)* And no doubt he enjoys some – *financial* support?

GEORGE No doubt he does.

ELIZABETH How generous you are!

GEORGE As you must be aware, Elizabeth, the best arrangements work both ways.

ELIZABETH So how will his being in Parliament benefit you?

GEORGE It's always useful to have the ear of an MP – in matters of trade, legislation, legal matters and so forth—

ELIZABETH Legal matters? I see *(as if it's just occurred)* – I wonder what he might do in a case like Ross's.

George is on the alert at once. What's her agenda?

ELIZABETH *(cont'd)* Of course I know little of such things, but I doubt he'd want a fellow-gentleman to come to grief. What civilized man would?

A momentary flinch from George. The thought of her thinking him 'uncivilized' is not pleasant.

ELIZABETH *(cont'd)* Although – practically speaking – what could he do? Except, I suppose, put a word in the right ear—? *(beat)* As an MP – *(then)* except he's not yet an MP—

GEORGE No, indeed—

ELIZABETH So I suppose the power of influence remains with you.

CUT TO:

19: INT. PASCOE'S OFFICE – DAY 3

If Ross thinks he's in for an easy ride, he's mistaken.

PASCOE So you've made no arrangements.

ROSS None whatsoever.

PASCOE *(He hands Ross a piece of paper.)* Jeffrey Clymer KC. Your defence. He'll meet you in Bodmin.

ROSS *(laughing)* Will he?

PASCOE Next, your finances.

Ross is marvelling at the sheer audacity of Pascoe.

PASCOE *(cont'd)* You're chief shareholder in Wheal Leisure. Other than that you have no income. Your tenants regularly default on their rents. Your house is mortgaged and you have outstanding debts of one thousand pounds at interest of forty per cent.

ROSS My wife will be sorry she wed me!

PASCOE Your wife deserves better. Have you made a will? *(beat)* Of course not. *(getting out pen and paper)* I need a list of all your assets.

ROSS *(amused)* That shouldn't take long!

CUT TO:

20: EXT. TRURO HARBOUR – DAY 3

George and Elizabeth continue their walk. George realizes the conversation has taken him into dangerous waters.

GEORGE Are you suggesting *I* intervene?

ELIZABETH I suppose the question is – what could be the benefit – to you?

GEORGE I fail to see one.

ELIZABETH And yet *family* gratitude cannot be underestimated—

GEORGE The *family* means little to me. You alone are the person I care to please.

ELIZABETH It distresses me to think of my cousin at risk of his life. So many matters would be left unresolved.

She doesn't elaborate. And George doesn't ask her.

ELIZABETH *(cont'd) (as if it's just occurred)* How difficult would it be to have him come before a 'sympathetic' judge?

GEORGE There are ways of 'encouraging' such sympathy. But does Ross ask it of me?

ELIZABETH You know, you and Ross are more alike than you know—

GEORGE I have said so! I said it to *him*!

ELIZABETH I do not think he could fail to feel gratitude – if he felt himself beholden – if he could see his benefactor in a new light—

George nods thoughtfully. Her arguments are swaying him. And a plan is already taking shape in her mind.

CUT TO:

21: EXT. KILLEWARREN – DAY 3

Caroline, carrying Horace, steps down from her carriage. Servants are unloading vast piles of luggage. Ray Penvenen comes out.

CAROLINE Uncle Ray!

RAY PENVENEN My dear!

They embrace warmly. He notes her luggage.

RAY PENVENEN *(cont'd) (ironic)* I see you travel light, niece. How long d'you intend to stay?

CAROLINE That depends. If Horace and I get bored, we may be forced to return to London!

RAY PENVENEN No doubt you're much in demand there.

CAROLINE An heiress is much in demand *everywhere*! Especially one who is not yet of age!

RAY PENVENEN Why so?

CAROLINE It's assumed she must do the bidding of her wealthy uncle and marry where he chooses!

Now Unwin comes forward and greets Ray.

RAY PENVENEN Well, Unwin? Are you confident?

CAROLINE Of winning his seat – or my hand?

UNWIN Both, I trust!

Caroline tinkles with laughter at the very idea and runs inside. Unwin looks rather foolish. Ray shrugs as if to say, 'That's what you're letting yourself in for!'

UNWIN *(cont'd)* I hope we can come to terms soon, sir.

RAY PENVENEN I hope so too. *(not without affection)* She runs rings round her old guardian! I'm sure a younger man would benefit from the exercise!

CUT TO:

22: INT. TRENWITH HOUSE, LIBRARY – DAY 3

Elizabeth takes paper, pen and ink and begins to write a short note: 'My dear Demelza . . .'

CUT TO:

23: INT. NAMPARA HOUSE, ROSS & DEMELZA'S BEDROOM – NIGHT 3

Ross is getting ready for bed – as if he hadn't a care in the world. Demelza marvels at his blasé attitude.

ROSS Did I mention I saw Unwin Trevaunance? Our would-be MP?

No response from Demelza. Ross continues blithely.

ROSS *(cont'd)* And his intended. Our neighbour Ray Penvenen's niece. No doubt she's here for the election in Bodmin.

He continues to get ready for bed.

DEMELZA I've never been to Bodmin.

ROSS Be grateful *you're* not going *now*.

DEMELZA Why?

ROSS The election takes place the same day as the assizes. The town will be seething.

DEMELZA With who?

ROSS Oh, the great and the good! Those who wish to stare or be stared at!

DEMELZA Will Elizabeth go?

ROSS I shouldn't think so.

Demelza hesitates. She has a delicate subject to broach.

DEMELZA She sent us a note.

Ross looks up, surprised. And suspicious.

ROSS What could she want?

DEMELZA Same as I. *(beat)* As you did promise me after Julia died. That we all be reconciled.

ROSS *(surprised)* You still want that?

DEMELZA With the trial nigh upon us, mebbe I'll be glad o' the friendship—

ROSS Even though they cost us Julia?

DEMELZA Nay, Ross, you cannot lay it all at their door—

ROSS Can I not?

DEMELZA 'Tis why I d' wish to make peace – *despite* all we lost. Will it not mean Julia did'n die in vain?

Ross eyes her closely. He can see how much this means to Demelza. She hands him the note.

DEMELZA *(cont'd)* She say tomorrow at two.

Ross nods. We sense he might be swayed.

CUT TO:

24: EXT. TRENWITH HOUSE – DAY 3A

(Wide) Ross and Demelza walk arm in arm up the drive to Trenwith. It's reminiscent of their first visit to Trenwith the Christmas after they were married. Demelza is nervous and Ross is wary. Now the front door is opened by Elizabeth.

ELIZABETH It's good of you both to come.

She seems flushed and nervous – almost guilty – as if she has some hidden agenda. Ross and Demelza exchange a glance.

CUT TO:

25: INT. TRENWITH HOUSE, GREAT HALL – DAY 3A

Demelza and Ross follow Elizabeth into the Great Hall. Ross is especially wary. Something about this, about Elizabeth's nervousness, doesn't feel right. Ross glances round. Aunt Agatha is (apparently) asleep in her chair.

ROSS Is Francis here?

ELIZABETH Somewhere hereabouts. I wanted to speak with you first. To ask if some help might be given – when you come to court. I hope you will take the gesture with the kindness in which it's intended—

ROSS Gesture?

George walks into the room behind Ross and Demelza. Huge surprise – and awkwardness. George bows politely, though he, too, is wary.

ELIZABETH George might know the judge who will hear your case—

George and Ross regard each other with suspicion. Demelza is shocked. Elizabeth a bundle of nerves.

ROSS *(amused)* How convenient.

ELIZABETH And thought that perhaps he could be—

GEORGE Pointed in the right direction?

Ross looks at George, half-incredulous, half-amused.

ROSS For a price, no doubt.

GEORGE Not one you would *personally* need to pay.

Ross locks eyes with George. Is George seriously offering to bribe a judge for him? To his astonishment, he realizes that he is. And he knows exactly what the cost would be. A truce. Even friendship.

ROSS But I see that I would. And it strikes me as more than my liberty's worth.

Eyeball to eyeball. Ross making sure George is in no doubt as to his meaning. George isn't.

ROSS *(cont'd)* Demelza, we're leaving.

As Ross is about to walk out, Francis appears. He's utterly shocked to walk into this gathering.

FRANCIS Ross? *(then)* Elizabeth? What's the meaning of this?

ELIZABETH I thought – if there was something we could do – to help Ross—

FRANCIS 'We'?

DEMELZA We appreciate the thought—

ROSS But not the method.

Ross walks out. Demelza follows. George is stony-faced. Francis is gutted. Are these seriously the lengths to which Elizabeth will go to help Ross?

FRANCIS You'll excuse us, George.

GEORGE Of course.

He bows and goes out. Elizabeth is left to face Francis.

ELIZABETH I thought it the least we could do. For Demelza's sake.

FRANCIS Demelza's. Of course.

It's a defining moment for him. Clearly he believes that Elizabeth still cares for Ross. He smiles sadly and leaves. Aunt Agatha opens her eyes (she's been awake all the time), raises an eyebrow as if to say, 'Well, that went well, didn't it?' Elizabeth remains. It's all gone horribly wrong.

CUT TO:

26: EXT. TRENWITH HOUSE – DAY 3A

Ross stalks angrily down the drive followed by Demelza. As they reach the gates, Ross turns and sees George come out of the front door.

DEMELZA Do 'ee think Elizabeth *meant* f'r 'im to call?

ROSS Obviously.

DEMELZA But what could she hope—?

ROSS I've no time to waste in idle speculation. The subject is closed.

He walks off – but not before he and George have exchanged a final hostile glance. Demelza follows after him.

CUT TO:

27: INT. NAMPARA HOUSE, HALLWAY – DAY 3A

Returning from Trenwith, Ross storms through the front door, followed by Demelza. He's furious.

ROSS It beggars belief! Could they seriously imagine I'd stoop to beg favours of that upstart poodle? If I wished to prostitute myself, I'd sooner grovel to Ray Penvenen – who's actually *acquainted* with Judge Lister!

DEMELZA *(suddenly alert)* Is he?

ROSS It really is the end for me and Francis!

DEMELZA Where are you going?

ROSS To the mine. Where it's still possible to do an *honest* day's work!

Demelza remains. An idea has occurred to her.

CUT TO:

28: EXT. WARLEGGAN HOUSE – DAY 4

Dawn establisher.

CUT TO:

29: INT. WARLEGGAN HOUSE, GEORGE'S DEN – DAY 4

George is reading a document to Tankard.

GEORGE 'A known Jacobin and revolutionary . . . fomenter of unrest and affray . . . once escaped justice by taking the king's shilling . . . fathered numerous bastards . . . bedded and wedded his scullery maid upon whom he got his latest brat – this creature being a notorious doxy from a family of murderers and thieves—'

TANKARD Our friend 'Anonymous' has an engaging style. How many copies?

GEORGE Enough to paper all Truro and Bodmin?

Tankard gives George a look which says, 'You're determined to get him convicted, aren't you?'

GEORGE *(cont'd)* I merely wish to see justice done.

TANKARD If he's found guilty, he could hang.

GEORGE If he hangs, he'll have only himself to blame. *(then)* I do not make the laws, sir.

Tankard's look clearly says: 'No, but you know how to manipulate them.'

CUT TO:

30: EXT. OPEN COUNTRYSIDE – DAY 4

Two sinister-looking figures, like horsemen of the apocalypse, ride purposefully across the countryside. They are Tankard and George's 'enforcer', the loutish Tom Harry.

CUT TO:

31: EXT. SAWLE VILLAGE – DAY 4

Prudie is washing clothes in a stream when she is accosted by Tom Harry and Tankard.

TANKARD Prudence Paynter?

Prudie eyes him suspiciously and says nothing.

TANKARD *(cont'd)* My name is Tankard. Acting for the Crown in the case of Rex versus Poldark. *(no reply)* What d'y'recall of the night of the shipwreck?

PRUDIE What shipwreck?

TOM HARRY Sithee, woman – when there's riot and robbery like there was that night—

TANKARD The law says naught of those who follow if it can lay hold of those who *lead*. But if it cannot prove the ringleader, it must smoke out the *bystander* – who is guilty simply by *being there* and doing nothing to prevent the crime.

TOM HARRY So 'tis best for all concerned that the right man should stand in the assizes.

PRUDIE The right man?

He raises his eyebrows as if to say, 'We both know who I mean.' Prudie eyes him narrowly, as if considering what will be to her best advantage.

PRUDIE *(cont'd)* Ross Poldark?

TOM HARRY Ross Poldark.

PRUDIE Well, why did'n 'ee say so i' th' first place?

They look at her hopefully. Tankard gets out his notebook ready to make note of her evidence.

PRUDIE *(cont'd)* I never see'd sight nor sound of 'im.

She goes back to washing clothes.

CUT TO:

32: INT. NAMPARA HOUSE, KITCHEN – DAY 4

Ross whistles cheerily as he cuts a piece of pie, wraps it up and prepares to leave for the mine. Demelza watches him beadily. But instead of addressing Ross she addresses Garrick.

DEMELZA *(to Garrick)* So tomorrow we be free, Garrick. Once Mister Ross leaves for Bodmin.

ROSS So soon? I've scarce given it thought.

DEMELZA *(to Garrick)* An' tomorrow night we lay cosy by the fire – while he lies in Bodmin Jail!

ROSS Having first met Clymer, my counsel. For what that's worth!

DEMELZA *(A thought occurs.)* Will – Mr Penvenen go to Bodmin?

ROSS To the election? Undoubtedly. If only to keep an eye on his niece.

Ross waves cheerily, picks up his pie and goes out. Demelza's mind is working overtime.

DEMELZA *(to Garrick)* Well, if he won't help himself, I must do it for 'im!

CUT TO:

33: EXT. CLIFF-TOP PATHWAY – DAY 4

Demelza walks purposefully towards Killewarren.

CUT TO:

34: EXT. KILLEWARREN – DAY 4

Demelza knocks on the door of a large house. A servant opens.

DEMELZA Mistress Poldark to see Mr Penvenen.

CUT TO:

35: EXT. SAWLE VILLAGE – DAY 4

Tankard and Tom Harry ride by the village and encounter Jud.

TANKARD Jud Paynter?

JUD Niver 'eard of 'im.

TANKARD You were on Hendrawna Beach the night of the shipwreck.

JUD Was I?

TOM HARRY Ye don't recall? P'raps this'll jog your memory.

He offers Jud a swig from a bottle of brandy. It's halfway to Jud's mouth when Prudie marches up, seizes the bottle and thrusts it back at Tom Harry. Then she boots Jud up the arse and frogmarches him away.

PRUDIE Get off 'ome, ye bladderwrackin' pifflin' piece of offal!

CUT TO:

36: INT. KILLEWARREN – DAY 4

Demelza sits waiting for Ray Penvenen, fanning herself, looking faint. Ray appears. This visit is unexpected and he doesn't quite know how to respond.

RAY PENVENEN Mistress Poldark – I – don't believe I've had the pleasure—

DEMELZA *(offering her hand)* Forgive the intrusion, sir – I was taken queasy as I was out walking – an' yours was the first house I came upon.

She gives him a winning smile.

CUT TO:

37: INT. WARLEGGAN HOUSE, GEORGE'S DEN – DAY 4

George pours wine for Unwin, who sniffs and tastes it in the manner of a wine buff/bore.

GEORGE Now, sir, let us discuss precisely how you and I can work together – to our mutual advantage.

CUT TO:

38: INT. WHEAL LEISURE – DAY 4

Ross is working alongside Zacky, Paul and Charlie. He's working as if his life depended on it – something which doesn't go unnoticed by Zacky, Paul and Charlie. Eventually . . .

ZACKY 'Tis no use, Ross.

Ross stops, looks at Zacky, puzzled.

ZACKY *(cont'd)* The lode 'ave petered out. We know'd it a week ago but—

ROSS I swear there's more.

ZACKY There's no sense persistin'. 'Tis all work'd out.

ROSS So we give up?

ZACKY We move on.

Ross stops and looks at him. He knows Zacky means this in more ways than one. But can he?

ROSS Easier said than done.

Zacky nods. He knows what Ross is referring to. He pats him on the back, in consolation.

ZACKY Bitter thing, to lose a child.

ROSS Demelza bears it better than I. She expects less of life – so finds consolation where I find none. *(then)* I haven't even had the heart to move Julia's crib.

It's said without bitterness or self-pity. An observation. A fact of life.
CUT TO:

39: INT. KILLEWARREN – DAY 4

Ray hands Demelza a glass of canary.

DEMELZA You have a fine estate, sir.

RAY PENVENEN It keeps me occupied. I have mining interests, of course, but truth be told, I much prefer my cows. They're more reliable!

DEMELZA Oh, there we agree, sir! An' d'you have a special favourite?

RAY PENVENEN Minta. She's my prize. But, alas, she's sick. Calved two days ago and today she's barely fit to stand. Teeth rattling, tail awry—

DEMELZA Oh? Would you like for me to look at her?

RAY PENVENEN You, ma'am?

DEMELZA I've a little in the way of animal learning.

Ray is taken aback, but seriously impressed.

CUT TO:

40: EXT. WHEAL LEISURE – DAY 4

Paul and Zacky are walking with Ross.

PAUL All set for the trial?

ROSS I've not given it much thought.

ZACKY The Crown has. An attorney was in Sawle last night – askin' questions, offerin' money—

PAUL Is that lawful?

ROSS Not remotely. But it shows the Crown's intent.

Paul and Zacky exchange a glance. As we pull back we reveal George on horseback, watching from a distance, unnoticed. He rides on.

CUT TO:

41: INT. KILLEWARREN, SHIPPON – DAY 4

Demelza is staring intently at Ray's prize cow Minta. Screwing up her face with concentration, she makes a firm pronouncement.

DEMELZA Tail shot.

Ray appears from behind the cow.

RAY PENVENEN I never heard of such a thing. Is there a cure?

DEMELZA *(confidently)* There is. *(then)* Slit open the tail – 'bout a foot from the end – bind there a well-salted onion – leave f'r a week – meantime, making a cordial of rosemary, juniper, coltsfoot, cardamon . . .

Ray warms further to Demelza.

CUT TO:

42: EXT. GRAMBLER MINE – DAY 4

Francis stands looking at the derelict Grambler mine. Written on his face are feelings of self-loathing. Presently Elizabeth rides up. She says nothing but Francis believes he knows what she's thinking.

FRANCIS How pitiful it looks. *(beat)* Is. *(then)* Whereas *Ross's* mine . . . *(no reply)* Of course Ross would never gamble away his most precious asset. Ross is too wise, too clever – *(beat)* even when he's accused of wrecking and riot, people still revere him! What must he do before he's despised?

ELIZABETH You *wish* him to be despised?

FRANCIS At least he could keep me company!

ELIZABETH Who despises you?

FRANCIS Aside from myself?

He spurs his horse and rides away. Elizabeth gives Grambler one final look, then heads home (in the opposite direction to the one Francis took).

CUT TO:

43: EXT. CLIFF-TOP PATHWAY – DAY 4

Ross is riding home from the mine when he sees Francis up ahead on horseback. Ross hopes to avoid him, but Francis rides to meet him.

FRANCIS Ross! This is well met! May I walk with you a while?

ROSS I'm pressed for time. I leave for Bodmin tomorrow.

FRANCIS The encounter yesterday – was not of my doing—

ROSS So I gathered.

FRANCIS Yet still I'd hope we could put past quarrels behind us—

ROSS I'd hoped so too, but I find now I cannot.

Ross rides off. Francis speeds after him.

FRANCIS Ross – *(catching up with him)* Ross, if things should go amiss in court – how is Demelza fixed?

ROSS How is that your concern?

FRANCIS Only that – I'd hope she would feel she could turn to me—

This offer is so surprising it brings Ross to a standstill.

ROSS For what?

FRANCIS If your sentence is prison – or worse – she'd be entirely alone, with no source of income—

ROSS *(ironic)* Whereas you yourself are swimming in guineas?

FRANCIS I've a little put by – some six hundred pounds – if the need arose—

ROSS Why would you offer it?

FRANCIS I don't forget what we owe Demelza. *(no reply)* In saving our son—

ROSS She lost our daughter. *(laughs)* There's justice for you!

FRANCIS I hope you'll fare better in court.

ROSS I wouldn't bet my house on it! Or yours. If you still own it.

Ross rides away. Francis remains, feeling more wretched than before.
CUT TO:

44: EXT. KILLEWARREN – DAY 4

Ray is escorting Demelza from the house.

RAY PENVENEN I cannot thank you enough.

DEMELZA Thank me when the cow is mended!

RAY PENVENEN I hope you're not too downcast – about your husband's coming trial?

DEMELZA Truly, I fear the worst.

She looks tearful. Ray looks sympathetic.

DEMELZA *(cont'd) (then, casually)* If one only knew who the judge would be—

RAY PENVENEN Why, that's no secret, ma'am. 'Tis Justice Wentworth Lister.

DEMELZA Oh! Are you – acquainted with him?

RAY PENVENEN A stern fellow – though generally accounted fair.

DEMELZA It d' puzzle me exceedingly how a judge can be expected to listen to a case and get to the bottom of it, all in a matter of hours. Does he never ask for the truth in private before the trial begins?

RAY PENVENEN *(laughs)* No – but perhaps he should!

DEMELZA *(laughs)* Do 'ee think so?

RAY PENVENEN If it came from someone like you, ma'am, how he could object?

They're both laughing now. Clearly Ray is joking. Equally clearly, Demelza doesn't realize this, has taken him at his word and is forming a plan!

DEMELZA Will you be in Bodmin for the assizes?

RAY PENVENEN For the election, ma'am.

DEMELZA I hope we may meet again, sir.

She offers her hand to Ray. He kisses it. She walks away from the house. As she passes through the gates, Unwin and Caroline arrive in their carriage. They glance quizzically at Demelza. Demelza flashes Unwin a winning smile. As they arrive outside Killewarren:

CAROLINE Who was that, Uncle?

RAY PENVENEN Ross Poldark's wife.

CAROLINE What did she want?

RAY PENVENEN She didn't appear to want anything.

UNWIN I doubt that, sir. She looks like a dangerous woman to me.

CUT TO:

45: INT. TRENWITH HOUSE, LIBRARY – DAY 4

Elizabeth returns to find Aunt Agatha reading a newspaper.

AUNT AGATHA Riot and mayhem – Paris ablaze. Unruly beggars, the French.

ELIZABETH I worry for Ross.

AUNT AGATHA Is he travelling to France? Have we run out of brandy?

ELIZABETH No, Aunt. I mean, with his actions on the night of the wrecking – the Crown may feel obliged to take a stand—

AUNT AGATHA Fiddlesticks! My nephew's a hothead – not a revolutionary.

ELIZABETH But there are those who may wish to *paint* him as such.

Mrs Tabb comes in, followed by George.

GEORGE *(kissing Elizabeth's hand)* Elizabeth, you look ravishing today. *(to Aunt Agatha)* You too of course, ma'am.

AUNT AGATHA I do not. And nor, may I say, do you. Quite pasty-faced. Consequence of sitting too long indoors, fingering coin.

GEORGE *(to Elizabeth)* I've brought a small gift for my godson.

ELIZABETH Oh, that's kind of you, George.

Elizabeth looks out of the window and sees Geoffrey Charles cantering around on a hobby-horse.

CUT TO:

46: EXT. TRENWITH HOUSE – DAY 4

A dejected Francis rides up the drive. He sees Geoffrey Charles cantering around on his new hobby-horse.

GEOFFREY CHARLES Papa, look! My very own horse! Uncle George bought it for me.

FRANCIS *(trying to contain his displeasure)* Did he?

Francis dismounts and goes into the house.

CUT TO:

47: INT. TRENWITH HOUSE, LIBRARY – DAY 4

Francis comes in.

FRANCIS Well, well, the great George Warleggan! Dispensing bounty! Are you keeping him sweet, Elizabeth? If you don't, we may find ourselves homeless!

George smiles patiently – and reassuringly at Elizabeth.

GEORGE That will never happen.

Francis helps himself to a drink – and doesn't offer George one.

FRANCIS I saw my cousin just now. He was not eager to exchange pleasantries.

AUNT AGATHA No doubt he's thinking of the trial. *(to George, challenging)* D'you think he'll be acquitted?

GEORGE I don't see how he *can* be. So many witnesses to his activities that night—

A snort of derision from Aunt Agatha.

GEORGE *(cont'd)* And the fact that he's treated the law with contempt on previous occasions—

ELIZABETH I know of no previous occasions.

AUNT AGATHA Nor is the court supposed to.

FRANCIS But it will not be left in ignorance.

He gives Elizabeth a pamphlet.

FRANCIS *(cont'd)* As I came past Sawle, a villager showed me this pretty paper.

ELIZABETH *(reads)* 'The true and sensational life of Captain R. P. Adventurer, seducer, wrecker and suspected murderer'?

Elizabeth looks horrified. Francis looks pointedly at George. George shrugs and smiles amiably.

GEORGE Yes, I've seen them about. They're not important.

FRANCIS Except to Ross.

ELIZABETH But if this is believed, it will prejudice the jury—

GEORGE Pay it no heed, Elizabeth. These scurrilous sheets are always defaming one person or another.

FRANCIS But *this* author has gone to some trouble and expense. You wouldn't know him, would you, George?

GEORGE *(smiles)* I imagine he must be desperate to earn his money in such a manner. Only a bankrupt would sell his services that way.

A look between George and Francis. Francis flushes. Clearly George's remark has hit home. Elizabeth can see it, but isn't sure why. But one thing is certain: this incident has not endeared George to her. He knows it. He tries to catch her eye but she refuses to look at him.

CUT TO:

48: INT. DWIGHT'S COTTAGE – NIGHT 4

Medical instruments, medical text books, specimens in bottles, etc. are seen about the room. Dwight is pacing, practising a speech under his breath. A knock at the door. Ross enters.

ROSS I've asked Demelza not to come to Bodmin tomorrow.

DWIGHT So you and I will ride together? Perhaps as we go, some brilliant defence will occur to me!

Ross notes the paper Dwight's holding.

ROSS *(amused)* That's my character reference?

DWIGHT *(screwing it up)* I've no idea what to say! I was not on the beach, so cannot refute the charges – but from what I hear, they're not easily dismissed.

ROSS Salvaging spoils from a wreck? No jury in Cornwall would convict me!

DWIGHT Assaulting a customs official?

ROSS Not guilty! *(then)* You doubt me?

DWIGHT We both know you're capable of it!

Ross tries to laugh but is forced to admit the truth of this. He helps himself to rum and pours Dwight one.

DWIGHT *(cont'd)* Your situation is not good, Ross.

ROSS I've seen worse! *We've* seen worse!

DWIGHT On the battlefields of Virginia?

ROSS *(indicating his scar)* I salute you for saving my face!

DWIGHT Saving your *neck* may not be so easy!

A look between them. This is not a pleasant thought.

CUT TO:

49: EXT. CLIFF-TOP PATHWAY – DUSK 4

The sun sets as Ross rides home along the cliff tops. He can see Nampara far away in the distance.

CUT TO:

50: EXT. NAMPARA FIELDS – DUSK 4

Ross rides through his fields towards Nampara, which is glowing in the last rays of the setting sun. In the windows candles burn warmly. Ross halts to take in the sight. From inside come the distant notes of the spinet being played.

CUT TO:

51: INT. NAMPARA, PARLOUR – DUSK 4

Demelza is playing the spinet. Ross stands in the doorway unseen and watches her a while. She's still dressed up from her visit to Ray Penvenen.

ROSS *(creeping up on her)* Who's this fine lady and what has she done with my wife?

DEMELZA Judas!

ROSS There she is! For a moment I thought I'd lost her!

DEMELZA Why? 'Cos she's prink'd up to the nines an' her fizzog powdered?

ROSS Clearly I needn't worry about you when I'm gone. There'll be a line of suitors from here to Penzance.

DEMELZA So I should hope.

ROSS And how shall you decide?

DEMELZA I was thinkin' I shouldn't entertain a man without a title. At very least a baronet, hopefully a lord?

Ross laughs and kisses the back of her neck.

CUT TO:

52: EXT. SAWLE KIDDLEY – DUSK 4

Jud reels out of the kiddley (sounds of laughter and music within) and staggers off into the gathering dusk.

CUT TO:

53: EXT. COUNTRY ROAD – DUSK 4

The drunken Jud is stumbling homewards, singing to himself.

JUD *(sings)*

The old grey duck
She stawl her nest
And laid down in the field,
And when the young ones
They came forth
They had no tail nor bills

They had no tail nor bills,
They had no tail nor bills . . .

Presently he hears approaching hoof-beats and is overtaken by Tank-
ard and Tom Harry. He looks at them warily.

JUD *(cont'd)* Yer barkin' up the wrong door. I be a peaceable
law-biding son-of-a-nun – an' 'oo-ever says I ain't be a filthy,
festerin', forky-tongue—

TANKARD 'Tis said that you and your good wife were once
servants of Captain Poldark—

JUD An' 'is father afore 'im.

TANKARD And that after working faithfully all those years
you were turned out without a word—

JUD 'Tweren't right, I'll say that!

TANKARD And that he often used his horsewhip and near
drowned your wife under the pump—

JUD Monstry ingratitude.

TANKARD Assault and battery is against the law.

TOM HARRY Ye do understand the law?

JUD An Englishman's castle is his habeas corpse and thou
shalt not ascend thy neighbour's goat?

TANKARD So you understand that your duty under the law is
to report what you saw on the night of the wreck—

JUD Wreck? Wreck?

TANKARD Come, man, we know you were there—

TOM HARRY With Poldark—

TANKARD We know you took part in the riot and pillaging, we know you played a part in resisting officers of the Crown—

JUD Never 'eard such loitch—

TANKARD But we're willing to overlook all that if you will turn King's evidence.

Jud eyes them narrowly. This is something he hadn't expected.

TANKARD *(cont'd)* We've a weight of testimony against Poldark, but we wish to make it watertight. You owe him no loyalty. 'Tis common sense to testify against him – as well as your common duty—

Jud walks off.

TOM HARRY Also . . . we'd make it worth your while.

Jud continues walking, but his interest is piqued.

CUT TO:

54: INT. TRENWITH HOUSE, CORRIDOR – NIGHT 4

Elizabeth comes upstairs to bed. At her bedroom door she finds Francis waiting.

FRANCIS May I join you a while?

ELIZABETH *(hesitates, then)* Perhaps another night? *(then)* Goodnight, Francis.

FRANCIS Goodnight.

Elizabeth goes into her room and closes the door. Francis lingers, as if hoping she'll change her mind. Then retires to his own room.

CUT TO:

55: EXT. NAMPARA HOUSE – NIGHT 4

The moon is high in the sky. A single light shines in an upstairs window. Presently it is extinguished.

CUT TO:

56: INT. NAMPARA, ROSS & DEMELZA'S
BEDROOM – NIGHT 4

Ross and Demelza undress each other and head for the bed – for what could be the last time.

CUT TO:

57: EXT. NAMPARA HOUSE – DAY 5

A spectacular dawn breaks over the house.

CUT TO:

58: INT. NAMPARA, ROSS & DEMELZA'S
BEDROOM – DAY 5

Demelza wakes to find Ross's place beside her is empty. From outside, bird song and the sound of wood being chopped.

CUT TO:

59: EXT. NAMPARA HOUSE – DAY 5

Ross is chopping wood. As he looks around him, at the sights and features of his land (the cobwebs on the hedgerows, the dew on the grass, the thistles and flora), he seems to see everything in the most intricate and exquisite detail, as if the most ordinary things have become extraordinary. He looks up at the house . . . and sees Demelza framed in the front door, watching him. She is suffused by sunlight, an exquisite vision of loveliness.

DEMELZA So you leave me abed like the Queen o' Sheba while you see to the chores?

ROSS Is it not my duty to cherish my wife while I'm here – and to provide firewood for when I'm not?

She smiles at him. A moment of deep connection between them.

DEMELZA I wish we could stay like this for ever.

ROSS I wish it too. *(then)* I'm only glad for your sake that you'll not see me in court.

DEMELZA No, Ross.

ROSS *(eyeing her closely)* You *will* stay here?

DEMELZA Yes, Ross. If that's what you wish.

Ross puts his arm round her and they go into the house. He is slightly surprised that she hasn't argued.

CUT TO:

60: INT. TRENWITH, GREAT HALL – DAY 5

Francis is dressed in travelling clothes.

FRANCIS *(calling out)* Elizabeth? I'm leaving for Bodmin.

Elizabeth comes in.

ELIZABETH Shall I not come with you?

FRANCIS A court is no place for a lady.

Elizabeth would like to argue but thinks better of it. Francis eyes her closely. He thinks he knows why she's upset.

FRANCIS *(cont'd)* A terrible thought, is it not? A world without Ross.

ELIZABETH I wonder how Demelza would bear it.

FRANCIS How would any of us bear it? *(beat)* For which of us does not secretly adore him?

Elizabeth looks at Francis in surprise.

FRANCIS *(cont'd) (a sad smile)* You see? You do not even trouble to deny it.

ELIZABETH I should not need to.

Francis looks at her, willing her to deny it. And she, for all she would like to, is unable. And in that moment they – and we – see the tragedy of their entire relationship. There's no animosity between them now, just sadness.

FRANCIS How different might our lives have been?

ELIZABETH Had Ross not returned from the war?

FRANCIS Had he not gone away in the first place.

And they both know what that means. Elizabeth would never even have given Francis a second glance. It seems to confirm Francis in some decision he's already made.

FRANCIS *(cont'd)* Goodbye, my dear. God bless you.

He walks out. Elizabeth is momentarily nonplussed by the gentleness of his parting words. Then something makes her blood run cold.

ELIZABETH Francis—?

She runs out after him.

CUT TO:

61: EXT. TRENWITH HOUSE – DAY 5

Elizabeth comes out of the house in time to see Francis ride away down the drive. She opens her mouth to call after him – but decides against. She's worrying unnecessarily. Isn't she?

CUT TO:

62: EXT. NAMPARA HOUSE – DAY 5

Ross's horse is saddled ready to depart. Demelza stands beside it. Ross comes out, moves to take Demelza in his arms. She pushes him away.

DEMELZA You'll come home again.

ROSS I promise. You will see me soon.

She nods. He gets on his horse and rides away.

DEMELZA *(to herself)* Sooner than you think!

CUT TO:

63: INT. DWIGHT'S COTTAGE – DAY 5

Dwight packs his bags for Bodmin. He looks anxious.

CUT TO:

64: EXT. DWIGHT'S COTTAGE – DAY 5

Dwight is saddling his horse and prepares to leave for Bodmin.

CUT TO:

65: EXT. OPEN COUNTRYSIDE – DAY 5

Ross gallops for Bodmin across spectacular open countryside. Presently he is joined by another rider. It's Dwight. They continue their gallop together.

CUT TO:

66: INT. NAMPARA, ROSS & DEMELZA'S BEDROOM – DAY 5

Demelza is packing to leave. She packs her very best dress. The sight of Julia's empty crib catches her eye. She takes a rose from a vase beside her bed and scatters the petals across Julia's pillow.

CUT TO:

67: INT. SAWLE KIDDLEY – DAY 5

Jud is drinking. Tom Harry and Tankard come in and sit down at his table.

TANKARD Ross Poldark is gentry. By making example of your former master, the law deters lesser men from following in his footsteps.

JUD Mebbe. Mebbe not. But I'm still waitin' to hear, what's in it for me?

Tom Harry and Tankard exchange a glance. They're beginning to find Jud very tiresome.

TANKARD Brandy.

JUD Guineas.

TANKARD Five.

Jud snorts with derision.

TANKARD *(cont'd)* Ten. *(another snort from Jud)* Ten now. Ten after the trial.

JUD The Crown d' love a jest!

Jud gets up and goes out.

CUT TO:

68: EXT. BARGUS CROSSROADS – DAY 5

Demelza waits by the gibbet at the crossroads. Presently a stage coach appears in the distance. As it arrives we see it's the coach from Falmouth. It stops. Demelza gets in.

CUT TO:

69: INT. COACH – DAY 5

Demelza gets into the coach. It's very crowded. One of the other passengers is Verity.

VERITY I've saved you a place, my dear!

Demelza squeezes in beside Verity. They are delighted to see each other and embrace warmly.

VERITY *(cont'd)* You *did* tell Ross you're coming?

DEMELZA O' course not!

Verity smiles. This is the Demelza she knows and loves.

CUT TO:

70: INT. COACH – DAY 5

Caroline and Ray are travelling to Bodmin. Caroline is feeding Horace titbits.

RAY PENVENEN You spoil him.

CAROLINE How else could I persuade him to come to Bodmin with me? Indeed he wonders why either of us must go *at all*.

RAY PENVENEN Because tonight is election night – and as Unwin's intended you are expected to be at his side.

Caroline yawns and looks bored. Ray checks his pocket-watch.

RAY PENVENEN *(cont'd)* We'll be arriving shortly.

CAROLINE And Horace will wish to go straight to our lodgings – where he and I will spend an agreeable evening eating jellies!

Ray shakes his head in dismay.

CAROLINE *(cont'd)* What? You'd prefer me to catch cold in some draughty assembly rooms, watching dreary men voting and spouting nonsense? *(then)* I may venture out later. If Horace can spare me. *(then, to Horace)* Bodmin, Horace! What a dull-sounding place! I'm sure nothing of moment ever happens there!

CUT TO:

71: EXT. SQUARE, BODMIN – DAY 5

Welcome to Bodmin! We go with Ross as, with Dwight at his side, he enters a bustling square, brimming with people, in town for the election and for the assizes. A town crier's voice announces the election: 'Hear ye! Hear ye! By the sheriff's precept – notice of election – The major and aldermen of the borough – and the Speaker of the House of Commons – do command, issue and proclaim on Monday seventh day of September in the year of our Lord seventeen hundred and ninety . . .' People from all walks of life cross his path – from beggars to bankers to baronets and everything in between. Women dressed in high fashion loom into view, then beggar women dressed in rags. Already this feels like a step up from Truro – both in terms of numbers and in terms of the mood of the crowd. There's already a faint air of hostility here, as if something is brewing. Flags of the various election factions hang over the Assembly Rooms. Everywhere men are handing out election pamphlets. Ross and Dwight walk through the square – Ross on his way to rendezvous with his defence KC and Dwight on his way to his lodgings. They halt, shake hands, Dwight wishes Ross luck, they part and walk in different directions. We go with Ross. He comes across a man handing out pamphlets. He takes one, thinking it's an election flyer, but instead finds a pamphlet like the one Francis showed Elizabeth: 'The true and sensational life of Captain R. P. Adventurer, seducer, wrecker and suspected murderer'. Incredulous – who would go to such trouble? – Ross screws it up and walks on.

CUT TO:

72: INT. ASSEMBLY ROOMS, BODMIN – DAY 5

Caroline and Unwin enter the Assembly Rooms.

UNWIN If you could give me the slightest encouragement of your readiness to entertain my affections—

CAROLINE I can do no such thing since I'm not convinced I'd make a suitable parliamentary wife.

UNWIN I think you'd be perfection. Imagine yourself at my side tonight, waving from the balcony at the crowds below.

CAROLINE Smiling and simpering – and holding my tongue. For it wouldn't do for me to have opinions, would it?

UNWIN Parliamentary wives are assumed to share their *husband's* opinions.

CAROLINE That seems an equitable arrangement. I share your opinions and you share my fortune.

UNWIN I care nothing for your fortune, Caroline.

CAROLINE And I even less for your opinions!

She walks off, laughing. Unwin is ambushed by a man who thrusts a pamphlet into his hand. Still reading the pamphlet, he notices Ray and George and walks towards them.

UNWIN Have you seen this? I thought it was an election pamphlet, but it appears to be an assassination of Ross Poldark's character.

George takes it, pretends to read it, as if for the first time. He grimaces in dismay.

GEORGE How unfortunate.

CUT TO:

73: INT. CROWN INN, BODMIN – DAY 5.5

Ross comes into the inn and sees a small, combative bulldog of a man sitting in the corner, his papers spread on the table before him. He knows at once who this is – and the man, JEFFREY CLYMER KC, seeing him, immediately offers his hand.

CLYMER Jeffrey Clymer, King's Counsel. I'm here to see if we can wriggle you off the hook.

He invites Ross to sit down. As Ross does so, Clymer consults his papers.

CLYMER *(cont'd)* Wrecking. Inciting a riot. Attacking a customs official.

ROSS *(amused)* Impressive.

Clymer bristles, eyes Ross narrowly. This isn't going to be easy. He restrains himself.

CLYMER Following to your arrest, your statement to the examining magistrate was – unhelpful.

ROSS I answered truthfully. Is that not what the law requires?

CLYMER The 'truth', sir, is relative. So are 'the facts'. A common misconception is that 'truth' is the same as 'innocence'. It is not. My job is to position the 'truth' so that you do not pay for it with your life. So let me be clear: anything other than absolute contrition would be sheer folly.

He packs up the papers and gets to his feet.

CLYMER *(cont'd)* I'll visit you in jail with a list of the witnesses who are to appear against you.

ROSS And those *for* me?

CLYMER A shorter list. Friends and workers, whose testimony, presumed biased, will easily be dismissed. Meanwhile, I advise you to reconsider your attitude. It's no detriment to me if you choose to run your neck into a noose. But I suspect it might be to *yours.*

CUT TO:

74: INT. DWIGHT'S LODGINGS, BODMIN – DAY 5

Dwight has just arrived and is being shown to his room by a servant when the landlord appears behind them.

LANDLORD Beg pardon, sur, be you a surgeon or such like?

DWIGHT I am.

LANDLORD There's someone took mortal sick at Priory House.

DWIGHT I'll go at once.

CUT TO:

75: INT. PRIORY HOUSE, BODMIN – DAY 5

Dwight is shown in and finds Caroline reclining on a chaise.

DWIGHT I'm a physician, ma'am. May I be of service?

CAROLINE I hope so. My darling little Horace has had two fits and now he's barely breathing. Will you attend on him, please?

She reveals a small black pug curled up on a cushion.

DWIGHT Your footman made a mistake. It would be a farrier you sent him for.

CAROLINE It is not my custom to employ a horse doctor for Horace. I want the best advice and I'm willing to pay for it. What is your fee?

Dwight is trying to contain his irritation and doesn't immediately reply.

CAROLINE *(cont'd)* But perhaps you do not know your trade well enough. If you're a beginner, perhaps you should leave and we'll call someone else.

DWIGHT That was what I was about to suggest.

He walks towards the door. Caroline is almost prepared to let him go. But at the last moment:

CAROLINE Wait—

Dwight turns back. Caroline's demeanour softens.

CAROLINE *(cont'd)* Have you never had a dog of your own?

DWIGHT Yes—

CAROLINE And would you have let him die on a point of – formality?

Caroline looks at him beseechingly. He finds himself coming back into the room.

DWIGHT How old is he?

CAROLINE Twelve months.

DWIGHT Fits are not uncommon at that age. An aunt of mine had a spaniel—

Reluctantly he swallows his pride and examines Horace. Caroline watches anxiously.

DWIGHT *(cont'd)* His pulse is steady and there's no sign of fever. Nonetheless, I'd advise a *lowering* system of treatment – no more sweetmeats or pastries—

CAROLINE Oh but he loves to eat—

DWIGHT Plenty of running and jumping. Dogs do not need to be carried. *(He writes out a prescription.)* Have a druggist make up this paregoric of black cherry water and Theban opium.

CAROLINE Thank you.

He hands her the prescription.

CAROLINE *(cont'd)* You were saying? *(beat)* About your aunt's spaniel?

DWIGHT Oh – he – used to have fits – when she played the spinet. *(beat)* One hesitates to say whether he was musical, or the reverse.

Caroline's face breaks into a smile.

CAROLINE What is your name?

CUT TO:

76: INT. CROWN INN, BODMIN – DAY 5

Francis is trying to get a room at the inn.

FRANCIS Not a single room in the entire inn? Are you quite sure?

The landlord shrugs apologetically. As Francis turns away, Dwight walks in.

FRANCIS *(cont'd)* Enys! Are you here for the trial?

DWIGHT I am indeed. And you?

FRANCIS I thought to look in. D'you know where I can get a room for the night? This place is full and the town is fermenting with people.

DWIGHT You may be unlucky. I trust your sister had the foresight to reserve her room at the White Lion.

FRANCIS *(surprised)* Verity's here?

DWIGHT I saw her go in just now with Demelza. Is your wife with you?

FRANCIS Elizabeth prefers to remain at Trenwith. *(then)* I hope Ross's counsel knows his business.

DWIGHT We'll know better tomorrow.

He's about to walk off. Then . . .

DWIGHT *(cont'd)* If you should be without a place to sleep tonight, I'm at the London Inn, beside the church.

FRANCIS You may be held to that.

As Francis heads out he passes a man who is handing out pamphlets. Francis takes one, glances at it – and realizes it's one of the anti-Ross pamphlets. Furious at the way George is trying to ruin Ross, Francis decides he must now take matters into his own hands.

CUT TO:

77: INT. WHITE LION INN, BODMIN, BEDROOM – DAY 5

Verity and Demelza are shown into their room by a servant. They put their luggage down and begin to unpack.

DEMELZA So tell me more of Andrew. Where is he?

VERITY At sea, or he would have joined me.

DEMELZA And all's well?

VERITY We could not be happier. *(beat)* But for one thing—

DEMELZA Yes?

VERITY The cost to *you* – of bringing us together—

DEMELZA And to you. The rift 'twixt you and Francis—

VERITY Is painful – but so much less than your loss of Julia.

Verity squeezes her hand. A moment between them.

VERITY *(cont'd)* I know you forgive me. I wish I forgave myself.

DEMELZA Her death was not your fault.

VERITY Nor yours.

DEMELZA I fear we're both too hard on ourselves.

A nod of acknowledgement between them. Then, to break the moment:

VERITY But this town is a *boiling*. I'd forgot it was election week.

DEMELZA I lately met one of the candidates. A friend of our neighbour Penvenen. *(then, trying to sound casual)* Indeed I must later go out on an errand.

VERITY Without an escort? With the streets full of drunkards?

DEMELZA 'Tis for Ross I must do it.

VERITY Would he wish you to?

Demelza struggles with her conscience. Can she really bring herself to lie to Verity? She decides that she can.

DEMELZA O' course he would.

CUT TO:

78: INT. ASSEMBLY ROOMS, BODMIN – DAY 5

Francis comes in and spots George at a table with Ray (reading the pamphlet from earlier) and Unwin.

RAY PENVENEN A terrible thing. A man of his standing? And that young wife of his – to think of her a widow—

He seems genuinely distressed at the thought. Now George spots Francis.

GEORGE *(amiably)* Francis! Are you joining us?

FRANCIS Will I not be interrupting your council of war?

GEORGE Against whom?

FRANCIS My cousin? As declared in your recent literary effort?

He puts the pamphlet down on the table. George hurriedly gets up and draws Francis aside so that Unwin and Ray won't hear their conversation.

FRANCIS *(cont'd)* 'Tis a piece of fiction entirely worthy of you!

George leads Francis ever further out of earshot.

FRANCIS *(cont'd)* So tell me – what could induce you to throw your weight *behind* Ross instead of against him?

GEORGE The very same question your wife asked me!

Though this reminder is a dagger to Francis's heart, he's damned if he'll let George know it.

GEORGE *(cont'd)* Naturally I could not consider it. Ross has offered me insolence once too often.

FRANCIS In that case, may I offer you *advice?*

GEORGE By all means.

FRANCIS You may flaunt your guineas on lavish garments and fancy carriages—

George bristles but says nothing.

FRANCIS *(cont'd)* You may purchase a coat of arms and deck out your servants in gaudy livery. You may buy your way into every club and mine and drawing room in the county. But what you will never buy is nobility – or breeding – or even common decency.

George looks at Francis as if Francis has taken leave of his senses.

GEORGE Are you quite certain you don't wish to apologize, Francis? Given the nature of our – association?

FRANCIS You own me. I acknowledge that. My indebtedness to you has long muddied the waters between us. So I trust that any confusion about my feelings is now entirely cleared up?

A moment between them. George is close to punching Francis. Francis is daring him to do so. George resists.

CUT TO:

79: EXT. CLIFF-TOP PATHWAY – DAY 5

Elizabeth walks along the cliff tops. She's debating whether to go to Bodmin.

CUT TO:

80: INT. ASSEMBLY ROOMS, BODMIN – DAY 5

The Assembly Rooms are filling up. George makes a beeline for Caroline, Unwin and Ray.

CAROLINE Mr Warleggan! I see that Unwin speaks the truth. He cannot stir an inch without you.

GEORGE He says the same of you.

CAROLINE Of course! We're both indispensable to his ascent in the world. I as a hunting trophy—

RAY PENVENEN Caroline—

CAROLINE And you as a – how to describe you? Benefactor? Sponsor? Paymaster?

GEORGE I'm certainly lending my support to his campaign—

UNWIN *(to Caroline)* Shall we go out and wave to the crowd?

CAROLINE And I am lending mine to his arm. I wonder which of us stands to gain the most?

They go out. George follows.

CUT TO:

81: EXT. SQUARE, BODMIN – DAY 5

Ross walks through the masses in the square. It will soon be time to present himself at the prison. He savours these final moments of free-dom, seeing individuals in the crowd rather than nameless faces: a drunken man, a begging child, two wealthy gentlemen, a destitute mother and baby, an urchin reminiscent of the young Demelza . . . and Tom Harry, who quickly walks in another direction. As Ross gets nearer to the Assembly Rooms, he sees Ray, Unwin, Caroline and George (alongside Michael Chenhalls, Hugh Dagge and various other officials) up on the hustings platform. George is swaggering amidst the upper echelons of society. It's a fitting illustration of where they now both are: George on high and Ross down below. He walks on, pushes his way through the crowds and disappears.

CUT TO:

82: INT. WHITE LION INN, BODMIN, BEDROOM – DAY 5

Demelza is getting dressed up to go out. She's really making an effort. Verity watches her anxiously.

VERITY Are you sure Ross meant you to go out alone? You're a lady after all—

DEMELZA But I was brought up a miner's daughter. An' there's naught a few drunkards can do that I couldn't give 'em back!

She puts on her cloak and goes out.

CUT TO:

83: INT. CROWN INN, BODMIN – DAY 5

Tom Harry pays a few coins to three men: Vigus, Oliver and Fiddick. Tankard makes notes in his notebook. Now Jud comes in, takes one look at them and skulks off into a corner. Has he come to an agreement with them or hasn't he? Crouched over a table now, shielding his activity from prying eyes, Jud begins to count out fifteen gold sovereigns. Suddenly he glances up and sees Prudie come in. He hastily hides the coins. Prudie comes over, suspicious.

PRUDIE What 'ee be up to, 'ee lizardy lousedy pissabed?

JUD Up to? I? Innocent as a new-mown babe!

Prudie snorts with derision and clips him round the head.

CUT TO:

84: INT. WHITE LION INN, BODMIN, BEDROOM – DAY 5

Verity is reading by the window when there's a knock at the door. Expecting Demelza, Verity goes to open it.

VERITY What did you forget, cousin? Oh—!

Francis pushes past her into the room.

FRANCIS Have you brandy or rum?

VERITY There's port—

FRANCIS Demelza's tipple. Where is she?

VERITY She went out. How are you, brother? Are you staying here?

FRANCIS The London inn – or some such—

He takes a swig of port then surveys her as if for the first time.

FRANCIS *(cont'd)* Well, sister, how does it feel to be married to a drunken brute?

VERITY Francis, I hoped—

FRANCIS That I was come to make peace? With my sister, perhaps. Not with a Mistress *Blamey*! Tell me, is he worth the loss of your home and family?

VERITY We're happy, Francis. And I hope the day will come when you'll be glad for me – and allow me home to Trenwith.

FRANCIS As soon as you like! Without him.

Verity's face falls. Francis watches her carefully.

FRANCIS *(cont'd)* Oh, do I disappoint you? I disappoint most people! Father, Elizabeth – *myself*! Why do I amount to precisely nothing? Whereas *Ross* – Ross is considered such a threat, men will spend a fortune to get him hanged! And yet I envy him!

VERITY You cannot.

FRANCIS If I were going to stand before my judges, I'd give 'em a piece of my mind! Francis Poldark Esquire, of Trenwith! And it wouldn't be the first time today!

Something in his tone makes Verity look at him more closely. He is flushed and though drunk, almost triumphant.

FRANCIS *(cont'd)* I met a man handing out pamphlets – defaming Ross in the grossest manner. I happen to know the author so I paid him a visit. And left him in no doubt as to my opinion. *(beat)* George?

VERITY Was that wise? When he owns the very roof over your head?

FRANCIS Oh, no doubt he's planning this minute how to punish me. But he may be defrauded.

Francis stares into the dregs of his glass. Verity watches him. A sudden fear crosses her face.

VERITY Do not lose heart, Francis. Tomorrow's a new day.

FRANCIS *(smiles savagely)* And it may never come.

He downs the rest of his drink and goes out.

CUT TO:

85: INT. TRENWITH HOUSE, OAK ROOM – DAY 5

Aunt Agatha is playing solitaire when Elizabeth comes in. She seems agitated.

ELIZABETH I wonder if I shouldn't go to Bodmin?

AUNT AGATHA To what purpose?

ELIZABETH To be with Francis.

Aunt Agatha raises a sceptical eyebrow.

AUNT AGATHA And your cousin?

ELIZABETH Ross has Demelza.

Aunt Agatha nods and returns to her card game.

CUT TO:

86: EXT. SQUARE, BODMIN – DUSK 5

Demelza is shouldering her way through the crowd. Her POV of the crowds milling about, crossing her path. Up ahead a shower of coins (an election tradition) is tossed and people push and scramble to retrieve them, brawling with each other to get at them. We are reminded just how capable Demelza is of looking after herself. She braces herself as she inches sideways through the throng. One man turns angrily and is about to punch her. She squares up to him defiantly and he, realizing she's a lady (and seeing her defiant expression), decides against confrontation. As Demelza continues to push her way through, she hears a familiar voice:

TOM CARNE'S VOICE I am the voice crying in the wilderness. Make ye ready the ways of the Lord for the kingdom of God is at hand!

Suddenly Demelza and Tom Carne come face to face. Tom is carrying a placard which proclaims: 'Silks and feathers cannot Vice disguise'.

DEMELZA Judas! Father?

TOM CARNE So now 'ee be cast into the pit, daughter, into this nest of vipers? Thy child is buried, thy 'usband's to 'ang! See now the wages of sin!

DEMELZA I know of no sin.

TOM CARNE Do 'ee live a goodly life? Do 'ee ne'er cozen nor deceive? E'en with th' best intentions? 'Tis the way the foul fiend works!

Demelza looks self-conscious. Surely this is what she's doing right now – something deceitful? Tom is convinced he's hit a raw nerve.

TOM CARNE *(cont'd)* Turn again, daughter! 'Ee'll never be more 'n a miner's daughter, for all thy fancy feathers! Come 'ome an' live a pure life! We'll find 'ee a crust an' plenty chores to keep 'ee from idleness.

DEMELZA Thank 'ee, Father. I take the offer kindly but I hope 'twill not be needed.

She gives him a peck on the cheek and shoulders her way back into the crowd. Tom Carne continues on his way.

TOM CARNE Vengeance is mine, saith the Lord. For the day of calamity is at hand . . .

CUT TO:

87: EXT. ASSEMBLY ROOMS, BODMIN – DUSK 5

George is standing near the entrance to the Assembly Rooms, looking out into the crowded square. A note is handed to him. It reads: 'We have hopes that Paynter will be persuaded, given the right incentive.' Feeling very pleased with himself now, George idly watches the throng of people outside. He sees several groups of gentlemen escorting ladies, shielding them from the rabble and bringing them safely inside. Then he sees Demelza, pushing her way through the crowd, elbowing, shoving, almost digging a way through – heading straight for the Assembly Rooms. A delicious idea occurs to him.

There are several officials on the door, making sure the rabble don't enter. George strolls up to one and takes him aside.

GEORGE Be advised, sir. An infamous harlot is approaching and must on no account be admitted.

The official looks doubtful. 'But sir—' George halts him in his tracks.

GEORGE *(cont'd)* This is a house of gentility. Can such a person be permitted to pollute its corridors?

The official continues to look doubtful.

GEORGE *(cont'd)* See here, man—

He produces a pamphlet from his pocket. It's the defamation of Ross. He points to one of the lines:

GEORGE *(cont'd)* 'Notorious doxy'. This is she.

He points to Demelza, who is now fast approaching (but who hasn't seen George). The official still looks dubious.

GEORGE *(cont'd)* And as any man knows, if it's written down, it must be true.

The official seems to respond to this. He goes forward to meet Demelza. George now retires to a distance to watch.

HIS POV: Demelza approaches the entrance and finds her way barred. At first she looks surprised. Then she argues. Then she pleads. The official is now showing her the pamphlet. George is almost crying with laughter.

ON DEMELZA:

DEMELZA *(outraged)* I'm no scullery maid! 'Tis the grossest lie! I come to see Mr Penvenen – he did particularly ask for me—

A smirk between two of the officials – 'I'll bet he did!'

DEMELZA *(cont'd)* *(growing desperate)* I beg you to let me through. 'Tis all the reason I've come to Bodmin. My husband's life depends on it!

The officials laugh at each other. 'Husband? A likely story.' They close ranks and Demelza realizes there's no way she's getting in there tonight. Hot tears of rage fill her eyes. To salvage what's left of her pride, she turns and walks away.

ON GEORGE: Shaking with laughter. This has made his night.

CUT TO:

88: INT. DWIGHT'S LODGINGS, BODMIN – DUSK 6

Francis is being led upstairs by the landlord.

LANDLORD Are 'ee sure Dr Enys was agreeable t'ee sharin' his chamber?

FRANCIS He was insistent, man, so less of your insolence and show me the door.

LANDLORD 'Tis a small chamber, sur, and but a single bed.

FRANCIS I shall not be needing a bed.

The landlord halts before a door, opens it to allow Francis to go inside. Francis enters – and shuts the door in the landlord's face. Presently the sound of the door being locked from the inside is heard.

CUT TO:

89: EXT. BODMIN JAIL – DUSK 5

Ross pushes his way through the unruly crowds and presents himself at the dismal gates of the jail.

CUT TO:

90: INT. BODMIN JAIL, CELL – DUSK 5

Ross is escorted into his cell and left there. He can hear shouts and altercations increasing outside.

CUT TO:

91: INT. DWIGHT'S LODGINGS, BODMIN – DUSK 5

Francis sits at a desk writing a letter.

CUT TO:

92: INT. BODMIN JAIL, CELL – NIGHT 5

Ross paces restlessly. Presently the door opens and Clymer comes in. He slaps a document on the table.

CLYMER The list. Of those summoned to speak against you.

ROSS *(amused)* A long list.

He scans it. Looks surprised. Then philosophical.

CLYMER Some of these people are your friends?

ROSS I'd thought so.

He continues to scan the list. A look of disappointment crosses his face.

ROSS *(cont'd)* Jud Paynter?

CLYMER Know him?

ROSS He was my servant.

CLYMER Now he's the Crown's.

Ross pauses to let this blow land. Jud's betrayal hits him hard.

CLYMER *(cont'd)* And the testimony of a loyal servant against his former master—

ROSS Nail in the coffin.

CLYMER Precisely.

CUT TO:

93: INT. WHITE LION INN, BODMIN, BEDROOM – NIGHT 5

Verity is at the window listening to the increasing noise of the crowds in the street below. Now Demelza comes in.

VERITY Oh, my dear, I was so worried! The crowds in the square—

Then she takes in Demelza's utterly desolate expression.

VERITY *(cont'd)* What is it? Did all go well?

DEMELZA Not – exactly.

VERITY Francis was here—

DEMELZA What did he want?

VERITY I'm not sure—

CUT TO:

94: INT. BODMIN JAIL, CELL – NIGHT 5

Ross sits writing a letter by candlelight. It begins 'My most beloved wife Demelza . . .'

CUT TO:

95: INT. DWIGHT'S LODGINGS – NIGHT 5

Francis continues writing. In the silence of the room all we hear is the quill scratching upon the paper and the tick of a clock. From outside in the street comes the occasional outbreak of drunken laughter. Francis continues to write.

CUT TO:

96: INT. TRENWITH HOUSE, LIBRARY – NIGHT 5

The clock is ticking. Geoffrey Charles has fallen asleep in Elizabeth's arms. Aunt Agatha is at the table doing her tarot cards. She lays down a card: the Tower.

CUT TO:

97: INT. DWIGHT'S LODGINGS – NIGHT 5

The clock strikes. Francis finishes his letter, folds it up and seals it.

CUT TO:

98: INT. TRENWITH HOUSE, LIBRARY – NIGHT 5

The clock strikes. Aunt Agatha lays down another card: Justice.
CUT TO:

99: INT. WHITE LION INN, BODMIN, BEDROOM – NIGHT 5

A clock is striking outside. Verity remains anxious, Demelza distraught. Suddenly and without warning Demelza heads for the door.

VERITY My dear – where are you going?

DEMELZA I have one last thing I must try.

She grabs her cloak and goes out again.
CUT TO:

100: INT. DWIGHT'S LODGINGS – NIGHT 5

The clock strikes. Louder. Francis gets out a pistol, primes it. And raises it to his head.
CUT TO:

101: INT. TRENWITH HOUSE, LIBRARY – NIGHT 5

The clock strikes. Louder. Aunt Agatha lays down another card: Death.
CUT TO:

102: INT. BODMIN JAIL, CELL – NIGHT 5

The clock strikes. Deafening. Ross sits alone in his cell. Awaiting his fate. Outside the noise of the riots grows louder still.

Episode 2

1: EXT. HENDRAWNA BEACH (FLASHBACK) – DAY (SPRING 1789)

Spectacular panoramic views of a long, deserted beach at sunrise. We pick out two figures walking along through the surf. As we go closer, we see it's Demelza and Ross, walking hand in hand. They stop to watch the sun rise. Ross kisses her. The sunlight bathes them in gold and blinds them.

CUT TO:

2: INT. BODMIN JAIL, CELL – NIGHT 5 (AUTUMN 1790)

Ross is staring into a candle flame as he comes back to the present. He is sitting at a table with his back to the door. He returns to his letter to Demelza. It continues: '. . . if the worst should happen and we are parted never to meet again on this earth –' He pauses. There's no way he's actually going to die, is there? A knock at the door.

ROSS Save your breath, Mr Clymer. I'm in no mood—

GEORGE'S VOICE Sounds ominous.

Ross turns slowly in his chair. George is standing in the doorway. Incredibly he's smiling. Ross looks him in the eye – and returns his smile.

ROSS You bribed the jailer.

GEORGE Naturally.

Ross motions politely for George to sit down. George graciously accepts.

GEORGE *(cont'd)* I hope I'm not disturbing you?

ROSS I was writing to my wife.

It's all so civilized and measured. No raised voices. They could almost be old friends. In fact, this is the first time we've ever seen them sit across a table from each other.

GEORGE I have not come to fight, Ross. But to confess.

An expression of mild surprise from Ross.

GEORGE *(cont'd)* Confess myself disarmed. Impressed. Of course you might have guessed that Elizabeth would ask me to intervene. But would you guess that Francis did too? That Ray Penvenen tried to fight your corner? Alfred Barbary? Lord Devoran? How do you inspire such loyalty? It impresses me. I see its value. I could use it.

Ross says nothing. He continues to watch George as a cat watches a mouse.

GEORGE *(cont'd)* I could do what they ask me. Remove the hostile witnesses. Drop a word in the ear of the prosecution. I could even take the stand and give you a character reference. How would *that* sway the jury? The very man whose cousin perished? *(then)* What do you say, Ross? Will you meet me halfway? Will you take the hand of friendship?

He holds out his hand. Incredibly he seems sincere. Vulnerable even. Ross considers. It would be so easy to reach out to George, to accept his outstretched hand. He's almost there. And then he smiles.

ROSS Forgive me. Are you truly so deluded? Do you really think I would *ever* shake your hand?

For a moment there is a flicker of disappointment on George's face. Then he too smiles.

GEORGE No. Not for a single moment. But when you go to the gallows, I'll be able to say, hand on heart, to Elizabeth – I offered Ross Poldark my help and he turned me down. So thank you – for being every bit as predictable as I hoped you'd be.

ROSS And thank *you*. For reminding me what *can* and *cannot* be bought.

Ross returns to his letter, leaving George to puzzle out quite how insulting that last statement is. As George gets up to leave, Ross doesn't even look up.

CUT TO:

3: INT. CROWN INN, BODMIN – NIGHT 5

Dwight is having a quiet drink and making notes for his speech at the trial. All around him are rowdy, drunken commoners. Aggrieved voices complaining. One man – Jack Tripp – seems particularly vocal. At first Dwight is lost in his thoughts and doesn't notice who's talking: Paul, Jud and Prudie.

JACK TRIPP'S VOICE This election? 'Tis a joke! What diff'rence do it make?

PAUL'S VOICE Naught f' th' likes o' we—

JACK TRIPP'S VOICE Who suffers when mines close? Not politicians—

PAUL'S VOICE Who starves when corn gets shipp'd abroad?

JACK TRIPP'S VOICE Not fancy folk—

PRUDIE'S VOICE Stuff'd t' th' gizzards wi' beef – while we scrape by on black bread an' beech leaves!

Dwight, about to leave, notices Paul, Jud and Prudie.

PAUL In France they wud'n stand f'r it!

JACK TRIPP 'Twill 'appen 'ere soon enough! Bin out there, 'ave 'ee? (*i.e. the square outside*) 'Tis like a powder keg!

Dwight passes them on his way out.

PRUDIE Dr Enys! Wha' brings 'ee here?

DWIGHT Same as you, Prudie.

PAUL To speak f'r Cap'n Ross?

DWIGHT As I'm sure we all will.

Murmurs of assent from everyone. Except Jud, who remains remarkably quiet and studies the bottom of his mug of ale.

DWIGHT *(cont'd)* Mr Paynter, are you ill?

JUD Dammit, can a man not study th'innards of a jug without bein' clepp'd malingerer?

DWIGHT I commend you to your studies.

JACK TRIPP Be goin' out there? 'Ave a care! 'Twill take but a spark an'—

He mimes an explosion. Dwight nods in acknowledgement and goes out.

CUT TO:

4: EXT. ASSEMBLY ROOMS, BODMIN – NIGHT 5

Demelza is fighting her way through the crowds towards the Assembly Rooms. This time the mood on the street is rowdier and more hostile than ever. Demelza's expression is absolutely resolute. She puts her head down and shoulders her way through – much to the surprise of the people she barges aside. Now, as she approaches the Assembly Rooms, she hangs back. She locates the officials who had previously denied her entry. She scans the crowd and waits for a group of well-heeled guests to arrive. Then she puts up the hood on her cloak and sneaks in alongside them.

CUT TO:

5: INT. TRENWITH HOUSE, LIBRARY – NIGHT 5

Aunt Agatha is gathering up her cards. Elizabeth comes in, sees her. It's the final straw.

ELIZABETH For pity's sake! Must we always have these dire predictions?

Aunt Agatha looks up calmly as if Elizabeth has taken leave of her senses.

ELIZABETH *(cont'd)* Not once have I known you forecast an outcome which was remotely cheering!

AUNT AGATHA *(calmly)* I am not divining the future. I am entertaining myself with a game of Snap!

Calmly Aunt Agatha continues to shuffle her cards. Then:

AUNT AGATHA *(cont'd)* Go to Bodmin, Elizabeth. You will never be satisfied till you do.

CUT TO:

6: INT. WHITE LION INN, BODMIN, BEDROOM – NIGHT 5

Verity is unable to sleep. She is fretting over her encounter with Francis. Now she takes pen and paper and begins to scribble a note: 'My dear Francis . . .'

VERITY *(VO)* 'My dear Francis, you will think me foolish, but I would be glad of your assurance that you do not intend to do yourself a harm . . .'

She pauses. Then, convincing herself she's overreacting, she screws up the piece of paper.

CUT TO:

7: INT. ASSEMBLY ROOMS, BODMIN – NIGHT 5

The Assembly Rooms are bursting at the seams with people awaiting the election results. Demelza pushes her way through the throng, anxiously scanning the crowds in search of her target. Finally, to her relief, she sees him: across the room, chatting with Unwin and Caroline: Ray Penvenen. She hangs back, studying her prey, mulling over her ambush tactics. She is near enough to overhear the following:

CAROLINE What a jovial sort is George Warleggan. I wonder if he'll be so jolly if his investment fails?

RAY PENVENEN Investment—?

CAROLINE Has he not purchased votes for Unwin to the tune of two thousand pounds? But will not his rivals be trying to do the same? Dear me, how awkward. Still, I suppose it's worth it if your aim is to influence Parliament without ever stepping out of Cornwall.

Unwin is looking at Ray with an imploring look which says, 'Can't you get her to keep her voice down?'

CAROLINE *(cont'd)* *(laughing)* I told you I'd make a bad parliamentary wife!

Now Demelza decides to take courage and walks towards them.

RAY PENVENEN Mistress Poldark, how delightful!

DEMELZA Mr Penvenen! To think of us meeting again so soon!

RAY PENVENEN May I introduce my niece, Caroline? Mistress Demelza Poldark of Nampara. And Mr Unwin Trevaunance.

They all bow to each other.

CAROLINE Are you here for the election, ma'am?

DEMELZA No, ma'am, for the assizes.

CAROLINE Oh yes, Unwin, were you not telling me there was a Poldark to be tried this week?

DEMELZA That's my husband, ma'am.

CAROLINE And is he guilty? What did he do?

Unwin clears his throat loudly to silence Caroline.

CAROLINE *(cont'd)* *(blithely)* Well, if I were the judge, I'd sentence him to be returned to his wife without delay!

A loud commotion is heard from outside.

UNWIN That must be the crowd, clamouring for me. Will you join me outside?

CAROLINE Why not? I like a baying mob.

They head off. Demelza remains with Ray.

RAY PENVENEN I was about to send word, ma'am. My cow Minta's near-recovered! If there was any way I could show my gratitude—?

DEMELZA *(with a smile)* Well, since you mention it—

CUT TO:

8: INT. ASSEMBLY ROOMS, BODMIN – NIGHT 5

RAY PENVENEN Influence? I've no influence of that sort. It would prejudice your husband's case, not help it!

DEMELZA But if it was put the right way—?

RAY PENVENEN If it was put *any* way! No, ma'am, I wouldn't dream of trying to persuade a judge. Believe me, the law is above that sort of thing.

DEMELZA But politics is not? *(seeing him look confused)* Just now I heard your niece say that George Warleggan paid two thousand pounds to get Unwin elected?

RAY PENVENEN Ah – yes—

DEMELZA So why is it right to pay for votes but wrong to ask a favour of a judge?

RAY PENVENEN (*urging her to keep her voice down*) Believe me, ma'am, I sympathize. I hope the court will look kindly on your husband. But the surest way of attaining the *opposite*, would be to try and influence the judge.

DEMELZA (*seemingly defeated*) I see. Yes. I do see that. Forgive me, sir. I'm a little despairing.

She bows, turns, makes to leave. And then:

DEMELZA (*cont'd*) Is he a kindly man? In appearance, I mean?

RAY PENVENEN Justice Lister? Somewhat severe.

DEMELZA Small and stout?

RAY PENVENEN Tall and lean.

He's unaware that Demelza is now scanning the room, her eyes darting about to see if anyone fits this description. She spots a possible contender.

DEMELZA An' likes his port?

RAY PENVENEN Resolutely sober.

Demelza's eyes light on a tall, thin, grim-faced, soberly dressed man in his early fifties who is standing alone, drinking water – and whose manner seems to deter approach. She knows at once this is Justice Wentworth Lister. Her heart sinks.

CUT TO:

9: INT. BODMIN JAIL, CELL – NIGHT 5

Ross is pacing, restless, fired up from his encounter with George. He can hear the clamour of restive crowds outside in the square. Clymer is shown in. He seems ruffled.

ROSS Sounds lively out there.

CLYMER The rabble are out in force tonight.

He slams his bag down on the table and begins to unload documents and papers.

ROSS You've been busy.

CLYMER Your defence is proving more of a challenge than I'd anticipated.

ROSS *(laughs)* And to think I might have been able to assist it!

CLYMER How?

ROSS A man called earlier. A person of considerable influence. Offering to remove hostile witnesses and speak on my behalf.

CLYMER You should bite his hand off.

ROSS Doubtless you're right. But the cost was more than I could stomach. D'you have the document from Harris Pascoe?

Clymer gets out a document and gives it to Ross.

CLYMER Your Last Will and Testament?

CUT TO:

10: INT. TRENWITH HOUSE, ELIZABETH'S ROOM – NIGHT 6

Geoffrey Charles is sleeping. Elizabeth kisses his forehead.

ELIZABETH Sssshhhhh, my darling. I'll return soon. And bring Papa with me.

She gets up and goes out.

CUT TO:

11: INT. ASSEMBLY ROOMS, BODMIN – NIGHT 5

Dwight is pushing through the crowds inside the Assembly Rooms. He sees Unwin, Ray, George and Caroline across the room. George is urging Unwin to go out into the square (ready for the election results announcement). As they head out, Caroline, who is bringing up the rear of the party, catches sight of Dwight and goes over to him.

CAROLINE Are you stalking me, Dr Enys?

DWIGHT Not at all, ma'am. But now I'm here, may I be of service?

CAROLINE Can you prescribe something to keep me awake?

DWIGHT You find the election boring?

CAROLINE Exceedingly dull. And the rabble out there insufferable.

A roar goes up outside as the election results begin to be announced ('Gentlemen! I have here the results of the election for the Bodmin County constituency of Cornwall . . .')

DWIGHT Oh, I grant you it seems unpleasant. But take each man for himself and he's likeable enough.

CAROLINE Are you a Jacobin, like Ross Poldark?

DWIGHT It's clear you don't know Ross Poldark.

CAROLINE No, but I expect to tomorrow, and hope for better entertainment than I've had tonight.

DWIGHT Perhaps you're the sort who takes a window at Tyburn for the pleasure of seeing someone choked to death?

CAROLINE Is it any business of yours if I am?

DWIGHT No, I'm thankful not.

(In the background the announcement has continued: '. . . the total number of votes for each candidate was as follows: Chenhalls,

Michael: two thousand, two hundred and fifty; Dagge, Hugh: one thousand, two hundred and three; Trevaunance, Unwin: one thousand, two hundred and three.') Uproar has greeted the end of this announcement.

CAROLINE In any case, there's violence here to be had – *and* the promise of bloodshed! Shall we avail ourselves?

She heads out. Dwight hesitates then, against his better judgement, follows.

CUT TO:

12: INT. ASSEMBLY ROOMS, BODMIN – NIGHT 5

Demelza is edging closer to Justice Lister. She contrives to be standing right behind him when he turns to put his glass on a table – and accidentally steps on her foot. Demelza gives a ladylike squeal.

JUSTICE LISTER Dear madam! My deepest apologies. Are you hurt?

DEMELZA Only my dignity, sir!

JUSTICE LISTER May I assist you to a chair? Some port, perhaps?

DEMELZA I never touch it, sir.

Justice Lister gives a small smile of approval. Demelza's in!

CUT TO:

13: EXT. ASSEMBLY ROOMS, BODMIN – NIGHT 5

Confusion and uproar follow the election announcement. Some people are arguing. There is even a suggestion of fisticuffs. Unwin is looking daggers at his rival Hugh Dagge and the outright winner Michael Chenhalls.

RAY PENVENEN A most farcical state of affairs! Three candidates for two seats?

GEORGE We had to give 'em *some* result! And since neither candidate's prepared to give way—

UNWIN There'll be pressure on *me* to stand aside—

GEORGE There can be no question of that. The key is to regard yourself as selected – and act accordingly.

UNWIN But how? I'm tied in second place!

At this moment Michael Chenhalls is being hoisted onto a chair by his supporters and carried off into the crowd.

GEORGE The chair, man! Take a second chair! Claim your seat before Dagge gets a chance to contest it!

UNWIN *(aside to Ray)* I must claim something – or Caroline won't look twice at me.

RAY PENVENEN She barely looks twice at you *now*!

GEORGE Come, now! There's no time to lose!

George is summoning a chair, helping Unwin into it and dispatching it into the crowd, whilst Hugh Dagge is looking outraged. Caroline and Dwight come out of the Assembly Rooms in time to see Unwin being chaired away, looking more than a little nervous.

CUT TO:

14: EXT. ASSEMBLY ROOMS, BODMIN – NIGHT 5

Unwin is looking nervous as he is chaired through the crowds. He can sense hostility – and though he's waving and smiling gamely, he's feeling increasingly uneasy. Suddenly there's a surge from the crowd and several overtly hostile people converge on him. One of them is Jack Tripp.

JACK TRIPP Who are ye?

UNWIN Er – well, I – er—

JACK TRIPP D'ye know me? D'ye speak for me?

UNWIN I'm your elected member—

JACK TRIPP Who elected ye? Did I? Did any here?

The crowd chimes in: 'Not I', 'We didn't!', 'Not us!', etc.

JACK TRIPP *(cont'd)* Ye don' speak for me! But mebbe *this* will!

He throws a heap of dung in Unwin's face.

CUT TO:

15: EXT. ASSEMBLY ROOMS, BODMIN – NIGHT 5

CAROLINE *(trying not to laugh)* Lord, I hope he's brought his rose water!

CUT TO:

16: EXT. ASSEMBLY ROOMS, BODMIN – NIGHT 5

Unwin is being pelted with more dung. Several members of the crowd join in (though Jack Tripp is the prime culprit). Unwin yelps as he flails about trying to protect himself. Soldiers now push forward. Jack Tripp is seized by two and marched off. Others clear a way for Unwin and his chair to make a hasty retreat back to the Assembly Rooms. Caroline and Dwight draw aside as Unwin is bustled inside. Now they make their way into the Assembly Rooms.

CUT TO:

17: INT. ASSEMBLY ROOMS, BODMIN – NIGHT 5

Caroline and Dwight enter the Assembly Rooms. Caroline has been hugely entertained by the spectacle.

CAROLINE Is it always like this in Bodmin?

DWIGHT I couldn't say. I live near Truro. I'm only here for tomorrow's trial.

CAROLINE You speak for Ross Poldark? *(Dwight nods.)* I look forward to seeing how you acquit yourself.

DWIGHT Happily it's not I who is on trial.

CAROLINE Are you quite certain of that?

DWIGHT You flatter yourself, ma'am.

CAROLINE Are all men so odiously conceited?

DWIGHT I shouldn't put conceit as the particular property of one sex.

CAROLINE No? Well, how gracious of you to correct me, sir! I wonder you're so solicitous for one you so clearly despise.

DWIGHT You're mistaken, madam. I neither solicit nor despise.

He bows curtly and departs, frustrated at himself for even giving her the time of day. Caroline watches him go. Deeply intrigued.

CUT TO:

18: INT. BODMIN JAIL, CELL – NIGHT 5

Ross is pacing, reading through the document, watched by Clymer.

ROSS *(laughing)* If there's to be a reckoning, it's as well to have one's affairs in order! *(beat)* Little as there is of value. My household effects, my shares in Wheal Leisure—

CLYMER Mr Pascoe mentions a 'Wheal Grace'—

ROSS My father's old mine. It's derelict.

CLYMER But still yours – and still deemed an asset.

ROSS Not by me! I deem it a worthless hole in the ground! *(cheerfully)* But by all means let me bequeath it to my wife, along with all my other debts and liabilities! *(It finally dawns.)* I've really left her nothing.

It's not a pleasing thought. He takes the will and signs it.

CUT TO:

19: INT. ASSEMBLY ROOMS, BODMIN – NIGHT 5

Ray and George are looking across at Unwin, who has returned and is spraying himself with perfume in an attempt to fumigate himself after the dung assault.

GEORGE Mission accomplished. Unwin has established his claim.

RAY PENVENEN Almost at the cost of his life!

GEORGE Cheap at the price!

RAY PENVENEN That rabble – have they no respect for their betters – or the law? I tell you, someone needs to take them by the scruff of the neck— *(suddenly)* Good God – what is the woman doing?

CUT TO:

20: INT. ASSEMBLY ROOMS, BODMIN – NIGHT 5

DEMELZA A judge? How fascinating! I'm sure I'd not have the first notion of how to go about such a thing!

CUT TO:

21: INT. ASSEMBLY ROOMS, BODMIN – NIGHT 5

RAY PENVENEN She'll hang her husband if she's not careful!

George is suddenly on alert. Seeing Demelza with Judge Lister, he knows exactly how to turn it to his advantage.

CUT TO:

22: INT. ASSEMBLY ROOMS, BODMIN – NIGHT 5

DEMELZA So let me ask your lordship – how can a body judge – if a person be tellin' the truth?

JUSTICE LISTER Well—

DEMELZA For some of 'em's so downright convincin' – an' have all th' evidence to back 'em up – but how if the evidence be *false*?

CUT TO:

23: INT. ASSEMBLY ROOMS, BODMIN – NIGHT 5

George is edging nearer to where Judge Lister and Demelza are talking.
CUT TO:

24: INT. ASSEMBLY ROOMS, BODMIN – NIGHT 5

DEMELZA Say f'r instance, that a body did know the truth – about an accused? Wouldn't he – or she – be obliged to speak?

JUSTICE LISTER Most assuredly. In the appropriate place. Which would be the court.

Now George is edging through the crowds, getting closer so that presently he's in earshot. Now out of the corner of her eye Demelza spots him. She knows it's now or never.

DEMELZA Then put the case, sir – that a body – know'd some other body – who paid money – so that other bodies might speak lies – against the body who that other body wished to injure—

JUSTICE LISTER You list a great many bodies, ma'am. Are any of them here now?

DEMELZA Well in truth – since your lordship do ask me d'rectly—

But it's too late. George is already upon them.

GEORGE Mistress Demelza, what a pleasure to see you. And your lordship – out unusually late?

JUSTICE LISTER Indeed, sir. Though not unagreeably detained.

A nod at Demelza – who smiles back at him.

GEORGE *(to Demelza)* You must be grateful for the distraction, ma'am. Were you speaking of your husband? *(to Justice Lister)* Of course you will meet him tomorrow.

JUSTICE LISTER Sir?

GEORGE Ross Poldark? When he comes before you in court. *(feigning innocence)* Oh, I see – you were not aware?

JUSTICE LISTER No, sir, I was not.

He looks coldly at Demelza, now realizing exactly the purpose of her engaging him in conversation.

JUSTICE LISTER *(cont'd)* You'll pardon me, ma'am, sir. I must retire.

GEORGE Let me accompany you.

They both bow to Demelza and leave.

GEORGE *(cont'd) (as they go)* What d'you make of this assault on our newly elected MP? Barely escaped with his life! If this goes on we'll have revolution on our hands!

JUSTICE LISTER In Cornwall?

GEORGE People are fearful, sir. People are wondering when a clear message will be sent. Those who stir up disorder should expect the severest penalty. Would you not agree?

Demelza remains, appalled at the catastrophic failure of her attempt – and its possible consequences.

JACK TRIPP *(VO)* There'll be a reckoning, mark 'ee!

CUT TO:

25: INT. BODMIN JAIL, CELL – NIGHT 5

The sounds of unrest outside continue. Ross and Clymer are sitting at the table, looking at Clymer's documents as they hear voices out in the corridor.

JACK TRIPP'S VOICE Commons don' 'old wi' bein' tramp'd underfoot! Bring down th' fancy folks an' let th' poor rise!

Ross looks through the bars of his cell and sees Jack Tripp being bundled through into a neighbouring cell, scuffling and struggling with the soldiers who have brought him.

JACK TRIPP Nay, 'ee shan't muzzle me! I'm a free man – I've a right to speak!

A soldier brings a weapon crashing down on Jack Tripp's head and knocks him out cold.

ROSS Apparently not.

Ross returns to the table. Clymer looks dismayed.

CLYMER This has not helped our cause.

Ross has no idea what he means. Yet.

CUT TO:

26: INT. DWIGHT'S LODGINGS – NIGHT 5

Dwight is heading for his room when the landlord appears behind him.

LANDLORD Beg pardon, sur, there's a gentleman within—

DWIGHT In my chamber?

LANDLORD Say 'ee did 'vite 'im to share, should he find no other lodgings.

DWIGHT *(remembering)* A Mr Francis Poldark? Oh, yes, I did say so.

The landlord withdraws. Dwight taps at the door to alert Francis of his arrival, then lifts the latch to go in. But the door is locked from the inside. Dwight rattles the door, knocks again, louder. No answer.

CUT TO:

27: INT. BODMIN JAIL, CELL – NIGHT 5

The sounds of riot continue outside. Clymer fishes out a document and hands it to Ross.

CLYMER This is the statement I've prepared for you. You may find it a little contrite for your taste.

Ross glances at the document, then smiles.

ROSS There are limits – even if one's neck is at stake.

CLYMER So you'd go to the gallows on a point of principle? Of course it's your life to do as you please.

Ross continues to read, to shake his head in disgust.

CLYMER *(cont'd)* Got a wife? Got a family? Don't think it's worth making this concession for their sake?

Ross looks up, thoughtful. Is he prepared to do that?

ROSS I appreciate your efforts. But I cannot put my name to beggary and flattery.

CLYMER Dammit, man, you have no choice! The case against you is too strong. It's not a question of *whether* you'll be found guilty, but *when!* – and what the sentence will be! All you can do is paint a penitent figure so you may escape the worst. *(seeing Ross unmoved)* The worst, I tell you! *(then)* Perhaps you will consider *that* before you sleep tonight.

Clymer goes out.

CUT TO:

28: INT. DWIGHT'S LODGINGS – NIGHT 5

Dwight returns with the landlord, who has another key which he puts into the lock.

LANDLORD Locked, sir. From the *inside.*

The landlord continues to twiddle the key in the lock (to no avail), while Dwight continues to knock at the door.

DWIGHT We may need to break it down.

LANDLORD Nay, 'twill damage it – an' who's to pay—

DWIGHT Dammit, man, Mister Poldark may be ill. He may even be—

Unexpectedly the door opens. Francis is actually alive!

CUT TO:

29: INT. ASSEMBLY ROOMS, BODMIN – NIGHT 5

As she is on her way out, Demelza encounters George, who is returning. She knows she should ignore his smug grin, but somehow she just can't.

DEMELZA I heard just now that Unwin Trevaunance will go to Parliament.

GEORGE As an elected MP, yes.

DEMELZA And yet – forgive my ignorance but ought not such a person be – as 'twere – a man of the *people*?

GEORGE What a curious idea.

DEMELZA Is it? That a man who be corrupt – and spineless – with no care for the people – be elected to *speak for* the people?

GEORGE It may seem strange to you—

DEMELZA No more than that Ross – who d' truly care for people – might hang on account of a spineless an' corrupt justice. D'you think that's fair?

GEORGE It's the way of the world.

George is about to walk off. Then:

DEMELZA Why do you hate him? What has he ever done to deserve it?

GEORGE I doubt you'd understand.

DEMELZA Because I am not so well bred as you? I'm a miner's daughter. You're a blacksmith's grandson. What's the difference?

GEORGE The difference is, you will always be a miner's daughter. Whereas I am a gentleman.

DEMELZA And I a gentleman's wife.

GEORGE Soon to be a gentleman's widow?

Tired of the conversation, George bows and walks past her back into the Assembly Rooms. Demelza hangs on to her dignity long enough for him to disappear, then her face crumples.

CUT TO:

30: INT. DWIGHT'S LODGINGS – NIGHT 5

Dwight glances around the room – at a letter propped up on the table addressed to 'Elizabeth Poldark', at Francis's bloodless face and distracted manner.

FRANCIS Are you a fatalist, Enys? Do you believe we're masters of our own destiny?

DWIGHT Well, I—

Francis sweeps aside some papers and reveals the pistol.

FRANCIS Five minutes ago I pointed this at my head. It misfired. Since then I've been debating whether to try again. *(then)* Oh, I agree, it's in very poor taste – to make use of your hospitality for such a purpose. Anyway, the thing's not done – so for now you have a talkative companion instead of a silent one.

DWIGHT I don't understand. Why would you wish—? *(then)* You're young, propertied, respected, you have a beautiful wife, a healthy son—

FRANCIS Stop! Or I shall weep for joy!

Dwight moves to take the pistol away. Francis puts his hand on it to prevent him.

FRANCIS *(cont'd)* Shall we have some brandy? At any rate I can do no damage till I have fresh powder.

DWIGHT I hope you will reconsider.

He pours brandy for both of them. Francis raises his glass.

FRANCIS Here's to the devil! Lord knows whose side he has been on tonight.

CUT TO:

31: INT. BODMIN JAIL, CELL – NIGHT 5

Ross paces his cell like a caged tiger, listening to the sounds of riot outside. Against his better judgement, he begins to read Clymer's document.

CUT TO:

32: INT. WHITE LION INN, BODMIN, BEDROOM – NIGHT 5

Demelza lets herself into the darkened room. She tiptoes across and sits on the bed. Distraught. Verity stirs.

VERITY Did you have better luck?

DEMELZA If anything I've made it worse.

VERITY What did you hope to achieve?

DEMELZA I don' know. Anything. *(then)* I lost my child, Verity. How would I bear it if I lost Ross too?

CUT TO:

33: EXT. BODMIN MOOR – DAY 6

Daybreak. Rain is falling, the sky is dark, the clouds are heavy. Distant thunder continues to rumble. A coach rattles its way towards

Bodmin. As we get closer we see that one of the passengers is Elizabeth.
CUT TO:

34: INT. BODMIN JAIL – DAY 6

Ross dresses in preparation for his trial. Sounds of rain falling and distant thunder. Outside in the corridor he hears voices, the clang of a cell door and a voice shouting, 'You! Tripp! On your feet now!' Ross goes to the door of his cell. Through the bars he can see the bruised, bedraggled and dazed Jack Tripp being led out of his cell.

ROSS D'you go before the court?

JACK TRIPP With head held high!

ROSS And sore, no doubt!

JACK TRIPP Not fer long. The noose is a great curer fer 'eadaches!

ROSS I wish you justice – if there's any to be found.

JACK TRIPP Which there ain't – as we both d' know. So luck it must be!

ROSS For both of us, then!

A moment between them. Then Jack Tripp is led away.
CUT TO:

35: INT. DWIGHT'S LODGINGS – DAY 6

Rain is falling as Francis, already awake and dressed, is sitting at the desk, cleaning his pistol – aware that Dwight is watching him.

FRANCIS Why not ask? Am I cleaning it to put away? Or do I intend to use it again?

DWIGHT Do you?

FRANCIS *(smiles)* If I see a suitable target.

CUT TO:

36: EXT. SQUARE, BODMIN – DAY 6

George walks briskly across the square. Presently he meets with Tankard.

GEORGE Everything in order?

TANKARD Witnesses primed. And we've augmented the crowd with persons who – share our view of the accused. And will not scruple to make their voices heard!

GEORGE And his lordship—?

TANKARD Is immune to persuasion.

GEORGE On the contrary, I believe he was persuaded last night. Without a penny changing hands.

George and Tankard walk off, just as Elizabeth is seen arriving (George doesn't see her). Crowds are milling everywhere. In contrast to Demelza, Elizabeth is completely out of her comfort zone and struggles to make her way through towards the court.

CUT TO:

37: EXT. ASSIZES COURT, BODMIN – DAY 6

Elizabeth arrives. Crowds are milling everywhere. The mood of unrest is still in evidence. Soldiers mingle with the crowds, trying to keep order. The sense that at any moment it could all erupt again. Meanwhile, outside the court, people are pushing and jostling to get in. Nervous and full of dread, Demelza and Verity arrive and go in together.

JUSTICE LISTER *(VO)* As ringleader and instigator of the affray, in which you did unlawfully, riotously, and tumultuously assemble together . . .

CUT TO:

38: INT. ASSIZES COURT, BODMIN – DAY 6

As Demelza and Verity go in and find seats Justice Wentworth Lister, resplendent in his robes, is speaking.

JUSTICE LISTER . . . in direct contravention of the Riot Act of 1714, you have been found guilty.

Jack Tripp is in the dock.

JUSTICE LISTER *(cont'd)* It only now remains for me to pass the dreadful sentence of the law, which is that you be taken from hence to a place of execution, where you shall be hanged by the neck until you die.

Howls of protest from some people in court. Roars of approval from others. Jack Tripp is taken away. Demelza is visibly shaken by this sentence. Not that she knows Jack Tripp personally – but the severity of the sentencing does not bode well for Justice Lister's 'mercy'.

CUT TO:

39: INT. BODMIN JAIL, CORRIDOR – DAY 6

Jack Tripp, being led down to the cells, meets Ross being led from them. A look between them. Sympathy from Ross. A shrug from Jack Tripp. Life is cheap. It's what he'd expected.

CUT TO:

40: INT. ASSIZES COURT, BODMIN – DAY 6

Demelza glances round and sees Unwin and Caroline. Unwin is full of swagger, waving and greeting people as if he's now Prime Minister. Elsewhere Demelza spots Tankard and Tom Harry (though she doesn't recognize these two). Then she sees Francis and Dwight. Then Zacky, Paul and Henshawe. Then, finally, George, in a corner of the balcony by himself. The room is seething, tension is mounting. Sellers of hot pasties, chestnuts and lemonade jostle with spectators. Demelza looks across at the jury. They look stern and forbidding. Demelza feels as if she is about to faint. All sounds in the room seem to be distorted. She can see Justice Lister speaking but no words seem to come out of his mouth. Then suddenly she is jolted back to the present.

CLERK OF THE COURT Call Ross Poldark.

Demelza's head swims, she grips Verity to steady herself. Now Ross is led into the court. He looks pale but defiant. He doesn't look at the crowd so does not see Demelza. Several people in the crowd shout: 'There he is! There's the murderer!', 'Justice! Justice for Matthew Sanson', 'Hang him!' Verity and Demelza are shocked.

VERITY Why do they cry murder? That is not the charge.

Zacky and Paul look outraged at the tactics of the Warleggan supporters.

CLERK OF THE COURT Order! Silence in court!

The jury members glance at each other. Clearly the shouted accusations about Ross are troubling and difficult to ignore. George remains impassive. Not betraying the smallest glimmer of the satisfaction he secretly feels. Gradually the noise subsides. Now the Clerk of the Court steps up and reads the indictment.

CLERK OF THE COURT *(cont'd)* Ross Vennor Poldark, you stand accused that on the seventh of January, you did incite divers peaceable citizens to riot. And furthermore, wilfully and with malice aforethought, did plunder, steal and take away divers goods belonging to a ship in distress. And furthermore . . .

The speech seems to fade away into white noise and the cries of the Warleggan supporters ('Disgraceful', 'Hang him', 'Criminal', 'Murderer', etc.) as Verity turns to Demelza.

VERITY So many against him?

DEMELZA Only the ones paid by George.

VERITY But if the jury believe them?

Demelza's expression gives its own answer. The Clerk of the Court winds up his address:

CLERK OF THE COURT . . . without care, without conscience, without the fear of God before his eyes. *(then)* Culprit, how do you plead?

ROSS Not guilty.

Muttering of 'Disgraceful', 'Shameful', 'He must be made an example of' from the Warleggan supporters. Unnoticed by anyone Elizabeth slips into the back of the balcony and takes her seat. Now the prosecuting counsel, Henry Bull, KC, steps up. Bull pauses to survey the court as if it were his kingdom. But when he speaks, his manner is more engaging than that of the Clerk of the Court. He speaks to the jury as if they were friends, appealing to their sense of fair play rather than hectoring or lecturing them.

HENRY BULL Gentlemen of the jury. You'll recall, in the last great gale of winter, a ship got into distress and was driven ashore on Hendrawna Beach, just below the house of the accused.

Murmuring from the court.

HENRY BULL *(cont'd)* Here is a man comfortably circumstanced, a mine and landowner with an ancient family name. You might expect that such a man's first thought would be for the safety of the poor souls aboard. Instead, he sought to rouse the lawless spirits of the district so that when the wreck came in it could be plundered with the utmost dispatch.

Zacky and Paul look outraged at this depiction of them and their motives.

HENRY BULL *(cont'd)* Witnesses will testify that the accused personally directed the plunder – and that survivors from the wreck were beaten as they struggled ashore.

PAUL That's a lie!

HENRY BULL When a contingent of excise men and soldiers arrived, the prisoner warned them not to interfere and threatened them with violence if they did. When they nonetheless went down to the beach, they were set upon by the accused – and one received near-fatal injuries.

Demelza is shaking her head in disbelief. George remains impassive, watching as if with casual interest.

Dwight glances up and sees Caroline on the balcony. She is watching with keen interest. Unwin, at her shoulder, seems to be making witty remarks to her. None of which she appears to hear. Until, seeing Dwight, she decides to take an interest in Unwin and laughs at some remark he's made. Dwight is disgusted – at Caroline's frivolity – and at himself for caring.

HENRY BULL *(cont'd)* It's no exaggeration to suggest that what we have here is a lawless revolutionary. Self-serving, contemptuous of his class and careless of others' property. Of all the crimes committed that night, this man was the instigator and chief perpetrator.

Outrage from Zacky and Paul, quiet dismay from Henshawe. Applause and cheers from the Warleggan supporters. Demelza and Verity are looking increasingly horrified at Bull's recitation. Dwight cannot stop himself from glancing up at Caroline, who is watching, fascinated, apparently enjoying the entire spectacle.

HENRY BULL *(cont'd)* It is not within my scope to call attention to the previous acts of lawlessness which have marred the accused's character . . .

CLYMER *(leaping to his feet)* Objection!

Uproar in the court. Roars of disapproval from Ross's supporters: 'Unfair!', 'Irrelevant!', 'Outrageous!' The Warleggan supporters begin shouting: 'Murderer', 'Drunkard', 'Seducer', 'Renegade', 'Liar', 'Thief', 'Brigand'. Some brandish George's pamphlets, some read aloud from them. Zacky and Paul start scuffling with some Warleggan supporters.

JUSTICE LISTER Confine yourself to the *present allegations*, Mr Bull.

HENRY BULL *(bows and turns to the jury)* But it is relevant to draw conclusions from statements made by him at the time of his arrest – which attempt to *justify* his actions and which brand him an obvious admirer of the bloodshed and tyranny in France!

More uproar in the court. 'Disgraceful!', 'Too true!', 'The man's a revolutionary', 'Send him back to France!', 'We don't want him here!', etc. The members of the jury are looking grim-faced and implacable.

HENRY BULL *(cont'd)* As a gentleman, this man should set an example. That instead he should side with the rabble—

Zacky and Paul are incensed by this description.

HENRY BULL *(cont'd)* – encouraging them in acts of violence they would not otherwise have the intelligence to conceive.

PAUL I'll 'conceive' 'im!

HENRY BULL Such a man is a danger to us all. The Crown, the country and justice itself demands the severest penalty!

Demelza is suddenly overcome with nausea and has to flee the court.

CUT TO:

41: EXT. ASSIZES COURT, BODMIN – DAY 6

Discontented commoners stand in huddles, muttering darkly amongst themselves in the wake of Jack Tripp's sentence. Demelza, sniffing at her smelling salts, tries to steady herself and stave off the nausea which threatens to engulf her. An alarming thought now occurs. Involuntarily her hand cradles her stomach. Surely, at this time, of all times, she can't be pregnant again? And yet she knows beyond all doubt that she is. And then Elizabeth appears, fanning herself. It's an unexpected meeting and it catches them both off-guard.

ELIZABETH Oh! Demelza! Is it not intolerable in there? I could scarce breathe.

DEMELZA Nor I.

They pause, both aware that they have nothing and everything to say to each other.

ELIZABETH I – came for Francis—

Demelza nods. Awkwardness. Both know it's not entirely true.

DEMELZA I never thanked you – for tending me – in my sickness.

ELIZABETH You saved my son. And at such a cost. *(then)* How can you bear it?

DEMELZA *(blurting it out)* I'm with child again.

There, it's said – and Demelza can hardly believe she's said it. But now she has, suddenly it seems real.

ELIZABETH Is – Ross glad?

DEMELZA I've not told him. If things go ill today—

ELIZABETH Pray God they do not.

DEMELZA *(gestures vaguely towards the court)* I – must—

ELIZABETH Of course.

Demelza goes back into the court. Elizabeth waits a moment, then follows.

CUT TO:

42: INT. ASSIZES COURT, BODMIN – DAY 6

As Demelza returns to the court room she realizes that the first witness has been called and is being examined by Henry Bull. By now her nausea and light-headedness are causing her to see everything through a peculiar haze. Nick Vigus is being questioned.

HENRY BULL 'Roused from sleep', you say?

NICK VIGUS Aye, sur. By 'im, sur.

HENRY BULL Saying what?

NICK VIGUS 'Pickin's for all! Hendrawna Beach! Wreck comin' in! Strip 'er to the last plank!'

HENRY BULL And when you reached Hendrawna Beach, what did you see the accused do?

NICK VIGUS Pluck cargo from the sea – pile it on the strand – direct others to do th' same—

HENRY BULL Did you see him assault the customs officer?

NICK VIGUS Aye, sur. Assault, sur. Terrible thing, sur.

PAUL G'eat liar!

ZACKY Never 'eard such randigal!

NICK VIGUS Not as I seen it wi' me own eyes – but I 'eard tell of it – aye, 'twas th' talk o' the beach that night.

Demelza closes her eyes as the room seems to swim before her. When she opens them again, Ross is looking at her. He looks surprised. Why is she here when he expressly told her not to come? But now she is, he's glad of it. As they lock eyes, the testimony of other prosecution witnesses continues.

HENRY BULL'S VOICE Did you see the prisoner attack the customs officer?

ELI CLEMMOW 'Es, sur. See'd 'im strike a blow cross 'is pate – and kick 'im when 'e's down.

Ross and Demelza look at each other in disbelief. Then they hear: 'Call Jud Paynter.' Resignation. This is very disappointing indeed.

CUT TO:

43: INT. ASSIZES COURT, BODMIN – DAY 6

Jud is in the witness box, shuffling and sniffing and wiping his nose on his sleeve.

JUD So there's Prudie – that's the wife – snorin' fit t' rouse the dead—

Prudie in the crowd swells with self-importance.

JUD *(cont'd)* – when along come Cap'n Ross – shoutin', 'Ship ashore down Hendrawna!' –

Demelza shakes her head in dismay.

DEMELZA I can't believe he would turn against Ross like this.

Jud is looking pleased with himself, as if he's just delivered some earth-shattering news. Now he halts.

HENRY BULL Yes? *(no reply)* What else did he do?

JUD Do?

HENRY BULL Did he urge you to do anything?

JUD Urge? Did he? Oh, aye, 'e sez to I, 'Do 'ee go run an' roust all th' village – an' head f' th' shore.'

HENRY BULL Did he give a reason?

JUD Reason, sur? Aye, sur. 'Come now,' sez 'e – 'sharp as 'ee can – for likely thur's women an' childer aboard an' they must be saved from a watery grave . . .'

Prudie is nodding her approval. Henry Bull looks up, confused. Then consults his notes. Then looks back at Jud.

HENRY BULL Come, man, recollect yourself. Think what you are saying.

Jud stares up at the ceiling as if for inspiration. Then:

JUD Aye, that's what 'e said sure 'nough.

HENRY BULL *(trying not to sound riled)* And I tell you, man, to think again. What you say is not in accordance with your sworn statement.

A murmur of surprise in the court. Zacky, Paul and Henshawe exchange looks of disbelief. Prudie looks outraged.

HENRY BULL *(cont'd) (to the judge)* If I have your permission? *(He reads from Jud's original statement.)* 'When Captain Poldark came to my house he told me to hurry and rouse the village because there was a wreck and the sooner it was stripped the better before the authorities turned up.'

Prudie looks unimpressed. Jud looks up to the ceiling again for inspiration. Then . . .

JUD Nay, sur, I never 'eard such words in my life an' I never thought 'em neither.

Henshawe stifles a smirk of amusement. Prudie looks relieved.

HENRY BULL I would remind you, Paynter, this statement was made before witnesses and read aloud to you before you signed.

JUD Aye, well, I'm 'ard of hearing. 'Tis more 'n like I misheard what they said – and they misheard what I said.

Prudie is nodding in agreement. Zacky, Paul and Henshawe are now struggling to contain their mirth.

HENRY BULL *(to Jud)* In your statement you say you saw Poldark strike John Coppard the excise man.

JUD Nay, don't know nothin' about that neither.

JUSTICE LISTER Mr Bull, I would have thought it was clear that this witness is useless. Plainly he has committed perjury – either now or when he gave his original statement. I suggest you turn him out of the box and get on with your case.

Reluctantly Henry Bull signals to some court officials and Jud is unceremoniously bundled out of the witness box and led out of court.

Despite himself, Ross is rather amused by Jud's performance.

Zacky, Paul and Henshawe are struggling to contain their amusement. Prudie isn't quite sure what's happened. She has a nasty feeling Jud had been intending to testify against Ross.

George remains outwardly calm but inwardly seething. He rises from his place and leaves the balcony.

CUT TO:

44: INT. ASSIZES COURT, BODMIN, CORRIDOR – DAY 6

George is greeted by Tankard – who knows he is in trouble.

TANKARD We could not possibly have foreseen . . .

GEORGE I beg to differ. These people have peculiar loyalties. You should have brandished less carrot and more stick. Without him, our hand is considerably weakened. What of Captain Bray? Did you manage to prevail *there*?

CUT TO:

45: INT. ASSIZES COURT, BODMIN – DAY 6

HENRY BULL Describe, Captain Bray, the sight which met your eyes when you came ashore on the night of January the seventh.

CAPTAIN BRAY Like Dante's Inferno.

DISSOLVE TO:

46: EXT. HENDRAWNA BEACH (FLASHBACK) – NIGHT (WINTER 1789)

Ross walks through hell-on-a-beach, a broken man, not caring where he's going or what's happening around him. People are fighting, grappling each other for cargo, reeling around drunkenly, swigging brandy, stuffing themselves with food . . .

CAPTAIN BRAY *(VO)* Drunken men cavorting, mules staggering beneath spoils from the ship . . . All semblance of order gone . . . 'twas as close to Hell as I ever hope to come . . .

DISSOLVE TO:

47: INT. ASSIZES COURT, BODMIN – DAY 6 (AUTUMN 1790)

HENRY BULL And your passengers and crew?

CAPTAIN BRAY Confronted by viciousness of the grossest kind. I had to stand guard to prevent 'em being torn to pieces.

HENRY BULL Thank you, Captain Bray. Your description would strike a chill into the heart of any decent human being.

Henry Bull stands down. Ross whispers something to Clymer.

CLYMER The prisoner begs leave to question the witness.

JUSTICE LISTER Granted.

Ross gets to his feet.

ROSS Captain Bray, do you recall seeing me on the beach that night?

CAPTAIN BRAY You came and offered me and my passengers shelter in your house.

ROSS Did you, while on the beach, hear or see me encouraging anyone to wreck your ship?

CAPTAIN BRAY It was dark, sir – but I don't believe I'd set eyes on you until that moment.

ROSS Did you see the meeting of myself and the captain of the soldiers?

CAPTAIN BRAY As I recall, you warned him not to go down to the beach.

ROSS Did I accompany you into my house?

CAPTAIN BRAY You did.

ROSS Thank you.

Ross sits down. Captain Bray is preparing to leave the stand when Henry Bull jumps up.

HENRY BULL One moment, Captain. How long did the accused stay with you when you entered the house?

CAPTAIN BRAY About ten minutes. He said his wife was ill and he needed to tend her.

HENRY BULL And when did you see him again?

CAPTAIN BRAY About two hours later.

HENRY BULL So there was nothing to prevent him leaving the house as soon as you were settled and returning to the beach to attack the excise men?

CAPTAIN BRAY I suppose not.

HENRY BULL Thank you. You may stand down.

Demelza feels nausea coming in waves now. She fears that at any moment she will faint. She fixes her eyes on Ross to steady herself – and thus it is his face only she sees while a stream of other prosecution witnesses line up to give their evidence – their voices echoing and overlaying each other:

HENRY BULL'S VOICE Ephraim Oliver, you were on the beach on the night of January seventh last. What did you see?

EPHRAIM OLIVER That man strike the gauger 'cross his skull – and kick 'im t' th' ground an' leave 'im f' dead—

HENRY BULL'S VOICE William Fiddick, how close were you to the accused when he struck John Coppard, the excise man?

WILLIAM FIDDICK'S VOICE Close as you be to me, sur – an' felt the blow like 'twas across me own 'ead—

HENRY BULL'S VOICE Sergeant Tremayne, the prisoner warned you not to go to the beach. And yet you did so. Why was that?

SERGEANT TREMAYNE'S VOICE I felt he was casting doubts upon my resolve and goading me to do so.

HENRY BULL'S VOICE In effect laying a trap for you?

SERGEANT TREMAYNE'S VOICE 'Twas my belief, sir.

Ross returns to the present, shaking his head in disbelief.

HENRY BULL Let us come finally to the statement which the prisoner made at his arrest. In it he gives a very clear account of himself. If I may read some of the choicest phrases . . . Asked if he encouraged the riot which broke out on the beach . . .

CUT TO:

48: INT. TRURO JAIL – NIGHT 1 (SPRING 1790)

ROSS I did not consider it a riot.

CUT TO:

49: INT. ASSIZES COURT, BODMIN – DAY 6 (AUTUMN 1790)

HENRY BULL Asked if he approved of plunder and lawlessness:

CUT TO:

50: INT. TRURO JAIL – NIGHT 1 (SPRING 1790)

ROSS Do you approve of whole families being without sufficient food to keep them alive?

CUT TO:

51: INT. ASSIZES COURT, BODMIN – DAY 6 (AUTUMN 1790)

HENRY BULL Asked what part he played in the death of Matthew Sanson:

CUT TO:

52: INT. TRURO JAIL – NIGHT 1 (SPRING 1790)

ROSS Regrettably none whatsoever.

CUT TO:

53: INT. ASSIZES COURT, BODMIN – DAY 6
(AUTUMN 1790)

HENRY BULL If you have ever heard a more damning indictment from a prisoner's own mouth, I would frankly be amazed. Your lordship, gentlemen of the jury, the Crown rests its case.

Assorted reactions from the court. Applause and approbation from the Warleggan supporters. Disgust and outrage from Ross's. The Clerk of the Court tries to restore order.

CLERK OF THE COURT Silence!

DEMELZA *(to Verity)* Witnesses for the defence?

VERITY Are there any?

CLERK OF THE COURT Call Dwight Enys.

Dwight comes up and takes the stand, involuntarily glancing up at the balcony and seeing Caroline looking down at him. She smiles mischievously as if to say, 'You will make this entertaining, won't you?' Annoyed at himself for even engaging with her, Dwight turns back to the judge.

DWIGHT My Lord, I am the physician who attended Captain Poldark's wife and child during their attack of the putrid throat. At that time I was constantly in the house and can testify that Captain Poldark had no sleep for almost a week. His only child died and was buried the day before the wreck. On the day itself, I formed the opinion that he had suffered a mental breakdown. I consider that any strangeness in his actions should almost entirely be attributed to that.

Silence. The whole court is listening more intently now and even signals from Tom Harry cannot raise any murmurs of discontent from the crowd. Henry Bull gets to his feet, puffs himself out like a bird arranging its plumage – and sets out to dismantle Dwight.

HENRY BULL You are an apothecary?

DWIGHT A physician, sir. A licentiate of the London College of Physicians. And a Cornishman by birth.

This last statement brings a murmur of approbation from the court.

HENRY BULL And an expert in mental afflictions?

DWIGHT I did not say so.

HENRY BULL Then your views on the subject can hardly be expected to carry much weight.

Reactions from the court. Muffled sniggers from the Warleggan stooges. Dwight glances involuntarily at Caroline – she raises her eyebrows as if in a challenge – and decides he's not going to allow himself to be made a fool of.

DWIGHT I believe they can, sir. In my view, Captain Poldark was – temporarily – through grief and lack of sleep – not himself.

HENRY BULL Do you consider that anyone who loses a child and a few days' sleep is justified in creating a riot?

DWIGHT I do not believe he created the riot.

HENRY BULL We require your opinion as a *physician* – not as a friend or drinking companion.

DWIGHT I speak *purely* as a physician – and base my opinion on clinical observation. Captain Poldark was unsteady on his feet and disordered in his remarks.

HENRY BULL Perhaps he was drunk.

DWIGHT He had not touched drink for several days. *(now addressing the judge and jury directly)* My lord, when his infant daughter died, a great many people came for the funeral. All of society, from highest to low. He's held in very great esteem, you see. But with his wife ill, it was impossible to give them any refreshment. This weighed heavy on his mind.

DISSOLVE TO:

54: INT. NAMPARA HOUSE, ROSS & DEMELZA'S BEDROOM (FLASHBACK) – DAY (WINTER 1789)

Impressionistic images of Ross sitting beside the unconscious, still feverish Demelza, holding her hand. Dwight watching. Ross barely aware of him. It's as if he's in a trance, unaware of anything and anyone around him.

ROSS So many came.

DWIGHT They care for you.

ROSS I should have provided for them. It's the custom after a burial. The winter's been savage – and the least I could've done was fed and watered them.

DWIGHT But—

ROSS I should have provided for them.

DISSOLVE TO:

55: INT. ASSIZES COURT, BODMIN – DAY 6 (AUTUMN 1790)

HENRY BULL And I suggest that he *did* provide for them. In rousing the rabble and leading them to the wreck, he both assuaged his conscience and filled his larder with pillage goods.

Loud roars of approval from the Warleggan stooges.

DWIGHT *(shouting to make himself heard)* That was not my meaning, sir.

Urged on by Tom Harry, the Warleggan stooges continue to roar their approval . . .

HENRY BULL Thank you, sir. You paint a very clear picture of the prisoner's state of mind.

The clamour continues to rise. Dwight hesitates. Has he helped or hindered Ross? He glances at Ross, who nods and gives a faint smile of appreciation. As Dwight leaves the stand, he glances up at Caroline. She applauds ironically. Meanwhile, the noise in the court has become deafening. Cries of 'Poldark's a disgrace', 'Punish him!', 'We demand justice!', 'Hang the Jacobin!', etc. In return, Zacky and Paul start scrapping with the Warleggan stooges again. As Paul lays into one, more join in. Then Zacky joins in. Henshawe attempts to calm things down.

JUSTICE LISTER Enough! Remove these persons from the court.

On the balcony, a puffed-up Unwin is raring to show how important he is.

UNWIN Quite right! They should be taken out and whipped!

Various officers of the court now come and remove the Warleggan supporters – and Zacky and Paul – from the court, amidst further protests. Tom Harry casts a glance at George but his expression has returned to its former impassive self. Justice Lister motions to the Clerk of the Court.

CLERK OF THE COURT The court will take a short adjournment.

Everyone rises as Justice Lister goes out. The din subsides. The spectators shift and stretch their legs. The sellers of sweetmeats and lemonade come rushing in and are besieged by hungry and thirsty spectators. Elizabeth leaves the court and goes outside. Unwin is still posturing on the balcony.

UNWIN When I'm in Westminster I shall issue a decree that all such people should be shot.

Caroline stifles a yawn.

CUT TO:

56: EXT. ASSIZES COURT, BODMIN – DAY 6
(AUTUMN 1790)

Groups of Commoners continue to stand in discontented huddles, bemoaning the fate of Jack Tripp. Elizabeth is taking the air when Francis comes out. He is surprised to see her – though he immediately thinks he knows why she's here.

FRANCIS You could not bear to keep away.

ELIZABETH I was concerned.

FRANCIS For me?

ELIZABETH Do I not have cause?

FRANCIS As you see, I am well. So had you not better return to Trenwith?

ELIZABETH Having come so far, I may as well stay.

FRANCIS Ross will be gratified.

ELIZABETH Are *you?*

A look between them. Neither Francis nor Elizabeth is sure that she has come for Francis, not Ross.

CUT TO:

57: INT. ASSIZES COURT, BODMIN – DAY 6

Ross has remained in his seat. Now he remembers the document Clymer had prepared for him. The first words Ross reads are: 'My Lord, gentlemen of the jury, I can only apologize that this case has taken so much of your time already. I will try to take as little more as may be necessary to beg your clemency – and the jury's understanding . . .' Clymer leans over to him.

CLYMER Are you resolved?

ROSS To prostrate myself and beg for mercy?

Ross shrugs but doesn't commit himself either way.

CLYMER Good God, man, do you not see what is happening? You stand accused of riot and lawlessness. Last night in this very town, what broke out? Riot! Affray! That man who was sentenced to hang. Of what was he accused?

Ross shrugs. He can see which way this is leading.

CLYMER *(cont'd)* This country lives in dread of France. Because of last night, because of that man, this court must be seen to set an example. That man will hang tonight. And unless you have a care, so will you . . . So that is why you must grovel. Under no circumstances must you be seen to sympathize or condone. As a gentleman you have the power to distance yourself from the mob. Do so now or you will not live to see the sun rise tomorrow.

Ross looks across to see how Demelza is faring. She looks up. She smiles at him. A look intended to give him courage. Suddenly there is a murmur of expectation. People rush to re-take their seats. Judge Lister is returning. A silence falls upon the court. Ross stands. He is holding Clymer's defence document. He hesitates. Opens it. Pauses. Then begins to read, with an appropriately humble and contrite tone:

ROSS My Lord, gentlemen of the jury, I can only apologize that this case has taken so much of your time. I will try to take as little more as may be necessary to beg your clemency – and the jury's understanding . . .

TOM CARNE'S VOICE Understandin'? What understandin' do he deserve?

Ross halts, surprised. Looks round. Demelza looks horrified. She recognizes the voice. Now Tom Carne, who has been sitting, unnoticed, in the midst of the crowd, gets to his feet.

TOM CARNE Let the court beware this man! The devil in

gent's clothing! He stole my daughter, debauch'd an' left her unfit for neither man nor beast!

JUSTICE LISTER *(wearily)* Remove this man.

TOM CARNE And when I did go to th' rescue o' my child, this man did viciously assault I – a poor God-fearing creature in his dotage – with fists and with weapons—

ON CAROLINE: Looking with renewed interest at Ross. This is new information for her.

Two officers of the court come to remove Tom Carne – but even as he's being led out, he won't be silenced.

TOM CARNE *(cont'd)* I tell 'ee, this man do think hisself above the law – do think he may take what he please an' ne'er pay th' price ferrit.

ON ELIZABETH: Tom's words give her pause for thought. Could they be true?

TOM CARNE *(cont'd)* I do implore the court to see justice be done! In the name of I an' all who've suffered at his hands! An' most especially my lost daughter . . .

ON DEMELZA: Horrified by what Tom is saying.

TOM CARNE *(cont'd)* . . . who 'ave placed her trust in 'im an' who will surely come to regret it!

Tom Carne is finally removed from the court. Demelza and Verity look horrified. This could not have come at a worse time.

ON THE JURY: Looking scandalized.

ON GEORGE: Looking delighted.

Ross notices George's smile of delight. A moment between them. A stand-off. Then George looks away.

JUSTICE LISTER *(to Ross)* Continue with your plea, sir.

Ross consults his prepared speech again.

ROSS It is true that on January the seventh I saw a wreck

come in – that I rode and told several villagers – that a number of people came upon the beach and items were carried away.

Ross glances up and sees George smirking at him, enjoying his discomfort and looking forward to seeing Ross grovel. In that moment, Ross decides that he cannot and will not.

ROSS *(cont'd)* Though not by me.

Now, to Clymer's dismay, Ross puts away the defence document.

ROSS *(cont'd)* My house was searched and none were found. Why? Because I took none.

Clymer is signalling desperately to Ross, urging him to return to the prepared speech. Ross ignores him. Demelza and Verity exchange a glance. They can see that Ross is already going off-message.

ROSS *(cont'd)* The counsel speaks of 'lawless rabble'. Had he been there I believe he would have seen a different picture. The people of Sawle, Mellin and Grambler who came upon the beach that day were ordinary people – no more or less law-abiding loyal subjects than any here. As to what happened when those people saw the wreck – I ask you to think of the traditions of our county. That attempts are made to lure ships onto rocks by means of false lights is a lie spread only by the prejudiced or ignorant. But that people scour the beaches for flotsam – and look on the leavings of the tide as their own especial benison – this is commonly known. The law says this flotsam belongs to the Crown – or to this lord or that merchant.

George gives the slightest perceptible nod of agreement.

ROSS *(cont'd)* But in times of dire need, these pickings – great or small – are the means of keeping ordinary people alive! What else would you have them do? After they've rescued the crew and brought goods ashore – often at risk of their own lives – are they to sit by and await the arrival of the excise

men? To watch them carry off the goods that they themselves
have salvaged? The law, of course, says yes. But when fathers
have seen their children without a crust for their bellies or a
rag for their backs, can you expect them to reason as they
should?

George looks unconvinced and unimpressed.

Caroline looks faintly amused.

The members of the jury look unmoved.

*He consults Clymer's document again. Clymer looks hopeful. But then
dismayed as Ross promptly discards it.*

ROSS *(cont'd)* Counsel has suggested that I am a revolutionary
– that these people are revolutionaries – branded with a
desire to overthrow authority. Nothing could be further from
the truth. We are Cornishmen. Headstrong sometimes. But
steadfast. Slow to anger, loath to judge. Quick to come to
another's aid, willing to share what little we have.

*A perceptible shift in the mood of the crowd. Less hostility now towards
Ross. Demelza is looking proud of Ross's declaration.*

ROSS *(cont'd)* You ask if I was in my right mind? You've heard
evidence that I was not.

*Dwight looks hopeful – that his testimony may have strengthened
Ross's case.*

ROSS *(cont'd)* But is it insanity to think that rich pickings
strewn across a beach are better used to sustain those in need
than returned to those whose only goal is profit?

*The crowd are beginning to nod their approval and agreement with
Ross's sentiments.*

ROSS *(cont'd)* I cannot believe it. I will not believe it. And so
I make no apology for my actions. In truth, I would do the
same again.

CLYMER *(under his breath)* No, no, no, no, no, no . . .

Uproar in the court. Verity is shaking her head in despair. Demelza is close to tears, proud of Ross whilst fearing he has signed his own death warrant. Mayhem reigns.

DWIGHT I've heard speeches that were more penitent.

FRANCIS But rarely more eloquent?

Dwight nods his agreement. It's clear they both admire Ross's stance whilst fearing it will have unfortunate consequences. George is struggling to contain his feelings of triumph. Ross glances up and for the first time sees Elizabeth. He gives the smallest perceptible nod. Which she returns. He's grateful for her presence and support. Now he turns back to Clymer.

ROSS My apologies.

Clymer takes the defence document back. He does not trust himself to reply.

ROSS *(cont'd)* What next?

CLYMER The Judge's summing up. I would not expect much . . . benevolence.

ON FRANCIS & DWIGHT:

FRANCIS 'The quality of mercy is not strained'!

Dwight looks at him in surprise, not at first realizing Francis is quoting Shakespeare.

FRANCIS *(cont'd)* 'It droppeth as the gentle rain from heaven upon the place beneath—' *(then)* And God knows it droppeth sometimes on those who least deserve it!

A moment between Dwight and Francis. Both know what Francis is referring to. A hush falls as Justice Lister prepares to give his summing-up. He glances at Demelza. Though his face is impassive, Demelza fears the worst. George looks smug, convinced that Ross has condemned himself out of his own mouth. Ross looks stoic, calm, resolved to face whatever comes. Demelza and Verity clutch each other's hand for support.

JUSTICE LISTER Gentlemen of the jury, this man stands accused of riot, wrecking and assaulting an officer of the Crown. On the charge of assault, you have heard witnesses swear he was the culprit. Others have sworn he could not possibly have been. It was a dark night and there may have been confusion. So let me remind you that where there is reasonable doubt, the law dictates that the accused should have the benefit of it.

Murmuring from the court. This is an unexpected – but welcome – development. George is gritting his teeth. This is not the opening he could have wished for. Demelza and Verity confer excitedly.

VERITY This is a good beginning.

Dwight and Francis confer likewise.

DWIGHT Better than we'd hoped?

JUSTICE LISTER As to the charges of riot and wrecking, these are very differently based.

George nods thoughtfully. This sounds more promising. Demelza's heart sinks. Something in Justice Lister's tone strikes a chill into her.

JUSTICE LISTER *(cont'd)* The prisoner admits that he summoned people to the wreck, carried items from the sea and directed others to do the same. He admits that a riot broke out but denies inciting or participating in it. But in law, if you are satisfied that a riot took place, you need only be satisfied that the prisoner was involved, to find him guilty as a principal.

Demelza feels her heart getting colder and colder.

JUSTICE LISTER *(cont'd)* It therefore remains for you to decide: first, whether or not the prisoner was on the beach at the time of the wreck; second, whether he was there with others with intent to strip the wreck; third, whether such a pillaging, riot and assault took place.

Murmurs of surprise from the crowd. This is an unexpected development. Francis and Dwight look dismayed as it begins to dawn on them that Justice Lister is actually directing the jury to find Ross guilty. George is unable to conceal a smug smile. Demelza is horrified at the direction this is taking. Clymer is shaking his head: this is exactly what he predicted.

Ross's heart sinks. Doubts beginning to creep in. Perhaps he should have grovelled after all.

JUSTICE LISTER *(cont'd)* The prisoner has attempted to find mitigating circumstances in the distress generally prevailing among the poor, devoting a part of his final plea to a defence of his own country folk. You may consider this an admirable sentiment, but you would be failing in your duty if you allowed it to influence your judgement in any way.

As directed, the jury look stern and unmoved.

JUSTICE LISTER *(cont'd)* *(to the jury)* So will you now consider your verdict?

The jury put their heads together and whisper feverishly.

JUSTICE LISTER *(cont'd)* You may retire if you wish.

The foreman of the jury consults with his fellow-jurors, then nods his agreement. Justice Lister stands up and walks out. Demelza is aghast.

DEMELZA I thought to help him.

VERITY My dear?

DEMELZA I thought to show the judge there were those who wish'd him ill.

VERITY *(horrified)* You spoke to the judge?

DEMELZA Judas! What have I done?

Francis and Dwight confer.

DWIGHT Bad, is it not?

FRANCIS Very bad. Not that I don't admire his stubbornness – but he'll pay for it.

George leaves the balcony and goes out.

CUT TO:

58: EXT. SQUARE, BODMIN – DAY 6

Disaffected commoners are milling about. The mood of discontent has not dispersed. George emerges into the square where presently he is joined by a jubilant Tankard.

TANKARD We could not have hoped for a better judge! Poldark must surely hang!

GEORGE Yes.

Something in George's tone makes Tankard look more closely at him.

TANKARD That is what you wanted?

For a brief moment a look of doubt crosses George's face. Is this really what he wants? Almost immediately the thought is banished – and business takes over.

GEORGE The mine he will leave to his wife.

TANKARD We can soon acquire the shares. Was she not his kitchen maid? She will give us no trouble.

GEORGE Do not believe it.

TANKARD You'll be celebrating tonight.

GEORGE I certainly intend to.

He walks back towards the court. On his way back he meets Elizabeth.

GEORGE *(cont'd)* I did my best. As you requested. I offered him my help.

ELIZABETH Did you order those pamphlets?

GEORGE Of course not! How could you think – Elizabeth, give me *some* credit.

ELIZABETH Francis is sure you did.

GEORGE On my honour, Elizabeth.

Elizabeth studies him a moment. Then walks off.

CUT TO:

59: INT. ASSIZES COURT, BODMIN – DAY 6

Ross remains seated. Clymer is tidying up his papers.

ROSS Will I have a chance to say goodbye to my wife?

CLYMER You will be removed from court and taken directly to your fate.

ROSS *(to Henry Bull)* I congratulate you on your eloquence. You almost convinced me I was guilty!

The two men actually laugh. Startled and surprised looks from Demelza. From Verity. From Dwight.

HENRY BULL In truth, I believe there's nothing you or anyone could have said which would have changed the old man's mind. He seems determined to make an example of you.

Ross nods philosophically. He can almost see the funny side.

CUT TO:

60: INT. ASSIZES COURT, BODMIN – DAY 6

Demelza sits staring at her hands. She toys with her wedding ring. Then all around her there is a buzz and a bustle of activity as people rush to return to their seats. Still Demelza doesn't look up. People push past her. Still she toys with her ring. Finally Verity nudges her.

VERITY They're coming back.

Demelza looks up. The jury are now filing in slowly, looking self-conscious, almost guilty. The foreman himself looks particularly sorrowful. The court stands as Justice Lister comes back and takes his seat. The atmosphere is strained to breaking point. The Clerk of the Court gets to his feet and signals Ross to do the same.

CLERK OF THE COURT Gentlemen of the jury, have you reached a verdict?

FOREMAN *(nervously)* We have.

CLERK OF THE COURT Do you find the prisoner guilty or not guilty?

The Foreman clears his throat nervously. The tension is unbearable.

FOREMAN We find him – *(He struggles to get the words out.)* not guilty – on all three charges.

A moment's stunned silence. Then uproar in court. Ross closes his eyes. Relief floods him. He struggles to contain it. Verity and Demelza fall weeping into each other's arms. Francis and Dwight struggle to contain their elation. George goes white. Tight-lipped, he gets up and goes out. Caroline is smiling. This has been most entertaining. Elizabeth is struggling to hold back tears of relief.

Tussles break out between those sympathetic to Ross and those suborned by the Warleggans. Even the sensible and restrained Henshawe is now getting involved. Ross opens his eyes. He looks across to Demelza. She is weeping uncontrollably. Demelza rushes forward, pushes her way through the crowd and falls into Ross's arms.

Elizabeth watches. Her face is impassive but it's a defining moment for her. Ross is not even aware that she's there. She turns and walks out.

Caroline watches with amusement from the balcony. She sees Dwight looking up at her, immediately turns away and begins chatting to Unwin. Dwight exits, convinced that he has imagined the frisson he'd felt between them.

Mayhem reigns.

CUT TO:

61: EXT. ASSIZES COURT, BODMIN – DAY 6

People pour out of the court. Verity finds herself swept along on a tide of people – and comes face to face with Francis. Both are so overjoyed at Ross's deliverance that they almost forget the bone of contention between them.

VERITY I thought we'd lost him!

FRANCIS I was sure of it!

VERITY Oh, Francis – dear brother – *(then)* can we not take heart from this? Is there not hope in it for all?

FRANCIS Hope?

VERITY Of a reconciling?

FRANCIS Gladly.

He takes her hands and squeezes them affectionately.

FRANCIS *(cont'd)* For you and I. But your husband? While I live and breathe – it will never happen.

And he walks away, leaving her tearful and disappointed once again. Now Ross and Demelza emerge to be congratulated by various members of the public. Henshawe comes, shakes Ross's hand.

HENSHAWE Seems I shan't be rid of you yet, Captain. A pity. I was looking forward to dealing with the *sensible* side of the family! *(i.e. Demelza)*

They all laugh. As they walk off, Francis now meets up with Elizabeth.

FRANCIS So he will come home after all.

ELIZABETH Yes.

She struggles not to let her tears show.

FRANCIS Oh, don't stop on my account. *(then)* I wonder if you would have wept so prettily had *I* not come home.

ELIZABETH Why would you not have come home, Francis?

They face each other – and for a moment we think Francis will open his heart and tell Elizabeth how close he had come to taking his own life. But at the final moment . . .

FRANCIS Let's not distress ourselves to no purpose. I *am* coming home. *(beat)* And so is Ross. And tomorrow the sun will rise again. So let us count our blessings.

He takes her hand, puts it under his arm and leads her away. It is a small – very small – move towards reconciliation.

CUT TO:

62: EXT. BARGUS CROSSROADS – DUSK 6

Ross, Demelza and Dwight pass Bargus Crossroads as they ride home.
CUT TO:

63: EXT. HENDRAWNA BEACH – DUSK 6

Spectacular panoramic views of the beach, sea and sky at sunset. Ross, Demelza and Dwight ride home along Hendrawna Beach. They are in a daze and cannot speak. As they ride they see in the distance a small fire with various people around it. The distant sound of a fiddle is heard. Some of the people look up. They seem to recognize Ross and Demelza. They begin to run towards them.

MRS ZACKY *(to Ross)* Is it true? Are 'ee safe?

ZACKY Is't over an' are 'ee free?

ROSS It would appear so.

Ross dismounts and is embraced by well-wishers: Mrs Zacky, Jinny and Beth Daniel clasp his hands, Ted, Zacky and other men embrace him. Ted (the fiddler) breaks into a triumphant tune to celebrate. Demelza dismounts and embraces the women. Dwight dismounts and joins in the celebrations.

JINNY Will 'ee join us?

ZACKY Leave 'em be, Jinny, they'll be wantin' to be away home.

ROSS True, Zacky. To the place I never thought I'd see again.

He puts his arm round Demelza, and leading his horse, begins to walk up the beach. The others leave their fire and accompany them as a guard of honour, with Ted playing fiddle alongside them.

CUT TO:

64: EXT. NAMPARA HOUSE – DUSK 6

Ross and Demelza, alone now, walk across the fields towards the shadowy outline of Nampara House, silhouetted against the darkening sky. The moon is high in the sky. As they approach the house they are suddenly startled by two figures who emerge from the darkness.

DEMELZA Judas!

It's Jud and Prudie. They look humble and contrite. Ross eyes them narrowly. He knows what they want – realizes they're too scared to ask for it – and isn't minded to give them an easy ride. He ignores them completely, ties up his horse and instead addresses Demelza.

ROSS I might venture to town tomorrow. I've a notion to engage a couple of servants.

DEMELZA *(immediately catching on)* What sorts would 'ee be lookin' for?

ROSS Fiendishly hardworking. Pitifully grateful. Exceedingly cheap. If you hear of any such, tell them to make themselves known to me.

Without a glance at Jud and Prudie, Ross goes into the house. Dem-
elza follows, trying not to laugh. The door closes. Jud and Prudie look
at each other for a moment . . . then barge each other over in their
haste to get to the front door. Which they hammer on eagerly.

CUT TO:

65: EXT. WARLEGGAN HOUSE – NIGHT 6

A carriage draws up outside the front door. A postilion gets down and
opens the carriage door. George gets out. Stony-faced. He ignores his
servants and goes into the house.

CUT TO:

66: INT. WARLEGGAN HOUSE, GEORGE'S DEN – NIGHT 6

George storms into his den. Tankard follows.

GEORGE How? How did he get off? How could the accursed
jury disregard all the evidence and find him not guilty?
(exploding) And to think I let my uncle persuade me against
pressing a charge of murder!

TANKARD I tell you there was not an atom of proof and we
could not have manufactured it!

GEORGE And Paynter recanted! He will pay for it shortly!

TANKARD What now? Do we accept defeat?

GEORGE By no means. *(He pours himself some brandy and sips it
thoughtfully.)* Wheal Leisure is his one real asset. We must set
about buying up shares. When I control the mine, I control
Ross.

TANKARD And Francis?

George scowls at the very mention of Francis's name.

TANKARD *(cont'd)* His finances are in your hands. You can break him tomorrow.

GEORGE I could. But for the moment I intend to make no move at all.

TANKARD You care nothing for his good will.

GEORGE Not *his*. But there is another person to consider.

CUT TO:

67: INT. TRENWITH HOUSE, LIBRARY – NIGHT 6

Elizabeth comes in, followed by Francis, to greet Aunt Agatha.

FRANCIS Not guilty!

Aunt Agatha casually holds up a tarot card. It's the Sun.

AUNT AGATHA As I expected.

Francis escorts Elizabeth to a seat beside the fire.

FRANCIS Sit here, my dear. Shall I bring you a glass of wine?

ELIZABETH Thank you.

She sits. We sense an uneasy truce between them. Something has changed – and even Aunt Agatha is aware of it.

CUT TO:

68: INT. KILLEWARREN, PARLOUR – NIGHT 6

Ray hands Caroline and Unwin a glass of wine.

RAY PENVENEN *(toasting Unwin)* To Westminster.

CAROLINE To Ross Poldark!

UNWIN You must toast as your uncle bids you, Caroline. You are his ward and must obey his wishes.

CAROLINE And what are his wishes?

UNWIN *(puffing himself up)* Why, for you to engage yourself to a man of substance and repute.

CAROLINE Oh, I intend to, I assure you!

They all toast.

CUT TO:

69: EXT. HENDRAWNA BEACH – NIGHT 6

Dwight sits drinking with Mrs Zacky, Zacky, Ted, Jinny & co. They toast to Ross.

CUT TO:

70: INT. WARLEGGAN HOUSE, GEORGE'S DEN – NIGHT 6

George pours himself a glass of wine. He is feeling encouraged by his new plans. Until:

TANKARD We overlook one thing. *(beat)* Ross Poldark is alive. *(beat)* And must be aware of our attempts to render him otherwise.

GEORGE And?

TANKARD He never struck me as a man who would take such things lying down. After all he's a soldier—

GEORGE A renegade—

Tankard nods. He doesn't care to press the point further.

GEORGE *(cont'd)* Your point?

TANKARD That in failing to get him hanged, you have left yourself – exposed?

A flicker of fear crosses George's face. This is the first time it has dawned on him.

CUT TO:

71: INT. WARLEGGAN HOUSE, GEORGE'S ROOM – NIGHT 6

George gets into bed. Before he blows the candle out, he opens the drawer of a bedside table and checks something. Lying there is a pistol.

CUT TO:

72: EXT. WARLEGGAN HOUSE – NIGHT 6

Outside George's bedroom window a shadow moves. It looks sinister. But it's only Tom Harry. On guard duty.

CUT TO:

73: INT. NAMPARA HOUSE, ROSS & DEMELZA'S BEDROOM – NIGHT 6

Demelza lays a few violets on the pillow of Julia's empty crib. She is ready for bed. She sits on the bed now, combing out her hair. Ross comes in and begins to undress.

DEMELZA I did not care for Bodmin. *This* is all I desire. You, me – our house – candles burning – the scent of new-picked violets. Maybe it's because I'm of common stock that I'm easily pleased.

ROSS Common stock you are not.

DEMELZA Nor was Julia.

She's looking now at Julia's empty crib and the violets scattered across the pillow. Julia's name has been spoken and for a while neither speaks. Then . . .

DEMELZA *(cont'd)* There *is* one thing I desire. *(beat)* A child in the crib?

ROSS To take her place?

DEMELZA Not to make us forget her, but—

ROSS Do not wish it.

DEMELZA Not – ever?

ROSS Not for now. With our future so uncertain.

This is a blow for Demelza. She lets it land. But then, pragmatic as ever, she rallies.

DEMELZA Our future looks kinder than we ever expected.

ROSS Much kinder.

He comes and sits beside her on the bed, takes the comb from her hand.

ROSS *(cont'd)* I believe we agreed you would not come to Bodmin?

DEMELZA Yes, Ross, I believe we did.

ROSS Have I told you what I feel about a disobedient wife?

DEMELZA Have I told you what I feel about a reckless husband?

They smile at each other and begin to kiss.

Episode 3

1: EXT. NAMPARA FIELDS – DAY 7 (AUTUMN 1790)

Spectacular views of open countryside on a glorious autumn morning. A distant figure is piling out hay from a cart, which is yoked to a horse. Also visible are two cows and an ox. As we go closer we see Ross. His expression is determined but upbeat. He appreciates the beauty of the morning and the detail of his surroundings; the birds wheeling across the sky, the autumn leaves blown by the wind.

CUT TO:

2: EXT. NAMPARA FIELDS – DAY 7

Ross comes over the crest of the hill, leading the horse and hay cart home. As he does so, his attention is caught by the distant outline of Wheal Leisure. He halts. A thought occurs to him. A plan begins to form in his mind.

CUT TO:

3: EXT. NAMPARA COVE – DAY 7

Bare toes paddle in the surf. Demelza is revealed. She seems thoughtful, wistful. Hand on her belly. The tiniest bump. A secret smile.

CUT TO:

4: EXT. DWIGHT'S COTTAGE – DAY 7

A solitary figure, sleeves rolled up, is chopping wood outside his lonely cottage. It's Dwight. In the distance he sees two well-dressed figures on horseback. One of them is Caroline. She doesn't appear to have noticed him.

CUT TO:

5: EXT. OPEN COUNTRYSIDE – DAY 7

Caroline and her maid Hicks are on horseback. Contrary to Dwight's assumption, Caroline has noticed him.

CAROLINE What a sweet little cottage! I wish I lived in such a place. *(then)* Doubtless you think I wouldn't last five minutes!

Hicks says nothing. Caroline smiles archly.

CUT TO:

6: INT. WARLEGGAN HOUSE – DAY 7

George is boxing with a boxing instructor. He is straining to land punches on the boxing instructor who is an accomplished sportsman, though clearly under instructions to go easy on George. Tankard appears, watches the proceedings.

TANKARD I applaud your foresight. It's as well to be prepared.

GEORGE For what?

TANKARD Any – encounter? – with those who might wish us – ill?

GEORGE Ross Poldark would not dare lay a finger on me.

TANKARD Even though we tried to get him hanged?

GEORGE We failed. Did you forget?

George returns to his boxing with renewed vigour.

TANKARD But on that score – as we've agreed, there are other ways to choke a man.

GEORGE I look forward to hearing of your progress.

Tankard nods and goes out. George redoubles his efforts against his boxing instructor. He (George) is still clumsier and slower than his instructor. It frustrates him.

CUT TO:

7: INT. NAMPARA HOUSE, LIBRARY – DAY 7

Ross comes in and begins to rifle through some papers. Presently he finds what he's looking for: an old map of the local mining area. It shows some ancient workings – the old Trevorgie workings, long since abandoned. He traces their extent – and sees that they connect up with the Wheal Leisure workings.

ROSS *(under his breath)* Yes!

He's excited by this discovery. There's a knock at the door and a grovelling Jud comes in, saluting.

JUD Beggin' yer pardon, Cap'n, sur, 'tis a letter, so please 'ee.

Ross takes the letter, suspicious of Jud's newfound subservience (from being allowed back to Nampara). Jud peers at the map over Ross's shoulder.

JUD *(cont'd)* Ah, the ole Trevorgie workin's? 'Tis a fine thought!

ROSS What is?

JUD Whatever 'ee be thinkin'.

ROSS I'm thinking of thrashing you from here to Sawle.

JUD *(saluting)* Aye, sur. Whatever 'ee say, much obliged, sur.

Jud salutes and scuttles out before Ross can make good his threat. Ross opens the letter. Pascoe's voice reads: 'My dear Ross, I write to remind you that your loan of One Thousand Pounds with interest at forty per cent is shortly due for repayment. Your friend, Harris Pascoe.'

ROSS *(to himself)* All I need!

DEMELZA'S VOICE What is?

Demelza comes in. Ross immediately hides the letter and deflects her question.

ROSS Jud! His grovelling is killing me!

He starts to gather up his stuff, including the map.

DEMELZA You're away somewhere?

ROSS Truro. For the Wheal Leisure shareholders' meeting.

DEMELZA Oh – 'tis only – since the trial—

Ross continues to gather his things. Demelza is clearly itching to talk to him.

DEMELZA *(cont'd)* I've scarce seen you – let alone had chance to speak. You seem always about some business or other—

ROSS *(laughing)* The mine? The harvest? Would you have me neglect our affairs?

DEMELZA No, but—

ROSS We'll talk. Soon. I promise.

He kisses her briefly in passing as he goes out. Demelza remains. Frustrated.

CUT TO:

8: EXT. NAMPARA COVE – DAY 7

Demelza is collecting driftwood. A passing rider (Captain McNeil) is glimpsed up on the headland in the distance, too far away for us to see who it is. But whoever it is has halted and is watching her.

CUT TO:

9: INT. RED LION INN, MEETING ROOM – DAY 7

On the old map, a finger traces the workings of the Wheal Leisure out towards the old Trevorgie workings. The finger is Henshawe's. He, Ross and Zacky exchange glances. Henshawe nods his agreement. They seem cautiously optimistic. They are clustered round the top of the table, awaiting the arrival of the Wheal Leisure shareholders. Presently Horace Treneglos, Mr Renfrew, Mr Aukitt and various other shareholders come in. Affable greetings are exchanged. As they take their seats, Mr Renfrew passes a note to Ross. Ross glances at it briefly, frowns, shows it to Zacky. Zacky curses under his breath. The shareholders settle. Ross addresses the meeting.

ROSS Gentlemen, welcome to the quarterly meeting of the Wheal Leisure shareholders. Before we begin, I must make you aware that Mrs Jacqueline Tregidden has sold her shares. *(beat)* To a Mr Coke.

A murmur of interest from the other shareholders (the name 'Coke' does not mean anything to them yet).

ROSS *(cont'd)* Since Mrs Tregidden always trusted us to get on with our business without her interference, let's hope this gentleman will do the same.

Everyone laughs their agreement. The door opens. Tankard comes in.

TANKARD Good day t'you, gentlemen. My name is Tankard. Acting on behalf of Mr Coke.

HORACE TRENEGLOS *(aside)* Mr *Warleggan*, more like!

Looks are exchanged between the shareholders. This is a known

Warleggan man. Tankard smiles. He knows exactly what they're all thinking.

TANKARD *(to Ross)* Pray go on with the business, sir. I'm most eager to hear what you have to say.

Ross, Henshawe and Zacky exchange concerned looks as Tankard takes his place at the foot of the table. Ross knows he has no option but to continue as normal.

CUT TO:

10: EXT. TRENWITH HOUSE GROUNDS – DAY 7

A Warleggan servant in gaudy livery waits outside the front door. Presently Elizabeth comes out. She's about to hand a note to the servant when Francis appears from the gardens. He's dressed in working clothes and is accompanied by Geoffrey Charles. He pretends to be dazzled by the sight of the servant.

FRANCIS *(to Geoffrey Charles)* Shield your eyes, boy! The dazzle of Warleggan livery can blind a man!

The servant shuffles uncomfortably.

ELIZABETH George has invited us to a soirée. I've sent our regrets.

FRANCIS Surely not?

Elizabeth looks puzzled. Is this not what Francis wants?

FRANCIS *(cont'd)* After he was so assiduous in trying to get our cousin hanged? *(to the servant)* Pray convey our *delight* in declining his invitation.

The servant bows and departs. Francis raises an amused eyebrow at Elizabeth. Then . . .

FRANCIS *(cont'd)* *(to Geoffrey Charles)* Now then, boy, would you like to do your lessons? Or help me in the fields!

GEOFFREY CHARLES The fields! The fields!

FRANCIS Is the correct answer! Come then, boy.

He swoops Geoffrey Charles up, puts him on his shoulders and starts trotting off towards the fields.

FRANCIS *(cont'd)* D'you think Mama will be able to catch us? I don't think she will!

He breaks into a jog. Geoffrey Charles shrieks with laughter. Elizabeth watches them go, astonished by Francis's new-found zest for life.

CUT TO:

11: INT. RED LION INN, MEETING ROOM – DAY 7

The shareholders' meeting continues. Ross is acutely aware of the newcomer Tankard.

ROSS Gentlemen, it's four years since we opened Wheal Leisure. We started with fifty men – now we employ a hundred. We're not prosperous – but we consistently show a small profit—

HORACE TRENEGLOS Though none of us is getting fat on it!

Murmurs and wry smiles of agreement from round the table.

ROSS But that could change if another lode of copper could be found. Mr Henshawe?

HENSHAWE 'Tis common knowledge that the ancient Trevorgie workings – abandoned half a century back when the owner died – were never worked out. The old shafts caved in long ago – 'tis impossible to reach 'em above grass. But if you look at this old map – and compare it with the current map o' th' Wheal Leisure workings – you'll see that we've extended considerably in the direction of Trevorgie.

A murmur of interest and curiosity from the shareholders. Tankard remains impassive.

ROSS My proposal is this: we divert our quarterly profits into starting an exploratory tunnel – to see if we can join up with the old Trevorgie workings and access the untapped copper.

More murmurs of interest from the shareholders. Tankard alone seems unmoved.

TANKARD And who's to do the digging? Will it take men away from the day-to-day working? Can you guarantee that copper will be found? How will this affect my client's dividends?

Ross reins himself in and forces himself to be polite.

ROSS As you know, sir, there are no guarantees in mining. But Captain Henshawe will personally supervise the venture. A small team – including myself – will be led by Zacky Martin. And we'll take on six extra men to cover them.

The other shareholders consult amongst themselves. Eventually . . .

HORACE TRENEGLOS Well, I can't see what harm it'll do. Six extra men? I doubt their wages'll bankrupt us!

ZACKY *(wry)* Ye can be sure o' that, sir!

HORACE TRENEGLOS And if, at the end of six months, we've struck no copper . . . well, we're no worse off than we are today.

HENSHAWE And may be considerably better.

HORACE TRENEGLOS *(considers, then)* I'm in favour. Who's with me?

Ross, Henshawe, Zacky and all but Tankard and Aukitt raise their hands. Ross smiles with satisfaction. Until he sees Tankard – who has caught Aukitt's eye. Ross considers the implications of this new involvement.

CUT TO:

12: EXT. TRURO STREET – DAY 7

Zacky, Henshawe and Ross walk along the street.

HENSHAWE George Warleggan finally has a spy in the camp.

ROSS It was bound to happen eventually. But provided the other shareholders hold firm, Tankard – and George – can be kept in check.

ZACKY Last thing 'ee need now – with all the rumours goin' about!

ROSS Rumours?

Zacky and Henshawe exchange an embarrassed look.

HENSHAWE The parlous state o' your finances?

ROSS Have people nothing better to gossip about?

Zacky and Henshawe shrug in embarrassment.

ROSS *(cont'd)* Well, if you'll excuse me, gentlemen, I must return to my haymaking!

ZACKY When's the last time 'ee took a day off?

ROSS *(laughs)* When I sat in jail, awaiting trial?

Henshawe and Zacky laugh. The three part.

CUT TO:

13: INT. WARLEGGAN HOUSE – DAY 7

George is dressing after his boxing lesson when Unwin sweeps in.

UNWIN I have a new mission!

George eyes him wearily and prepares to be underwhelmed.

UNWIN *(cont'd)* To bring order and civility to Cornwall! Since the riots at Bodmin, I've felt personally compelled to take a stand.

GEORGE I can imagine.

UNWIN So I've summoned an expert in public order and will be taking his advice as to how such a debacle can be avoided in the future.

GEORGE I should have thought that was obvious. One simply removes the provocation. Which, in this case, was you. And since you will shortly be leaving for London—

UNWIN Will I?

GEORGE Have we not discussed this? The imperative for you to claim your seat in Parliament *ahead* of the other pretenders?

UNWIN Oh! Yes, yes – indeed – although Caroline intends to remain in Cornwall. And if I wish to press my suit— *(then)* Ah, there's the carriage. Georgie, *au revoir!*

And to George's annoyance, Unwin sweeps out, crossing with a servant who brings a note. As George opens it, he glances out of the window.

HIS POV: A carriage has drawn up and Caroline is sitting in it. She looks like a spoilt princess, an impression not diminished when Unwin tries to kiss her hand and she withdraws it petulantly. Caroline glances up and sees George looking at her. She smiles flirtatiously, letting her look linger as the carriage is driven away.

Now George turns his attention to the note. It's from Elizabeth. He frowns. Tankard comes in.

GEORGE Elizabeth Poldark 'regrets'. *(then)* This is Francis's doing.

TANKARD Why waste your time on these people? Surely Unwin is of more use?

GEORGE Unwin is proving less of an asset than I'd hoped. All manner of promises made in exchange for votes – and I begin to fear they've been wasted. What is the use of having an MP in your pocket if he's too obtuse to do your bidding?

TANKARD He's pliable. Is that not an asset?

GEORGE Only if yoked to wit and intelligence – which in this case it is not. *(then)* How was the meeting?

TANKARD Illuminating.

GEORGE Tell me. *(then)* Oh, but first, summon Tom Harry. There's another small matter which needs clearing up.

CUT TO:

14: INT. SAWLE KIDDLEY – DAY 7

Jud sits at a table, haranguing a group of customers who have clearly heard it all before. Prudie, in particular, interjects with regular snorts of derision and eye-rolling.

JUD Ross Poldark do owe me 'is life! I tell 'ee, 'tis down t' me that Ross Poldark walks this earth a free man! When 'Is Worshipfulness the judge say t' me, 'Mester Paynter', he sez: 'Did this man do wrong or no?' – and I sez, 'Sithee Your Honourableness, Ross Poldark is as innocent as a new-dropped babe in its first wettels.' An' sez 'Is Majestical Worship: 'Mester Paynter, 'tis your testimony an' yours alone 'ave set this man free.'

CUT TO:

15: EXT. NAMPARA HOUSE – DAY 7

Returning home with her driftwood, Demelza hears the sound of a horse's hooves behind her. She smiles, assuming it's Ross – so is surprised when she is overtaken by . . .

DEMELZA *(surprised)* Captain McNeil!

CAPTAIN MCNEIL Mistress Poldark! Have you recovered from your husband's ordeal?

DEMELZA I give thanks daily f'r 'is acquittal, sir.

CAPTAIN MCNEIL Doubtless he'll be a wiser man for it? No more sailing close to the wind? Devoting himself to home and family?

DEMELZA *(a sarcastic smile)* You know Ross.

CAPTAIN MCNEIL Is he at home?

DEMELZA In town.

CAPTAIN MCNEIL I'm in the neighbourhood at the behest of Unwin Trevaunance – advising on matters of local security. But I trust I may drop in and take a glass of rum with my old army comrade?

DEMELZA I doubt Ross'd object!

CAPTAIN MCNEIL Or indeed my old comrade's *wife*!

He leaps down off his horse and takes the armful of driftwood from Demelza.

CAPTAIN MCNEIL *(cont'd)* Allow me, ma'am.

Taken aback by his boldness, though not displeased by his attention, Demelza smiles her acquiescence and leads the way to Nampara.

CUT TO:

16: EXT. TRENWITH, BARN – DAY 7

Francis, alongside two male servants, is bringing hay into the barn, helped by Mrs Tabb, a servant girl and Geoffrey Charles. Elizabeth watches from a distance. Aunt Agatha appears at her shoulder, looking puzzled.

ELIZABETH Is something amiss?

AUNT AGATHA Francis's head? Did something drop on it? He's not been right since he returned from Bodmin!

Elizabeth considers this.

ELIZABETH He *is* changed. And I do not know how or why. But we must be glad of it.

She loops her arm through Aunt Agatha's and walks with her.

AUNT AGATHA And will he let little Verity come home?

ELIZABETH In that he is not changed, Aunt. I only wish he were.

CUT TO:

17: INT. NAMPARA HOUSE, PARLOUR – DAY 7

Captain McNeil sits in Ross's chair. Prudie brings in a tray with two glasses and a bottle of rum. She glances suspiciously at McNeil. She senses what Demelza as yet does not – that McNeil is very keen on her.

PRUDIE Cap'n Ross be 'ome soon, i' bla'.

DEMELZA *(as she hands McNeil a glass of rum)* I hope so – for Captain McNeil has called 'specially to see him.

Prudie's expression tells us she doesn't believe that for a moment. She goes out.

CAPTAIN MCNEIL *(to Demelza)* Your health, ma'am.

They drink. Then . . .

CAPTAIN MCNEIL *(cont'd)* In truth, 'twas also *you* I wished to see. On account of your skill at cow doctoring.

DEMELZA I've no such thing, sir!

CAPTAIN MCNEIL Ray Penvenen begs to differ. Whereas Sir Hugh Bodrugan simply *begs*. His prize cow Sheba is sick. He'd esteem it the greatest of favours if you'd cast your eye over the beast and prescribe a remedy. *(seeing her hesitate)* He asked for you particularly.

DEMELZA *(wry)* I don't doubt it.

CAPTAIN MCNEIL May I tell him that he need not hope in vain?

Their eyes meet briefly – and for a moment Demelza catches a glimpse of something beyond a friendly interest. She is both disconcerted and flattered. Before she can think how to respond, Ross walks in.

ROSS Captain McNeil?

McNeil leaps to his feet.

CAPTAIN MCNEIL An ambush, sir! Caught off-guard and in possession of the field!

He offers Ross his hand and shakes it warmly.

ROSS How are you, Captain? On manoeuvres hereabouts?

CAPTAIN MCNEIL Quartered with Sir Hugh at Werry House. Whither I'm attempting to lure your wife.

ROSS To what end?

DEMELZA Sir Hugh wants me to cure his cow – though I say I've no skill – despite my good luck with Penvenen's.

CAPTAIN MCNEIL *(to Ross)* Can I persuade you to lend your wife to such a cause?

ROSS Demelza has a mind of her own, sir – but since she's a special fondness for Sir Hugh, no doubt she'll be over directly.

It's said mischievously, but Demelza isn't impressed.

ROSS *(cont'd)* Excuse me, I've some mine figures to attend to.

As Ross goes off into the library we get the impression that McNeil's 'old comrade' ploy is wearing thin and that Ross is beginning to find his interest in Demelza increasingly tiresome.

CUT TO:

18: EXT. SAWLE COTTAGES – DAY 7

Caroline and Unwin are driving past in Caroline's carriage. Unwin tries to engage her attention but Caroline speaks only to Horace. As they pass a row of humble cottages, Caroline pouts with distaste.

CAROLINE Look, Horace, what beastly little hovels! Who could bear to live here?

UNWIN I urge you to quit this place and come to London – then these loathsome sights need not distress you.

As they pass by Caroline notices Dwight talking to Ted. He is too busy to notice Caroline. But she notices him.

CAROLINE I did not say I found *all* the sights loathsome hereabouts.

Unwin has no idea what she's talking about. And she has no intention of enlightening him.

CUT TO:

19: INT. NAMPARA HOUSE, LIBRARY – DAY 7

Ross is making drawings for the proposed new tunnel when Demelza appears.

DEMELZA Did you mislay your manners? Leavin' me alone to deal with our guest?

ROSS You appeared to be handling him admirably. I felt like an intruder.

DEMELZA Meaning what?

ROSS Oh Demelza, d'you really suppose he wants you to cure Bodrugan's cow? He makes his intentions very plain.

DEMELZA I think I ought to be able to judge that for myself.

ROSS No doubt you think so, but be careful his uniform doesn't dazzle you. It has that effect on some people.

DEMELZA Especially a common miner's daughter who don't know any better?

ROSS That's for you to demonstrate.

DEMELZA You're detestable – sayin' that!

ROSS I'm sure I didn't start this argument.

DEMELZA Oh no, you never do! You just give me cold shoulder an' sour looks an' despise everything that isn' up to your high-an'-mighty standards!

She runs out of the room and slams the door. Presently Prudie sticks her head round the door.

PRUDIE What 'ee bin sayin' t' upset the maid?

ROSS *(genuine)* I haven't the faintest idea.

CUT TO:

20: EXT. TRENWITH LAND – DAY 7

Demelza, still angry from her confrontation with Ross, is walking with Garrick. She strides across fields, crosses a stream and passes a copse of trees. Garrick goes charging off into the trees, on the scent of something. Demelza pauses to rest. Presently the snap of a twig makes her look up. It's Elizabeth. She's on the border of Nampara and Trenwith land.

ELIZABETH Demelza?

Demelza jumps. It's an awkward meeting.

ELIZABETH *(cont'd)* Are you well?

DEMELZA Quite well, thank 'ee. I came in search of Garrick. He scented rabbit an'— *(shouting)* Garrick, come to!

ELIZABETH Is – Ross recovered from the trial?

DEMELZA He rarely speaks of it.

ELIZABETH And – your news? *(Demelza's pregnancy)* The child? Is he pleased?

DEMELZA Not – exactly.

Elizabeth eyes Demelza closely. And guesses the truth.

ELIZABETH You've not told him.

Demelza's first instinct is to lie. But then . . .

DEMELZA He don't wish f'r another. Since Julia, he haven't the heart f'r it.

ELIZABETH And we're to blame.

DEMELZA That's not my b'lief.

ELIZABETH It's good of you to say so. But the fact that there's still discord between our families—

DEMELZA There is. An' I think 'twill not be lightly set aside. By Ross at least.

Elizabeth nods. There's very little else to say. Demelza is eager to get away.

DEMELZA *(cont'd) (shouting)* Garrick? *Garrick!*

To her relief Garrick comes racing out of the trees. An awkward nod between Demelza and Elizabeth – then Demelza strides away with Garrick at her heels.

CUT TO:

21: EXT. SAWLE KIDDLEY – DUSK 7

Jud reels out of the kiddley and is about to stagger off home when he spots two figures on horseback some distance away. It's Tankard and Tom Harry – and Jud knows exactly why they're here. He tries to sidle away – and when he thinks he's sufficiently out of sight, breaks into a jog.

CUT TO:

22: EXT. SAWLE VILLAGE – DUSK 7

Tom Harry and Tankard watch as Jud jogs off into the gathering gloom.

TANKARD It must be clean and swift – and out of sight—

TOM HARRY Giss on, man, you're talkin' to the master now!

They set off slowly after Jud.

CUT TO:

23: EXT. WHEAL LEISURE – DAY 8

Dawn breaks over Wheal Leisure. Presently Ross, Zacky, Paul, Ted and various others emerge from the mine, blackened and dirty, having done their first shift at the tunnel. They are greeted by Henshawe.

HENSHAWE A good night's work?

ZACKY A good deal nearer Trevorgie than this time yesterday!

HENSHAWE Go home and get some rest.

ROSS *(laughs)* None of that for the wicked! It's home to break-fast then away to Truro. My finances require urgent attention!

CUT TO:

24: INT. NAMPARA HOUSE, ROSS & DEMELZA'S
BEDROOM – DAY 8

Demelza is smoothing out the linens of Julia's crib bed. A brief pang – and a reminder of her current situation. She now knows she really must tell Ross she is pregnant. Ross comes in, he seems resolved to mend their disagreement of the day before.

ROSS Demelza—

DEMELZA Ross—

ROSS You first.

DEMELZA No, you.

ROSS I've been distracted of late. With the trial, Wheal Leisure. But there are things I've been wishing to say to you.

DEMELZA And I to you.

ROSS About our finances.

DEMELZA Oh.

Ross doesn't notice the note of disappointment in her voice.

ROSS My shares in Wheal Leisure are the only thing of value we have. I've begun this new tunnel to improve our chances of the mine becoming profitable – but still, our own coffers are almost bare.

DEMELZA They needn't be. You're Head Purser at the mine. Why won't you take a wage?

ROSS I prefer to plough every last penny back into the mine.

DEMELZA No one else works for nothin'.

ROSS That's their choice. And mine. *(before she can argue)* We have, however, a more pressing concern. Last year I asked Pascoe to find me a loan of one thousand pounds. The interest – at forty per cent – is due this week.

DEMELZA Four hundred pounds? How is *half* such a sum to be found?

Ross shrugs. He really has no idea.

DEMELZA *(cont'd)* What's to be done?

ROSS Ride to Truro, see if Pascoe's managed to get the loan

extended for another year. In the meantime, the more I work in the mine, the better our chances of reaching Trevorgie.

DEMELZA And the interest?

ROSS Look about you. See what you can bear to part with. *(beat)* Then look again.

He gets up and goes out. Demelza isn't thrilled to be presented with this sudden ultimatum. Then as she looks out of the window she sees their two cows in the field below. An idea occurs to her.

CUT TO:

25: EXT. WERRY HOUSE – DAY 8

Demelza walks up to Werry House – to be greeted by Sir Hugh and Captain McNeil.

SIR HUGH BODRUGAN Mistress Demelza! Have you come to steal my heart?

DEMELZA No, sir. I've come to visit your cow.

McNeil catches her eye and gives her an approving smile.

CUT TO:

26: EXT. TRENWITH HOUSE FIELDS – DAY 8

Francis is driving a cart laden with hay. Geoffrey Charles rides beside him. Francis offers the reins to Geoffrey Charles. The cart passes and almost runs over the discarded hobby-horse which George had given to Geoffrey Charles.

FRANCIS A real horse is much better than a hobby-horse, is it not?

Geoffrey Charles nods eagerly. Then . . .

GEOFFREY CHARLES Why does Uncle George not visit us now?

FRANCIS Uncle George is not our friend.

A pause. Then . . .

GEOFFREY CHARLES Is Uncle Ross our friend?

Francis considers this seriously.

FRANCIS In time, I hope he will be.

They drive on.

CUT TO:

27: INT. STABLES, WERRY HOUSE – DAY 8

Demelza examines Sir Hugh's cow, looks in its eyes, examines its mouth.

DEMELZA She d' look fair sick, Sir Hugh. What treatment has she had?

SIR HUGH BODRUGAN All manner of blisters, clysters, salves and poultices. All to no avail. But I've no doubt you'll give me better advice.

DEMELZA I will. *(beat)* Start afresh with a better beast.

CUT TO:

28: INT. TRENWITH HOUSE, LIBRARY – DAY 8

Elizabeth ushers Dwight into the library. Aunt Agatha sits apart, in a world of her own.

ELIZABETH You're quite the favourite with Mrs Tabb these days. She cannot abide Dr Choake.

DWIGHT I suspect she prefers the cheapness of my remedies.

ELIZABETH Or possibly their efficacy?

Dwight smiles and takes the acknowledgement.

ELIZABETH *(cont'd)* Aunt Agatha, Dr Enys has agreed to take tea with us.

Aunt Agatha gives a brief nod of acknowledgement.

ELIZABETH *(cont'd) (to Dwight)* You know how she loves to hear of the latest dread diseases!

They sit down. Elizabeth pours tea.

DWIGHT Is it my imagination or is Francis in better spirits these days?

AUNT AGATHA *(to no one in particular)* Scrofula! That's it! Great purple blotches and swellings of the neck—

ELIZABETH Since the trial, you would not know him. I cannot tell if it's because Ross was saved – or if something else happened while he was in Bodmin. *(then)* He shared your room the night before the trial. Did you notice any strangeness – of mood or behaviour?

DWIGHT I – not that I can recall.

ELIZABETH From something he said, I had the feeling— *(hesitates, then)* You may think me callous – or hysterical – but I could almost believe – that Francis had intended to kill himself.

Dwight says nothing. This in itself is enough for Elizabeth's fears to be confirmed.

ELIZABETH *(cont'd)* Did he?

DWIGHT You should not listen to malicious gossip.

AUNT AGATHA *(to no one in particular)* Throbbing great pustules and fiery carbuncles – never a good sign—

ELIZABETH *(to Dwight, smiling)* I wonder where you think I would hear such gossip? You see how we live here? We do not make or receive calls – even from our cousins at Nampara. I beg you to be honest with me.

DWIGHT Whatever occurred, be glad of it. He came to town a broken man. He returned – like that.

They look out of the window.

CUT TO:

29: EXT. TRENWITH HOUSE, GROUNDS – DAY 8

The distant sight of Francis, with Geoffrey Charles beside him, urging on the horse and cart, both of them screaming with laughter.

CUT TO:

30: EXT. WERRY HOUSE – DAY 8

Sir Hugh is escorting Demelza around the grounds.

SIR HUGH BODRUGAN This cow you speak of – your Emma—

DEMELZA She's our pride an' joy. So we could not let her go except at a goodly price.

SIR HUGH BODRUGAN *(laughing)* Not if the rumours be true! *(beat)* Your husband's financial difficulties? Of course I'm always happy to help a friend. And I could be persuaded to pay that 'goodly price' – if the terms were right.

DEMELZA What terms would you require?

SIR HUGH BODRUGAN Merely a kind of interest. Payable here – *(He touches her cheek.)* here – *(He touches her lips.)* and here! *(He grabs her and pulls her towards him.)* He attempts to kiss her. She struggles to escape his grasp.

DEMELZA Sir Hugh! You forget yourself!

SIR HUGH BODRUGAN On the contrary—

DEMELZA Then let this remind you – *(grappling to keep him at bay)* – Judas, I think my *dog* has better manners!

SIR HUGH BODRUGAN Woof! Woof!

DEMELZA Down, sir! Or must I box your ears and send you to the stables?

As she struggles to fend him off, McNeil appears.

CAPTAIN MCNEIL Sir Hugh – I believe you're wanted at the house. *(seeing him hesitate)* Urgently?

Sir Hugh seems to come to his senses. He bows and departs.

DEMELZA Sir Hugh gets a mite unruly sometimes.

CAPTAIN MCNEIL Should you decide to brave his company again, I will personally undertake to protect you from his – *enthusiasm.*

DEMELZA I'm obliged t' you, sir.

A brief moment between them. It's a welcome change to have someone so attentive when Ross is so distracted these days. Then Demelza curtseys and leaves. McNeil remains.

CUT TO:

31: INT. PASCOE'S BANK – DAY 8

Ross and Pascoe are dining together.

PASCOE It wasn't easy but I've secured agreement for your loan to be extended for another year. At the same exorbitant rate. *(beat)* Provided *this* year's interest is forthcoming tomorrow.

ROSS *(laughs)* A mere four hundred pounds!

PASCOE Quite so. *(then)* How went the shareholders' meeting?

ROSS Well enough. But for the appearance of a new share-holder.

PASCOE Tankard? The Warleggan proxy?

ROSS You heard.

PASCOE Are they on a mission to own the company?

ROSS No, sir. Just to own me.

CUT TO:

32: EXT. TRENWITH HOUSE – DAY 8

Elizabeth is saying goodbye to Dwight. Elizabeth raises a delicate sub-ject.

ELIZABETH You see much of Ross and Demelza?

DWIGHT Why d'you ask?

ELIZABETH I so wish our families could be reconciled – but Ross is determined to keep his distance.

Dwight nods thoughtfully but tries not to get embroiled.

ELIZABETH *(cont'd)* I wonder—? Might I ask you to speak to them on our behalf?

DWIGHT What could I say?

ELIZABETH Francis is to give a supper when the harvest is in. To our tenants – and friends. Would you ask Ross and Dem-elza to join us? To stay the night? You too are most welcome.

DWIGHT I'll happily carry the invitation. I cannot guarantee how it will be received.

CUT TO:

33: EXT. HENDRAWNA BEACH – DUSK 8

Ross and Demelza walk along the beach with Garrick.

ROSS I'm not overjoyed to think of Sir Hugh in possession of Emma.

DEMELZA Nor I – but you said she must be sold – and I've secured a buyer. So what else must go?

ROSS Not the oxen. Without them we cannot plough. But the chickens, the pigs—

DEMELZA The clock?

ROSS The carpet.

DEMELZA The settle?

ROSS At least one chair.

DEMELZA My brooch is worth a hundred pounds.

ROSS It was a gift. *(beat)* But it may need to be sold in the end.

Demelza nods stoically. Ross feels guilty. He tries to cheer her up.

ROSS *(cont'd)* I wonder what Garrick would fetch on the open market? One overgrown mongrel? Carnivorous—

DEMELZA Crockery breaker?

ROSS Stealer of pies? D'you suppose there'd be any takers?

A smile between them. They're united again.

CUT TO:

34: EXT. NAMPARA FIELDS (MONTAGE) – DAY 9

Ross hands over a halter to Sir Hugh's farmhand. On the other end is Emma, the cow. Into Ross's palm Sir Hugh counts money. Demelza holds up two chickens by the claws and gets money in return. Prudie looks on, dismayed; Jud stands muttering as Ross negotiates the sale of their prize sow. Money is counted out; Demelza and Prudie look sad and Jud scowls as Ross hands over a young calf. Demelza watches as Jud and Ross load the grandfather clock onto a cart.

CUT TO:

35: EXT. KILLEWARREN – DAY 9

Ray is tending his herd when he sees Caroline, dressed in her riding habit.

CAROLINE May I fetch you anything from Truro, Uncle?

RAY PENVENEN You're going with Unwin?

CAROLINE Good Lord, no! I'm in need of some *sensible* conversation!

RAY PENVENEN Hicks will escort you.

CAROLINE Oh, but—

RAY PENVENEN You cannot be roaming about the country-side unaccompanied, Caroline.

CAROLINE *(appears to acquiesce)* No, Uncle. Of course not. *(then)* So what may I bring you? Sugared almonds? Marzipan?

RAY PENVENEN You spoil your old uncle!

An affectionate smile between them. Caroline certainly knows how to wrap Ray round her little finger.

CUT TO:

36: EXT. MARKET PLACE – DAY 9

Caroline and Hicks walk through the market place. Then, without warning, as Hicks pauses to look at a stall, Caroline darts away and disappears into the crowds, leaving Hicks gesturing helplessly in her wake.

CUT TO:

37: EXT. OPEN COUNTRYSIDE – DAY 9

Ross and Demelza ride into town, pulling a cart which contains the grandfather clock, the carpet and several items of furniture.

CUT TO:

38: EXT. MARKET PLACE – DAY 9

Demelza and Ross ride into town with the cart. They hold their heads high as they ride. People watch them pass. They are obviously persons of quality and this is an interesting sight. Now George is revealed, unseen by them, watching from the door of the Red Lion. He struggles to conceal a smile of triumph. He is joined by Margaret.

GEORGE How the mighty are fallen. *(then)* Do you not find it diverting?

MARGARET *(smiles sadly, shakes her head)* I have a soft spot for him.

CUT TO:

39: EXT. TRURO, MARKET PLACE – DAY 9

Caroline is strolling through the market, glancing at the various stalls and street sellers. Her superior riding habit marks her out as a woman of wealth and quality. Now, to her delight, she spots Dwight, who is talking to some of his patients. Caroline watches with interest, enjoy-

ing Dwight's ease and expertise with his patients. As the patients walk off, Dwight now sees Caroline.

CAROLINE Dr Enys! What a lucky encounter.

DWIGHT How are you, Miss Penvenen?

CAROLINE I have a tingling in my throat. D'you think it could be serious?

DWIGHT I very much doubt it. You seem otherwise in the peak of health.

CAROLINE I hope it's not that hideous complaint – what is it called? *Morbus strangulatorius?*

DWIGHT If it were the putrid throat you'd soon know it.

CAROLINE Oh, is that what Ross Poldark's daughter had? He's not exactly blessed with luck, is he?

DWIGHT No. And that doesn't seem about to change.

As they look, Ross and Demelza appear with their horse and cart. They notice Dwight and Caroline. They acknowledge Dwight with warmth and Caroline with politeness – and walk on.

CAROLINE How humiliating it must be for him. *(beat)* Less for her, I suppose.

DWIGHT I doubt either of them see it that way. *(then)* Would you excuse me, ma'am? I have patients to see to.

He bows and walks away. Caroline remains, watching Ross and Demelza, intrigued.

CUT TO:

40: EXT. TRURO, MARKET PLACE (MONTAGE) – DAY 9

Ross unfurls the carpet to be valued; Demelza places the pair of candlesticks before a merchant; Ross hands over the grandfather clock; Demelza lays down a pewter bowl. As she does so she glances up and

sees Caroline watching from a distance. Demelza nods in acknowledgement. Caroline smiles. Ross receives money in exchange for a
chair; Ross lays down the ruby brooch. The goldsmith examines it.
Demelza is almost in tears as she watches him. The goldsmith counts
out some money to Ross. Demelza looks imploringly at the goldsmith
as if beseeching him for more. He counts out one more note. Ross takes
it. Choked, but not wanting Ross to see how upset she is, Demelza
walks away. And thus comes unexpectedly face to face with George.
It's not a welcome encounter for either party.

GEORGE Mistress Poldark—

DEMELZA Mr Warleggan.

As Ross joins them:

GEORGE Ross! How are you? You don't look at all well. Can
it be the anxieties of the trial?

ROSS Nor you, George. Can you have had some disappointment?

GEORGE None that I know of.

ROSS Perhaps it is yet to come.

A moment between them. Eyeball to eyeball. George goes pale. Demelza
grabs Ross's arm and steers him away.

CUT TO:

41: INT. PASCOE'S BANK – DAY 9

The clock strikes five. Just before the close of business, Ross and Demelza count out four hundred pounds.

PASCOE How did you manage it?

ROSS (cheerfully) Oh, it was quite straightforward. We sold
pretty much everything we own.

CUT TO:

42: EXT. OPEN COUNTRYSIDE – DUSK 9

Ross and Demelza return home with the empty cart.

CUT TO:

43: EXT. WOODED COPSE – DUSK 9

Jud is making his way home when he hears the snap of a twig behind him. He freezes. If he doesn't move perhaps he won't be seen? Finally he turns . . . and sees Tankard and Tom Harry.

TANKARD Mr Paynter—

JUD 'Oo, sur? Me, sur? Nay, not I, sur.

He tries to walk off. Tankard bars his way.

TANKARD You recall the bargain we struck some time ago?

JUD Bargain? I niver struck no such thing! Don't hold with 'em, does I?

TOM HARRY In exchange for testifying against Ross Poldark?

They're closing in on him now. Jud starts to panic.

JUD Nay, sur, p'raps I do recall something now—

They close in further.

JUD *(cont'd)* Thinkin' it over, p'r'aps I wasn't meself in court – mebbe it did slip me mind. In which case 'tis on'y fair I give 'ee back yer guineas. *(fumbling in his pockets)* Ten, were it?

TOM HARRY Fifteen. But that is not what we have come for.

JUD For what, then?

TOM HARRY This.

Suddenly he whacks Jud across the head and fells him to the ground.

Watched by Tankard, Tom continues to lay into Jud, who howls and tries in vain to protect himself.

CUT TO:

44: INT. NAMPARA HOUSE, PARLOUR – DUSK 9

Ross and Demelza contemplate their supper: a meagre bowl of thin broth and a bowl of windfall apples. Ross takes a spoonful of broth.

ROSS *(feigning appreciation)* Mmmmmmmmmm.

Demelza is trying to summon up the courage to tell Ross of her pregnancy.

DEMELZA Ross – I bin wantin' to speak of somethin' but haven't yet found the right moment—

Before she can continue, Prudie comes in.

PRUDIE Surgeon's 'ere.

Dwight comes in.

DEMELZA Oh! Dwight!

PRUDIE I hope 'ee 've eaten!

Dwight sees the meagre supper and the threadbare room. Prudie goes out, scowling. She can't forgive Ross for having sold all their home comforts. Ross offers Dwight the bowl of apples.

ROSS Admiring our harvest?

DWIGHT I hope to augment it. With an invitation—

DEMELZA Oh?

DWIGHT From Trenwith.

CUT TO:

45: INT. NAMPARA HOUSE, ROSS & DEMELZA'S BEDROOM – NIGHT 9

Demelza and Ross are getting ready for bed.

ROSS Obviously we won't accept.

Demelza is silent. This is exactly what she expected. But Ross appears to need to justify his decision.

ROSS *(cont'd)* We surely can't forget that it's thanks to them we lost Julia? Or that George is still their bosom friend?

DEMELZA Is he?

ROSS You'd have us overlook it?

DEMELZA Have I said so? In truth I'm in no haste to go to Trenwith.

ROSS Then we're in accord.

DEMELZA Do appear so.

Before he can react to the strange tone of her reply, there's a loud hammering on the door downstairs, and presently an anguished shriek from Prudie.

CUT TO:

46: INT. NAMPARA HOUSE, HALLWAY – NIGHT 9

Ross and Demelza rush downstairs to find Prudie wailing.

PRUDIE Dead! He'm dead! He'm mortal dead!

CUT TO:

47: INT. NAMPARA HOUSE, LIBRARY – NIGHT 9

The bloodied, bruised, dead body of Jud is laid out on a table. Ross, Paul, Zacky, Ted, Beth Daniel and Mrs Zacky stare in shocked silence at it. Prudie collapses wailing into Demelza's arms.

PRUDIE 'Oo could do such a thing? He 'ad no enemies – he were the sweetest, kindliest, most peaceable cove a body could meet! An' never a cross word did pass 'is lips—

A few raised eyebrows at this.

PRUDIE *(cont'd)* An' I now left a widder – all forlorn – wi' not a penny in the world – not e'en t' bury the poor soul – God rest it!

PAUL There *is* this . . . *(hesitates, then)* When we moved 'im, these fell out of 'is pockets.

He hands Prudie fifteen gold sovereigns. When she sees them, her eyes widen. At first Ross is as puzzled as everyone else.

PRUDIE Gold? Sov'reigns? *Gold sov'reigns?* Where'd 'e get such—?

ROSS Where indeed?

Demelza shoots a glance at Ross. What does he suspect? Suddenly Prudie snaps out of her distress.

PRUDIE Why, th' mizzerly, mazzerly stinkin' black worm! He 'ad 'em about 'im an' never tell'd me?

ZACKY *(to Ross)* Reckon 'tis from the Trade?

ROSS Unlikely.

PRUDIE I'll crown 'im senseless! Tan th' arse off 'im! Knock 'im sideways down Stippy-Stappy Lane! *(then, remembering to feel grief)* Then give 'im a rare good buryin'. *(warming to the idea)* Rum an' vittles – hymns an' viols – widder's weeds for poor ole Prudie. 'Tis a matter of lookin' *respectable*, 'tis. We mus' give the ole man a send-off fitty ways.

CUT TO:

48: INT. NAMPARA HOUSE, KITCHEN – NIGHT 9

Ross and Demelza at the table, while in the library Mrs Zacky and Beth Daniel help Prudie with the washing and laying out of Jud. Ross is struggling to come to terms with Jud's demise.

ROSS I've known him since I was a child. He was the most useless servant under the sun – but he taught me to smoke a pipe – and cheat at loo— *(then a thought occurs)* They left the money.

DEMELZA Yes?

ROSS Then it was no random attack.

DEMELZA What, then?

ROSS Vengeance?

DEMELZA For what?

ROSS You were in court. You heard his original statement. He was ready to testify against me.

DEMELZA But then he did not.

ROSS What if he was paid to speak against me – hence the fifteen guineas – then changed his mind?

A moment while they let the implications of this land. Then they go back into the library, where the preparation of Jud continues. Prudie is already warming to her new role as grieving widow.

PRUDIE *(gives Mrs Zacky some sovereigns)* Take these an' axe Will Nanfan t' fix 'im a buryin' box? The finest, sithee? *(handing over more coins)* An' this for the feast, shall 'ave five casks of rum, six tetty pies, five capons, three legs o' mutton, six damson tarts an' a jug o' custard. *(to Beth Daniel)* An' do 'ee go call 'is friends in Sawle an' Mellin t' come and drink and feast 'is passin' this night tomorrow?

The two women depart, leaving Prudie to continue the laying out. Demelza comes to help her. Too distressed to linger, Ross leaves.

CUT TO:

49: INT. NAMPARA HOUSE, PARLOUR – NIGHT 9

Demelza comes in to find Ross drinking brandy, lost in thought.

DEMELZA Would George wreck all we have? The family, the business – now our servant—?

ROSS That seems to be his aim.

DEMELZA Can we do nothing?

Ross considers carefully, takes another drink.

ROSS Some things cannot be mended. *(beat)* But some can.

Demelza eyes him closely. What does he mean?

CUT TO:

50: EXT. TRENWITH HOUSE, FIELDS – DAY 10

Francis is leading the line of men scything – with more authority and aptitude than we've ever seen before. Elizabeth is watching with Geoffrey Charles.

CUT TO:

51: EXT. TRENWITH LAND – DAY 10

Ross and Demelza walk across the fields to Trenwith. Both seem wary, in two minds about the wisdom of what they're about to do.

ROSS It suits George to have me and Francis at odds – but I'm damned if I'll let him call the tune in my own family.

They are passing the boundary of Trenwith and Poldark land, crossing the bridge over the stream, by the copse of trees. Demelza is feeling nauseous – and none too attractive in an old gown.

DEMELZA It d' feel wrong to be feastin' an' drinking, with Jud lyin' cold in his weeds.

ROSS You can bet Prudie will be consoling herself with gin and mutton! And tomorrow we'll be at the burial.

They walk on in silence. Demelza looks down at her gown.

DEMELZA I look like a ragamuffin.

ROSS It's not the Lord Lieutenant's Ball!

DEMELZA *Some* folks'll be dressin' up.

ROSS Apparently not.

He draws her attention to the sight ahead of them.

THEIR POV: A distant view of Elizabeth. Even though she's wearing an old dress, she looks gorgeous, her hair loose, her face glowing. Her face lights up when she sees them approach. Francis's even more so. Unable to believe his eyes, he waves delightedly at them.

CUT TO:

52: EXT. TRENWITH HOUSE, FIELDS – DAY 10

Francis and Elizabeth watch Ross and Demelza approach.

FRANCIS *(to Elizabeth)* This is your doing?

ELIZABETH You're not displeased?

FRANCIS Far from it!

He goes forward (still hesitant, unsure of his reception) to greet Ross and Demelza.

FRANCIS *(cont'd)* Cousin! An unexpected pleasure.

Ross is wary but allows Francis to shake his hand. Francis kisses Demelza's hand, then escorts her to Elizabeth, who comes forward to greet her.

ELIZABETH Thank you for bringing him. It means the world to Francis.

Demelza forces herself to smile but, glancing sideways at Elizabeth, feels dull and dowdy again. And clearly Ross is not immune to Elizabeth's glowing appearance. He takes her hand and kisses it.

ROSS *(to Elizabeth)* You look well, cousin.

ELIZABETH We're both so glad to see you, Ross. Are we not, Francis?

FRANCIS Beyond measure.

And we can see he's absolutely genuine.

CUT TO:

53: EXT. TRENWITH HOUSE, FIELDS – DAY 10

Villagers, tenants, servants, family (including Ross, Demelza, Francis, Elizabeth, Geoffrey Charles, Aunt Agatha) and guests (including Dwight) gather in a circle in the field for the ceremony of 'Crying the Neck'. The last sheaf of corn is standing. Francis is urged by his tenants and servants to be the one to lift the last sheaf of corn. He seems reluctant. They are cheerfully insistent. (Ross observes this and exchanges a look with Elizabeth.) Finally Francis acquiesces, steps forward and lifts the sheaf of corn above his head.

FRANCIS I 'ave 'n! I 'ave 'n! I 'ave 'n!

EVERYONE What 'ave 'ee? What 'ave 'ee? What 'ave 'ee?

FRANCIS A neck! A neck! A neck!

EVERYONE Hurrah! Hurrah! Hurrah!

Francis hands the sheaf to Geoffrey Charles, who holds it above his head and, guided by Francis, leads the way from the field towards Trenwith. Francis beckons Elizabeth, she takes his arm and they follow Geoffrey Charles. A piper falls in behind them and starts to play. Demelza takes Ross's arm and the rest of the crowd follow.

CUT TO:

54: INT. TRENWITH, GREAT HALL – DAY 10

The 'neck' of corn adorns a long table where harvest offerings and simple food and drink are laid out. Tenants, villagers, servants and guests all mingle, eating and drinking. Francis plays the host. Ross chats with Aunt Agatha. Demelza is feeling nauseous and is finding the whole event something of a trial. Elizabeth is mingling with her guests. Mrs Chynoweth arrives.

MRS CHYNOWETH *(unimpressed)* I was expecting a small private gathering. Instead I find myself ambushed by *sans-culottes*!

ELIZABETH *(laughing)* Hardly, Mama! These are our tenants and friends.

MRS CHYNOWETH Trust me, a few crusts will not curry favour when they turn on you. Ask the Marquis de Launay – if you can find his head!

Elizabeth laughs and summons Francis to greet his mother-in-law. Incredibly, he does so without complaint.

FRANCIS You look radiant, mater-in-law!

MRS CHYNOWETH Are you quite well, Francis?

FRANCIS Never better! *(then)* Come, friends! Shall we have dancing? I think we shall!

Country dance music starts. Francis takes Elizabeth's hand and leads her to the dance.

ON ROSS: Observing them. Finding himself uncharacteristically uncomfortable. What is he feeling? Could it be a pang of jealousy? Mrs Chynoweth gives Ross a sneer of triumph as she notices his expression. The dancing begins. Elizabeth and Francis are full of energy. Dwight is dragged into the dance by an eager village girl. Aunt Agatha insists on dancing with Ross! Demelza is invited to dance by Horace Treneglos – and despite feeling nauseous, obliges.

CUT TO:

55: INT. NAMPARA HOUSE, KITCHEN – DUSK 10

Ted plays a mournful tune as Prudie – in widow's weeds – is brought into the kitchen, supported by Mrs Zacky and Zacky. A table is groaning with food and drink. Prudie is escorted to a throne-like chair, a flagon of gin is placed in her hand and she prepares to receive a steady stream of mourners as if she were head of state.

CUT TO:

56: INT. WARLEGGAN HOUSE, GEORGE'S DEN – DUSK 10

George, dressed to go out, is incandescent with rage.

GEORGE I ordered you to scare him, not assassinate him!

TANKARD Tom got a little carried away—

GEORGE This is disastrous!

TANKARD You think Poldark will know who's behind it?

GEORGE I wouldn't be surprised if he's outside my house right *now*!

There's a loud hammering on the door. George almost leaps out of his skin. He rushes to his desk and takes out his pistol. He is poised to fire when Unwin prances in, oblivious, and does a twirl.

UNWIN How d'you like my coat? I ordered my tailor to make it the double of Prinny's! You most definitely need one, George. *(then)* Well? Shall we go? My intended will be impatient to see me.

George covertly puts the pistol away.

GEORGE By all means.

TANKARD *(low)* Will you require Tom to escort you?

GEORGE *(low)* At a distance.

Tankard nods – 'Leave it with me.' George and Unwin go out.

CUT TO:

57: INT. KILLEWARREN, PARLOUR – DUSK 10

Caroline is sitting by a window, rubbing her throat. A knock at the door.

CAROLINE *(sounding hoarse)* Come in.

Ray appears.

RAY PENVENEN My dear? Our guests will be arriving soon.

CAROLINE I have such a pain.

RAY PENVENEN But Tom Choake was just here. Did he not bleed you?

CAROLINE For a sore throat?

RAY PENVENEN You dismissed him.

CAROLINE Would you have me submit to his butchery?

RAY PENVENEN So what do you propose?

CUT TO:

58: INT. TRENWITH HOUSE, LIBRARY – DUSK 10

Francis escorts Ross and Dwight from the Great Hall.

FRANCIS May I offer you some port? This is the last bottle of the eighty-three. When that's done we'll have to resort to cheap gin! *(as he serves them)* Did you hear that I quarrelled with George?

ROSS No. What was the cause?

FRANCIS Oh, these things sink in slowly. At first you barely notice – then one day you wake up to the realization that the man who has been your friend for years is a complete and utter blackguard.

ROSS I don't disagree. Indeed, I strongly suspect he's behind the assault on Jud.

DWIGHT What will you do?

ROSS Till I can prove it? Nothing. But when I do—

Dwight and Francis are left in no doubt about Ross's intentions. Now a servant appears with a letter that is given to Dwight. He opens it.

DWIGHT There's someone ill at Killewarren.

FRANCIS Tell them to be ill at a more convenient time!

DWIGHT They cannot be sure but – it's a complaint of the throat.

A look goes round them all. Dwight leaps to his feet. Ross, Francis and Dwight are all thinking the same thing. Is this the putrid throat?

DWIGHT *(cont'd)* I'll go at once.

CUT TO:

59: INT. TRENWITH, OAK ROOM – DUSK 10

Demelza has taken refuge in the Oak Room. She sits fanning herself. Aunt Agatha appears.

AUNT AGATHA Elizabeth? Where's my port?

Elizabeth appears, followed by Mrs Chynoweth, who barely acknowledges Demelza's presence.

MRS CHYNOWETH . . . and Lady Whitworth says that fashions in London and Bath are now verging on the indecent!

ELIZABETH *(laughing)* What exactly does that mean?

MRS CHYNOWETH Bosoms! Acres of 'em – exposed like capons on a platter!

AUNT AGATHA *(to Demelza)* You look pale, child. Are you unwell?

DEMELZA No – that is – I b'lieve I may be sickenin' for something.

Elizabeth and Demelza exchange a glance.

AUNT AGATHA *(oblivious)* Get Elizabeth to mix you a rouge – a little cinnabar ground with mercury? Elizabeth goes out so seldom, she has no need of it.

MRS CHYNOWETH It's criminal that this should be the highlight of your social calendar, Elizabeth! I know I would be driven quite mad if I had only farmhands and kitchen maids to converse with.

It's quite clearly aimed at Demelza – but she is already feeling so wretched, she could hardly feel much worse.

DEMELZA If you'll pardon me – I must take a breath of air.

She gets up and goes out.

CUT TO:

60: INT. KILLEWARREN – DUSK 11

George and Unwin arrive at the Penvenen gathering and are shown into a reception room. This harvest supper is an altogether more lavish affair than the Trenwith supper. A buffet of rich, exotic food is laid out. Servants are on hand to dispense food and drink. The guests are all aristocrats and gentry. Amongst them we see Sir Hugh Bodrugan, Captain McNeil, Margaret and Mr Aukitt.

SIR HUGH BODRUGAN Dammit, but I'm partial to a harvest supper. Gladdens the heart to eat the fruits of one's labours!

CAPTAIN MCNEIL Remind me when you were last in your fields with a scythe, sir?

Everyone roars with laughter.

MARGARET And I hear you have a new cow, Sir Hugh?

SIR HUGH BODRUGAN Ah, Demelza Poldark's Emma? What a beauty. I think she's taken quite a fancy to me!

CAPTAIN MCNEIL If only he could say the same for Demelza Poldark!

More braying laughter from Sir Hugh and the guests. George scans the room. Though there are several well-dressed ladies there, Caroline is not amongst them.

GEORGE Is Miss Penvenen not here?

UNWIN Nor her uncle. Most irregular! Invited to supper and not a sign of the hosts! Shall we go hunt them down?

Then he sees Captain McNeil and summons him over.

UNWIN *(cont'd)* Ah, McNeil, what news? Can we now rest easy in our beds, knowing you've purged the district of violence?

CAPTAIN MCNEIL I lay claim to no such thing, sir. Only last night we had a murder on our doorstep.

GEORGE Surely not?

CAPTAIN MCNEIL Captain Poldark's manservant.

UNWIN Oh, a *lackey*! I thought for a moment it was someone important!

He whacks George round the shoulders and roars with laughter at his own wit.

CUT TO:

61: INT. NAMPARA HOUSE, KITCHEN – DUSK 10

Prudie is knocking back the gin whilst continuing to receive a stream of commiserations. Zacky and Paul exchange a glance: they suspect that Prudie is enjoying being the centre of attention. Then . . .

PRUDIE *(rapping the table)* Paul Daniel? Where 'ee be?

Paul comes over to Prudie.

PRUDIE *(cont'd)* Do 'ee go draw th' spigot o' th' next keg o' brandy. I've an urge t' address th' conflagration!

Paul goes out. Prudie summons Mrs Zacky and Zacky to help her to her feet. She bangs the table to call for silence. Then addresses the mourners.

PRUDIE *(cont'd)* Jud Paynter – 'e wear a white sepulchre – a cloamin' ole tomcat! Y'd as lief trust a beaver! But now 'e's passed on – to flowery fields and green meads – and when Paul Daniel come back, we'll raise a toast an' send 'im on his way—

Suddenly Paul reappears in the doorway. He looks horror-struck.

PAUL 'E's gone!

PRUDIE We know that, fool!

PAUL From his slab! 'Tis empty! The corpse ain't there!

Uproar in the room. Then everyone makes a beeline for the library.
CUT TO:

62: INT. NAMPARA HOUSE, LIBRARY – DUSK 10

The mourners burst into the library.
THEIR POV:
A winding sheet is all that remains lying on the table. Prudie lets out a prolonged howl.
CUT TO:

63: EXT. TRENWITH HOUSE – DUSK 10

Demelza is fanning herself, trying to stave off nausea, when a distraught Prudie appears.
DEMELZA What is it?
PRUDIE 'Tis they body stealers! They've robbed me o' my ole man!
CUT TO:

64: INT. KILLEWARREN – NIGHT 10

Dwight is admitted and is greeted by an anxious Ray.
RAY PENVENEN My niece has been ill for three days. Dr Choake attended her, but she grows worse and insisted on sending for you. Will you come with me?
Ray escorts Dwight upstairs. Now George appears with Unwin.
UNWIN Adams or Wyatt?

GEORGE For what?

UNWIN Our house in London. Caroline will want the latest thing. And she can well afford it. I wonder if it shouldn't be Wyatt? His Pantheon in Oxford Street has pleasing dimensions.

GEORGE Perhaps you'd better *secure* the lady before you start spending her fortune.

Irritated, he walks away from Unwin – and spots William Aukitt. Who just happens to be a Wheal Leisure shareholder.

GEORGE *(cont'd)* Mr Aukitt, remind me, do you still have shares in Wheal Leisure? How goes it?

CUT TO:

65: INT. KILLEWARREN, CAROLINE'S ROOM – NIGHT 10

Caroline is sitting on a chaise as Ray ushers Dwight in. She looks weak and pale but smiles sardonically – then lifts up a cover to reveal Horace asleep on a cushion beside her. Dwight smiles, comes over, sits on the bed and feels her pulse.

DWIGHT Did Dr Choake attempt a diagnosis?

RAY PENVENEN Quinsy.

DWIGHT With or without fever?

RAY PENVENEN Without, but she can hardly swallow.

CAROLINE Is it the putrid throat?

DWIGHT That we will shortly ascertain. Will you open your mouth, please?

Caroline obeys. Dwight leans forward and examines her throat, pushing her tongue down with a spoon and holding a candle close so that it can shed some light. He's acutely aware of Caroline's proximity. Ray, genuinely concerned for her, looks on. Suddenly Dwight catches sight of something in Caroline's throat. He withdraws the spoon. He looks concerned. Caroline catches his look.

CAROLINE Will I die?

DWIGHT *(to Ray)* Might a servant fetch me some warm water and salt?

RAY PENVENEN I'll see it done directly.

Ray goes out. Left alone with Caroline, Dwight is determined to retain his authority. He opens his bag of instruments – and selects a pair of tweezers.

DWIGHT I think I might be able to help you but you must keep absolutely still. Can you do that?

Caroline nods meekly.

CUT TO:

66: INT. TRENWITH HOUSE, LIBRARY – NIGHT 10

Flushed with drink and optimism, Francis leans forward to Ross.

FRANCIS May I tell you a secret? *(Ross nods)* Old Fred Pendarves? Mine Captain at Grambler in my father's day? For a month now I've had him prospecting over my land.

ROSS To what end?

FRANCIS Oh Ross, you know I'll never make a farmer. I do my best but in truth I can't tell the nose of a cow from its tail! Mining. That's what I keep coming back to. That's what *he* wanted for me.

He gestures to the portrait of Charles on the wall. They both toast Charles.

FRANCIS *(cont'd)* God knows, he'd be as surprised as me to think that any of what he taught me had sunk in. But that's the truth of it. I must start mining again.

ROSS Well, don't let me deter you – but even a hole in the ground costs money.

FRANCIS Oh, I *have* money. *(beat)* A few hundred – put by. *(then)* Had things gone badly at the trial, I'd have given it to Demelza. Now I'm minded to spend it on a final attempt to secure my own destiny. If only to spite George.

ROSS I think the best revenge would be to succeed in your own right – *despite* his interventions.

CUT TO:

67: INT. NAMPARA HOUSE, LIBRARY – NIGHT 10

Prudie shows Demelza the empty table where Jud's body had lain. Prudie flings herself upon it and weeps.

CUT TO:

68: INT. KILLEWARREN, CAROLINE'S ROOM – NIGHT 10

Dwight is leaning very close to Caroline. Both of them are keenly aware of each other's closeness. Caroline has her mouth open and Dwight is delving inside.

DWIGHT Almost there . . . *(then)* All done. Now rinse your mouth with salt water.

He withdraws the tweezers and before Caroline can say anything, he gives her a bowl of water. She does as she's told.

DWIGHT *(cont'd)* It will get easier now. I've nothing here but if your man will come with me, I'll give him something to soothe the throat.

Caroline is clutching her throat in amazement.

CAROLINE What did you do?

DWIGHT When did you last eat fish, Miss Penvenen?

CAROLINE Three days ago?

DWIGHT You must be more careful in future.

Now he shows her what he removed from her throat: a tiny piece of sharp fish bone. Caroline stares at it in astonishment. Dwight is feeling pleased with himself. He can see that Caroline is seriously impressed – and that emboldens him further.

DWIGHT *(cont'd)* Can I do anything for Horace while I'm here?

CAROLINE *(with a smile)* Horace and I are both eternally in your debt, Dr Enys.

CUT TO:

69: INT. KILLEWARREN, HALLWAY – NIGHT 10

A flushed and bright-eyed Dwight comes down the stairs and is about to depart when he encounters a drunk and disorderly Mr Aukitt who is being supported by Margaret. He seems agitated and barely able to stand.

DWIGHT Mr Aukitt? May I be of assistance?

Aukitt looks dazed. He is shaking his head in disbelief and muttering to himself.

DWIGHT *(cont'd)* What ails him?

MARGARET *(amused)* A fatal encounter. I doubt you can save him.

Dwight takes Aukitt by the arm and steers him to the outside where he can get some fresh air. Margaret returns to the party.

CUT TO:

70: INT. KILLEWARREN – NIGHT 10

Caroline comes downstairs to join the party. Seeing her descend, Unwin starts to make his way over to her. Only to find Caroline is ignoring him and heading straight for George.

GEORGE Miss Penvenen, I trust you're on the mend?

CAROLINE I believe I am, sir.

She flashes him a dazzling smile. Unwin tries to butt in but Caroline shows no interest in him.

CUT TO:

71: INT. TRENWITH HOUSE, LIBRARY – NIGHT 10

Francis tops up Ross's glass, but – unusually – doesn't pour any for himself.

FRANCIS The ladies have deserted us.

ROSS Perhaps we bore them!

FRANCIS I think I must go to bed. I find I'm less able to hold my liquor these days. No, finish your port. God knows when I'll be able to offer you more of it! *(then)* Thank you, cousin.

ROSS For what?

FRANCIS I never thought to see you under my roof again.

ROSS I never thought to be here.

It's a big moment. Though nothing is said, they silently acknowledge the bond between them. They shake hands. Francis goes out; Ross remains, thoughtful.

CUT TO:

72: INT. NAMPARA HOUSE, KITCHEN – NIGHT 10

Prudie sits at the table being comforted by Demelza, Zacky, Paul, four other mourners – and the brandy.

PRUDIE 'Tis the shame of it! To 'ave an 'usband – an' then to not 'ave an 'usband – I'll never live it down.

DEMELZA Sssshhh now.

PRUDIE But what about the buryin'? Y' can't 'ave a buryin' without a body.

DEMELZA No.

PRUDIE So now I ain't jus' robbed o' my 'usband, I'm robbed o' the pleasure of seein' 'im planted i' th' ground!

ZACKY Tragedy.

PAUL Terrible.

Suddenly Prudie's eyes widen. She's seen something in the doorway. She points, starts to scream – and then faints. The four other mourners erupt in shrieks of terror and are falling over each other in their panic to escape. Demelza, Zacky and Paul turn to look behind them . . . and see Jud, looking dazed and bewildered, dressed in his funeral shroud. Very much alive.

CUT TO:

73: INT. TRENWITH HOUSE, LIBRARY – NIGHT 10

Ross is lost in his thoughts, drinking rum by the fire, when Dwight returns.

DWIGHT Have I missed all the fun?

ROSS You appear to have had some of your own.

A nod to Dwight's flushed face.

DWIGHT Oh! – It must be the ride and the night air.

ROSS Was it the putrid throat?

DWIGHT Thankfully not. *(then)* I *did* have to sedate William Aukitt though. He was so agitated he could barely speak.

ROSS What ailed him?

DWIGHT A fit of the Warleggans? He'd been talking to George – and before he knew it he'd signed away some shares.

ROSS *(alarmed)* Oh?

DWIGHT In a mining venture. *(seeing Ross's look of dismay)* He did not *specify* Wheal Leisure.

ROSS Did George look happy?

DWIGHT Yes?

Ross shrugs, resigned. They both know which mine it is.

CUT TO:

74: INT. NAMPARA HOUSE, KITCHEN – NIGHT 10

Demelza, Zacky, Mrs Zacky, Paul, Beth, Ted and Prudie stare at Jud in disbelief.

ZACKY So 'ee were lyin' on the table—?

JUD With a terrible thirst an' dreamin' o' gin. So I carts off to Jake's kiddley for some ale – an' what 'appens? They all ups an' screams like stuck pigs, a-fallin' o'er each other to get out the door. So I drinks me fill an' comes 'ome to Prudie. *(with a glare at Prudie)* An' what does I find? Folks a-feastin', drinkin', fligged out in fancy black! – at *my expense*! An' naught left but two kegs o' brandy an' a windin' sheet! Tedn' right, tedn' fair, tedn' just, tedn' fitty!

Suddenly he seizes the two kegs of rum and a pie from the table and heads for the door. In the doorway he pauses.

JUD *(cont'd)* Truly I say unto 'ee – a prophet is never honoured in 'is own land.

And with a flourish he stalks through the door and slams it behind him. Demelza, Paul, Zacky, Prudie, etc. look at each other in amazement.

CUT TO:

75: INT. WARLEGGAN HOUSE – NIGHT 10

George returns home. A footman tries to help him with his coat. George gestures him away and hastens upstairs.

CUT TO:

76: INT. WARLEGGAN HOUSE, GEORGE'S ROOM – NIGHT 10

George comes in, takes off his coat, surveys himself in the mirror. Clenches his fists into boxing stance and strikes an imaginary punch at an imaginary enemy.

CUT TO:

77: INT. TRENWITH HOUSE, LIBRARY – NIGHT 10

Ross pours himself another glass, sits staring into the fire. Elizabeth comes in. Both of them are caught off-guard.

ELIZABETH Oh! – Ross – I thought everyone had retired.

ROSS I thought so too. Is Demelza about?

ELIZABETH I think she was feeling unwell and went up early. I thought I'd clear the table.

ROSS Let me help you.

They begin to clear together – both of them suddenly a little self-conscious, finding themselves alone together for the first time in a long while.

ELIZABETH I must thank you for coming.

ROSS It was a good day.

ELIZABETH Heaven knows how we've paid for it. But Francis was insistent.

ROSS The Poldarks have fallen low! *(then)* You must be sorry you married into the family!

ELIZABETH *(laughing)* Do you think I should answer that?

ROSS *(laughing)* Perhaps I should not have asked it?

A brief moment of eye contact between them . . . then they return to the task.

CUT TO:

78: EXT. TRENWITH HOUSE – NIGHT 10

Demelza returns through the gates and makes her way up the path. She's tired now and looking forward to bed.

CUT TO:

79: INT. TRENWITH HOUSE, LIBRARY – NIGHT 10

Ross and Elizabeth continue clearing the table. Both seem acutely aware of each other, both trying to seem blasé about being in such close proximity – and neither really succeeding. Then . . .

ROSS Francis tells me he has some money put by. I'm surprised he doesn't use it for this household.

ELIZABETH Oh no, he's quite adamant. It's a 'special sum' – to be used for a 'special purpose'.

ROSS Does George know he has it?

ELIZABETH George gave it him.

ROSS *(surprised)* Did he?

ELIZABETH In recompense for his gaming losses – to Matthew Sanson.

ROSS D'you believe that?

ELIZABETH Should I not?

ROSS George is not known for his philanthropy.

Ross continues in silence a while. Then . . .

ROSS *(cont'd)* Francis is changed.

ELIZABETH Yes.

ROSS And you, I think.

ELIZABETH *(laughing)* For the better?

ROSS *(laughs)* I wouldn't go that far! Remember, there was a time when you were already *perfect. (beat)* To me, I mean.

There. It's been said. Both of them know it's moved things on to another level of intimacy.

CUT TO:

80: INT. TRENWITH HOUSE, HALLWAY – NIGHT 10

Demelza, returning to the house, tiptoes inside, closes the door quietly. And hears Ross and Elizabeth talking . . .

CUT TO:

81: INT. TRENWITH HOUSE, LIBRARY – NIGHT 10

ELIZABETH That was long ago. *(beat)* And you've been more than happy since. *(beat)* With Demelza.

ROSS And you've grown up.

ELIZABETH Not too much, I hope!

ROSS Today in the fields you looked like a girl of sixteen. *(then)* Your age when I first knew you.

ELIZABETH These past months have changed me – have made me appreciate what I have rather than what I lack.

ROSS Very wise. After all, there's no point thinking about what might have been . . .

CUT TO:

82: INT. TRENWITH HOUSE, HALLWAY – NIGHT 10

Demelza is listening, out of sight.

CUT TO:

83: INT. TRENWITH HOUSE, LIBRARY – NIGHT 10

ELIZABETH But you and I would never have been happy together. Our characters are too different.

ROSS True. But cannot love overcome such obstacles? *(then)* And surely there's a greater impediment? You're a lady – and could never have played the scullery maid.

ELIZABETH *(smiling)* Perhaps I have hidden talents.

ROSS I don't dispute that. For somehow you've managed to bring the light back to Francis's eyes.

ELIZABETH I cannot imagine how.

ROSS Can you not?

They are very close now . . .

CUT TO:

84: INT. TRENWITH HOUSE, HALLWAY – NIGHT 10

Demelza listens with rising dismay.

CUT TO:

85: INT. TRENWITH HOUSE, LIBRARY – NIGHT 10

Ross and Elizabeth are closer still. Looking into each other's eyes, they could almost be about to kiss. Or could they? Suddenly it's clear Elizabeth has no intention of going there again. She smiles, steps away and the moment passes.

ELIZABETH You should go to bed, Ross. *(seeing him hesitate)* Demelza will be thinking you've gone astray.

The mention of Demelza brings Ross to his senses. He nods his agreement.

ELIZABETH *(cont'd)* Goodnight, then.

Elizabeth takes a tray of glasses and walks out of the room. Ross remains, thoughtful.

CUT TO:

86: INT. TRENWITH HOUSE, HALLWAY – NIGHT 10

Distraught, Demelza tiptoes off upstairs to the bedroom.

CUT TO:

87: INT. TRENWITH HOUSE, GUEST BEDROOM – NIGHT 10

Ross comes in. To find Demelza still awake.

ROSS *(surprised)* You're awake? I thought you'd retired long ago.

DEMELZA I went out.

ROSS Out?

DEMELZA Prudie came. *(beat)* Jud's alive.

ROSS *What?*

DEMELZA At least till Prudie do kill 'im again!

ROSS Jud's *alive?* But – *how?* What happened?

DEMELZA Ask me tomorrow. I'm weary to the bone.

ROSS But – are you sure?

DEMELZA I see'd him with me own eyes.

She turns over and tries to go to sleep. Something in her resigned tone makes Ross uneasy. He starts to get undressed. Demelza waits to see if he will say anything about Elizabeth. He doesn't. Eventually . . .

DEMELZA *(cont'd) (nonchalantly)* Elizabeth looked well tonight.

ROSS She did.

DEMELZA Her mother thinks were she not wed to Francis, she'd have half the aristocracy at her feet.

ROSS But she is wed to Francis. *(beat)* And seems content to be so.

They are both silent a while. Lost in their own thoughts. Then Ross glances at Demelza – feels guilty at his treacherous thoughts and his neglectful behaviour to her of late – and becomes more conciliatory towards her. He sits down on the bed beside her.

ROSS *(cont'd)* D'you remember our first visit here? That Christmas?

DEMELZA When you first told me you loved me?

ROSS And you told me you were with child?

Here it is. The perfect opportunity for Demelza to tell him of her pregnancy. And she almost takes it. But for some reason she can't explain, she continues to hold back.

DEMELZA 'Twas different then. You were *glad* I was with child. We were in our first days of love. And you would never've looked twice at another woman.

He looks at her surprised. Put on the spot, he doesn't even deny it. Instead . . .

ROSS Oh, Demelza, what man does not occasionally look at another woman? *(before she can argue)* What woman does not occasionally look at another man? And what man or woman of sense does not have qualms about bringing a child into the world?

Demelza glances at him guiltily. He sees her look of panic. For a moment he's confused. And then he guesses the truth.

ROSS *(cont'd)* Demelza—?

DEMELZA Yes, Ross? *(exploding)* Yes, Ross! An' I know you don't want it! – I know it's just another burden to you! But there's no preventing it now – so all we can do is—

ROSS How long have you known?

DEMELZA Since the trial?

ROSS Good God! And not to tell me—?

DEMELZA You said you didn't want another! After Julia—

ROSS Nor did I! Nor do I! The very thought of it – a child to grow into our hearts and then be lost to us again? Could you bear it? I could not. Nor could you.

Demelza is silent. She acknowledges the truth of his argument. But then:

ROSS *(cont'd)* But if a child is *coming* . . . that's different.

DEMELZA How is it different?

ROSS A child is not a thought. A child is flesh and blood. *(He takes her hand.)* And if you can risk your heart again—

DEMELZA I can.

ROSS Then so can I.

A moment of connection between them. He kisses her. Not passionately but with utmost tenderness. They are tentatively reconciled.

Episode 4

A bird alights on a crumbling tower which is all that is left of the derelict mine Wheal Grace. The wind whistles around it. Wild flowers and grasses bob in the breeze. The lonely cry of a gull is heard. We pull back until the crumbling edifice is a tiny speck in a lonely land-scape. At the far edge of the frame a man on horseback leads a line of six prisoners, guarded by two soldiers.

CUT TO:

2: EXT. CLIFF-TOP PATH – DAY 11

Customs Officer Vercoe, on horseback, leads a line of six bedraggled men, guarded by two soldiers. Presently he sees two figures walking along the path towards them.

HIS POV: Demelza and Ross walking arm in arm. Demelza is seven months pregnant and glowing with health. She and Ross seem close and enjoying each other's company. Seeing Vercoe, who he knows and isn't fond of, Ross forces himself to be pleasant.

ROSS Mr Vercoe.

VERCOE Captain Poldark.

ROSS May I ask where these men are headed?

VERCOE Truro Jail.

ROSS Their crime?

VERCOE Importing goods without paying the required duty? Some call it 'Free Trading'.

ROSS *(pleasantly)* Some call it the only way to afford life's necessities.

VERCOE Brandy? Gin? Are these essentials?

ROSS Salt is.

VERCOE It's my duty to enforce the law, Captain.

ROSS Your commitment is heartwarming.

Ross smiles benignly, but Vercoe senses the edge behind the pleasant tone. He leads his procession on. After he's gone:

DEMELZA Shouldn't rile 'im.

ROSS Couldn't resist.

They both suppress a grin. After a while the path splits in two: one way leads to Nampara Cove, the other to the distant Wheal Leisure.

ROSS *(cont'd)* I'm wanted at the mine. There's fuses to set.

DEMELZA *(teasing)* You'd abandon me? S'pose I met a foot-pad on the way home?

ROSS God help him.

Demelza hits Ross playfully. Laughing, they go their separate ways. We go with Demelza. As she glances back to make sure Ross isn't watching her, we know she's up to something. Instead of returning to Nampara, she heads off down towards Nampara Cove.

CUT TO:

3: EXT. NAMPARA COVE – DAY 11

Spectacular views of open sea and sky. A lone rowing boat is glimpsed out in the bay. As we go in closer we realize the rower is Demelza. She looks up towards land as a loud explosion is heard.

CUT TO:

4: EXT. WHEAL LEISURE – DAY 11

The huge explosion reverberates underground.
CUT TO:

5: INT. WHEAL LEISURE TUNNEL – DAY 11

Ross, Henshawe, Zacky, Paul and Ted are covered with dust from the explosion in the tunnel. They wait for the dust to clear, then Ross leads the way down the tunnel towards where the explosives were set. They peer through the hole made by the explosion – but there's only darkness.

ROSS *(frustrated)* Still not through?

PAUL Can't be far off.

ZACKY Can almost *smell* Trevorgie, th' other side o' that iron-stone!

HENSHAWE Another blast should do the trick.

ZACKY *(to Ross)* Will the shareholders keep faith with us?

ROSS They're sensible men – most of them – and I intend to make a robust argument.

HENSHAWE So we carry on?

ROSS We carry on.

CUT TO:

6: INT. WARLEGGAN HOUSE – DAY 11

George is sparring with his boxing instructor. The instructor isn't giving his all, but just enough to make it tough for George. As the instructor eases off, Tankard comes in with Tom Harry.

GEORGE They've broken through?

TANKARD Almost.

GEORGE They will. Ross Poldark is tenacious.

The sparring continues.

GEORGE *(cont'd)* Ultimately I expect Wheal Leisure to do very well for me.

TOM HARRY Why else would 'ee buy shares in it?

George raises his eyebrows wearily at Tankard. Tom Harry is so slow!

GEORGE On whose land does Wheal Leisure sit? Who is its main shareholder? *(beat)* And his latest scheme is about to come to fruition? *(beat)* It's just too easy.

Even Tankard has no idea what George is planning next. But he's about to find out.

CUT TO:

7: EXT. NAMPARA COVE – DAY 11

Demelza pulls the boat ashore and secures it, reaches in and lifts out her catch. In a good mood, and believing herself unobserved, she sings as she makes her way up the beach.

DEMELZA *(sings)*

Hal-an-tow, jolly rumbalow,
We were up long before the day-O,
To welcome in the summer,
To welcome in the May-O,
The summer is a-coming in
And winter's gone away-O . . .

She is shocked out of her reverie by an unexpected voice.

ELIZABETH'S VOICE Is that wise—?

DEMELZA *(leaping out of her skin)* Judas!

She sees Elizabeth walking along the beach with Geoffrey Charles.

ELIZABETH With the currents so strong hereabouts?

DEMELZA I know 'em well enough.

ELIZABETH Would Ross be happy?

DEMELZA He'll be happy wi' *these*! *(holding up her fish)* An' who's to tell 'im where I got 'em?

A moment's stand-off between them. Then Demelza bows and walks off. Elizabeth isn't quite sure why things have cooled between them. She's unaware that Demelza overheard her conversation with Ross (Episode 3) and now doesn't trust her an inch!

CUT TO:

8: INT. NAMPARA HOUSE, KITCHEN – DAY 11

Demelza comes in with her fish. Prudie and Jinny are making pastry. Prudie raises an eyebrow at Demelza's catch. Demelza returns her look defiantly. Nothing further needs to be said.

JINNY *(to Prudie)* How long will Jud be gone?

PRUDIE Don' talk t' me o' that slinkin' g'eat lurker! Any excuse to shirk 'is chores an' study th' inside o' Sally Chill-off's kiddley.

DEMELZA *(to Jinny)* 'Keepin' 'is head down', he says.

JINNY 'Keepin 'is throat oil'd', more like!

PRUDIE I'll keep 'is head down!

She slams down a fish with such force that Demelza and Jinny jump.

CUT TO:

9: EXT. WHEAL LEISURE – DAY 11

Ted, Paul and Zacky emerge from the mine followed by Ross. For the first time we notice that Paul has bruised arms and Ted has a trickle of blood from his nose. Ross looks concerned.

ROSS Were you hurt in the blast?

PAUL 'Tis bruisin' I 'ave all th' time – same as Ted.

Ross looks at Ted, at the trickle of blood from his nose, and also the bruising and blotches.

ROSS *(to Zacky)* What is it?

ZACKY *(He shrugs; he has no idea.)* Like a plague, Ross. Half th' mine's afflicted—

PAUL 'Alf the village beside—

ROSS *(to Zacky)* Should we send these men home?

ZACKY They cannot afford to lose their pitches—

ROSS They won't, of course – but we need 'em fit. *(then)* Get Dwight Enys.

CAROLINE *(VO)* Dwight Enys is a scoundrel!

CUT TO:

10: INT. KILLEWARREN, PARLOUR – DAY 11

Caroline is pacing up and down.

CAROLINE For all he knows I might be dead!

Ray, reading, glances up at his niece.

RAY PENVENEN I think I would have informed him, had that been the case.

Caroline continues to pace. She begins to compose a letter in her head.

CAROLINE *(VO)* 'Dr Enys, having saved my life some months ago, you appear to have no further interest in my recovery . . .'

She stalks out.

CUT TO:

11: INT. KILLEWARREN, CAROLINE'S ROOM – DAY 11

Caroline is at her writing desk, penning a letter.

CAROLINE *(composing her letter)* 'I would nonetheless esteem it a favour if you would call to assure yourself of my full recovery and to receive payment for your skill. Unless, of course, you have more important matters to attend . . .'

CUT TO:

12: EXT. WHEAL LEISURE – DAY 11

A long line of ragged and bedraggled miners, fisher folk and balmaidens line up to see Dwight, among them Ted, Paul and Charlie Kempthorne. With the exception of Charlie, they all look deathly pale, listless and have bruises and blotches all over their bodies.

DWIGHT I can't account for these symptoms. Swelling, bruising, bleeding gums, listlessness . . .

ROSS Is it the dust? The foul air of the mine?

DWIGHT I wondered that – but some of these people are fisher folk. It's perplexing. Now Charlie comes to be examined.

CHARLIE KEMPTHORNE Here'm one o' your successes!

DWIGHT Your symptoms were entirely different. I could diagnose the complaint—

CHARLIE KEMPTHORNE *(proudly)* Consumptives!

DWIGHT Phthisis. And therefore treat it.

CHARLIE KEMPTHORNE I d' lead a cleanly life now, surgeon. Walkin', fresh air, asses' milk – not t' mention my sailmaking – it do wonders for th' lungs!

ROSS Your daughters must be delighted.

CHARLIE KEMPTHORNE They surely are, Cap'n!

DWIGHT I wish all my patients were as responsive as you, Charlie.

Charlie looks pleased with himself. The other miners look even worse by comparison.

CUT TO:

13: EXT. TRENWITH HOUSE, FIELDS – DAY 11

Francis is walking his land, holding before him a virgula divinatoria *(divining rod).*

AUNT AGATHA *(VO)* What is that contraption?

Francis looks up and sees Elizabeth and Aunt Agatha watching him at the window.

ELIZABETH *(VO)* A *virgula divinatoria*. It's believed to sniff out metal.

AUNT AGATHA *(VO)* Could it sniff out mutton? That *would* be a find these days!

CUT TO:

14: INT. TRENWITH HOUSE, LIBRARY – DAY 11

Aunt Agatha and Elizabeth look through the window.

AUNT AGATHA That upstart Warleggan hasn't called of late.

ELIZABETH He and Francis have quarrelled.

AUNT AGATHA I wonder he doesn't call in your loans. *(beat)* But perhaps he has other plans.

ELIZABETH Such as?

AUNT AGATHA Should I know how the Devil's mind works? *(then)* You'd better keep him sweet.

ELIZABETH I've no influence over George.

Aunt Agatha raises a scornful eyebrow. This gives Elizabeth pause for thought. Should she be actively trying to keep George sweet as Aunt Agatha has suggested? Now Francis comes in, cheerfully brandishing the virgula divinatoria. *Aunt Agatha eyes him narrowly.*

AUNT AGATHA I've summoned Dr Choake.

FRANCIS Are you unwell?

AUNT AGATHA I am *never* unwell. It's *you* he comes to see.

A glance between Elizabeth and Francis. They both agree Aunt Agatha is out of line. But Francis declines to be riled.

FRANCIS I find myself in excellent health, thank you, Aunt. And will improve further when we have a working mine to our name. And are no longer reliant on Warleggan charity!

He smiles and goes out. Aunt Agatha looks displeased.

AUNT AGATHA Little Verity should be here. She'd know what to do.

CUT TO:

15: EXT. TRURO HARBOUR – DAY 11

Verity is walking with Andrew along the harbour wall.

ANDREW Will you join me aboard next week?

VERITY People will think me a bad wife! To be always galli-vanting off and sunning myself in Lisbon!

ANDREW That makes you a *good* wife. For acceding to your husband's wishes! *(then)* Yet I think they are yours too?

VERITY You know they are.

They walk on. Then:

ANDREW I've had word from James.

VERITY *(suddenly nervous)* Oh?

ANDREW His ship was diverted to Penang.

VERITY And Esther?

ANDREW Remains with her governess in Plymouth. But when James returns, they will both come and visit us. *(Verity looks doubtful)* I shall insist.

They walk on a little. Then:

VERITY Do you ever think the price was too high? Your children shun us. My brother disowns us.

ANDREW We have at least *one* friend! To whom we owe everything.

CUT TO:

16: EXT. MARKET PLACE – DAY 11

Demelza and Verity walk through the market.

VERITY Of course we're happy. I could not be more so.

DEMELZA And yet?

VERITY My brother will not forgive me. And Andrew's chil-dren will not meet me. Not that I blame them. I've replaced their dear departed mother. They must hate me!

DEMELZA But when they meet you—

VERITY I begin to think that will never happen. *(then)* And if they will not accept me now, how much worse will it be if Andrew and I have a child of our own?

DEMELZA Are you—?

VERITY No. Not yet. But children are the natural consequence of marriage, are they not?

DEMELZA *(with a smile)* It would appear so.

CUT TO:

17: EXT. WHEAL LEISURE – DAY 11

Dwight is examining a bal-maiden's bruised arm. He's concerned and puzzled. Ross draws him aside.

ROSS Could someone have caused the bruises?

DWIGHT She says they come of their own accord. But how? I can't fathom it. Is it paludal fever? Is it purpura? *(then)* I've tried fresh air, sunlight, goat's milk, nutmeg – perhaps what I *should* try is a different profession!

Ross tries to rally him.

ROSS The navy, perhaps? You'd enjoy ships' rations! Salt pork, dried biscuit, weevils—

DWIGHT No doubt! And be all the healthier for it! *(then)* Of course – *(then)* of *course!*

ROSS What?

DWIGHT Biscuit – salt – no fresh fruit – no green vegetables! I thank you, Ross!

ROSS For what?

DWIGHT Helping me diagnose the complaint.

Ross looks utterly baffled.

DWIGHT *(cont'd)* *(triumphant)* Scurvy!

Delighted with himself, Dwight returns to his patient, the bal-maiden. A messenger comes up to Ross with a letter. Ross glances at it, smiles to himself, then takes it to Dwight.

ROSS This just came for you. *(pointedly)* From Killewarren.

Dwight flushes as he takes the note. Embarrassed, he scans it briefly, crunches it up and puts it in his pocket. Ross is amused at his discomfort.

ROSS *(cont'd)* *(teasing)* Will there be any reply?

CUT TO:

18: INT. KILLEWARREN, PARLOUR – DAY 11

Caroline is reading Dwight's reply.

DWIGHT *(VO)* 'Dear Madam, I am happy to hear of your recovery but be assured, as to payment, I am amply recompensed by the knowledge of your gratitude.'

Caroline, piqued by the brevity of the reply, begins another letter to Dwight.

CAROLINE 'To you, Dr Enys, no doubt the saving of my life seems a very small service. To me it assumes a slightly greater significance. I therefore enclose a guinea, which is the smallest value, little as I esteem myself, that I can put upon your services—'

Caroline is interrupted by the arrival of George.

GEORGE Miss Penvenen! I called in the hope of finding Unwin.

CAROLINE How careless of you to lose him. Is he your man or not?

GEORGE I do not own him, ma'am.

CAROLINE But I thought that was *precisely* what you did.

George struggles not to smile.

GEORGE I trust you've recovered from your indisposition?

CAROLINE Dr Enys saved me!

GEORGE How fortunate.

CAROLINE Tell me – is he a gentleman?

GEORGE By birth – if not by habit. He has a peculiar affection for the common man.

CAROLINE Like his friend Ross Poldark!

GEORGE Both would do better to cultivate people of their own station.

CAROLINE Like Elizabeth Poldark? *She's* a favourite, I hear.

GEORGE Of Ross?

CAROLINE And yourself, I believe.

GEORGE I find I'm less inclined to favour the *fading* gentry when there are more robust specimens at hand!

Taking the compliment personally, Caroline extends her hand for George to kiss. A moment between them. Then George bows and takes his leave. Caroline returns to Dwight's letter – and her reply.

CAROLINE *(writing)* 'Be so kind as to attend me today, as I have been without medical attention since your visit . . .'

CUT TO:

19: EXT. MARKET PLACE – DAY 11

Verity is saying goodbye to Demelza.

VERITY Do you think Elizabeth could ever be persuaded to meet me here? Even for half an hour? With Geoffrey Charles?

DEMELZA Would she do that? Behind Francis's back?

VERITY No, she would never. But I do miss them so terribly and—

Suddenly she stops dead, seems about to burst into tears. Francis is walking down the street in their direction. He sees them. He slows down. Is he coming over? Verity looks hopeful. Demelza too. Francis hesitates – he's on the verge of coming over – then seems to think better of it and only nods in curt acknowledgement. Demelza is dismayed and Verity distraught.

VERITY *(cont'd)* You see? He will never be reconciled.

CUT TO:

20: EXT. COUNTRY ROAD – DAY 11

Ross is riding towards Truro when he rounds a corner and comes face to face with George who is coming from Killewarren. George is momentarily caught off-guard. He tries to edge past Ross – but Ross blocks his way.

ROSS You seem in haste, George. Have you urgent business afoot?

GEORGE All my business is urgent.

ROSS Including your assault-by-proxy?

GEORGE Excuse me?

ROSS My servant Jud Paynter, a witness at the trial, was attacked and left for dead. Fortunately he recovered.

GEORGE How is that *my* concern?

ROSS Only that it would be a mistake to imagine such intimidation could continue to be one-sided.

GEORGE Is that a threat, Ross? Is it?

But Ross has already ridden on, leaving George posturing ineffectually and feeling that once again Ross has the upper hand.

CUT TO:

21: INT. KILLEWARREN, PARLOUR – DAY 11

Caroline is standing at the window, stroking Horace, as Dwight is shown into the room.

CAROLINE How kind of you to call, Dr Enys. I've been waiting above three months!

DWIGHT I apologize, Miss Penvenen. I've been busy with my other patients.

CAROLINE Doubtless they're more important than I.

DWIGHT Only in so far as their conditions are more serious.

CAROLINE Well? Are you going to examine my throat or not?

He moves towards her. She looks him directly in the eye – a challenge, an encouragement. The sexual tension crackles between them.

DWIGHT Open your mouth. *(then)* Wider, please.

She does so. Dwight can hardly breathe, so electric is the tension between them. Eventually he pulls away.

DWIGHT *(cont'd) (brisk and businesslike)* Most satisfactory. You will have no further trouble.

CAROLINE How brusque you are today! *(then)* Is your friend Ross Poldark so peremptory?

DWIGHT He has little time for pleasantries, if that's what you mean.

CAROLINE *(undeterred)* Do you ride, Dr Enys? For pleasure, that is?

DWIGHT I'm sure you'll appreciate I have very little time when I'm taken up with—

CAROLINE More serious complaints. So tell me, what are they?

DWIGHT Scrofula, phthisis, scurvy—

CAROLINE What can be done for them?

DWIGHT For scrofula, nothing. For scurvy – a doctor's drugs are useless but simple foods – green vegetables, fresh fruit – can effect an almost immediate cure. But these are precisely what the poor cannot afford, so they bleed and die.

CAROLINE Why do they not spend less on gin and more on oranges?

DWIGHT Oranges, when they can be had, cost threepence apiece. Gin costs less than sixpence a quart. Yet many are as sober as you or I.

CAROLINE But shall you do any good by attempting to save these people? They will only multiply and there'll be even more mouths to feed. Of course it's sad to see them die, but at least it keeps the numbers in check. Oh, do I shock you?

DWIGHT Only by your assumption that *you* will not be included in this stocktaking.

CAROLINE But of course I won't! I'm a Penvenen, so am rich and privileged!

DWIGHT Will you excuse me, madam? My patients require me.

He bows and heads for the door. At the door he halts and places something down on a small table there.

DWIGHT *(cont'd)* I shall take the liberty of returning your fee.

CAROLINE You consider yourself tainted by it?

DWIGHT I bid you good day.

He strides out – clearly disgusted by her attitude – but even more disgusted that it hasn't diminished his own attraction towards her.

ON CAROLINE: A playful smile of amusement tells us she's not at all upset by Dwight's behaviour.

CUT TO:

22: EXT. NAMPARA HOUSE – DAY 12

Dawn establisher. Birds sing in the hedgerows. Primroses and wood anemones begin to blossom. Buds begin to burst on the trees.

CUT TO:

23: INT. NAMPARA HOUSE, LIBRARY/KITCHEN – DAY 12

Ross is upbeat as he prepares to leave for town. In the parlour he can hear Jinny, Prudie and Demelza gossiping together as they gut and prepare Demelza's latest catch of fish.

ON ROSS: In the library, gathering his paperwork, only half-listening to the conversation in the parlour.

JINNY In Sawle las' night 'ey say another drop was ambush'd—

PRUDIE Cargo lost an' four more sent t' Bodmin Jail—

DEMELZA Since the riots in Bodmin, the district's been crawlin' wi' soldiers—

Still gathering his belongings, Ross's interest is caught by this observation.

PRUDIE And now they'm clean out o' salt from Padstow to St Ives—

DEMELZA Bode ill f' when th' shoals come in—

PRUDIE Fish won't keep—

DEMELZA Fish won't sell—

PRUDIE Zacky Martin say if it weren't fer th' *mine*—

JINNY Mam says if it weren't for *Mister Ross*—

ON ROSS: Not entirely thrilled to have the weight and expectations of an entire community on his shoulders! Now he comes through into the kitchen, sees what they're doing. Prudie tries to hide the fish, but only succeeds in drawing more attention to it.

ROSS Where are these from?

DEMELZA *(nonchalant)* Nampara Cove?

ROSS You went out in the boat?

DEMELZA No, I whistled an' they came a-dancin' at me out the waves!

ROSS Have you no sense?

DEMELZA Yes. *And* an extra mouth to feed!

ROSS Then perhaps you'll do it the courtesy of taking more care of yourself in future. *(before she can argue)* I won't be home late. The shareholders' meeting should be fairly straight-forward.

He gathers his things and goes out. To take out her frustration, Demelza defiantly hacks off the head of a fish. It's clear she has no intention of obeying Ross's orders.

CUT TO:

24: INT. RED LION INN, MEETING ROOM – DAY 12

There's a bustle of optimism as the shareholders arrive for the Wheal Leisure board meeting. Horace Treneglos and several other share-holders cluster round Ross and Henshawe, chatting, so it is not until they all sit down that Ross notices Tankard sitting silent and impassive at the far end of the table. Nevertheless, he's sure nothing can spoil the optimism of the day.

ROSS Gentlemen, we have good things to report. Mr Henshawe?

HENSHAWE Our latest excavations have taken us to within what we calculate to be *feet* o' the old Trevorgie copper lode. Now I admit this has taken longer than we'd hoped, but it's my belief that the next blast will see us break through.

A murmur of excitement and approval from all the shareholders (except Tankard).

ROSS So it only remains for us to secure your approval to divert this quarter's profits – for the *last* time – to pay for this final push. Do we have everyone's agreement?

Shareholders are nodding, hands are about to be raised, when Tankard clears his throat.

TANKARD Eight weeks—

ROSS Yes?

TANKARD Beyond your wildest estimate. And still you're not through?

ROSS Ironstone's no respecter of time or money.

TANKARD But we shareholders must be, surely? Each quarter we've seen our profits diverted into a scheme which has so far yielded precisely nothing. Optimism's one thing – but what if you've got your bearings wrong and bypassed the old workings altogether?

A murmur of concern from the other shareholders. This thought had not occurred to them.

ROSS There's not a man in these parts who knows the workings better than Captain Henshawe—

TANKARD But if *he's* wrong? You might dig on for *years* and never connect.

More murmurs of concern and dismay.

HENSHAWE *(confident)* I say we put it to the vote. Those in favour of continuing—?

Henshawe, Ross and Horace Treneglos raise their hands. To Ross's dismay, none of the other shareholders raise their hands.

HENSHAWE *(cont'd)* Those against?

Tankard and the other shareholders raise their hands. Ross, Henshawe and Horace Treneglos are outvoted. Ross and Henshawe can hardly believe it.

HENSHAWE *(cont'd) (low, to Ross)* Shall we close the meeting? There's little else to report.

TANKARD *(loud)* One moment, sir—

The murmur of voices stops. Tankard has suddenly assumed a position of power in this gathering which no one can be unaware of.

TANKARD *(cont'd)* You will no doubt have noted the absence of Mr Renfrew?

Murmuring from the other shareholders. This is in fact the first time they've noted his absence.

TANKARD *(cont'd)* As of yesterday, he is no longer a shareholder. Having sold his shares to me.

Shocked responses from the other shareholders. Henshawe glances at Ross. Ross doesn't trust himself to speak.

CUT TO:

25: INT. WARLEGGAN HOUSE – DAY 12

George is standing at his window as Tankard hands him the report from the shareholders' meeting.

GEORGE Was he furious?

TANKARD Not to me. But then he knows I am not the *actual* owner of the shares.

George nods with satisfaction. As he glances out of the window he sees

Elizabeth riding past on the road outside. Without a word he walks out.

CUT TO:

26: EXT. DWIGHT'S COTTAGE – DAY 12

Dwight comes out of his cottage carrying a tray of misshapen, half-rotten windfall apples. He is surprised to see Caroline, on horseback, looking down on him from the upper path.

CAROLINE Dr Enys, are you now a pedlar? *(She looks at the apples with distaste.)* I don't envy your customers!

DWIGHT They're for my patients. When these are gone, there'll be nothing till next harvest.

CAROLINE And do your patients enjoy worms and mould?

DWIGHT *(smiles)* Beggars cannot be choosers.

He walks away and begins to load the apples into his saddlebags. Caroline smiles to herself. She's had an idea.

CUT TO:

27: EXT. NAMPARA HOUSE – DAY 12

Ross arrives home to find an unfamiliar horse tethered outside the front door.

CUT TO:

28: INT. NAMPARA HOUSE, PARLOUR – DAY 12

Ross comes in to find Demelza pouring tea for (the extremely portly, shabbily dressed, though in gentleman's clothes) Mr Trencrom.

ROSS Mr Trencrom.

TRENCROM Captain Poldark.

CUT TO:

29: EXT. WARLEGGAN HOUSE – DAY 12

Elizabeth, having ridden past the Warleggan House, gives a brief glance which tells us her being here is entirely deliberate and not the chance passing George assumes it is. Presently George catches up with her. As he overtakes her:

GEORGE You pass my house without paying a call? How have I offended you?

ELIZABETH As I think you know, George, since the trial—

GEORGE The trial? But is that not behind us now? Cannot we move forward? Rekindle our former connection?

ELIZABETH I'm not sure how possible—

GEORGE Please. At least return with me and take some refreshment?

CUT TO:

30: INT. NAMPARA HOUSE, PARLOUR – DAY 12

Demelza is watching Ross and Trencrom carefully, trying to assess their relationship (if any).

ROSS What can I do for you, Mr Trencrom?

TRENCROM Can a man not call, in neighbourly fashion – enquire after your affairs, see how they prosper, speak a little of his own—

ROSS Suppose you speak first of *yours*, so I may come to a quicker understanding of your interest in *mine*?

*Ross smiles affably. He and Mr Trencrom seem to know and under-
stand each other. Demelza begins to have her suspicions.*

CUT TO:

31: INT. WARLEGGAN HOUSE – DAY 12

*George and Elizabeth are served tea by a gaudily dressed servant.
Once they're alone:*

GEORGE I'm sad that you've declined my invitations of late.

ELIZABETH We decline *all* invitations. We simply cannot
afford to return the hospitality.

GEORGE May I venture to suggest that I am a 'special case'?
(no reply) And difficult as things are at Trenwith, they could –
I'm sure you realize – be so much worse.

Elizabeth knows exactly what George is referring to.

ELIZABETH And if Francis cannot say so, allow me to convey
the thanks of the entire family.

GEORGE Not the *entire* family, surely?

CUT TO:

32: INT. NAMPARA HOUSE, PARLOUR – DAY 12

*Ross is lounging back in his chair. He knows what Trencrom is going
to say – and he's not going to make it easy for him.*

TRENCROM My affairs d' far from prosper. Oh, business is
brisk as far as *consumption* goes. The difficulty comes with the
supply.

ROSS So I hear.

TRENCROM What do you hear?

ROSS That the customs officers at St Ann's are determined to let nothing slip ashore? That all your attempts to 'persuade' 'em with a share of the profits have fallen on deaf ears?

TRENCROM But now this crack-down from on high means that every time we find a new landing place, we're met by gaugers and military. All cargo confiscated – crew barely 'scaped with their lives. So here's the thing, we've run out of navigable inlets.

ROSS And I possess the only one for miles.

CUT TO:

33: INT. WARLEGGAN HOUSE – DAY 12

George and Elizabeth continue their talk. George prepares to drop his bombshell.

GEORGE *(casually)* Actually, I expect to be seeing a good deal of Ross in future. *(beat)* I've increased my shareholding in his mine.

ELIZABETH Oh—

GEORGE So I hope I won't have cause to inflict 'undue pressure' on him. *(beat)* Or on Francis, for that matter.

ELIZABETH What might cause you to?

GEORGE I wonder.

He smiles at her. It seems affable enough, but Elizabeth now realizes she has wandered into deeper waters than she'd anticipated.

CUT TO:

34: INT. NAMPARA HOUSE, PARLOUR – DAY 12

Demelza is horrified by Trencrom's suggestion and expects Ross to dismiss it.

TRENCROM Your cove is not ideal but we could land there safely on still nights. I'd handle the distribution and all you'd need to do is draw your curtains.

ROSS And what, d'you think, would induce me to do so?

DEMELZA Ross—

TRENCROM We could discuss a lump sum per cargo. How does – fifty pounds sound?

ROSS I see you've not lost your sense of humour.

TRENCROM Is that such a poor offer? What would you suggest?

ROSS Two hundred pounds per cargo.

DEMELZA Ross—

TRENCROM My dear sir! Impossible. It would make the journey almost without profit—

ROSS Not to mention salt.

TRENCROM Salt?

ROSS There's less profit in salt than in brandy or tea.

TRENCROM And less call for it amongst my more – genteel – customers.

ROSS Two hundred pounds. And six casks of salt. That's my price. Take it or leave it.

CUT TO:

35: INT. WARLEGGAN HOUSE – DAY 12

Elizabeth waits nervously for George to name his price.

ELIZABETH What is it you seek, George?

GEORGE Your friendship? A renewal of our former intimacy?

(beat) A gradual increase in it? *(no reply)* Is that too much to ask? Particularly if it safeguards those you love?

CUT TO:

36: INT. NAMPARA HOUSE, PARLOUR – DAY 12

Ross and Trencrom shake hands. Demelza is furious. She storms out of the room.

CUT TO:

37: INT. WARLEGGAN HOUSE – DAY 12

George waits expectantly, convinced he has Elizabeth over a barrel. But in the end:

ELIZABETH I do not believe Francis would be happy about my visiting here often. *(beat)* If at all.

GEORGE A pity. *(beat)* A very great pity.

Elizabeth gets up and goes out, knowing she's not improved matters, fearing she's made them worse.

CUT TO:

38: INT. NAMPARA HOUSE, HALLWAY – NIGHT 12

Ross shuts the door on the departing Trencrom.

DEMELZA Two hundred pound – for lettin' tub-carriers use our cove? That won't buy you out of prison!

ROSS I don't intend to be there.

DEMELZA I can't stand it all over again! The frettin', the not sleepin', the picturin' you hangin' at Bargus Crossroads!

ROSS And were we not in dire straits, I wouldn't do it. But today I learned that George has bought up more of Wheal Leisure. With two hundred pounds we can at least keep our heads above water. And Sawle can salt its pilchards.

DEMELZA An' why is it fine for you to run risks while I may not even take a boat out in calm waters?

ROSS Believe me, I've every intention of keeping on the right side of the law. Or at least the *blind* side!

To put an end to the conversation, he goes out. Demelza is fuming. We can tell she's not going to take this lying down.

CUT TO:

39: EXT. WHEAL LEISURE – DAY 13

Dawn breaks over Wheal Leisure.

CUT TO:

40: EXT. WHEAL LEISURE – DAY 13

Miners line up ready for the next shift. Amongst them are Ted and Paul. They continue to look blotchy, bloodshot, pale, an odd one with blood trickling from the nose. Ross and Zacky appear from the mine office.

ZACKY 'Tis a cryin' shame we stopped th' tunnel. In my bones I could feel we were close.

ROSS *(looking out across the land)* Where d'you estimate we'd got to?

ZACKY *(scanning the land)* Nigh on that clump o' trees?

He points across the land. They all look where he's indicating.

THEIR POV: In the middle distance, a clump of trees. And in the far distance, the broken tower of Wheal Grace.

ROSS Halfway towards Wheal Grace?

ZACKY I'd say so. *(then)* Yer father's old mine.

They both look at it a while. Gradually the same thought strikes both of them.

ROSS It never occurred to me till now how close it is to the old Trevorgie workings.

ZACKY Reckon 'twouldn't hurt to have a closer look at Trevorgie from that end. Mebbe the old men found a way through that we know nothin' of—

ROSS Is that what Mark meant? The night he went away to France—?

CUT TO:

41: EXT. NAMPARA COVE (FLASHBACK) – NIGHT (SUMMER 1787)

Mark is crouched in the dark beside Ross and Paul.

MARK There's money in that mine. Copper. I never see'd a more keenly lode.

PAUL Where is it?

MARK On the east face. 'Twill be under water most times.

CUT TO:

42: EXT. WHEAL LEISURE – DAY 13 (SPRING 1791)

ZACKY Y' think he might've wandered into Trevorgie?

ROSS Could he?

ZACKY But if it's all under water—

ROSS With no way of draining it—

ZACKY We'd need one o' those new-fangled pumping-engines—

ROSS Which cost.

Ross nods. Thoughtful.

ROSS *(cont'd)* Let me think on it. If I decide to take it further, I'll come back to you.

Zacky nods his agreement. They're not getting carried away with excitement. Yet.

CUT TO:

43: EXT. DERELICT MINE (WHEAL GRACE) – DAY 13

Ross sits down among the piles of stones outside the derelict Wheal Grace and ponders. It's a defining moment for him. Here among the whispering grasses and lonely cries of sea birds, he knows where his future lies. But not how to get there. After a while Francis rides up.

FRANCIS What are you up to?

ROSS *(laughs)* Daydreaming.

Francis eyes him narrowly. And in that moment he knows exactly what Ross is thinking.

FRANCIS Wheal Grace? You wouldn't think to resurrect her?

ROSS *(laughs)* If my finances ever match my ambitions!

FRANCIS The curse of the Poldarks! Plenty of one and none of the other!

A moment of connection between them. They understand each other very well. It's a game-changing moment. Though neither of them realizes it yet.

CUT TO:

44: INT. ANDREW & VERITY'S HOUSE – DAY 13

Andrew bursts through the door carrying an armful of packages.

ANDREW Almonds, sugar, oranges, chocolate—

VERITY You spoil me!

ANDREW May I not? But in fact it is not all for you. The sugar is for James, the chocolate for Esther! They come in a month! *(then)* Are you happy now?

VERITY Yes! Of course!

But as she forces a smile, we see in her eyes absolute terror.

CUT TO:

45: INT. KILLEWARREN, PARLOUR – DAY 13

Caroline comes in to find Ray reading a letter.

RAY PENVENEN From Unwin. Pressing the subject of an engagement. Now he's an MP—

CAROLINE His coffers need to keep pace with his ambitions?

RAY PENVENEN For shame, Caroline! One must not assume mercenary motives. I would hope that both of you are marrying for love.

CAROLINE *(bursts out laughing)* You think Unwin *loves* me?

RAY PENVENEN You do not?

CAROLINE I think he loves my twenty thousand pounds!

RAY PENVENEN I'd be sorry to think so.

Caroline is on her way out again when a thought occurs.

CAROLINE Does it not strike you as odd? I'm an heiress, yet I've no money of my own. Suppose you give me some?

RAY PENVENEN *(somewhat taken aback)* Well – I've – no objection to advancing you something – though Lord knows what you'd spend it on. Your every need is catered for—

CAROLINE Fifty pounds?

RAY PENVENEN *Fifty?!*

CAROLINE What's the use of being rich if one can't have a flutter now and then?

RAY PENVENEN You know I disapprove of gaming.

CAROLINE Oh, but this would be a new type of gambling, Uncle. It appeals to me and I have a fancy to indulge the whim.

She turns the full force of her smile on him. Ray looks as if he might be swayed.

CUT TO:

46: INT. TRENWITH HOUSE, LIBRARY – DAY 13

Francis is taking off his gloves when Geoffrey Charles runs in, followed by Elizabeth. Geoffrey Charles runs to Francis, who scoops him up into his arms.

FRANCIS I saw Ross.

ELIZABETH Was he well?

FRANCIS He's considering a new venture.

ELIZABETH Of what nature?

FRANCIS Oh, mining, of course! What else?

He picks up the virgula divinatoria *which has been left on the table.*

FRANCIS *(cont'd)* Whether we like it or not, it's in our blood. *(then, to Geoffrey Charles)* Come, boy. Shall we see if we can strike lucky?

He takes Geoffrey Charles's hand and they go out.

CUT TO:

47: EXT. NAMPARA HOUSE – DAY 14

Time has passed. Spring is more advanced. The trees are in leaf. Three horses are tethered outside the house. Inside the library, men's voices, laughter and conversation can be heard.

CUT TO:

48: INT. NAMPARA HOUSE, KITCHEN – DAY 14

Demelza is making rushlights with Prudie and Jinny. She's now eight months pregnant. She hears laughter and the hubbub of conversation (Ross, Francis, Zacky and Henshawe) coming from the library.

PRUDIE Someone's full o' cheer.

DEMELZA Always is when he's up an' doin'. 'Tis sittin' still he can't abide.

CUT TO:

49: INT. NAMPARA HOUSE, LIBRARY – DAY 14

Ross, Zacky and Henshawe cluster round the desk on which are an ancient map, several samples of copper and a book: Pryce's Mineralogia Cornubiensis. *Ross is showing them something on the map.*

ROSS This section's mostly shallow but the lower level's flooded—

HENSHAWE We'd surely need an engine—

ROSS Those two young engineers in Redruth—

ZACKY Trevithick and Bull?

ROSS They've some interesting new ideas—

HENSHAWE At a price—

ZACKY An' we don' yet know if there's ore enough to make it worthwhile—

ROSS Is it worth the risk? We have these samples – this map – Mark's word—

ZACKY Your pig-headedness!

ROSS And against that?

HENSHAWE Time? Money? Common sense?

They all laugh.

CUT TO:

50: INT. NAMPARA HOUSE, KITCHEN – DAY 14

Demelza hears the laughter coming from the library and smiles to herself. She is glad to see that Ross, despite their straitened circumstances, is full of purpose. Now she hears him bidding farewell to Zacky and Henshawe. Then he comes in.

DEMELZA Is it a secret or can we all be told?

ROSS *(smiles)* All in good time. But for tonight—

He helps himself to food.

ROSS *(cont'd)* You should draw the curtains early – and ignore any sounds outside.

DEMELZA An' where will *you* be?

ROSS Taking delivery of the cargo.

DEMELZA Ross, no! You cannot!

ROSS Already arranged.

DEMELZA Then *dis*-arrange it!

But Ross has already walked out of the room. Demelza is open-mouthed with fury.

CUT TO:

51: EXT. NAMPARA HOUSE – NIGHT 14

Darkness falls. A owl calls. Candles burn in the windows. Prudie draws a curtain.

CUT TO:

52: INT. NAMPARA HOUSE, PARLOUR – NIGHT 14

Demelza and Jinny sit mending as Prudie draws the curtains. Restless, unable to concentrate, Demelza picks up Ross's book: Pryce's Mineralogia Cornubiensis. *Tight-lipped and longing to vent her spleen, she forces herself to read the book.*

CUT TO:

53: INT. NAMPARA HOUSE, PARLOUR – NIGHT 14

No sound is heard except the loud snoring of the sleeping Garrick. Prudie and Jinny sense a storm of rage brewing from Demelza, who finds it increasingly difficult to concentrate on her book.

CUT TO:

54: EXT. NAMPARA GULLY – NIGHT 14

Ross, Paul, Ted and Charlie Kempthorne are returning from the shore, carrying goods, leading two mules laden with contraband.

Ross is shouldering a cask of salt. They keep glancing about nervously. They keep their voices low.

CHARLIE KEMPTHORNE So far, so good.

TED So I should hope. Who else could know about this?

PAUL Yet the other landings up the coast were surprised—

TED Mr Trencrom did advise us to trust no one.

They all look round at each other. The idea that they could at any moment be discovered is an unnerving thought. Suddenly:

CHARLIE KEMPTHORNE Gaugers!

Everyone falls silent. They can hear the sound of hooves approaching. Panicked looks are exchanged.

PAUL How many?

They listen. The hoof beats get closer.

CHARLIE KEMPTHORNE Jus' th' one?

A look of alarm. They're all thinking the same thing.

TED Vercoe!

Panic breaks out. People are inclined to scatter.

ROSS I'll head him off.

PAUL Nay, Ross. If he see you 'ere, yer good as hanged.

TED *I'll* go.

ROSS *(detaining him)* He'll know at once what you're up to. I can at least try to talk him round.

Ross is about to head off when Paul detains him.

PAUL Wait!

They fall silent, listening intently. To their amazement the sound of hoof beats starts to recede. They breathe a sigh of relief. The crisis is past.

CUT TO:

55: INT. NAMPARA HOUSE, PARLOUR – NIGHT 14

Demelza hears noises outside: passing footsteps and the low bray of a donkey.

PRUDIE If they varmints come a-troachin' 'cross our flower beds—!

Garrick starts barking. Demelza is a bundle of nerves. Gradually the noises die away and Demelza, Prudie and Jinny almost start to relax. Then Demelza almost jumps out of her skin as the door opens and Ross returns.

ROSS It's over.

Relief at seeing him safely home now gives way to fury that he's caused her such anxiety.

DEMELZA *Is* it?

Something in her tone makes Prudie and Jinny scuttle out swiftly. Ross can see that he's about to get a roasting, so he attempts to defuse it.

ROSS Demelza, try to see this in a rational light. I'm home. The tide is high. There're no footprints on the beach. There'll be salt for the pilchards. And we are two hundred pounds less in debt than we were this morning. Is that not cause to celebrate?

DEMELZA That you go against my wishes?

ROSS For the good of us both—

DEMELZA That you take risks you need not take?

ROSS On this occasion—

DEMELZA That you think you may do as you please while I always do as you bid me?

ROSS Well—

DEMELZA Think again.

She walks out, summoning Garrick to follow her.

CUT TO:

56: EXT. TRURO HARBOUR – DAY 16

Dawn establisher. Seagulls wheeling above the harbour.

CUT TO:

57: INT. ANDREW & VERITY'S HOUSE – DAY 15

Verity is bustling around, arranging and rearranging items on the table, flowers, bowls of oranges, teacups, etc. Andrew comes in, ready to depart.

ANDREW Well, my love? *The Thunderer* docks at noon. I'll collect James, then meet Esther off the Plymouth coach and we'll be with you by two.

Verity nods, forcing herself to look excited.

ANDREW *(cont'd)* Do not make yourself uneasy. They will adore you as much as I do!

Verity nods, tries to look brave. And fails.

CUT TO:

58: EXT. CLIFF TOPS – DAY 15

Caroline, dressed in hunting garb, is galloping along the cliff tops, enjoying the air and the landscape. She is a very able rider and enjoys taking rocks and streams in her stride.

CUT TO:

59: EXT. WHEAL LEISURE – DAY 15

Caroline looks down on Wheal Leisure, unseen. A cart loaded with sacks has just arrived. Satisfied, she now turns and begins to canter away. She sees someone approaching.

CAROLINE Captain Poldark!

ROSS Miss Penvenen? Are you lost?

CAROLINE Do I look it?

ROSS You're far from home.

CAROLINE Perhaps I enjoy my own company.

ROSS You should make the most of it. I hear you're to be married soon.

CAROLINE D'you recommend the estate?

ROSS Where both parties agree.

CAROLINE We cannot all follow our hearts.

ROSS Surely an heiress can?

CAROLINE *(laughs)* What an amusing idea! *(then)* Excuse me, I'm late for the hunt.

She rides off. Ross continues towards Wheal Leisure.

CUT TO:

60: EXT. WHEAL LEISURE – DAY 15

Ross arrives at Wheal Leisure in time to see a line of Dwight's patients waiting – and Dwight talking to a man who has brought a cart full of twelve bulging sacks.

DWIGHT Ross! Is it you I have to thank for this windfall?

ROSS What is it?

DWIGHT Oranges!

ROSS I think we both know I am not your mysterious bene-factor.

Dwight smiles to himself. He knows there's only one other person it could be.

CUT TO:

61: INT. KILLEWARREN, RECEPTION ROOM – DAY 15

Caroline, still dressed in hunting garb, is laughing in disbelief.

CAROLINE *Oranges?*

DWIGHT Oranges.

CAROLINE If I made you a gift, it would be a better instru-ment for removing fish bones. You bruised my mouth with your fingers, remember?

She looks at him long and hard without batting an eyelid. A moment of connection between them.

DWIGHT I knew it was you. I'm very grateful. They'll be life-saving.

CAROLINE *(laughing)* Good heavens, you don't imagine I care about the fate of a few fishwives, do you?

Dwight looks at her, utterly perplexed.

CAROLINE *(cont'd)* You wouldn't take my guinea!

DWIGHT So—?

CAROLINE I knew your conscience wouldn't let you refuse a gift for your starving patients! So you see, now you're under obligation to *me*!

DWIGHT Is that where you prefer your men?

They're standing close together now.

CAROLINE You're rather impertinent.

DWIGHT I like you very much too.

The sexual frisson between them is intense. The moment is broken by the entry of Unwin, followed by George (both in hunting gear: George is sporting a very gaudy neckcloth which is adorned with a ruby).

UNWIN *There* you are, Caroline! The fox escaped us but— *(seeing Dwight)* Dr Enys.

Dwight bows to Unwin and George. Unwin is oblivious, but George immediately picks something up – and can't resist putting Dwight in his place.

GEORGE Dr Enys, I hear you're rather good at curing dogs.

Dwight bows politely, determined not to get riled.

GEORGE *(cont'd) (to Caroline)* Did you notice Horace has a little spot on his ear?

CAROLINE *(genuinely concerned)* Has he?

GEORGE Perhaps Dr Enys might take a look at it after we've gone?

DWIGHT *(refusing to be provoked, to Caroline)* For twelve bags of oranges he shall have the best attention I can give him.

Caroline smiles. A moment between them. Then she sweeps out, followed by Unwin and George.

CUT TO:

62: EXT. RED LION INN – DAY 15

Ross arrives at the Red Lion.

CUT TO:

63: INT. RED LION INN, MEETING ROOM – DAY 15

Ross arrives at the spring shareholders' meeting. The shareholders take their seats. At the end of the table Tankard's chair remains empty.

HENSHAWE Do we wait for Mr Tankard?

ROSS He knows the time of the meeting. Proceed, Mr Henshawe.

HENSHAWE Last month we sent two parcels of red copper to auction. This month we'll have two, maybe three. The question is, do we take on extra men, aside from those back on tribute since the closing of the tunnel? Mr Tankard is not here, so we must take a vote without him. Gentlemen—

At that moment the door opens and George enters. He is still dressed in hunting gear, including the gaudy neckcloth which is adorned with a ruby. The other shareholders look shabby in comparison.

GEORGE Forgive my tardiness. The fox led us a merry dance, but we got him in the end.

He smiles affably and takes the vacant chair. For a moment no one speaks. George is visibly enjoying their discomfort. Then:

GEORGE *(cont'd)* You were expecting Mr Tankard? He will no longer attend. I feel, as a principal shareholder, it befits me to take a more robust interest from now on. Perhaps you would kindly outline your suggestions and I shall give them my best consideration.

The shareholders all look at Ross. Ross's face is impassive. There is a moment's silence. Then Ross calmly gets up and walks out.

CUT TO:

64: INT. NAMPARA HOUSE, KITCHEN – DAY 15

Demelza opens the larder. It's bare except for the remains of a single fish. Jinny appears behind her. She knows exactly what Demelza's thinking.

JINNY Mister Ross won' like—

DEMELZA *(defiant)* Mister Ross won' be told. Will he?

JINNY No, mistress.

She goes out. Jinny knows she doesn't dare disobey Demelza.

CUT TO:

65: EXT. WHEAL LEISURE – DAY 15

Ross stands looking at Wheal Leisure. He is genuinely close to tears. He now knows it's slipping away from him. Zacky and Paul approach.

PAUL What do it mean?

ROSS It means we cannot move an inch without his say so.

Ross stares mournfully at the mine. He looks broken, defeated. Zacky pats him consolingly on the back.

ZACKY Nothin' t' be done.

Ross looks at Zacky – and his expression changes. Zacky knows that expression. He's seen it many times before.

ZACKY *(cont'd)* Or is there?

CUT TO:

66: INT. PASCOE'S BANK – DAY 15

ROSS You will sell half my shares in Wheal Leisure.

PASCOE *(genuinely shocked)* If you wish—

ROSS You will demand the very highest price. I know for certain George will pay.

Pascoe is astonished but he can see that Ross is deadly serious.

PASCOE I think it's for the best. Indeed, had you done so a year ago— *(then, realizing this is a touchy subject)* Still, it's not too late to pay off your debts and start afresh.

ROSS Very true. But that's not, in fact, how I intend to use the money.

CUT TO:

67: EXT. TRENWITH HOUSE – DAY 15

Ross gallops up to Trenwith. He leaps off his horse, hammers on the door.

CUT TO:

68: INT. TRENWITH HOUSE, GREAT HALL – DAY 15

Ross is shown in – and is greeted by Elizabeth.

ELIZABETH Ross – it's good to see you—

ROSS Is Francis here?

ELIZABETH Yes, he's—

Francis comes in. He's delighted to see Ross.

FRANCIS I thought I heard your voice! Is this a social call?

ROSS Not exactly.

CUT TO:

69: INT. TRENWITH HOUSE, LIBRARY – DAY 15

ROSS I'm opening Wheal Grace.

FRANCIS What? You don't mean it! That's cheerful news!

ROSS Henshawe and I have been down. The lower level's flooded, so we'll need an engine. But we reckon there's enough ore in the shallows to get us going.

FRANCIS Who's investing the money?

ROSS I've sold half my shares in Wheal Leisure and can realize six hundred pounds.

FRANCIS Six hundred—

ROSS You told me more than once about the money you had put by—

FRANCIS Yes—

ROSS With twelve hundred pounds we could do a great deal.

FRANCIS You're suggesting we go into partnership?

ROSS Yes.

For a moment Francis is speechless.

ROSS *(cont'd)* It's a risk. In more ways than one. George has a long arm—

FRANCIS To hell with George!

ROSS And you may well lose your money.

FRANCIS I like a gamble.

ROSS One can gamble on a man as well as a mine.

FRANCIS I can't guarantee the *mine.*

Ross digests the implications of this – that Francis is saying Ross can trust him.

ROSS Well, if that's how you feel, let's shake hands on it.

Francis is overwhelmed. He's almost about to kiss Ross, so delighted is he by this offer. But something makes him hesitate.

FRANCIS Ross – before you take this forward – there are certain things I should tell you—

ROSS Past things?

FRANCIS *(nods)* And I shouldn't feel I could proceed unless you were fully apprised of—

ROSS If it's past, let's forget it. I don't think I want to hear it.

FRANCIS If that's the case, I don't think I want to hear it myself!

Ross puts out his hand. Francis takes it.

ROSS To the Poldarks.

FRANCIS The Poldarks.

CUT TO:

70: INT. TRENWITH HOUSE, GREAT HALL – DAY 15

Elizabeth is listening to the conversation. She can sense Francis and Ross's excitement – but wonders what implications this has for her.

CUT TO:

71: INT. ANDREW & VERITY'S HOUSE – DAY 15

Verity is embroidering. There is a knock at the door. Verity is not expecting her guests so soon, so assumes it's a message or tradesperson. But when she opens the door she sees a sullen-looking girl of sixteen. It's Esther Blamey.

ESTHER I'm Esther.

VERITY Oh! Oh, my dear. You come too soon! No, I meant – I did not expect you till this afternoon—

ESTHER I came on the early coach. Is my father here?

VERITY He's – gone to meet your brother. Won't you come in? Oh my dear, it's so good to meet you at last.

Esther bows sullenly and comes inside. She's clearly here on sufferance and seems determined not to like Verity. Verity almost screams aloud in panic.

CUT TO:

72: INT. PASCOE'S BANK – DAY 15

Ross and Francis sit opposite Pascoe.

PASCOE You wish me to draw up the deeds of partnership. Will it just be the two of you? No other shareholders?

Ross and Francis exchange a look.

ROSS None whatsoever.

FRANCIS There is one further point. I want my shares in the mine to be vested in my son's name.

PASCOE But he's still a child, isn't he?

FRANCIS If George learns of our partnership, he may try to get at Ross through me. If the shares belong to Geoffrey Charles, George cannot touch them.

PASCOE As you wish.

CUT TO:

73: EXT. TRURO STREET – DAY 15

Ross and Francis emerge from Pascoe's and stroll down the street. Both are trying not to smile. Francis seems particularly buoyant.

FRANCIS I've a fancy to buy a nosegay for Elizabeth.

ROSS Violets?

FRANCIS Her favourite! Well remembered!

And there's no sense of any jealousy between them any more. Then:

FRANCIS *(cont'd)* Shall we meet at the Red Lion then ride home together?

ROSS By all means.

Francis strides off, in chirpy mood. Ross, equally cheerful, heads for the Red Lion.

CUT TO:

74: EXT. NAMPARA COVE – DAY 15

Demelza, accompanied by Garrick, drags the boat into the surf and clambers aboard.

CUT TO:

75: INT. RED LION INN – DAY 15

Brimming with optimism, Ross walks into the Red Lion – where the first person he encounters . . . is George. Ross nods in brief acknowledgement and is all for sidestepping him, but George flexes his malacca cane and stands his ground.

GEORGE You may be interested to know I've just purchased more shares in Wheal Leisure.

ROSS I wish you joy of them.

GEORGE Ah, so the rumours are true? You and Francis are going into business together.

ROSS I see you have your ear to the ground. Or should it be the keyhole?

GEORGE I'm surprised to hear you're pinning your hopes on Wheal Grace. What d'you hope to find there? Gold?

ROSS No. Freedom to call our souls our own.

He's about to walk off. George calls after him.

GEORGE I suppose you know where Francis got the money he's investing?

ROSS Yes – and we're very much obliged to you.

GEORGE Yes, we paid it to him for services rendered. In exchange for the names of the Carnmore Copper Company shareholders. Six hundred pounds – or should I say thirty pieces of silver?

There is a moment's silence. Then – as if in slow motion – Ross reaches out and grabs George by his neckcloth, drags George towards him and begins to choke him. George struggles, his face purpling with rage, then, with an almighty effort, he manages to free his hand to hit Ross across the head with his malacca cane. Ross grabs George's hand and crushes it, forcing it to drop the cane. George is now flailing and punching and kicking. The two of them are ricocheting across the room now, scattering tables and chairs. People are screaming and shouting. George tries to gouge out Ross's eyes with his thumbs. Enraged, Ross slams George down onto a table. George rips the front of Ross's shirt. Ross grabs George and flings him across the room. George flies into a table which splinters beneath him and leaves him twisting and groaning on the floor. Ross is bleeding from a cut on his forehead and his mouth. The landlord rushes in, appalled, tries to remonstrate with Ross, but Ross pushes him aside and walks out. People rush to assist George. Utterly humiliated, he pushes them away and staggers to his feet.

CUT TO:

76: EXT. NAMPARA COVE, OPEN SEA – DAY 15

Demelza makes her first catch. As she reels it in, she feels a small twinge of pain in her back. It passes quickly. She thinks nothing of it.
CUT TO:

77: INT. ANDREW & VERITY'S HOUSE – DAY 15

Verity is desperately trying to make conversation.

VERITY I don't think you're at all like your father, are you, my dear?

ESTHER No, ma'am. I favour my mother. She was very beautiful. More so than—

It's clear she was about to compare her with Verity. She restrains herself. Then:

ESTHER *(cont'd)* After she died, people tried to poison me against her. But I know better. She was a saint.

VERITY Of course. And I know I could never replace her. But I hope you'll come to look upon me as a loving friend.

Esther scowls as if to say, 'As if!' Verity wilts beneath her scorn.
CUT TO:

78: EXT. TRURO HARBOUR – DAY 15

Dwight, returning from a visit to his patients, spots Ross, who appears to be looking out to sea.

DWIGHT *(surprised)* Ross?

Ross turns, smiling, to reveal his bruised and bleeding face.
CUT TO:

79: EXT. NAMPARA COVE – DAY 15

Demelza pulls up another fish. As she does so she feels another twinge. This time it's low in her belly. She's not too concerned. She returns to her fishing.

CUT TO:

80: EXT. TRURO HARBOUR – DAY 15

Dwight is cleaning up Ross's cuts.

DWIGHT Could it be true?

ROSS Francis certainly had the money from George. And it's clear to me he has something on his conscience. But the thought that he'd deliberately sell my secrets to George— *(then)* But if it's true, how can I go into business with him?

DWIGHT But if you accuse him – and you're wrong—?

ROSS He'll never forgive me. So either way the partnership's doomed.

It's an appalling thought. Then Ross's reverie is broken by a voice he hasn't heard in a long time.

ANDREW'S VOICE Captain Poldark?

Ross turns to see Andrew Blamey walking towards him.

ROSS Captain Blamey!

ANDREW You've been in the wars?

ROSS My surgeon has patched me up. Dr Enys – Captain Andrew Blamey. My cousin Verity's husband.

DWIGHT Your servant, sir.

ANDREW And yours, sir.

Ross is thinking on his feet. Any minute now Francis will be here –

and he will meet Andrew. Shouldn't Ross try to get rid of Andrew to avoid that confrontation?

DWIGHT *(to Ross)* If I you're sure you'll survive, I've other patients to attend to.

Ross comes to a decision.

ROSS There is one further service you can render me.

He walks Dwight aside, whispers something in his ear. Dwight looks puzzled.

DWIGHT *(surprised)* Certainly, if you wish. Good day, Captain Blamey.

Dwight walks off. Ross now deliberately detains Andrew.

ROSS Is Verity well?

ANDREW Exceedingly. *(then)* That's not entirely true. She tries to conceal it but I know she grieves the loss of her family. But I'm the last person to intervene.

ROSS You are. However—

He has seen, over Blamey's shoulder, Dwight encountering Francis, passing on Ross's message and sending him in Ross's direction. Francis, not realizing who Blamey is, strides over.

FRANCIS *(laughing)* Enys tells me you're barred from the Red Lion!

Now Andrew turns and suddenly he and Francis find themselves face to face for the first time since Verity eloped. Francis looks as if he's about to explode.

FRANCIS *(cont'd)* You—

ROSS Walk with us, Francis. You look as if you need the air.

FRANCIS Thank you, I'll not trouble you in *this* company.

ROSS Francis, this is the very last moment to wipe out the past!

Something in Ross's voice has caught Francis's attention. Andrew only dimly perceives that something momentous, unconnected with himself, is at play here. Francis and Ross face each other – and in that moment Francis knows the price he must pay to have his sins (re. George and Carnmore) forgiven. For a moment we still think he will argue. But eventually, after an immense struggle:

FRANCIS *(to Andrew, an attempt at civility)* My sister seems to find her new life agreeable.

ANDREW And I will never give her cause to think otherwise.

FRANCIS Not that she takes account of *my* approval!

ANDREW She would dearly love it. That's why I also desire it.

Francis shuffles uneasily, still unable to bring himself to offer his hand to Andrew. The most he can do is to make civil conversation.

FRANCIS You've heard, I suppose, of my cousin's encounter with George Warleggan? Threw him across the Red Lion and broke his nose!

ROSS Not quite.

FRANCIS I congratulate you. I've longed to do the same myself!

ANDREW Verity told me of a developing feud. What was the cause of the quarrel today?

Ross and Francis look at each other. In that moment Francis knows that, in some way, he (Francis) was the cause of the quarrel. But Ross will give nothing away. Instead:

ROSS *(deadpan)* I took a dislike to his neckcloth.

CUT TO:

81: EXT. NAMPARA COVE – DAY 15

Demelza experiences another twinge. She can no longer ignore what this means.

DEMELZA *(to herself)* Time to go home.

She begins to turn the boat around.

CUT TO:

82: INT. ANDREW & VERITY'S HOUSE – DAY 15

Verity is sitting alone when the door opens and Andrew comes in. Verity leaps to her feet.

VERITY Oh, Andrew, I can't bear it! Esther despises me. When James comes, pray excuse me – I cannot face both of them together!

ANDREW My dear, this is James, my son.

Verity is almost ready to faint when a boisterous teenager, dressed in a smart midshipman's uniform, bounces in.

JAMES Good day t'ye, ma'am! I've heard a deal of good about you!

Without ceremony he flings his cap onto the table, puts his hands on Verity's shoulders, kisses her on the cheek, then enfolds her into a huge hug.

JAMES *(cont'd)* You'll pardon the liberty, ma'am, but one don't get a new mother every day of the week! *(shouting)* Come down, Esther! I know you'll be sulking – but this is our family now, so it's well to get used to it!

Andrew smiles and shrugs his shoulders.

JAMES *(cont'd)* D'ye have any rum, ma'am? I've a powerful thirst on me!

VERITY Of course!

She's almost crying with relief.

CUT TO:

83: INT. TRENWITH HOUSE, GREAT HALL – DAY 15

Francis has just returned and told Elizabeth of his meeting with Andrew Blamey.

ELIZABETH *(incredulous)* You *spoke* to him? Civilly?

FRANCIS *(grudgingly)* And shook his hand.

Elizabeth can hardly contain her amazement.

CUT TO:

84: EXT. NAMPARA COVE – DAY 15

Demelza is rowing with real determination now. Her teeth gritted, her face twisted with exertion and pain. She's starting to get worried.

DEMELZA We be fine – we be fine –

CUT TO:

85: INT. NAMPARA HOUSE, PARLOUR – DAY 15

Ross returns from Truro to find the house apparently empty. He puts down his saddlebags and pours himself a glass of brandy.

ROSS Demelza?

There's no answer. At first Ross is not unduly concerned.

ROSS *(cont'd)* Demelza? *(then)* Garrick?

Still no answer. Presently Jinny appears in the doorway.

ROSS *(cont'd)* Where's Garrick?

Jinny looks panic-stricken. Ross starts to get suspicious.

JINNY Sur – I tell'd mistress not t' go, but she wud'n hear I—

Suddenly Ross knows exactly where she is.

ROSS *(shouting)* Prudie?

Prudie appears in the doorway.

ROSS *(cont'd)* You let her go?

PRUDIE 'Ee ever tried stoppin' 'er?

Ross strides for the door.

CUT TO:

86: EXT. NAMPARA COVE – DAY 15

Demelza has managed to turn the boat round and is heading for the shore but her labour pains are so strong she keeps having to stop rowing. Gasping with pain now, she looks up and sees Ross running towards the beach.

CUT TO:

87: EXT. NAMPARA COVE – DAY 15

Ross rushes onto the beach. Out in the cove he can see Demelza struggling to bring the boat into the shore. She seems to be in pain. For a moment it doesn't dawn on Ross what's happening here. Then the penny drops. She's actually in labour! He strikes out into the waves, wading towards her. Demelza is doubled up in the boat, gasping with pain – but as she sees Ross coming towards her, she seizes the oars again and defiantly starts to row.

ROSS Give me the oars – Demelza!

DEMELZA I can manage—

ROSS *Give me the oars!*

Still she refuses. Ross grabs one of the oars.

ROSS *(cont'd)* You are the most stubborn, pig-headed—

DEMELZA Oh, *I* am?!

ROSS Where would you be if I hadn't come along?

DEMELZA *(still trying to fight him off)* Where would you be if I hadn't come along?!

She doubles up again as a contraction grips her.

DEMELZA *(cont'd)* *(through gritted teeth)* Brawlin' an' drinkin' an' dodgin' the noose—?

ROSS Let's examine my failings at a more convenient time, shall we?

Ross detaches the other oar from her and bundles her into his arms. She roars with pain as the contraction builds. He runs with Demelza in his arms out of the waves and up onto the beach. Still she struggles defiantly.

ROSS *(cont'd)* Stop wriggling—

DEMELZA You're hateful—

ROSS You're infuriating—

DEMELZA I could crown you—

ROSS By all means! Once you've delivered our child!

And their argument continues to rage as Ross runs up the dunes towards Nampara with Demelza in his arms.

CUT TO:

88: INT. NAMPARA HOUSE, PARLOUR – DAY 15

All is peaceful and quiet. Ross is pacing up and down, drinking brandy. Presently Dwight appears from upstairs, his sleeves rolled up. Ross looks at him expectantly.

DWIGHT It was a close call— *(then)* You have a son.

Ross races out of the room and tears upstairs.

CUT TO:

89: INT. ANDREW & VERITY'S HOUSE – DAY 15

Verity, Andrew, Esther and James are having supper. Esther is still reserved, but in response to a dig from James, she forces a small smile. Verity, still tearful, exchanges a look of relief with Andrew. Now a servant brings a note. Andrew opens it, smiles and hands it to Verity to read.

VERITY *(elated)* Jeremy!

CUT TO:

90: EXT. WHEAL LEISURE – DAY 16

George, on horseback, sits looking down at the bustling Wheal Leisure. To all appearances nothing has changed. Dwight continues to tend his patients. Zacky, Paul, Ted and the rest of the men eye George narrowly. They don't seem pleased with this change of owner-ship. George doesn't acknowledge their presence or make any attempt to engage with them. Now a carriage, loaded with luggage, drives by. It's Caroline. Unwin is following on his horse. Caroline orders the carriage to stop (next to George and within earshot of Dwight).

GEORGE Miss Penvenen, you're surely not deserting us?

UNWIN Help me to change her mind, George.

CAROLINE Don't trouble yourself. I must return to civiliza-tion. One can only take so many barbarians! *(then)* Oh, Dr Enys?

Dwight looks up.

CAROLINE *(cont'd)* I've ordered more oranges.

GEORGE Oranges?

UNWIN Oranges?

CAROLINE *(ignoring them)* Come and say goodbye to Horace.

Dwight comes over. Caroline picks up Horace and delivers him into Dwight's arms.

CAROLINE *(cont'd)* Goodbye, Dwight. Such a quaint name. One thinks of someone shy and unprogressive. I wonder if we'll ever meet again.

For a moment they lock eyes. Then Caroline retrieves Horace.

CAROLINE *(cont'd) (to her driver)* Drive on.

The carriage drives off. Unwin rushes after her, more of a lap dog than Horace. George waits a moment longer, eyes Dwight with suspicion. He senses that Dwight has more to hope for than Unwin. It's clear, however, that Dwight doesn't think so.

CUT TO:

91: INT. SAWLE CHURCH – DAY 16

Ross holds his son in his arms and looks down at the sleeping child. A tender father–son moment. Now he is joined by Demelza, Dwight, Francis and Elizabeth and Verity, who cluster round the font as the Reverend Odgers baptizes baby Jeremy. Glances between Francis and Ross, between Elizabeth and Demelza. Between Verity and Francis. They all sense how precarious this reconciliation is – but everyone seems determined to cement it.

CUT TO:

92: EXT. WHEAL GRACE – DAY 16

Ross and Demelza, Dwight, Verity and Andrew, Francis and Eliza-beth stand outside the beginnings of the reborn Wheal Grace. The tower, now being rebuilt, seems symbolic of their hopes for the future.

DEMELZA I never thought I'd see the day.

VERITY Nor I.

ANDREW Nor any of us.

Now Jinny comes up, as Demelza once did at the opening of Wheal Leisure, with a tray of drinks and hands them out.

ROSS To the Poldarks.

FRANCIS And Wheal Grace.

ALL The Poldarks. And Wheal Grace.

They all toast. Optimism and laughter. Only Demelza and Elizabeth exchange wary looks.

ROSS *(aside, to Dwight)* And Miss Penvenen's gone.

DWIGHT For good, I trust.

ROSS Are you sure?

DWIGHT Of my relief or that she won't return?

ROSS Both.

Verity and Andrew, Francis and Elizabeth wander off to inspect the new buildings. Dwight, sensing that Ross wants to be alone with Demelza, strolls after them. Ross and Demelza stand in silence, look-ing at the new mine which is beginning to take shape.

ROSS *(cont'd)* My father named this mine after my mother.

DEMELZA He did love 'er.

ROSS Yes.

DEMELZA Yet folks said he was a wastrel.

ROSS While she lived, she kept him steady. He set his course by her.

DEMELZA Like the North Star.

ROSS Like the North Star.

Ross nods thoughtfully. He sits down on a pile of stones. She comes and sits beside him. Not touching. Not looking at each other. Just sitting together side by side.

ROSS *(cont'd)* But I have no such need.

Demelza's face falls. She doesn't see he's teasing.

ROSS *(cont'd)* The North Star – is not the brightest in the sky.

DEMELZA What is?

ROSS The Dog Star. *(beat)* Which is fitting. *(beat)* Since I found my star in a dogfight!

Demelza tries – and fails – to suppress a smile. Still they don't look at each other. The two of them sit in companionable silence amongst the old stones of Wheal Grace. We pull back until Wheal Grace is a tiny speck in a sweeping landscape.

Episode 5

1: EXT. HENDRAWNA BEACH – DAY A (SUMMER 1766)

Two tiny figures run across a vast expanse of beach. As we go closer we see that they are two six-year-old boys. We don't realize it yet but one is Ross, the stronger and more powerful, who is being chased by Francis, the gentler and more fragile. Francis tears off after Ross, both boys laughing and having the time of their lives.

DISSOLVE TO:

2: EXT. HENDRAWNA BEACH – DAY 17 (SPRING 1792)

Ross walks along the beach on his way to Wheal Grace. He is thoughtful (as he recalls the previous scene from his childhood) but upbeat and optimistic.

CUT TO:

3: EXT. WHEAL GRACE – DAY 17

A new pumping engine dominates the mine. A figure sits outside it, immersed in a pamphlet. It's Francis. The book is revealed to be Pryce's Mineralogia Cornubiensis: A Treatise on Minerals, Mines and Mining. *Francis is dressed in work clothes. He waves his book cheerfully as Ross approaches.*

FRANCIS My father would be amazed.

ROSS At our new engine?

FRANCIS At my reading matter?

ROSS I think he would approve of both!

Francis glows at the implied praise. They survey their new mine with its shiny new technology. For the first time we sense they are truly equal partners.

CUT TO:

4: EXT. SAWLE VILLAGE – DAY 17

Demelza approaches the village. She is met by the sight of Ted Carkeek and two other men being marched away by Vercoe and two soldiers. Betty Carkeek, weeping, is clinging to Ted, till the soldiers push her away and she is comforted by Rosina Hoblyn. Her father Jacka Hoblyn, Nick Vigus and Charlie Kempthorne watch in dismay.

DEMELZA Where were they caught?

ROSINA Tregunna Cove—

DEMELZA *(surprised) Tregunna*—?

JACKA 'Ee may well be surprised!

CHARLIE Las' place *anyone*'d expect a landin'—

NICK 'Tis why we chose it – 'tis full o' rocks an' teasy currents.

DEMELZA So was it just – ill luck?

BETTY Or did someone betray us?

They all look at each other. It's an alarming thought.

CUT TO:

5: INT. WARLEGGAN HOUSE, GEORGE'S DEN – DAY 17

Cary is dropping titbits of chicken into his dog Ambrose's mouth as George strolls in. He's looking stylish and confident – and unimpressed to find Cary as slovenly as ever.

CARY The prodigal returns! How was London?

GEORGE Invigorating. *(beat)* And home to many fine banks. I wonder, is it not time we had one of our own in Truro?

Cary nods. He's certainly not averse to the idea. Then:

CARY I have news. *(beat)* Of an interesting document—

GEORGE Oh?

CARY A promissory note – for the sum of one thousand pounds, with interest at forty per cent. The lender believes it will never be repaid. If we offered to buy the debt—

GEORGE Why would we do that?

CARY Because the *debtor* would then be at our mercy?

CUT TO:

6: EXT. WHEAL GRACE – DAY 17

Ross contemplates the new pumping engine with satisfaction.

ROSS Trevithick makes bold claims for this engine.

FRANCIS Fifty fathoms! Can it really drain so deep?

ROSS I hope so. Since we've just sunk the last of our capital into it!

Henshawe appears, with Paul and two other miners, ready for work.

FRANCIS Gentlemen! It's a pleasure to have you with us on our adventure.

He shakes hands with Paul and Henshawe and the two others.

PAUL Pleasure's ours, Mr Poldark.

HENSHAWE An' to be frank, the joy's gone out of Leisure. Since George Warleggan acquired more shares.

PAUL There's talk o' lower earnin's – even closures—

ROSS That won't happen while I still have a stake.

HENSHAWE Your stake is now so small as to be insignificant. As is mine. All we can do is take our dividends and watch others make decisions.

FRANCIS How does it feel, Ross, to lose your first love?

ROSS Painful! – at first – but now my affections lie with Grace. She may be temperamental, but at least she's mine! *(then)* Ours. *(then)* Shall we go to work?

He puts his arm round Francis's shoulder and they are heading for the mine entrance when a Trenwith servant comes up with a message for Francis. Francis scans the letter.

FRANCIS You must excuse me. My *other* duty calls.

He hands the letter to Ross. Ross scans it and frowns.

CUT TO:

7: EXT. SAWLE VILLAGE – DAY 17

Outside Jacka Hoblyn's cottage, Jacka, Nick and Charlie Kempthorne (with his little daughters Lottie and May) congregate. A distressed Betty is given a herbal concoction by Dwight.

DWIGHT Sip it slowly, Betty. It will calm you.

Rosina limps up to them. Her knee is bandaged.

DWIGHT *(cont'd)* Rosina – how fares your knee?

ROSINA Still pains me, sur.

DWIGHT All the time?

ROSINA Only when it go stiff. 'Tis like someone turn a key an' lock it.

DWIGHT May I see?

Dwight examines Rosina's knee.

CHARLIE Dr Choake did advise t' cut it off.

DWIGHT A convenient solution. For *him*. *(to Rosina)* I want you to keep it bound for a week till I come to see you again.

JACKA I don' see's needful f'r 'ee to be fiddlin' with it so oft, surgeon. Rosina d' get along fine as she is.

DWIGHT If I can help your daughter, that's surely a good thing, is it not?

Unwilling to brook further discussion, Dwight packs up his bags. As he prepares to depart:

DWIGHT *(cont'd) (low)* Will any of you go to court?

CHARLIE An' see Ted sent f' transportation?

JACKA Or worse!

CHARLIE Don' say that!

NICK 'Tis gauger Vercoe to blame. He'll not turn a blind eye—

DWIGHT It baffles me why a man would *want* to hunt down his fellow-men—

JACKA An' now's talk of an informer.

DWIGHT *(alarmed)* Since when?

NICK Mr Trencrom sent word today—

JACKA An' 'tint like Trencrom t' raise false alarm.

DWIGHT But who could it be?

Charlie, Nick and Jacka look at each other – and at Dwight.

NICK Trencrom say it could be *anyone*.

CUT TO:

8: INT. KILLEWARREN – DAY 17

Caroline (with Horace) strides into Killewarren, followed by Unwin, followed by a line of servants bringing her luggage.

CAROLINE Was that a yawn, Horace? Shall you find this place awfully dreary after a year in London?

UNWIN We needn't stay long. Once our engagement's announced—

Ray Penvenen appears.

CAROLINE *(delighted)* Uncle Ray! You look younger than ever!

They embrace. Ray glances over Caroline's shoulder at Unwin.

RAY PENVENEN Well, my dear, are you ready to embrace your fate?

CAROLINE Do you suppose Mrs Figg has any marzipan? Poor Horace is ravenous! *(then, to Horace)* Oh, but that nice doctor told me not to give you sweetmeats. Shall we defy him? I think we must!

She sweeps out, leaving Ray to deal with Unwin.

RAY PENVENEN So she's agreed to your engagement?

UNWIN I *think* so – *(then)* You know how she hates to be pinned down—

RAY PENVENEN I seldom entertain, Unwin. And the sole reason for tonight's dinner is to make an announcement. You'd better be sure there *is* one!

Ray goes out, leaving Unwin floundering.

CUT TO:

9: INT. NAMPARA HOUSE, PARLOUR – DAY 17

Ross is gathering his things, ready to leave for town.

DEMELZA I don' think you should go.

ROSS Ted's one of my tenants – and workers—

DEMELZA An' a fellow free trader! How will it look if you seem t' sympathize? *(no reply)* As if you're involved! Which you are! Three drops in our cove already this year—

ROSS But this was *not* our cove. And no one can point the finger—

DEMELZA *Yet!* But if there's an informer about—

ROSS What would you have me do?

DEMELZA Not go to court! And tell Trencrom he may no longer use our cove—

ROSS And save himself our fee? So we have even *less* coming in? And must close Wheal Grace? Is that what you want?

Demelza shakes her head. She acknowledges it's an impossible dilemma.

DEMELZA But are ye not afeared? T' think o' one of our own betrayin' us?

ROSS I'm concerned, of course. I'll be on my guard. *(This is obviously not reassuring enough for Demelza.)* I'll look twice at even our closest friends!

DEMELZA But still go to court?

ROSS I think I must.

DEMELZA I'll get my cloak.

ROSS What are you doing?

DEMELZA Goin' along of 'ee.

And he can see from her expression (amused but defiant) that there'll be no arguing with her.

CUT TO:

10: INT. TRENWITH HOUSE, GREAT HALL – DAY 17

Underneath portraits of Charles and Francis, Francis, now formally attired, is tying his neckcloth. Elizabeth brings his coat. Aunt Agatha is at a table, playing cards. She looks very frail.

FRANCIS Do I look distinguished?

ELIZABETH Perhaps you should be aiming for 'severe'!

Francis tries out a stern expression. Elizabeth smiles. Aunt Agatha glances up.

AUNT AGATHA Mighty fligged out for the mine, Francis!

FRANCIS I'm due in court, Aunt.

AUNT AGATHA On what charge?

FRANCIS Carrying out my duties as a magistrate? You do recall I took over after Father died?

AUNT AGATHA I should think so too! There's been a Poldark on the bench since the days of William and Mary. Hang 'em all, I say!

FRANCIS I'll do my best, Aunt.

He goes out. Aunt Agatha erupts into a convulsion of coughing. Elizabeth looks concerned. This downturn in Aunt Agatha's health is a new development.

ELIZABETH That cough has worsened, Aunt. Would you have me call Dr Choake?

AUNT AGATHA If I wished to be bled to death! *(then)* I've already sent for someone.

ELIZABETH Dr Enys?

AUNT AGATHA Someone far more sensible.

CUT TO:

11: EXT. MARKET PLACE – DAY 17

Verity walks through the market place, carrying a travelling box.

George, strolling past, bows graciously to her and walks on. We go with him. Up ahead he sees Dwight who is talking to some patients. George strolls over.

GEORGE Dr Enys! How fares our little backwater?

DWIGHT A good deal duller than London, I imagine.

GEORGE You imagine right. Having just returned, I'm already yawning! Can you prescribe me a pick-me-up?

DWIGHT Do your mining interests not invigorate you?

GEORGE On the contrary.

DWIGHT But perhaps your 'interest' in Wheal Leisure is not in actual *mining*?

George bristles at Dwight's implication.

GEORGE Do I hear you're now physician at Killewarren?

DWIGHT Mr Penvenen keeps in good health. I rarely see him.

GEORGE Whereas I saw a good deal of his niece in London.

Dwight is visibly ruffled by this mention of Caroline. Nevertheless, he makes a brave attempt at remaining calm.

DWIGHT I trust she was well.

GEORGE You've not heard from her?

DWIGHT Nor did I expect to.

GEORGE Then I assume her arrival here today will not inconvenience you?

Dwight hesitates just enough for us to know he's very rattled by this news.

DWIGHT Not in the least. Good day to you, sir.

He walks on, ruffled and struggling to subdue his excitement. George remains.

CUT TO:

12: INT. MAGISTRATES' COURT, TRURO – DAY 17

Francis sits with Reverend Dr Halse on the bench. Three smugglers – Ted Carkeek and his two brothers – are up before them. Ross and Demelza sit at the back of the court, too far back to be seen by Francis or Reverend Dr Halse. Near the front are Jacka Hoblyn, Betty Carkeek, Charlie Kempthorne and Nick Vigus. Vercoe is giving evidence.

VERCOE An' that conclude my evidence, yer worship – only to add that I hope 'ee see fit to send these men to th' gallows – for how else do we break our shores of this iniquitous trade? For 'tis my belief that honest men are glad to pay their taxes when 'tis for good of king an' country – though some men think they be above the law.

REVEREND DR HALSE We thank you for your diligence, Mr Vercoe. You may stand down.

Now he turns to Francis.

REVEREND DR HALSE *(cont'd) (low)* A straightforward case, I think?

Reverend Halse and Francis confer. Ross and Demelza look anxious. Likewise Betty. Ted and his brothers look fearful.

REVEREND DR HALSE *(cont'd) (low)* In the context of the monstrous events still unfolding in France? Mob rule, lawlessness of the rabble – examples must be made—

Vercoe looks stern and smug. Charlie inscrutable. Nick surly and furtive.

FRANCIS I agree with you, sir. Events across the water make our judgements here all the more significant—

REVEREND DR HALSE And in these tinderbox conditions – where the least flame can spark a conflagration – my concern—

FRANCIS Which I share – is how to balance severity of judgement with the appearance of mercy—

REVEREND DR HALSE The *appearance*—?

FRANCIS For as you say, our duty is to allay rebellion, not stoke it.

REVEREND DR HALSE But the punishment—

FRANCIS Oh, I agree, sir – it must not be a crown of thorns for them to wear with pride—

REVEREND DR HALSE Yet if they *wish* to make martyrs of themselves—

FRANCIS Then let us disappoint them!

Reverend Dr Halse is looking rather bemused. This is not going the way he expected.

FRANCIS *(cont'd)* We both know the type. Bone idle. Scorn to do a decent day's work.

REVEREND DR HALSE One has only to look at them—

FRANCIS How clever, then, to sentence them to the very last thing they would seek? Ignominious, backbreaking, without a shred of honour—

Ross and Demelza watch as Reverend Dr Halse and Francis hammer it out. Ted and his brothers look fearful. Vercoe looks smug. Reverend Dr Halse's expression is implacable. The tension in the court is almost palpable. Reverend Dr Halse swells up with importance and delivers his judgement.

REVEREND DR HALSE Sentenced – to three months' hard labour.

Uproar in court. Some people are outraged by the leniency. Others cheer at it. Clearly Ted Carkeek and his brothers are hugely relieved – as are Betty, Nick, Charlie, Jacka, etc., who applaud their escape. Demelza is amazed. Ross is silent but impressed. Francis declines to allow himself the least smile of triumph.

CUT TO:

13: EXT. TRURO STREET – DAY 17

Ross and Demelza are walking home with Francis.

ROSS I take my hat off to you. You played him at his own game. Something *I've* never achieved!

DEMELZA *(joking)* But you can live with yourself?

FRANCIS Oh, I think so! I know for a fact that Halse has brandy in his cellars which came from such a run!

Ross is smiling and nodding his approval.

FRANCIS *(cont'd)* But don't let that reassure you. With an informer at large, this won't be the last case which comes before the court. And our friend Halse will be keen to make the next man pay!

Demelza nudges Ross as if to say, 'What have I told you?' They walk on.

CUT TO:

14: EXT. OPEN COUNTRYSIDE – DAY 17

Caroline is cantering across the countryside, enjoying her return to the wilds of Cornwall after her year in 'civilized' London. As she approaches some woods, she slows down. Suddenly a rider appears. It's Dwight. His appearance is so sudden that neither of them have time to take evasive action.

CAROLINE Why, Dr Enys! How diverting!

DWIGHT Miss Penvenen.

CAROLINE How is the scurvy in Sawle?

DWIGHT Better, I thank you. The potato crop did not fail this year – and there were apples—

CAROLINE But no oranges? Dear me, were there no other ladies hereabouts to whom you might appeal!? And tug on their heartstrings in the name of charity?

DWIGHT I hope you're in good health, Miss Penvenen. I bid you good day.

He moves to ride on, resolving to remain calm, though much to his dismay, all his old feelings have rushed to the surface. Caroline bars his way.

CAROLINE We meet after a year's absence and you haven't a civil word for me?

DWIGHT I'm old-fashioned in these matters, Miss Penvenen. I thought civility should be shown on both sides. Would you excuse me?

He spurs his horse and rides off. Caroline watches him go. Smiles to herself, by no means deterred by his brusqueness.

CUT TO:

15: EXT. TRENWITH HOUSE – DAY 17

Verity arrives at the door and Elizabeth and Geoffrey Charles rush out to embrace her.

ELIZABETH Verity!

VERITY My dears!

A joyful embrace between Elizabeth, Verity and Geoffrey Charles. Aunt Agatha is glimpsed at the window. Her face lights up at the sight of Verity.

VERITY *(cont'd)* How is she?

ELIZABETH All the better for seeing you.

Now Francis appears. A moment between him and Verity.

FRANCIS Well, sister—

VERITY Well, Francis—

FRANCIS It's good to have you home.

He comes forward and kisses her hands, then leads her, smiling, into the house.

CUT TO:

16: INT. NAMPARA HOUSE, ROSS & DEMELZA'S BEDROOM – DAY 17

Ross gasps as Demelza pours hot water over his back. He is bathing in a wooden tub. Demelza pours herself a glass of port, which she continues to sip as she gets ready for the Penvenen dinner. She's in a lively mood and decides to wind Ross up.

DEMELZA I cannot but admire Francis. *(seeing Ross's look of surprise)* Oh, he's not as handsome as some – nor as daring – but he has wisdom – an' he d' value his own skin. He'll mebbe live longer on that account.

ROSS Do *I* not have wisdom?

DEMELZA Can you tell if a man be a traitor to his friends or no?

Raised eyebrows from Ross. 'Not this again?'

ROSS Perhaps you wish you'd married my cousin?

DEMELZA He's a good man. He has things you lack. *(then)* Though you have things *he* lacks! *(then)* Put you together, 'twould make a complete man!

ROSS I see.

He grabs her hand and pulls her towards the tub.

ROSS *(cont'd)* Do I leave such a lot to be desired?

DEMELZA Yes, Ross. A lot to be desired.

She allows him to kiss her.

CUT TO:

17: EXT. KILLEWARREN – NIGHT 17

Ross and Demelza walk up to Killewarren. Demelza seems in high spirits.

ROSS You seem very lively tonight. Could it be the port?

DEMELZA Could it be us dining out after a year of turnip and tetty pie?

ROSS Take care you don't trip over.

DEMELZA P'raps if I did, my husband would pay me attention!

ROSS Have I been so neglectful of late?

DEMELZA Ask your other wife. Grace!

ROSS It's true, she's more taxing than you. Though not as lovely.

DEMELZA So tonight you'll have eyes for none but me?

ROSS Tonight I'll have eyes for none but you!

And then they immediately come face to face with Elizabeth and Francis. A brief moment of awkwardness between Elizabeth and Demelza, a glance which assesses each other's outfit.

ELIZABETH A new dress?

DEMELZA If only! You?

ELIZABETH How I wish!

Forced smiles and polite laughter. Neither Ross nor Francis notice it. They all go in together.

CUT TO:

18: INT. KILLEWARREN, GREAT HALL – NIGHT 17

Caroline is the glittering centre of attention with men fawning over her. Unwin has stationed himself at her shoulder but she barely seems to notice him. As Ross, Demelza, Francis and Elizabeth come in, Caroline flashes Ross a dazzling smile. Amongst the admirers who turn to see who she's smiling at is George. He and Ross see each other. George seems shocked but Ross retains his composure.

FRANCIS Awkward?

ROSS Not for me. Last time we met, he went head over heels. I doubt he'll be keen to repeat the experience.

And indeed George seems to have had that very thought. He contents himself with eyeing Ross coolly from a distance. Now Unwin links George's arm and steers him aside.

CUT TO:

19: INT. KILLEWARREN, CORRIDOR – NIGHT 17

Unwin has linked George's arm and steered him aside.

UNWIN D'you not agree that since I became an MP, Cornwall is a better place?

GEORGE In what regard?

UNWIN Why, only today we've seen the arrest of more smugglers—

GEORGE For which you take credit?

UNWIN Indirectly – since I've made it my mission to curb lawlessness among the vulgars.

GEORGE *(with a glance at Ross)* And among the gentry? *(then)* Which reminds me. May I seek your advice? As a civilizing influence against the ravages of barbarism?

Unwin, flattered, bows his agreement.

GEORGE *(cont'd)* There's something I'd like you to see. When do you return to Westminster?

UNWIN The minute I've secured Caroline's hand!

CUT TO:

20: INT. KILLEWARREN, GREAT HALL – NIGHT 17

Ray Penvenen approaches Demelza, offers her his arm and leads her to the dinner table. All the other guests now follow. As is the custom of the day, there are no place names and the guests are left to choose their own places. However, Ross, who has been chatting to fellow-guests on his way to the table, somehow finds himself next to Elizabeth. He hesitates. Should he sit here? Elizabeth turns and smiles at him. He decides he will. Even after all this time there's a frisson between them. Now Ross notices that Caroline is directly opposite him. She gives him an arch smile. He smiles back. Clearly these two find each other attractive. Elizabeth notices – and finds herself piqued. Demelza is seated at the other end of the table between Ray Penvenen and Captain McNeil. Unwin seats himself next to Caroline – much to her surprise.

CAROLINE Must you sit here, Unwin? Did you not have enough of my company in London?

UNWIN I hope to have it officially after tonight—

CAROLINE *(ignoring Unwin)* Captain Poldark, have you been getting into scrapes while I've been away? I was quite diverted by your last court appearance.

ROSS I try to avoid the place whenever possible, ma'am.

CAROLINE By leading a virtuous life?

ROSS Attempting to, ma'am. I fear the execution is often beyond me.

Demelza is watching this exchange with interest. But she is soon distracted by the keen attentions of Captain McNeil.

CAPTAIN MCNEIL As you see, I've returned, ma'am. I was plagued with a fever and have come back to convalesce.

DEMELZA Doubtless you'll enjoy exploring the coves hereabouts—

RAY PENVENEN Looking for smugglers?

DEMELZA Though surely his last visit had quite put 'em down?

CAPTAIN MCNEIL Aye, but they're damnably sly, ma'am. One can never be certain how they're disguised.

DEMELZA I hope you do not suppose *me* to be such a one!

Captain McNeil roars with laughter.

CAROLINE If the jest will bear repetition, I think you should share it!

DEMELZA 'Twas no jest on my part, ma'am. Captain McNeil assures me he's not here to catch smugglers – and I told him I did not know what *else* he could expect to catch!

Everyone laughs. Francis, meanwhile, addresses Ray Penvenen.

FRANCIS Are you in health, sir?

RAY PENVENEN I try to avoid physicians.

GEORGE Especially when they're young and inexperienced?

CAROLINE Young perhaps, but with radical new ideas.

GEORGE Radical often means unproven.

UNWIN And enthusiasm's no substitute for skill!

CAROLINE Nor self-interest for compassion?

Ross and Caroline exchange a smile – something which clearly piques Unwin – and Elizabeth.

CUT TO:

21: EXT. TRENWITH HOUSE – NIGHT 17

Dwight walks up to Trenwith.

CUT TO:

22: INT. TRENWITH HOUSE, GREAT HALL – NIGHT 17

Verity escorts Dwight through the great hall towards the library.

VERITY Aunt Agatha's very angry with me for calling you.

DWIGHT What troubles her?

VERITY A cough, sore throat – and, she tells me, a fever – but I can find no sign of it – which is why I sent for you.

CUT TO:

23: INT. TRENWITH HOUSE, LIBRARY – NIGHT 17

They go into the library where Aunt Agatha is sitting, bundled up in shawls.

AUNT AGATHA I need no physician. Little Verity's perfectly capable of tending me.

DWIGHT But when the time comes for her to return home—?

AUNT AGATHA This is her home! What is there to interest her elsewhere?

VERITY A husband?

AUNT AGATHA *(to Dwight)* Trenwith has never been the same since she left. Elizabeth does her best but—

VERITY *(interrupting)* Can you diagnose the complaint?

DWIGHT I'll do my best.

He opens his bag and begins to get out his instruments.

AUNT AGATHA *(to Dwight)* Are you married, sir?

DWIGHT I am not, ma'am.

AUNT AGATHA And no plans to be so?

DWIGHT I can't imagine who'd have me!

SOUND OVER: Caroline's laughter.

CUT TO:

24: INT. KILLEWARREN, GREAT HALL – NIGHT 17

The dinner is in progress. Caroline is laughing. She and Ross have just exchanged more pleasantries.

Elizabeth, seeking to re-establish her ascendancy, leans closer to Ross and speaks softly to him:

ELIZABETH She's very striking, isn't she? *(Ross nods)* Do you believe that what the eye does not admire, the heart does not desire?

ROSS It's always been so with me. *(beat)* As you should know.

ELIZABETH Should I? We see little of each other now. I'm not sure I know you at all.

ROSS Nor I, you. But that's hardly surprising. How much did we ever know of each other? Even before—

ELIZABETH Before you went away?

ROSS It seems a lifetime ago.

ELIZABETH In some ways.

ROSS It's only now that I realize how young you were when you promised to marry me.

ELIZABETH I should have been old enough to know my own mind.

ROSS Well – possibly, but— *(then)* Let us agree that you were young. And then you thought I was dead.

ELIZABETH Did I? *(beat)* Or did I think I loved Francis better?

Ross looks at her with surprise. Is she making fun of him?

ELIZABETH *(cont'd)* How soon I discovered my mistake!

ROSS This is some pleasant jest, surely?

ELIZABETH If it is, then it's against myself. *(then, seeing his amazement)* Is it so astonishing that a woman who changed her mind once could change it twice?

Ross looks at her with absolute incredulity. She's very cool and calm and seems to be enjoying her ascendency in the face of his utter bewilderment.

ELIZABETH *(cont'd)* You seem shocked. *(then)* Why should you be? Cannot a woman love two men? Cannot a man love two women? I'm with Francis. He's the father of my child, we're alike in many ways. But a piece of my heart will always be yours. As a piece of yours will always be mine.

They're very close now. It's as if no one else in the room exists, as if all sound has drained out of the space and all that's heard is the sound of their breathing. Eventually:

ROSS Where does this leave us?

ELIZABETH *(smiling)* With our hands tied. To other people.

Ross nods. He sees the sense of this. And then just when he thinks there can be no further twist in the tale:

ELIZABETH *(cont'd) (with a glance at Demelza, who is flirting with McNeil)* Of course, were that ever not to be the case—

Ross glances down the table to where Demelza is lapping up the attention of Ray and McNeil. He turns back to Elizabeth. The conversation hangs, fraught with possibility. Then a loud bray of laughter from Unwin cuts across the room and the moment breaks. As if she fears she's been too open, Elizabeth immediately turns to speak to the guest beside her. Ross is still reeling from the effects of their conversation.

With Ray and McNeil vying for her attention, Demelza looks up and can't help but notice that something in his conversation with Elizabeth has left Ross in utter turmoil.

CUT TO:

25: EXT. KILLEWARREN – NIGHT 17

After the dinner, Ross is outside on a terrace taking the air when he overhears Caroline and Unwin arguing.

UNWIN'S VOICE I must insist that you treat me with deference when we are married—

CAROLINE'S VOICE If the day ever comes—

UNWIN'S VOICE Then name it, Caroline, I beg you.

CAROLINE'S VOICE I deplore beggars.

UNWIN'S VOICE How vexing you are!

CAROLINE'S VOICE How dull you are! I'm not convinced I have the stamina for a lifetime of yawning!

Suddenly the door opens and a furious Unwin comes storming out, past Ross, and away into the darkness. Presently Caroline appears, perfectly composed and smiling. Ross bows and waits to allow her to pass. It's obvious that Ross has heard every word of her conversation with Unwin. She doesn't seem the least bit fazed.

CAROLINE How is your friend Dr Enys?

ROSS Wedded to his work, ma'am, with no time for distractions.

CAROLINE Would you count *me* a 'distraction'?

ROSS I shouldn't presume to connect you with Dr Enys in any way. Your stations could not be further apart.

CAROLINE You think he does not give me a second thought?

ROSS I think he will always be interested in your welfare. And will certainly wish you well on the occasion of your engagement. Which I'm led to believe is imminent?

CAROLINE I've heard that too. Shall we go in and see if Uncle Ray will enlighten us?

CUT TO:

26: INT. KILLEWARREN, GREAT HALL – NIGHT 17

The whole party is gathered (all except for Unwin who is nowhere to be seen). George continues to keep his distance from Ross and Francis.

RAY PENVENEN My friends, I thank you for joining me on this auspicious occasion. My niece Caroline, of whom I've had sole charge since she was a child, will soon no longer be under my care. In December she comes of age, but before that I believe I must resign her to the care of another—

He glances round and realizes Unwin is missing.

RAY PENVENEN *(cont'd)* Unwin? Where is he? Caroline—?

CAROLINE I believe I saw him heading for his horse. *(then)* Oh dear, I hope I haven't said anything to upset him.

Caroline's expression is one of wide-eyed innocence. Ross and Demelza exchange a glance. Ray is very unimpressed but Caroline is equal to his sternness.

CAROLINE *(cont'd)* Shall we have dancing?

CUT TO:

27: INT. TRENWITH HOUSE, GREAT HALL – NIGHT 17

Verity is escorting Dwight to the door.

VERITY Can you tell what ails her?

DWIGHT I have my suspicions. *(then)* I'll call again tomorrow. In the meantime—

VERITY What should I give her?

DWIGHT Honey, juniper, a little warm milk – and your very best attention.

He smiles as he says this. It's clear that he's already diagnosed the complaint – but Verity doesn't yet suspect what it is.

CUT TO:

28: INT. KILLEWARREN, GREAT HALL – NIGHT 17

Francis is dancing with Elizabeth. Ross is dancing with Demelza. Sexual tension crackles between them. George is watching. Caroline appears at his shoulder.

CAROLINE There's a novelty. A married couple who like each other's company. *(then)* But did they not marry for love?

GEORGE Allegedly.

CAROLINE You do not approve? Pray, what is your definition of a successful match?

GEORGE Where two people are of equal rank or fortune, marriage can be a mutually beneficial contract.

CAROLINE That's what I've been taught. None of this muddying the water with actual feelings!

She laughs and walks away. George is unsure whether he's been slapped down or has scored a point. As he turns away, unexpectedly he comes face to face with Francis.

GEORGE Francis, how good to see you.

FRANCIS I regret I cannot return the compliment.

GEORGE This spite is pointless, Francis. In your cousin I've come to expect no reason but—

FRANCIS Well, if that's reason, expect none from me.

Francis walks off. George turns . . . and finds himself face to face with Ross. George is caught off-guard, but Ross is relaxed and urbane.

ROSS Good evening, George.

GEORGE Ross – I – had not expected to see you here—

ROSS *(smiles)* Ray Penvenen will insist on inviting the riff-raff.

GEORGE I hope your new mine prospers.

ROSS It will.

GEORGE I wish I had your confidence.

ROSS Must you be envious even of that?

George flushes and opens his mouth to speak but Ross has already moved away. George is on the verge of calling after him, but in the nick of time, restrains himself. Caroline appears at his shoulder.

CAROLINE Shall you call him back?

GEORGE No need. One has only to endure in silence, to triumph.

CAROLINE To triumph? How will you manage that?

CUT TO:

29: INT. WARLEGGAN HOUSE – NIGHT 17

Seething from the events of the evening, George bursts into the room where Cary is lolling with Ambrose.

GEORGE We will use whatever means necessary to acquire that promissory note.

CUT TO:

30: INT. TRENWITH HOUSE, ELIZABETH'S ROOM – NIGHT 17

Elizabeth is getting ready for bed when Francis comes in with two glasses of wine.

FRANCIS May I join you?

Elizabeth smiles her agreement. Francis comes in and closes the door.

CUT TO:

31: INT. NAMPARA HOUSE, ROSS & DEMELZA'S BEDROOM – NIGHT 17

As Demelza unlaces the front of her dress, Ross comes up to unlace it for her.

ROSS McNeil was all attention tonight.

DEMELZA And Elizabeth. *(begins to untie the stock round his neck)* And Caroline Penvenen—

ROSS Yes?

DEMELZA She kept you in a corner, did she not? And would not let you come forth.

ROSS She kept me in no corner that I did not wish to be kept in.

Demelza tweaks the stock as if in playful reprimand.

ROSS *(cont'd)* On one subject I'm sure we can agree: Miss

Penvenen is a piece of work and we wouldn't wish her on anyone we liked.

Demelza unwinds the stock from Ross's neck. They begin to kiss.

CUT TO:

32: EXT. OPEN COUNTRYSIDE – DAWN 18

Early morning. Dwight rides out on his rounds.

CUT TO:

33: INT. WHEAL GRACE TUNNEL – DAY 18

Ross is heading for the exit, followed by Francis and Henshawe. They seem pleased.

ROSS Water levels have fallen at least a foot—

HENSHAWE By my calculation—

ROSS And you'll continue to monitor them?

HENSHAWE Surely. And the coal consumption.

FRANCIS But the engine appears to be working?

HENSHAWE Would appear so.

FRANCIS So what's our plan?

HENSHAWE Continue to drain. Tomorrow we blast. Then sift the ore – and if we're lucky—

FRANCIS Copper! The elusive Trevorgie lode!

Francis is very excited. He seizes Ross, then Henshawe, by the hand and shakes them enthusiastically.

FRANCIS *(cont'd)* I must go and tell Geoffrey Charles!

HENSHAWE Does he take an interest in mining?

FRANCIS Of course! For one day he'll step into my shoes!

Francis walks off.

HENSHAWE I don't mind sayin', when Mister Francis first came aboard I had my doubts, but he's shown himself more'n equal to the task.

Ross nods, pleased to hear Henshawe's endorsement. Then they hear noises of shouting and arguing.

ROSS What's that?

HENSHAWE 'Twill be ole Nick Vigus. There's tales about – folk say he's the informer—

ROSS That wouldn't surprise me.

He strides off down the tunnel to where Nick is being pushed around by several of the miners. They fall back when they see Ross.

ROSS *(cont'd)* Why do these men attack you, Nick?

NICK No idea, Cap'n. I a'nt done nothin'!

ROSS Why would they think you had?

NICK Damned if I know.

He starts to skulk away.

ROSS Damned you may be! I suspect they attack you for your habit of turning against your fellows.

NICK I, sur?

ROSS You, sir. Letting Jim Carter take the blame for your poaching escapade? Pocketing George Warleggan's guineas to testify against me in court?

NICK I bain't the informer, Cap'n. But since 'ee accuse me, let me ask, why shouldn't a man sell himself to the highest bidder? Times like this, 'tis every man for himself.

ROSS Some of us beg to differ, Nick. Betray us, you betray yourself. Wound one man, you wound us all.

NICK Fine words for gentlefolks t' spout – with no notion what it's like to live in squalor – ev'n if 'ey think 'ey do by slummin' with scullery maids!

Suddenly Ross snaps and launches himself at Nick, unleashing all his unexpressed rage (from the Jim Carter and the trial incidents). Henshawe and some of the other miners leap in to separate them.

HENSHAWE Cap'n Ross! Cap'n Ross! Leave 'im be!

Eventually Ross is pulled away – but not before Nick is left bruised and bleeding. Ross, seething, finally walks off.

ROSS Get Dr Enys to clean him up.

CUT TO:

34: EXT. WHEAL GRACE – DAY 18

Captain McNeil looks on as Nick Vigus staggers out of the mine and away from Wheal Grace, bruised and bleeding. He waits a moment, then casually rides after him.

CUT TO:

35: EXT. SAWLE VILLAGE – DAY 18

Dwight approaches Sawle Village. He walks towards a large cottage (Vercoe's). Presently Rosina comes limping down the lane.

ROSINA Dr Enys! 'Ave 'ee 'eard o' Nick Vigus? Cap'n Poldark did clout 'im, yet he swear he's no traitor.

DWIGHT Why would any suspect him?

ROSINA We all suspect each other, sir. D' make the blood run cold t' think one of our own be false!

Now Charlie Kempthorne appears.

CHARLIE Dr Enys! Do 'ee tell Rosina how my health is mended this past year – since I turn my hand t' sailmaking. I could provide 'ansome, should I chuse to wed again—

DWIGHT And you have someone in mind?

CHARLIE *(with a glance at Rosina)* Mebbe.

ROSINA *(smiling shyly at Dwight)* Mebbe *I* have someone in mind myself.

CHARLIE Nay, Rosina, don't 'ee flitter yer eyes at surgeon. He's not for thee.

DWIGHT Nor for any maid, sir. I'm wedded to my work.

Now he knocks on the door of the large cottage. Presently the door is opened by a sour-faced Vercoe.

CUT TO:

36: EXT. VERCOE'S COTTAGE – DAY 18

Dwight is attending four-year-old Hubert Vercoe (who is reading a children's book of numbers as Dwight examines him).

DWIGHT That's a pretty picture, Hubert. Did you colour it yourself?

Hubert nods shyly.

DWIGHT *(cont'd) (to Vercoe)* Give him ginger, oil of anise and clarified honey. That should settle his stomach.

Vercoe nods gruffly.

DWIGHT *(cont'd)* And you, sir? Are you sick?

VERCOE Only from the verdicts in court! I did pin my hopes on transportation.

DWIGHT You take your duty to heart.

VERCOE If I don't, who will? 'Tis a thankless task but I expect my patience to be rewarded. A reckoning is coming. Ye may be sure o' that.

CUT TO:

37: EXT. SAWLE VILLAGE – DAY 18

Dwight is thoughtful as he leaves Vercoe's house . . . and so is completely caught off-guard when he comes face to face with Caroline, who is walking by.

CAROLINE I thought I might find you here – tending your beloved fisher folk!

DWIGHT You'll excuse me, Miss Penvenen, I've no time to—

CAROLINE Let me apologize? *(then, laughing)* There! You weren't expecting that!

DWIGHT Frankly, no.

CAROLINE You accused me of being uncivil. I intend to prove you wrong.

Dwight struggles visibly. He knows he should just walk away and cut all ties before he gets further embroiled. But he finds himself powerless to resist her.

CUT TO:

38: INT. WARLEGGAN HOUSE, GEORGE'S DEN – DAY 18

George pours Unwin a brandy.

UNWIN I consider it a fortunate escape! An MP needs a wife who is biddable – and Caroline is—

GEORGE Anything but?

UNWIN But now I'm spared that vexation, I can pursue more worthy ventures—

GEORGE Like the civilizing of Cornwall? Well, there's no shortage of scope.

UNWIN No, indeed!

GEORGE In Truro, for instance, there are the vilest of hovels – a blight upon the face of our town!

UNWIN A monstrous carbuncle!

GEORGE Where, I ask, are our crescents, our pantheons, our *banks*? For it cannot have escaped your notice that Truro boasts not a single example to rival those of London.

UNWIN An omission which must be remedied!

GEORGE I wonder who owns those hovels? Presumably the corporation? Which has not the will nor the means to upgrade them? *(as if it's just occurred)* Picture in their stead, a bank – which lends to our town prestige, distinction. Which declares itself a temple – of progress and enterprise.

UNWIN And is this something you yourself would wish to pursue—?

GEORGE I had not considered it, but – *if* there were no objections – or impediments—

UNWIN Suppose I make it my mission to remove them?

GEORGE You could do such a thing?

UNWIN As a Member of Parliament, you will find that my influence is considerable.

George forces himself to look impressed. Unwin has no idea how expertly he's been manipulated.

CUT TO:

39: INT. TRENWITH HOUSE, GREAT HALL – DAY 18

Francis, dressed for the mine, comes in, whistling happily to himself. Elizabeth is doing her household accounts.

ELIZABETH *(teasing)* I wonder where *you're* going?

FRANCIS Am I so transparent?

ELIZABETH The mine is your new mistress!

FRANCIS And she is so close to paying *me* – instead of the other way round!

ELIZABETH That's greatly to be desired!

FRANCIS Particularly when it means we need no longer rely on George?

Elizabeth raises an amused eyebrow. Despite their bantering tone, this is still a touchy subject.

FRANCIS *(cont'd)* His partiality for you is all that keeps him from calling in our loans.

ELIZABETH You overestimate my charms.

FRANCIS Thank heavens I no longer underestimate my own!

He kisses her hand extravagantly and goes out.

CUT TO:

40: EXT. WOODLAND – DAY 18

Caroline and Dwight walk together. Dwight is silent. Caroline mistakes his reason for this.

CAROLINE D'you dislike me so very much?

DWIGHT 'Dislike'? *(considers this, then)* If coming between me and my work every day for the last twelve months – if being unable to forget your voice or the way you turn your head or the lights in your hair – if wanting to hear that you're married and dreading to hear that you're married – if that's dislike – then perhaps you can identify these symptoms for me?

Caroline ponders the question. But instead of giving a direct answer:

CAROLINE Do you never ride for pleasure?

DWIGHT Seldom.

CAROLINE I shall be waiting here just after eight tomorrow.

Without another word she turns and walks away, leaving Dwight dizzy with excitement and anticipation.

CUT TO:

41: INT. WARLEGGAN HOUSE – DAY 18

George is sparring alone when Cary strolls in.

CARY What price would you be willing to pay?

GEORGE Any.

CARY I thought so.

With a flourish of triumph Cary presents George with the promissory note. George examines it eagerly.

CARY *(cont'd)* What will you do with it?

GEORGE That will depend.

CUT TO:

42: INT. TRENWITH HOUSE, TURRET ROOM – DAY 18

Elizabeth is astonished to see George ride up to Trenwith.

CUT TO:

43: EXT. NAMPARA FIELDS – DAY 18

Demelza and Prudie are carrying hoes, heading back from working the fields. They're hot and bothered.

DEMELZA 'Spect Jud be waitin' for th' plantin' to finish 'fore he come sneakin' back?

PRUDIE Don' 'ee speak o' that lizard t' me! Keepin' 'is 'ead down? 'Voidin' a decent day's work, more like!

DEMELZA P'raps *he's* the informer!

PRUDIE That braggashans? Lip too loose t' keep 'is trap shut!

Now they see a rider in the distance approaching Nampara.

DEMELZA McNeil?

PRUDIE Varmint! Knowin' Cap'n Ross be away – and thinkin' to 'ave 'ee to 'imself?

DEMELZA And you think I'm so foolish as to let my vanity get the better o' my wits?

Prudie shrugs. Clearly she does think this. As they watch they see McNeil dismount and go to the front door. Presently Jinny lets him in.

CUT TO:

44: INT. NAMPARA HOUSE – DAY 18

Demelza serves tea to Captain McNeil. She's wary of him now, though she maintains all appearance of charm and civility.

CAPTAIN MCNEIL *(pleasantly)* While passing your husband's mine, I came upon a man who was bruised and bleeding. His name was Vigus.

DEMELZA I know him. He works there on tribute.

CAPTAIN MCNEIL He tells me there's a deal of ill-feeling about. On account of the rumours—

DEMELZA Rumours?

CAPTAIN MCNEIL Of an informer? Ah, but you're so out of the way here, perhaps the tales do not reach you. At any rate, the rumours make people tetchy. And whoever gave Vigus a beating must have strong suspicions as to his involvement in the Trade.

DEMELZA Were you able to discover who it was?

CAPTAIN MCNEIL I was not minded to at this stage. I hope the assailant will realize his error and not repeat it. *(then)* It makes me wonder, though – what must it be like to live with such a character? One can only feel for the man's wife, having such temper to contend with, such disregard for law or safety.

DEMELZA Ross will be delighted you've called. It's a pity he's not here to greet you himself.

CUT TO:

45: INT. TRENWITH HOUSE, LIBRARY – DAY 18

Elizabeth is nervous and doesn't sit down.

ELIZABETH I cannot believe you would call—

GEORGE After my reception from Francis last night? *(then)* I don't expect you to be disloyal to Francis, but don't you *personally* think this feud has gone on long enough?

ELIZABETH You know Francis when his mind is set. He holds you to blame for the prosecution of Ross—

GEORGE Oh, *Ross!* I wish I could enjoy the favour in your eyes that *he* does. But let me be frank with you. Ross and I have never seen eye to eye. On my part it's no more than a clash of personality. On his it's a disease. He plunges headlong from one disaster to another and blames me for all of them.

ELIZABETH I hardly think that's fair.

GEORGE On the one hand, he's utterly reckless; on the other, he assumes an absolute right to do as he pleases. It comes of being born into money. But with it comes lack of judgement. His ill-conceived smelting venture was doomed from the start. When he was out of pocket as a result, he was too proud to ask friends for assistance and instead signed a promissory note for one thousand pounds at forty per cent interest!

Elizabeth struggles not to look horrified at this revelation.

GEORGE *(cont'd)* Last year he sold half his shares in a *profitable* mine and coerced Francis into joining him in a folly his father had exhausted twenty years before! When he ultimately beggars himself and Francis with him, no doubt he'll accuse me of stealing the copper from his ground overnight!

ELIZABETH May I ask – how you learned of this promissory note?

GEORGE It came into the hands of my uncle Cary. The lender was so convinced of Ross's inability to repay it, he was willing to be rid of it at half its face value.

Elizabeth begins to compute the implications of this.

ELIZABETH What does your uncle intend to do?

GEORGE To let me deal with it. *(beat)* Perhaps you'd like me to make a gift of it to Ross?

ELIZABETH Would you?

GEORGE If I thought Ross would drop his enmity. Would that please you? I like to please you. Do you ask it of me?

ELIZABETH What would you ask in return?

GEORGE Merely to be admitted to your friendship again.

ELIZABETH *(with reluctance)* Let me see what I can do.

He kisses her hand lingeringly.

CUT TO:

46: INT. TRENWITH HOUSE, GREAT HALL – DAY 18

On his way out, and feeling he has made some progress, George comes face to face with Aunt Agatha.

AUNT AGATHA George Warleggan? I remember the first time Francis brought you here! – fligged out in your frills and fallallery!

GEORGE I remember it too—

AUNT AGATHA Speak up, boy, I'm a little deaf.

GEORGE *(smiling politely but not raising his voice)* And still above ground! There should be a law to kill off old crones—

AUNT AGATHA Velvets and silks you wore – 'twas plain your mother had no taste—

GEORGE *(still smiling)* If you were the last of the Poldarks I'd do it myself—

AUNT AGATHA And you, staring about like a bull-calf that had strayed from its stall—

GEORGE But never fear, your great-nephews are digging their own graves without my help!

Aunt Agatha offers her hand for him to kiss.

GEORGE *(cont'd)* Goodbye, old woman. I hope when I next call you'll be six feet below.

He walks out, smiling to himself. He crosses with Verity, coming in.

GEORGE *(cont'd)* Your aunt is not long for this world, I fear.

Verity looks suddenly worried.

VERITY Aunt Agatha—?

CUT TO:

47: EXT. NAMPARA HOUSE – DAY 18

Ross walks back from the mine to Nampara.

CUT TO:

48: INT. NAMPARA HOUSE – DAY 18

Ross comes in to find Demelza playing with Jeremy.

DEMELZA Captain McNeil was here.

ROSS Encouraged, no doubt, by your smiles of last night?

DEMELZA Driven, no doubt, by the sight of the bruisin' you gave Nick Vigus?

ROSS What does he know? That I gave a known turncoat a deserved beating?

DEMELZA That you take the law into your own hands?

Ross shakes his head dismissively. Demelza gets riled.

DEMELZA *(cont'd)* You think he comes here after me? What if he comes after *you*! What if he knows something?

ROSS Of what?

DEMELZA Your dealings with Trencrom? *(then)* And the more he comes calling—

ROSS The more he's likely to sniff something out? And you cannot now offer discouragement without arousing his suspicions as to why!

DEMELZA *(incredulous)* So *I'm* to blame?

ROSS You've been so warm to him thus far, it will look odd if you suddenly withdraw your favours.

DEMELZA I've been no more warm to him than you've been to Elizabeth!

She looks at him with a raised eyebrow. Ross has to concede she has a point.

CUT TO:

49: EXT. OPEN COUNTRYSIDE – DAY 18

Francis canters home through spectacular countryside.
CUT TO:

50: INT. TRENWITH HOUSE, GREAT HALL – DAY 18

A buoyant Francis returns from the mine, kisses Geoffrey Charles, joins Elizabeth, Verity and Aunt Agatha.

AUNT AGATHA You missed a treat. George Warleggan graced us with his presence.

FRANCIS What did he want?

ELIZABETH To be reconciled with you?

FRANCIS Is that why he called when my back was turned?

AUNT AGATHA Very pleasant he was, too. Hoped I'd soon be worm-fodder. And you and Ross with me!

No one appears to take this seriously.

ELIZABETH I know he's been vicious in his pursuit of Ross, but I begin to think he would make amends if he could.

FRANCIS How?

ELIZABETH By not taking advantage of the power he holds—

VERITY What power does he hold over *Ross?*

There's a moment when Elizabeth might tell them of the promissory note. She thinks better of it.

ELIZABETH I – do not know of any specific threat to Ross – but to *us.* You know he owns the ground we walk on. What harm can it do to modify your hostility towards him? – If only to deter him from wielding power over us *all?*

Francis eyes her narrowly. He considers the implications of what she's saying.

FRANCIS Perhaps I'll ride over and see him.

ELIZABETH I think that would be for the best.

As Francis walks out:

AUNT AGATHA *(muttering to herself)* Wished me dead, he did. Called me old crone.

VERITY What's that, Aunt?

AUNT AGATHA Big mistake.

CUT TO:

51: EXT. WARLEGGAN HOUSE – NIGHT 18

Francis rides up to Warleggan House.
CUT TO:

52: INT. WARLEGGAN HOUSE, GEORGE'S DEN – NIGHT 18

George and Cary are relaxing when Francis is shown in.

FRANCIS (*pleasantly*) Elizabeth tells me you called today.

GEORGE I hope you took the visit in the spirit in which it was intended.

FRANCIS I believe I did. And in return I hope you will take what I have to say in the same spirit. You will never again set foot in my house. Nor approach me, or my family – including my son. He is no longer your godson. We are no longer your friends. You may turn us out of Trenwith if you wish. It will be a small price to pay to escape the noxiousness of your acquaintance.

He bows politely and walks out. Cary is open-mouthed with shock.

CARY Call in his loans. Turn 'em out into the fields!

GEORGE I will not make Elizabeth suffer for her husband's folly. And in fact, thanks to that promissory note, I do not need to.

George pours himself another glass of port and returns to staring into the fire.

CUT TO:

53: EXT. TRENWITH HOUSE – DAWN 19

Dawn breaks over Trenwith.

CUT TO:

54: INT. TRENWITH HOUSE, ELIZABETH'S ROOM – DAY 19

Francis, already dressed, stands in the doorway, contemplating the sleeping Elizabeth who has Geoffrey Charles slumbering beside her. He sits on the bed and brushes some strands of hair away from her face. She stirs but does not wake up. Geoffrey Charles opens his eyes.

FRANCIS Sssshh! Don't wake Mama. Papa must be at the mine early, to start the blasting. But he'll be home in time to read you a story.

He kisses Geoffrey Charles and leaves.

CUT TO:

55: EXT. WHEAL GRACE – DAY 19

Ross greets Francis outside the mine.

FRANCIS I've told Henshawe I'll set the fuses myself. Shall we go below?

ROSS By all means.

FRANCIS *(buoyant)* I've a feeling our fortunes will change today.

CUT TO:

55A: INT. TRENWITH HOUSE, LIBRARY – DAY 19

Dwight is examining Aunt Agatha. Verity and Elizabeth watch anxiously. Dwight looks serious. He beckons Verity and Elizabeth aside.

ELIZABETH Is it serious?

DWIGHT Yes. And physic will not cure it.

VERITY What will?

DWIGHT Something you cannot provide. *(to Verity)* Your presence here is what she craves. And you have a life elsewhere.

Verity and Elizabeth exchange a glance. They acknowledge the truth of this – and its implications.

VERITY So what's to be done?

DWIGHT In matters of the heart I think you must be the physician, ma'am.

Dwight bows and departs. Verity and Elizabeth exchange a glance. What is to be done? Elizabeth knows that this is Verity's decision alone. Verity hesitates – then goes over to Aunt Agatha. She's debating how to tackle this. Is she strong enough to put her own needs ahead of other people's? She waivers. Then:

VERITY I must leave you tomorrow, Aunt.

Aunt Agatha's face falls.

VERITY *(cont'd)* I have a husband and a home to return to.

AUNT AGATHA But they do not need you as Trenwith needs you. 'Tis not as if you have children—

Verity bites back a retort.

AUNT AGATHA *(cont'd)* And the cards – today they threaten some impending ill – which perhaps only you can prevent?

Aunt Agatha puts on a look of increased feebleness. Verity and Elizabeth exchange a look, trying not to smile.

VERITY Still, Aunt, I must go tomorrow.

Aunt Agatha is astonished. Even Verity can hardly believe she's been so bold.

VERITY *(cont'd)* But I'll return. More frequently. *(then)* We must both learn to give way a little.

Aunt Agatha scowls but we suspect she has new-found respect for Verity.

CUT TO:

56: INT. NAMPARA, BARN – DAY 19

Demelza is skinning a rabbit when Dwight canters past. He slows down when he sees her.

DEMELZA You're in haste.

DWIGHT I have a rendezvous with Caroline. *(then)* Don't excite yourself. It will come to nothing.

Raised eyebrows from Demelza.

DWIGHT *(cont'd)* We could not be less suited. She is an heiress – and I am—

DEMELZA As lowly as a kitchen maid?

Dwight smiles in acknowledgement of her comment.

DEMELZA *(cont'd)* May not a woman confer status as well as a man? Ross raised *me* up—

DWIGHT And Ross knows he was entirely the winner in that transaction!

DEMELZA Miss Penvenen may feel the same.

DWIGHT Miss Penvenen is engaged.

DEMELZA Then why has she asked to meet you? And why do you do her bidding?

DWIGHT A question I've asked myself a thousand times already!

Dwight rides off. Demelza continues with the rabbit. As she does so, she sees a rider approaching. Presently the rider dismounts and hands her a letter. It's addressed to Ross and marked urgent.

CUT TO:

57: EXT. WOODLAND – DAY 19

Caroline is standing by her horse, which is tethered to a tree. Dwight gallops to meet her, dismounts, tethers his horse. She watches him with a smile of amusement.

CAROLINE Uncle Ray is angry with me. I suspect he wants me safely locked away until my marriage.

DWIGHT Which is to be when?

CAROLINE Who knows? *(then)* At any rate, not Unwin.

Dwight looks at her, uncomprehending.

CAROLINE *(cont'd)* He jilted me. Or was it the other way round? Uncle Ray seems to think so.

Dwight is speechless. He opens his mouth to speak but then can't think what to say. Watching him gape and hesitate, Caroline regards him with amusement.

CAROLINE *(cont'd)* Tell me, who *is* Dwight Enys? Is he the strong, capable man who bestrides the sick room? Or the nervous, hesitant one I see here today? Which of them cares for Caroline Penvenen and wishes she would not go away?

DWIGHT You mock me.

CAROLINE Do I?

She is smiling at him and does indeed seem to be making fun of him. Nevertheless, he decides to answer her question.

DWIGHT You ask me who I am? A man with not the smallest fortune. Money was never plentiful and studying took all I had. There was no time for polite conversation or drawing-room chatter. I was never taught how to flirt or pay compliments. I hardly ever *met* women, except as cases. But as cases I know them well. So if you come to me with a sore throat or a bad knee, I know what to do and you think 'that man has confidence'. But if I meet you in a drawing room, you're a creature whose moods and manners I've never learned to decipher. I don't know the prescription for gallantry – and if you laugh at me, which you frequently do – I become tongue-tied and foolish. What I feel for you doesn't waiver between strength and weakness. It waivers between hope and despair.

CAROLINE Poor Dwight! Do I show such confidence and poise? How well I've been schooled! *(then, seeing he doesn't understand*) While you were learning to be a physician, I was learning to be an heiress! An heiress must know how to walk, to ride, to dress, to dance . . . The one thing she never learns about is the eligible marriage for which she's being prepared. You say you only know women as patients. I don't know men at *all.*

DWIGHT What would you *like* to know?

She studies him carefully before replying.

CAROLINE When I first met you in Bodmin – I wondered what it would be like to be kissed by you.

A moment between them – then Dwight pulls her towards him and kisses her. Startled at first, she soon acquiesces. Eventually she pushes him away and eyes him curiously.

DWIGHT And now, no doubt, you hate me.

CAROLINE And now, no doubt, I hate you.

They stand looking at each other a long while. Then:

CAROLINE *(cont'd)* I must go.

DWIGHT I'll never see you again.

CAROLINE Never. *(beat)* Till December.

DWIGHT But nothing will change.

CAROLINE One thing will change. In December I come of age.

She smiles, then walks towards her horse. Reeling from shock, Dwight remains a moment longer.

CUT TO:

58: EXT. WHEAL GRACE – DAY 19

A loud explosion is heard underground.

CUT TO:

59: INT. WHEAL GRACE – DAY 19

Ross and Francis make their way through the dust and rubble to where the blast went off. They peer into the darkness. Beyond it they can see murky water. They begin to examine some of the rubble which has come down in the explosion.

FRANCIS Anything?

ROSS What d'you make of this?

Francis holds his candle to a piece of rubble. There is a glint of something in the rock. Francis looks excited.

FRANCIS Is it—?

ROSS It's *something*. Let's collect more samples, take 'em above and examine them fully.

As they begin to gather suitable samples, they hear the crunch of footsteps in the tunnel. It's Paul Daniel.

PAUL Mistress Poldark above for 'ee, Cap'n. She say it's urgent.

Ross and Francis look concerned.

FRANCIS You go, Ross. I'll carry on here.

CUT TO:

60: EXT. WHEAL GRACE – DAY 19

Ross is met by Demelza, who hands him a letter. He reads it. Anxiety crosses his face but he struggles to remain calm.

ROSS It's from Pascoe. I'm wanted in Truro.

DEMELZA Is it bad news?

ROSS I'll know more when I've seen him.

Ross mounts his horse and rides off. Demelza looks anxious.

CUT TO:

61: INT. WHEAL GRACE – DAY 19

Working all alone, sifting patiently through the rock which has come down, Francis finds what definitely looks like a speck of copper on one of the samples. He can hardly contain his delight.

CUT TO:

62: EXT. TRENWITH GROUNDS – DAY 19

Elizabeth walks with Geoffrey Charles and Verity.

ELIZABETH Since it's to be your last night with us, I've asked Mrs Tabb for a special dessert!

She and Verity giggle and link arms.

GEOFFREY CHARLES When can I go down the mine, Mama?

ELIZABETH When copper is found?

VERITY Will it be?

ELIZABETH I've never seen Francis more convinced of anything.

VERITY Or more determined to be the one to find it?

ELIZABETH He's been so long in Ross's shadow – I think he wants to earn his admiration.

VERITY And yours?

CUT TO:

63: EXT. WHEAL GRACE – DAY 19

Francis emerges with several pieces of rock. Excited, he approaches Paul.

FRANCIS Have you seen Captain Henshawe? Or Zacky Martin?

PAUL Jus' missed 'em, sur. Can I be of service?

FRANCIS I'd like confirmation of something. But no matter. I'll ride over to Nampara and see if Ross has returned.

CUT TO:

64: INT. NAMPARA HOUSE – DAY 19

Demelza is laying the table as Francis arrives. Struggling to contain his excitement, he places some samples of copper on one of the dinner plates.

DEMELZA 'Tis never copper?

FRANCIS I hardly dare hope but – yes, I think it may be. Will you ask Ross to look when he returns?

DEMELZA Will you not stay to ask him yourself? He'll be that relieved.

FRANCIS It is my dearest wish. To be of use to him. *(then)* To make amends.

Something in his tone makes Demelza wary.

FRANCIS *(cont'd)* You do not ask me what amends I need to make.

DEMELZA I'm not sure I wish t' know.

FRANCIS Yet I think I must tell you.

DEMELZA There's no need, Francis—

FRANCIS *(ignoring her)* Years ago – when the Carnmore Copper Company was fighting for its life, George came to me one evening. Verity had just left. I blamed you for her marriage – and in my rage I gave George the names of the Carnmore shareholders.

He pauses to see if she looks surprised. She doesn't.

FRANCIS *(cont'd)* I suspect Ross – and you – already have some inkling – but I've never had the courage to tell you outright. *(then)* But you can't rebuild a friendship by ignoring what destroyed it. So now you know. *(then)* I'll go now.

DEMELZA Wait, Francis— *(He halts.)* If we break now, we'll hurt each other all the more. *(then)* One bad thing don't outweigh the many good. 'Tis the balance that counts.

FRANCIS You believe that? *(He looks at her in wonder and gratitude.)* I don't wonder Ross loves you.

DEMELZA Do you suppose he still does?

FRANCIS You doubt it?

DEMELZA Sometimes I think he loves Elizabeth better.

Francis contemplates Demelza – and smiles.

FRANCIS May I tell you something, Demelza?

DEMELZA Yes?

FRANCIS You have one failing – and that is that you don't think well enough of yourself. You came here as a miner's daughter, married into this ancient derelict family and took its standards as your own. So you mistake your own value, your own vitality. But Ross was a wise man when he chose you. If he's as clever as I think he is, he'll not forget it.

DEMELZA But Elizabeth – is so lovely – and well bred – and Ross's first love. How can I compete with perfection?

FRANCIS Whatever Elizabeth is or has, she's far from perfect.

He pauses to let that land. Then:

FRANCIS *(cont'd)* And you – must get rid of the notion that someone has done you a favour by taking you into our family. Will you do that?

DEMELZA I'll try.

FRANCIS *(getting up)* I must go. But I'll return – and tell Ross what I've told you. *(beat)* Then get down on my knees and beg his forgiveness.

DEMELZA He will make you get straight up again!

FRANCIS *(hopeful)* Will he?

DEMELZA Then he'll box your ears, pour you a brandy an' raise a toast to copper and Grace!

FRANCIS *(laughing)* Copper and Grace!

Overcome with emotion, he kisses Demelza's hand.

FRANCIS *(cont'd)* God bless you, Demelza.

He leaves. Demelza remains, shaken but moved.

CUT TO:

65: EXT. WHEAL GRACE – DAY 19

Francis arrives back at the mine. He meets Paul.

FRANCIS I'm going below to do more digging.

PAUL Do 'ee need me to go with 'ee, sur?

FRANCIS Thank you, no. I can manage. I shan't be gone long.

CUT TO:

66: INT. WHEAL GRACE, TUNNEL – DAY 19

Francis, carrying his pickaxe, makes his way past other miners. They seem to have a new respect for him and greet him cheerily with 'G'day,

Mister Poldark', 'G'day, sur', as he passes them and goes deeper into the tunnel.

CUT TO:

67: INT. WHEAL GRACE, TUNNEL – DAY 19

Francis gropes his way past the piles of blasted rubble. Holding his lamp in front of him, he spots a glint of something in the wall of the newly blasted cavern. Laying aside his pickaxe, he decides to follow it. He goes even deeper into the tunnel, following the faint vein of copper. But in his enthusiasm and excitement, looking up at the cavern ceiling, he fails to see the glint of something else up ahead: a deep gulley of water, the level of which has receded even further. His foot skids on the slimy rock, he slips and falls into the treacherous depths. The light goes out. The place is in almost complete darkness. He disappears beneath the water. He comes up for air, screaming.

FRANCIS Help me! Someone – help me!

He goes under again. More thrashing and flailing about. He comes back up and tries to scramble out. The sides of the gulley are too steep and too slippery. He casts about for something to hold onto. He manages to grasp hold of a rusty nail.

FRANCIS *(cont'd)* Is anybody there? Help me! Please!

CUT TO:

68: INT. TRENWITH HOUSE, GREAT HALL – DUSK 19

Elizabeth and Verity lay the table for supper, in anticipation of Francis's return. Verity glances up at the portrait of Francis on the wall and smiles to herself.

CUT TO:

69: INT. WHEAL GRACE – DUSK 19

Francis is still holding on to the rusty nail.

FRANCIS Is anybody there? Help me! *Help me!*

Weaker now, he closes his eyes:

DISSOLVE TO:

70: EXT. HENDRAWNA BEACH (FLASHBACK) – DAY A

Young Francis is standing on a sandbank, cut off by the tide.

YOUNG FRANCIS Ross! Ross, where are you? Ross, help me!

And suddenly, across the water, Young Ross comes wading, helps Francis climb onto his shoulders and carries him to safety.

CUT TO:

71: INT. NAMPARA HOUSE, PARLOUR – DUSK 19

Ross comes in. Demelza knows at once that the news is bad.

ROSS My debt is in the hands of the Warleggans. By Christmas I must find fourteen hundred pounds.

DEMELZA Or else?

ROSS I lose everything we own and go to debtors' prison.

For a moment they look at each other, speechless with horror. But before either of them can speak, Prudie comes in.

PRUDIE There be someone from Trenwith askin' for Mister Francis.

DEMELZA Is he not at the mine?

ROSS At this hour?

A brief glance between them – curiosity, not alarm at this point – then Ross gets up and goes out. Demelza follows.

CUT TO:

72: INT. WHEAL GRACE – DUSK 19

Francis, much weaker now, is still holding on. His eyes swim and he begins to hallucinate.

DISSOLVE TO:

73: INT. WHEAL GRACE – DUSK 19

Francis is slipping into unconsciousness. Suddenly he hears a voice calling his name.

ROSS'S VOICE Francis? Are you there? *Francis?*

He opens his eyes and sees Ross looking down at him.

FRANCIS Ross? I knew you'd come!

Ross reaches down a hand to help him out. Francis struggles to reach it. As he does so the image of Ross dissolves.

DISSOLVE TO:

74: INT. WHEAL GRACE – DUSK 19

Francis is still in the water and Ross is not there. Francis slips lower in the water. The nail comes away in his hand.

CUT TO:

75: INT. WHEAL GRACE, CHANGING HUT – DUSK 19

Ross discovers Francis's everyday clothes are still hanging up in the changing house. An awful thought begins to dawn:

ROSS I think he may still be down below.

He and Demelza look at each other. Neither speaks, nor dares to admit the gnawing anxiety which begins to make itself felt. Henshawe, having been sent for, now rushes up.

HENSHAWE Is it Mister Francis?

ROSS *(nods)* Will you come below with me? Demelza, wait here.

CUT TO:

76: INT. WHEAL GRACE – DUSK 19

Ross and Henshawe descend the shaft, followed by Zacky.
CUT TO:

77: EXT. WHEAL GRACE – DUSK 19

Demelza waits above ground. Her feeling of dread increases.
CUT TO:

78: INT. WHEAL GRACE – DUSK 19

Ross leads the way along the tunnel. He comes across Francis's abandoned pickaxe. He exchanges a glance with Henshawe and Zacky. They begin to fear the worst. They press on.

ROSS *(calling out)* Francis? *Francis?*

CUT TO:

79: EXT. WHEAL GRACE – NIGHT 19

Night is falling as Demelza waits anxiously outside the mine. More people are gathering. Prudie arrives with a shawl, which she wraps round Demelza's shoulders. Now Dwight arrives. He knows from their anxious faces that something is wrong.

DWIGHT Captain Henshawe sent for me. Is it an accident?

DEMELZA Francis is missing.

CUT TO:

80: INT. TRENWITH HOUSE, LIBRARY – NIGHT 19

Elizabeth waits with Geoffrey Charles and Verity, trying to remain calm. Verity is turning the pages of a book for Geoffrey Charles to look at. Aunt Agatha's fingers keep straying towards her tarot cards. She resolutely pulls them back. No one speaks. Nothing is heard but their breathing and the tick of the clock.

CUT TO:

81: INT. WHEAL GRACE – NIGHT 19

Ross leads the way down the tunnel till he comes to the deep gully of water. He shines the lamp across it. The light flickers upon a dark shape – a body floating face down in the water.

ROSS Oh God, no—

He scrambles into the water. Henshawe and Zacky hold their lamps aloft to light the way. Ross grabs Francis's body and hauls him to the side where Zacky and Henshawe drag him out. Ross clambers up, turns over the body of Francis. Francis's eyes are wide open but he has a peaceful look on his face. Ross closes Francis's eyes. He strokes the face of his dead cousin.

ROSS *(cont'd)* *(tenderly)* Why the hell didn't you learn to swim?

He cradles Francis in his arms and begins to weep.

82: INT. TRENWITH HOUSE, LIBRARY – NIGHT 19

Elizabeth, Verity and Aunt Agatha hear the sound of a horse's hooves.

VERITY *(to Geoffrey Charles, determinedly cheerful)* That's your father's horse. I'll see if his supper's ready.

ELIZABETH I'll go.

She gets up, with enforced calm, and heads for the door. Verity and Aunt Agatha exchange a glance. The tension is at breaking point.

CUT TO:

82A: INT. TRENWITH HOUSE – NIGHT 19

Elizabeth opens the door to Ross. One look at his face tells her all she needs to know.

CUT TO:

83: INT. CHURCH – DAY 20

A packed church is draped in mourning. Elizabeth, Geoffrey Charles and Verity stand in the front pew. Demelza is behind them, with

Prudie. All the great and the good (including George and Cary) – and some of the humble and poor – are there. Ted Carkeek pays a mournful tune on the violin as Francis's coffin is carried up the aisle on the shoulders of Ross, Dwight, Zacky and Paul. Elizabeth clutches Geoffrey Charles's hand. For a long while she seems to hold herself together. Then, as Ross, Henshawe, Zacky and Paul place the coffin on a bier, she begins to shake, to crumble, to sob. Ross hastens to stand beside her. She sways and leans against him. He takes her arm to steady her. Behind them Demelza can only watch as Ross holds Elizabeth close to him.

Episode 6

1: EXT. WHEAL GRACE – DAY 21 (WINTER 1792)

Ross stands alone at Wheal Grace. A solitary figure, without partner or support, on a day which is cold and comfortless.
CUT TO:

2: INT. WHEAL GRACE, TUNNEL – DAY 21

Ross descends the ladder and is met at the bottom by Henshawe.

HENSHAWE Still can't get used to Mister Francis bein' gone.

ROSS It breaks my heart to think of him – all fired up about those rock samples—

HENSHAWE When in the end 'twas only quartz, with schorl an' iron oxide mixed.

ROSS Fool's copper.

HENSHAWE Fool's copper.

A moment between them. Then they head off into the tunnel.
CUT TO:

3: INT. TRENWITH HOUSE, LIBRARY – DAY 21

A pale Elizabeth replaces a faded posy of flowers in a vase in front of the portrait of Francis. The atmosphere of Trenwith seems chilly and bleak. Elizabeth seems fragile but stoical. Presently she is joined by Verity. Both stand looking at the portrait. Verity is close to tears. Elizabeth, having paid her 'respects', squeezes Verity's arm and leaves. Left alone, Verity allows her tears to fall.

CUT TO:

4: EXT. WARLEGGAN HOUSE – DAY 21

George is watching as a line of servants unload lavish supplies in preparation for an extravagant Warleggan Christmas. George is in a good mood. He is humming a Christmas carol: 'In Dulci Jubilo'. Cary appears.

GEORGE Is it done?

Cary reads from a document.

CARY *(reads)* 'Mr Poldark, I give you notice that in a week your promissory note for one thousand pounds, plus interest at forty per cent, will fall due and must be paid in full.'

GEORGE The day after Christmas? Do they serve plum pudding in debtors' prison?

He smiles and hands the document back to Cary. A large basket of ripe peaches is carried past. George takes one, bites into it, nods approvingly.

CUT TO:

5: EXT. HENDRAWNA BEACH – DAY 21

A dead body has been washed up by the tide. For a while it seems as if no one has seen it. Then Rosina and Charlie are revealed, as if waiting for someone. Presently Dwight appears, carrying his case of instruments. They point him to the body.

DWIGHT Is it anyone we know?

CHARLIE Nay, sur. 'Tis thought he may be from the *Parthesia* as was wreck'd las' night off St Ann's.

ROSINA A cryin' waste o' life, do 'ee not think, Dr Enys?

DWIGHT I do indeed, Rosina. *(to Charlie)* Will you help me bring him ashore?

Dwight and Charlie drag the body out of the surf and into the dunes. One of the legs has a distinct tattoo. Dwight examines the man to confirm death.

DWIGHT *(cont'd) (to Charlie)* Take Rosina home. I'll see him buried.

Charlie offers Rosina his arm. She hesitates and looks to Dwight for his approval. Charlie notices her hesitation.

CHARLIE Nay, Rosina, 'tis needful 'ee take my arm – for fear thy lipsy leg do buckle b'neath 'ee.

Dwight nods his agreement. Rosina reluctantly takes Charlie's arm. Dwight waits till they've gone, then he crouches down beside the body, opens his medical bag and gets out an amputation knife.

CUT TO:

6: INT. NAMPARA HOUSE, KITCHEN – DAY 21

The kitchen looks bare and spartan. Demelza opens the doors to the larder. It's almost bare – just a few eggs, scraps of bread, scrag-ends of cheese. She looks at it ruefully. Then she reveals a concealed door at the back of the larder. Inside is a secret cache of cheeses, preserves, pickles, potatoes, etc. Into it she adds more pickles and preserves. Prudie comes up behind her.

DEMELZA Not a word t' Ross. I don' want him thinkin' I fear the worst.

PRUDIE 'Ee do fear th' worst! If 'ee go t' prison, we'll need more 'n a few tetties t' see us through!

DEMELZA Hush your creenin'! If this be his last Christmas here a while, I mean t' make it a goodly one.

PRUDIE Wi' just we? Or will there be 'guests'?

The raised eyebrows and the tone with which she says it makes us think she doesn't approve of the potential 'guest'.

CUT TO:

7: INT. TRENWITH HOUSE, GREAT HALL – DAY 21

Elizabeth comes in, looking fragile but exquisitely lovely in the mourning black of her riding habit. Trenwith feels cold today. Verity, now wrapped in a shawl, is helping Aunt Agatha (also in a shawl) to breakfast. As Elizabeth catches her reflection in a mirror, she frowns.

ELIZABETH I feel old.

AUNT AGATHA *(to Verity)* Ignore her. She says it to be contradicted.

ELIZABETH I say it because I look like an ancient black crow!

VERITY You're still a very beautiful woman, Elizabeth. As I'm sure you know. *(beat)* And if you doubt it, no doubt your visitor will be able to reassure you.

CUT TO:

8: EXT. TRENWITH HOUSE – DAY 21

Ross rides up to Trenwith.

CUT TO:

9: INT. TRENWITH HOUSE, GREAT HALL – DAY 21

Without realizing she's doing it, Elizabeth smooths her hair and lightly pinches her cheeks to give them colour. Verity eyes her narrowly but says nothing. Elizabeth notices.

ELIZABETH He comes to take Geoffrey Charles to the mine.

VERITY And you?

ELIZABETH I'm trustee of my son's shares in Wheal Grace. Which is why Ross brings me weekly reports—

AUNT AGATHA *(casually)* Sometimes *twice*-weekly—

ELIZABETH I rely on him to keep me informed—

VERITY I think it would be a mistake to become *too* reliant on him. *(beat)* For *both* your sakes.

Geoffrey Charles comes running in, dressed in riding garb.

GEOFFREY CHARLES Uncle Ross is here, Mama!

Elizabeth smiles and takes his hand.

ELIZABETH *(to Verity)* Who else can I depend on?

They go out. Verity seems resigned. She knows there is nothing she can say to stop this taking its course – whatever that course may be. Aunt Agatha, seemingly oblivious, tucks heartily into her breakfast.

CUT TO:

10: EXT. WHEAL GRACE – DAY 21

Ross, Elizabeth and Geoffrey Charles halt on the hillside overlooking Wheal Grace. Elizabeth seems small and fragile as she is blown by the cold wind.

ROSS Take my coat.

ELIZABETH I do not feel the cold.

ROSS I think you do. At any rate, you used to.

Elizabeth smiles in acknowledgement of a shared memory.

ELIZABETH At any rate, it's warmer than Trenwith! *(then)* I must learn to grow a thicker skin.

ROSS Can you?

ELIZABETH Sometimes. *(then)* I miss Francis.

ROSS I too.

ELIZABETH I never thought him the most practical of men, yet now I realize how much he dealt with. Matters of finance – the estate – the servants – decisions which now fall to me—

ROSS You must not hesitate to call upon me—

ELIZABETH Oh, I do. More often than I should. *(seeing him about to protest)* You have your own home – and wife and child. *(then)* You seek to share *my* troubles, yet never tell me your own. What of your debts? The promissory note which fell into George's hands?

ROSS Don't trouble yourself. The sum was much exaggerated.

ELIZABETH And the mine? How long can we continue with such poor yield?

ROSS For your sake and his I will squeeze out every last drop before it defeats us.

ELIZABETH *(to Geoffrey Charles)* Uncle Ross looks after us so well. Where would we be without him?

Elizabeth smiles gratefully, then turns her horse back to Trenwith. Ross looks a moment longer at Wheal Grace, then follows.

CUT TO:

11: INT. DWIGHT'S COTTAGE – DAY 21

Dwight is examining the tendons and ligaments of a severed leg. A visible tattoo tells us this is the leg of the man who was washed up drowned. Dwight is trying to work something out from the arrangement of the tendons and ligaments. Suddenly the penny drops.

DWIGHT *(to himself)* Of course. *It's obvious!*

CUT TO:

12: INT. HOBLYN'S COTTAGE – DAY 21

Dwight is manipulating Rosina's knee, watched by her father Jacka, Charlie and his daughters Lottie and May Kempthorne. Rosina is wincing and gritting her teeth, but is determined to be brave. Suddenly something in the knee clicks into place. Rosina gives a shriek of pain.

JACKA What do 'ee do to 'er?

Rosina is still gasping with pain.

DWIGHT *(to Rosina, ignoring Jacka)* Rosina? Can you stand?

Rosina hesitates. It's as if she daren't put her weight onto her leg.

DWIGHT *(cont'd)* Don't be afraid. I'll be here to catch you.

CHARLIE Nay, surgeon. If anyone shall, 'tis I—

ROSINA I think – I d' believe—

Hesitantly she puts her weight onto the injured leg. It holds firm. She takes a few tentative steps. The knee holds.

ROSINA *(cont'd) (in disbelief)* What did 'ee do?

She begins to walk, first with extreme caution, then with more purpose.

ROSINA *(cont'd)* 'Tis all mended. There be no pain.

DWIGHT There was a displacement. You've had it so long the muscles have withered and caused inflammation. I'll put a bandage on it for now, but soon you'll be able to manage without.

ROSINA 'Ee be an angel! How can I ever thank 'ee?

DWIGHT It's enough for me to know that I've helped you.

ROSINA 'Tis a miracle!

DWIGHT No. Basic anatomy.

A look between Dwight and Rosina. On Dwight's part, the delight of a physician who has effected a cure. On Rosina's, admiration bordering on hero-worship. Jacka notes the look. And isn't pleased by it.

CUT TO:

13: EXT. TRURO STREET – DAY 21

Ross rides along the street. He can't help but notice the ragged urchins and beggars who huddle around miserable fires or importune passers-by for alms. And there are soldiers on several places along the street. Their presence is not lost on Ross.

CUT TO:

14: INT. PASCOE'S OFFICE – DAY 21

ROSS There seem to be soldiers everywhere!

PASCOE Events across in France make the gentry nervous.

ROSS Events along the coast make the gaugers watchful. Has it arrived?

Pascoe shows Ross Cary's letter.

PASCOE As expected. The full amount, with interest. I did enquire whether they'd be willing to extend for another year—

ROSS I can guess their response.

PASCOE Quite so.

CUT TO:

15: EXT. TRENWITH HOUSE – DAY 21

George rides up to Trenwith.

CUT TO:

16: INT. TRENWITH HOUSE, LIBRARY – DAY 21

Aunt Agatha is scowling at George as he waits for Elizabeth to make an appearance.

AUNT AGATHA Ninety-five years of age! What d'you think of that?

GEORGE *(smiling)* I think it's high time the coffin-maker took measurements.

AUNT AGATHA Head of the family. Mistress of this house. And so I intend to remain.

She goes out.

GEORGE *(smiling)* Good luck with that, old hag. *(then)* Elizabeth! *(bows politely)* You look pale. Are you unwell? *(before she can answer)* I've brought a small token for my godson. I know you'll accept nothing for yourself.

ELIZABETH Well, I—

He hands her a box of candied fruits. Their very extravagance – and utter frivolousness – makes her lost for words.

GEORGE Are you looking forward to Christmas? *(before Elizabeth can disabuse him)* I wish I were. Entertaining on a grand scale is not my preference. But my uncle's very thick with Tony Boscoigne – and no doubt there's some scheme afoot to throw me under the hooves of his sisters! *(beat)* Or so your mother believes!

ELIZABETH *(surprised)* You've seen her?

GEORGE I – oh – I'd not intended to mention— *(as if being forced to admit it)* I have on occasion over the last few months prevailed upon her to dine with me. You know how much I admire her—

ELIZABETH She speaks highly of *you*—

GEORGE She has shared with me certain concerns—

ELIZABETH Oh?

GEORGE In the wake of Francis – forgive me – certain outstanding debts of his – accumulating interest – which must be dealt with—

ELIZABETH Of course.

GEORGE But not until you are out of mourning – and well beyond—

ELIZABETH You're very kind, George.

GEORGE As your *friend* it's the very least I can do.

He bows politely and leaves. Elizabeth is slightly stunned. This is a new George – one who is not so effusive and admiring. She's not sure she likes the change.

CUT TO:

17: INT. DEBTORS' PRISON – DAY 21

Ross is shown through into a row of individual cells. Richard Tonkin comes to the bars.

ROSS How are you, Tonkin?

TONKIN Good of you to call, Cap'n! Few others do. You've no notion how your visits have helped me through.

ROSS Not to mention this?

He hands him a bottle of rum.

TONKIN Bless you, sir.

ROSS When d'you expect to be released?

TONKIN Soon after Christmas.

ROSS Then it will be your turn to visit *me*! *(seeing his look of disbelief)* George Warleggan has a bill of mine which I cannot pay.

TONKIN But – surely – you have assets? Your shares in Wheal Leisure? Does the mine not prosper?

ROSS And yields small dividends – but these I must reserve for my wife. She'll have nothing else to live on.

TONKIN But would the Warleggans not exchange your shares for *some* portion of the debt?

ROSS My shares are worth about six hundred pounds. Not even *half* of what I owe. Besides, I would not give them the satisfaction.

TONKIN Then you will suffer.

ROSS *(cheerfully)* Then I will suffer.

CUT TO:

18: EXT. NAMPARA HOUSE – DAY 21

Large fallen and/or cut branches are scattered beneath a tree. Demelza is dragging them into a pile, then lashing a rope round them, ready to haul them home. Prudie is gathering smaller branches. As Demelza struggles to lash the branches together she grazes her hands.

DEMELZA Ah! Judas!

She examines her hands. They're full of splinters, cuts and calluses. Prudie grabs one and examines it.

DEMELZA *(cont'd)* Do 'ee read my fortune?

PRUDIE Aye, maid. It tell me, with hands like these, that Demelza Poldark is no lady!

They both laugh. Demelza licks her wounds.

CUT TO:

19: INT. CARRIAGE – DAY 21

CU: The very ladylike hands of Caroline Penvenen, folded neatly in her lap. Beside her Horace is sleeping. The carriage is piled high with luggage. There is a lady's maid with her. Caroline glances out of the window.

CAROLINE Horace, wake up, my sweet, we're nearly home!

CUT TO:

20: EXT. BARGUS CROSSROADS – DAY 21

The carriage rattles across the moors. As it approaches Bargus Crossroads, Caroline sees a rider coming across the moors in her direction. It's Ross, on his way home. He halts when he sees her.

ROSS Miss Penvenen?

CAROLINE Captain Poldark. Seven months away have given me an appetite for such sights.

ROSS And doubtless they for *you.*

CAROLINE I was most grieved to hear of your cousin's death.

ROSS Thank you. We miss him greatly.

CAROLINE He was your partner in the mine, I believe? Were you able to continue the venture?

ROSS It goes on.

CAROLINE Profitably?

ROSS Not profitably.

CAROLINE And how is Dr Enys?

ROSS A worker of miracles! As I came through Sawle, I heard tell of his curing a village girl of her lameness.

CAROLINE Rosina Hoblyn?

ROSS You know her?

CAROLINE Of her. But how was it done?

ROSS No doubt he'll be able to enlighten you better than I, ma'am.

He's about to ride on when Caroline detains him.

CAROLINE I don't suppose—

ROSS Yes?

CAROLINE You wouldn't accompany me to my uncle's house? He's not expecting me – and your presence may serve to mitigate the 'warmth' of my reception.

She flashes a dazzling smile at him – and Ross is powerless to resist.

CUT TO:

21: INT. TRENWITH HOUSE, ELIZABETH'S ROOM – DUSK 21

Elizabeth sits at her dressing table, examining her face in the mirror. She doesn't like what she sees. She frowns, then adopts a 'neutral' face, smoothing out the lines on her face.

GEOFFREY CHARLES Why don't you smile, Mama?

ELIZABETH Smiling makes lines upon the face, my love. *(She demonstrates.)* And lines make us look old. *(then)* So I must smile less. Not in public, but here, at home. *(then, putting him on her lap)* But when you see me *not* smiling, you mustn't think I'm sad or displeased with you. Only that I'm trying to spare my face— *(seeing him look confused)* It's important for a lady to look her best.

GEOFFREY CHARLES Why?

ELIZABETH You'll understand when you're older.

Geoffrey Charles looks at his mother in the mirror, over her shoulder. They make a charming tableau.

CUT TO:

22: INT. NAMPARA HOUSE, PARLOUR – DUSK 21

Ross returns from Truro and is so delighted to find Dwight there he barely notices Demelza, who has changed and prettified herself.

ROSS Dwight! This is a pleasant surprise. You'll stay to supper?

He goes to pick up Jeremy, who is playing on the floor. Dwight glances at Demelza. Her face betrays the smallest sign of disappointment (she had hoped to have Ross to herself).

DWIGHT *(a glance at Demelza)* If you're sure—

DEMELZA There's licky pie!

Ross puts Jeremy down to play again and he and Dwight take their places at the table. Demelza brings food to the table and serves.

ROSS I came just now from Killewarren. Ray Penvenen was up in arms—

DEMELZA At what?

ROSS His niece's arrival. He was not expecting her.

Dwight flushes and looks uncomfortable.

ROSS *(cont'd) (to Dwight)* Were *you?*

DWIGHT As a matter of fact – yes.

A pause. No one seems to know how to proceed – or whether Dwight wishes to be questioned further. Eventually:

DWIGHT *(cont'd)* The attachment's bad, I know – and it's my weakness that I cannot shake it. No doubt it will end badly and I'll have my just deserts.

ROSS Possibly. *(beat)* Though it seems to me fate does as it pleases – and it has nothing to do with our strength or our weakness.

Demelza watches Ross closely. To what is he referring? Is this connected in any way with Elizabeth?

ROSS *(cont'd)* Take Francis. Was there ever a sorrier or less deserved end? To walk out of this house and within an hour to drown like a dog in a well? And for *nothing!* That's what I most deplore – the wanton, useless *waste* of it. The quirks of fate which make nonsense of *all* our striving. You've seen me in the worst of it, Dwight. Julia's death and much beside. If you can see a difference between strength or weakness shown, you're a better man than I.

They eat in silence. Demelza is acutely aware that so far Ross has barely noticed her and has addressed all of the above to Dwight. Eventually:

DEMELZA That's true, Ross. But is that *all* the truth?

Ross turns to her, as if finally realizing she's there.

DEMELZA *(cont'd)* Luck's been against us, but it's also been *with* us. Grace is failing, but Leisure prospers. You were arrested, yet then acquitted. And if there was Julia, there's also Jeremy. Mebbe fate has deserted us – but Dwight may be more fortunate. Francis was not. But p'r'aps – *Elizabeth* will be?

A look between Ross and Demelza tells Dwight all he needs to know. Francis's death has had consequences for all of them.

CUT TO:

23: EXT. NAMPARA HOUSE – DAWN 22

A cold wintry dawn breaks over Nampara.

CUT TO:

24: INT. NAMPARA HOUSE, ROSS & DEMELZA'S BEDROOM – DAY 22

Demelza opens her eyes, turns over – and realizes Ross has already left the bed.

CUT TO:

25: EXT. WHEAL GRACE – DAY 22

Henshawe and Ross survey the mine. The engine seems to be making an unhealthy clanking noise.

HENSHAWE Something amiss with that engine.

ROSS I've sent for Trevithick.

HENSHAWE Is it worth the while – f' th' little she's yielding—?

ROSS I wondered that.

HENSHAWE 'Tis a cryin' shame we never found the lode Mark Daniel spoke of. *(then)* But perhaps he was mistook.

ROSS He was an experienced miner. He would know what he was looking at.

HENSHAWE Then it's a pity he can't be found and asked the question. *(beat)* Where?

Ross nods. It's clear from his expression that this has given him food for thought.

CUT TO:

26: INT. NAMPARA HOUSE, PARLOUR – DAY 22

Verity and Demelza sit by the fire. Jeremy plays on the floor.

VERITY Ross continues to vex society.

DEMELZA What's he done now?

VERITY What has he *not* done? Graced the Poldark family pew at church? Taken his seat as a magistrate on the bench? As head of the Poldark family, these things are expected of him.

DEMELZA Well, you know Ross and expectation! Besides, I have a suspicion he'd think he was *more* 'n fulfillin' his duties in *other* ways.

Verity gives her a searching look.

DEMELZA *(cont'd)* Towards Elizabeth, f'r instance?

VERITY Does that trouble you?

DEMELZA Ross never tells me what goes on in his meetings with her. And I never ask 'im.

VERITY But if you're concerned—?

DEMELZA It d' seem to me that havin' a husband is like goin' to church. Either you believe in something or you don't. If you don't, then why go at all? If you do, you've no cause to keep askin' for proof.

VERITY And do you – believe?

DEMELZA Most o' th' time.

She picks Jeremy up to play with him. She seems sanguine enough but Verity senses her deep unease.

CUT TO:

27: EXT. WOODLAND – DAY 22

Dwight rides through the woods till he sees a glade where Caroline, already dismounted, is standing. This is the first time they've met in seven months. He leaps off his horse and goes towards her. She turns, sees him. They fall into each other's arms. Eventually, reluctantly, they pull apart.

CAROLINE Seven months has seemed a lifetime.

DWIGHT Did my letters not satisfy you?

CAROLINE They evoked pleasure and pain in equal measure.

He moves to kiss her again. She turns her head away, half-teasing, half-distracted.

DWIGHT What is it?

CAROLINE Forgive me, I'm a little at sea. All I know for certain is that my uncle's furious. I'm my own mistress, yet no freer to follow my heart. But I'm here – and you're here – and perhaps that's all that matters.

Sensing her confusion, her need to acclimatize herself, he makes no move to kiss her again. She seems grateful for it.

CAROLINE *(cont'd)* I met your Captain Poldark again.

DWIGHT He told me.

CAROLINE Would you be jealous if I said I admire him greatly?

DWIGHT I admire him myself. He's an exceptional man and a dear friend. I only wish his circumstances were happier.

CAROLINE Is his cousin's pretty widow the 'circumstance' – or is it some other matter?

DWIGHT A financial matter.

CAROLINE And his wife? She seems to be universally adored. Is she the sort of woman that all men desire except her husband? It so often happens. No great incentive for marriage! Don't you think I should be ill advised to try it?

DWIGHT Not if you choose the right man.

CAROLINE Should I choose a miracle-worker?

Dwight smiles bashfully.

CAROLINE *(cont'd)* Who now has an adoring Rosina and a crowd of sickly miners battering at his door? There can't be many physicians of your calibre who use all their energies to help the poor. How do you live?

DWIGHT On an income of forty pounds a year from the two mines, plus whatever my patients can spare me. I agree it's very little.

CAROLINE But could you not set up in Oxford or Bath – where you may work among people of your own kind? Charity is a noble impulse – but should it not begin at home?

DWIGHT Even in Bath or Oxford the poor will always be in greater need of attention than the rich. Besides, I've no wish to become a society pet.

CAROLINE Is that what you think *I* am?

DWIGHT No, Caroline, I would never suggest that – or wish you to think—

CAROLINE That you are the most noble of men? Or I the most vacuous of women? *(before he can protest)* The sun has gone in. I'm cold. Let's ride.

She mounts her horse without waiting for his assistance.

DWIGHT Would you have me pretend to be other than I am?

CAROLINE I would have you believe you are better than you think. *(then)* Race me!

Without another word, she spurs her horse and races out of the wood. Caught off-guard only for a second, Dwight spurs his horse and races after her.

CUT TO:

28: EXT. OPEN COUNTRYSIDE – DAY 22

Caroline and Dwight crash through the undergrowth, clear a ditch then gallop across open fields. At first Caroline is out in front, then Dwight begins to gain and almost catches her. Then she takes another brook in her stride and outstrips him again. He redoubles his efforts and begins to gain on her once more. Soon they are racing neck and neck, Caroline laughing, Dwight determined. Eventually, as they gallop up a slope, by a clever manoeuvre, Dwight gains the upper hand and reaches the crest of a hill ahead of Caroline. Finally she joins him, both of them flushed and exhilarated.

CAROLINE You're an accomplished rider, Dr Enys. Clearly such talents would be wasted in city life.

DWIGHT I have other talents – which would not.

CAROLINE But you can't bear the thought of Bath.

DWIGHT And you can't bear the thought of marriage.

CAROLINE To a man of talent, anything is possible.

DWIGHT Without you, *nothing* is possible.

A moment between them, then without warning Caroline spurs her horse and rides away, leaving Dwight to follow in her wake.

CUT TO:

29: INT. SAWLE KIDDLEY – DAY 22

The kiddley is full. Ross sits with Trencrom in one corner. In another corner is Rosina, demonstrating to Charlie, Jacka, Ted and assorted villagers the miracle of her mended leg. Ross has just explained his mission to Trencrom.

TRENCROM Mark Daniel? 'Twould be too risky, I believe, for him to return to England. Have you asked my men for news of him?

ROSS I thought to come to you first.

Trencrom nods in acknowledgement of the courtesy.

ROSS *(cont'd)* Besides, I'm not sure whom to trust. The informer who answers to Vercoe might also report to McNeil.

TRENCROM McNeil claims convalescence, not the Trade, has brought him here.

ROSS You believe him?

TRENCROM Not a jot. *(then)* Our trusted band grows smaller. I've removed Vigus. Now I think to replace Hoblyn.

Ross glances over to where Jacka sits with Charlie, Rosina and various other villagers.

ROSS Why d'you suspect him?

TRENCROM I suspect everyone. 'Tis the safest way.

ROSS I think you're mistook. Jacka's a surly fellow, but I doubt he'd betray his friends.

TRENCROM Any man will betray his friends if the price is right.

Ted Carkeek is just passing.

ROSS As Ted knows to his cost. Ted! How are you? Recovered from your sentence?

TED Three months' hard labour did feel like three years! An' still I'm no closer to knowin' who betrayed me!

He heads off. Ross returns to his conversation with Trencrom.

TRENCROM But to Mark Daniel. I could put the word out? Get a letter to him?

ROSS I'd be most grateful.

TRENCROM And in exchange?

ROSS Yes—?

TRENCROM One drawback to your cove. You've always insisted, haven't you, that all must be done in a single night? Don't blame you. But 'tis deuced awkward. If we could store some of the goods – two, three days. Ten men do in three nights what thirty do in one. Less chance for the informer. Get the cargo ashore and *hide* it. If you catch my drift.

ROSS *(Slowly it dawns on him.)* Go on.

TRENCROM Your mine is not yet paying—

ROSS Do you wish me to confirm that or acknowledge the blackmail?

TRENCROM Oh please! Between friends? We work together. No wish to offend. Would be willing to make some small extra payment for the inconvenience. A goodwill gesture, so to speak.

Ross eyes Trencrom narrowly. After a pause:

ROSS How much of a gesture?

CUT TO:

30: INT. NAMPARA HOUSE, STABLE – DAY 22

Demelza is brushing out the stable. Ross has just told her of Trencrom's proposal.

DEMELZA A secret cache? On our land?

ROSS To store goods during a run – so they can be carried away at leisure—

DEMELZA Or *found* by the gaugers – and you carried away in chains!

ROSS In two weeks' time I shall be in chains regardless!

Demelza considers this a while. Then:

DEMELZA I dislike it, Ross.

ROSS If I go to prison for debt, this will mean more money coming in. And the quicker the debt is paid, the quicker I'm out again.

DEMELZA Unless the goods be found in our house, then you'll be in prison longer still!

ROSS The cache will be built in the library. It can be done in one night – with four or five to dig it – and six or eight to use it thereafter.

DEMELZA And the informer—?

ROSS Trencrom will hand-pick his men.

DEMELZA And in return?

ROSS Twenty-five guineas per cargo. *(beat)* And a promise to find Mark Daniel.

DEMELZA How will that help?

ROSS He's our last chance of finding copper. Of making the mine pay. If Grace fails, how will I repay the Warleggans?

DEMELZA Why can you not appeal to your friends? Ray Penvenen – Horace Treneglos – even Trencrom? Would they not put up the money to save you from bankruptcy?

ROSS The sum is too great—

DEMELZA You mean your pride is!

ROSS No one of sense, however much a friend, would loan money to a man with a failing mine. For the simple reason that they would never get it back. But if I could demonstrate that the mine might prosper, I could borrow against its better days. But till I find Mark Daniel—

Demelza is thoughtful. Ross senses she's softening.

ROSS *(cont'd)* Do I have your consent?

Something about his assumption that she will agree riles Demelza.

DEMELZA You durst ask me that? Knowin' full well you'd do exactly what you please, with or without my say?

Furious, she thrusts the broom at him and stalks out of the stable. Ross shakes his head, but he knows she has every right to be angry.

CUT TO:

31: INT. KILLEWARREN – NIGHT 22

Caroline is dining alone with Ray. He glances suspiciously at her. She pretends not to notice and continues to feed titbits to Horace. Eventually:

CAROLINE Were you ever involved in Ross Poldark's copper-smelting venture?

RAY PENVENEN I made a minor investment. It was an ill-conceived enterprise. Everyone lost money.

CAROLINE Except the Warleggans.

RAY PENVENEN Why d'you ask?

CAROLINE I believe Ross Poldark had some debts from that time. The Warleggans acquired them and are pressing for bankruptcy.

RAY PENVENEN You're very well informed.

CAROLINE Less than I'd like to be.

RAY PENVENEN *(terse)* No doubt Dr Enys could enlighten you further.

A tense moment. Then:

CAROLINE I believe I shall ride into Truro tomorrow. It's a poor place to shop but I need new buckles for my shoes.

RAY PENVENEN You are your own mistress now, Caroline.

CAROLINE So I am.

RAY PENVENEN Though I think you should not allow a natural pleasure in your new freedom to override the requirements of good conduct. *(beat)* To ride far and unattended in the company of a young man of eligible years is to invite comment of an unsavoury nature. No doubt it was innocently done, but it is neither fair to me, who may seem to countenance it, or to the young man, who may derive from it ambitions beyond his proper sphere.

CAROLINE Thank you for your concern, Uncle. If my conduct so troubles you, would it not be better for me to quit this house and live elsewhere?

RAY PENVENEN That would be an excellent solution – were it not for the affection we hold for each other.

CAROLINE *(to Horace)* Uncle Ray is becoming cross with me, Horace. There may shortly be angry words – which both of us will regret. Don't you think we had better change the subject?

RAY PENVENEN *(after a pause)* At what time tomorrow shall you require the carriage?

CAROLINE At nine, thank you, Uncle.

She gives him a beaming smile. Peace seems to be restored.

CUT TO:

32: INT. KILLEWARREN – NIGHT 22

Caroline has gone to bed. Ray is writing a letter.

RAY PENVENEN *(VO)* 'Dear Dr Enys, I should be obliged if you would attend on me tomorrow morning between ten-thirty and eleven . . .'

CUT TO:

33: INT. TRENWITH HOUSE, GREAT HALL – DAY 23

Verity comes in, carrying a small travelling box. Elizabeth, Aunt Agatha and Geoffrey Charles are at breakfast.

VERITY My dears, you do recall that I'm to return home today?

AUNT AGATHA Fiddlesticks! 'Tis nearly Christmas. A woman should be with her family at such time.

VERITY My husband would agree with you.

AUNT AGATHA Pooh! Men have business to attend to. I doubt he's even noticed you're gone.

VERITY His letters suggest otherwise *(heat)* In any case, I've missed him a great deal. And have every intention of making up for lost time!

Aunt Agatha is so astonished by this robust reply, she almost chokes on her breakfast.

VERITY *(cont'd)* *(to Elizabeth)* And you—

ELIZABETH I have an invitation to Nampara.

VERITY *(surprised)* Shall you accept?

ELIZABETH Geoffrey Charles is eager.

VERITY Are *you?*

ELIZABETH I think it will do me good to have more varied company.

She returns to her breakfast and avoids Verity's scrutiny. Verity joins them at breakfast. She is not reassured by this development.

CUT TO:

34: INT. WARLEGGAN HOUSE, GEORGE'S DEN – DAY 23

George is at his desk reading a document. Cary comes in. George waves the document at him.

GEORGE These guests—?

CARY Are chosen specifically for their use to us – in business, in society – in terms of the future—

GEORGE *(reads)* Arabella Trevelyan – the Honourable Maria Penrose – Eliza Courtney-Prowse? These girls must be all of seventeen.

CARY And prime breeding stock. You may examine their teeth, if you choose.

GEORGE I think I will ride to Trenwith.

He gets up to leave. Cary detains him.

CARY When will you call in the loans on that estate?

George halts, restrains himself from a sharp retort.

CARY *(cont'd)* What's to be gained by keeping in the good books of some poverty-stricken widow in her late twenties?

GEORGE I could alleviate her poverty if I chose. But I choose to let her feel it. She has made her bed. Now she must lie in it.

He walks out.

CUT TO:

35: INT. TRENWITH HOUSE, LIBRARY – DAY 23

A miserable fire sputters and hisses in the grate. Ross pokes at it.

ROSS This kindling is damp. Has it been seasoned?

ELIZABETH I've no idea.

ROSS *(smiles)* Of course not.

Then he sees the box of candied fruits.

ROSS *(cont'd)* I'm glad to see you allow yourself *some* luxuries.

ELIZABETH Oh – er – no – 'tis a present for Geoffrey Charles. *(beat)* From George.

ROSS Has he been here?

ELIZABETH I had to admit him, Ross. He's my chief creditor. It was difficult to see him without you here but he quite understood that you could not meet.

ROSS And his views on the debts?

ELIZABETH Very generous. They always have been. He offered to waive the interest indefinitely. Of course I could not accept.

ROSS Why not?

ELIZABETH There have been enough favours. I don't feel justified in accepting more.

ROSS That depends. If you refuse his favours out of loyalty to me, it's a mistaken loyalty. My quarrel with George is not your quarrel. If he wants to win your approval, let him. You don't have to *like* him. *(then)* If, on the other hand, you feel you would be compromised by accepting such favours – that by becoming his friend—

ELIZABETH I might alienate people I like better?

ROSS That you must decide for yourself.

ELIZABETH I already have.

Ross is quietly pleased. There is another frisson of connection between them. Elizabeth shivers and pulls her shawl more closely round her.

ROSS You're shivering.

He moves towards her. She pulls back.

ROSS *(cont'd)* I wish I could help you. This hardship is too much.

ELIZABETH For my own sake I can bear it. But for my son – for his future – *(then)* When Francis came into his estate, there was money to live on – comfort – dignity. It breaks my heart to think that Geoffrey Charles will have so little to his name.

ROSS It breaks my heart too.

Another intense moment of connection between them.

ELIZABETH Nothing to be done. Is there?

Out on Ross. His expression says: 'I wonder.'

CUT TO:

36: INT. PASCOE'S OFFICE – DAY 23

Pascoe and Ross meet by arrangement.

ROSS My remaining shares in Wheal Leisure. What would you say is their worth?

PASCOE Upward of six hundred pounds?

ROSS *(considers, then)* Sell them.

PASCOE You wish to devote the money to Wheal Grace.

ROSS No. To a special purpose. *(then)* Francis's widow and family are in dire need.

PASCOE More so than you?

ROSS Two years ago Francis sank his last six hundred pounds into Wheal Grace. I want Elizabeth Poldark to have it back.

PASCOE Will she accept it?

ROSS Of course not. Which is why I need your help. *(then)* When my shares in Leisure are sold, you will make an offer for Geoffrey Charles's holding in Wheal Grace. On behalf of an anonymous client whom you represent. Elizabeth will accept – and the money can be transferred to her.

PASCOE So – do I understand you aright? You are offering six hundred pounds for a half-share in a mine which is about to close?

ROSS Correct.

PASCOE As your banker and friend I must advise against. You cannot afford it. And you have your own wife and son to care for. Would it not seem as if you value your cousin-in-law's comfort ahead of hers?

ROSS It might. If I chose to tell her. Which I do not. *(then)* I am here. Francis is not. Demelza has resources which Elizabeth does not. She's a miner's daughter. She has learned to survive. Elizabeth – is a gentlewoman.

PASCOE And you are a madman.

ROSS A madman who can now order his life with a clear conscience.

CUT TO:

37: EXT. KILLEWARREN – DAY 23

Dwight rides across the fields towards Killewarren.
CUT TO:

38: INT. KILLEWARREN – DAY 23

Dwight is shown into the room where Ray sits waiting. He glances round, half-hoping to see Caroline. Ray notices.

RAY PENVENEN My niece is in Truro. I've taken the opportunity to summon you. I imagine you've some idea why?

DWIGHT I don't think it's for me to speculate, sir.

RAY PENVENEN I might wish you'd showed such delicacy in *all* your dealings.

DWIGHT I'm sorry you think I have not.

RAY PENVENEN I refer to your friendship with my niece.

DWIGHT In what way do you consider that offensive?

RAY PENVENEN Come, sir, you cannot be ignorant of the ways of the world. For some time now you've been paying her attentions. Have you considered how this might reflect upon her reputation?

DWIGHT Sir?

RAY PENVENEN Caroline is a delightful young woman – and a persuasive one – and capricious. 'Tis not uncommon for her to take a sudden liking to someone – and then to drop them just as swiftly.

DWIGHT And you suppose she will do that with me?

RAY PENVENEN Even if I did not, I should be opposed to these clandestine meetings. As for any serious attachment – to a young man of your station—?

DWIGHT I am a gentleman, sir.

RAY PENVENEN And she is an heiress. And too important a person to become entangled with a penniless country doctor.

DWIGHT Is that not for her to decide?

RAY PENVENEN Caroline must marry with my consent – or she will not inherit a penny. She has been brought up in the greatest possible luxury. D'you suppose she'll sacrifice that for the little you have to offer?

DWIGHT She has given me cause to suppose so—

RAY PENVENEN But it may be you think she has a private fortune of her own—

DWIGHT I neither know nor care what she has.

RAY PENVENEN Six thousand pounds, sir – is all you could hope to get if you married her.

Dwight is silent a moment. Ray mistakenly thinks his words have hit home.

DWIGHT Till now I've suffered your comments with a due degree of civility. But there are limits, sir. God knows I've never given you cause to suppose me a fortune-hunter – and if you imagine that no man without an eye to her inheritance could fall in love with your niece, then you greatly underrate her charms and insult us both.

RAY PENVENEN I trust I have made my views clear?

DWIGHT And in so doing you have given me hope. *(beat)* Caroline's fortune is less than I thought. I'm glad of it. A penniless doctor could wed such a fortune yet not be eclipsed by it.

RAY PENVENEN You will leave this house now and never return. You will cease all communication with my niece—

DWIGHT Caroline is of age, sir. Your control may be exercised within these walls, but not beyond.

RAY PENVENEN I see I have gravely mistaken your character, Dr Enys. But at least we now understand each other.

DWIGHT Yes, sir. We now understand each other.

Dwight walks out.

CUT TO:

39: EXT. TRENWITH HOUSE – DAY 23

A carriage waits at the door. Verity comes out with Elizabeth and Geoffrey Charles. Aunt Agatha is seen, scowling at the window. Verity kisses Geoffrey Charles goodbye.

VERITY Goodbye, little man. Look after Mama this Christmas. It's what your papa would wish.

Then she turns to Elizabeth.

VERITY *(cont'd)* You may think me interfering, but I urge you to let Ross and Demelza keep this Christmas to themselves.

ELIZABETH But—

VERITY For your sake as well as theirs.

Before Elizabeth can argue, Verity embraces her, then gets into the carriage. Elizabeth and Geoffrey Charles wave to her as she rides away. Elizabeth remains, thoughtful.

CUT TO:

40: INT. WARLEGGAN HOUSE, GEORGE'S DEN – DAY 23

George is at his desk, Cary is reading. A note is brought to George. He reads it.

GEORGE Tankard informs me some Wheal Leisure shares have just come onto the market.

They look at each other. Both are thinking the same thing: Let's buy them.

CUT TO:

41: INT. NAMPARA HOUSE, LIBRARY – DAY 23

Ross returns home to find Demelza standing by the door to the library, watching beadily as Zacky and Paul move some large oak chests and a rug away from the spot where the cache will be sited. She raises her eyebrow at him.

ROSS Nothing will happen till nightfall.

DEMELZA Well, that d' make *all* the difference!

ROSS Demelza—?

But she's already walked off upstairs.

CUT TO:

42: EXT. NAMPARA HOUSE – DUSK 23

Dusk is falling as a line of men, silhouetted against the darkening sky, walk up to Nampara, carrying spades and pickaxes. Amongst them are Paul, Zacky and Ted.

CUT TO:

43: INT. WARLEGGAN HOUSE – DUSK 23

George is entertaining Mrs Chynoweth. Cary looks bored but George is pulling out all the stops.

GEORGE London is so diverting. I may well take a house for the season next year. May I hope to be honoured by a visit from yourself?

MRS CHYNOWETH I'd be delighted, sir. And I'd like to think Elizabeth could be persuaded—

GEORGE Once she's out of mourning? But I dare not hope for it. She's been closeted away at Trenwith for so long. Yet society deserves to see more of its rarest treasures – yourself included—

Mrs Chynoweth simpers and smiles.

GEORGE *(cont'd)* Although, should we persuade her to venture, you must promise not to stand too close to her, for fear your combined brilliance should dazzle us all!

Cary raises his eyebrows and flicks a sliver of chicken to Ambrose.

CUT TO:

44: INT. NAMPARA HOUSE, LIBRARY – NIGHT 23

Demelza stands watching as Ross and the team build the cache. Some are digging a hole in the floor, others are constructing the wooden frame which will go inside. Ross is so immersed in the digging, he doesn't even notice Demelza, watching at the door. Presently, she adjourns to the kitchen.

CUT TO:

45: INT. NAMPARA HOUSE, KITCHEN – NIGHT 23

Demelza pours a glass of port for herself and Prudie.

DEMELZA What can I do? Can't beg for money. Can't earn it. Can't dig f'r it. Can't tell him *not* to dig! *(i.e. in the library)* What use am I? *(then)* He should've wed someone like Caroline Penvenen!

Prudie eyes her narrowly. Should she intervene or not? She decides she must.

PRUDIE I've know'd Cap'n Ross since he were a whelp. Since his mother died. She was a gentle soul. An' a wise. An' I know what she'd say.

DEMELZA What?

PRUDIE That her lad had met his match.

DEMELZA Mebbe that was true once. But now? Now I'm his torment!

PRUDIE And she would've said, serve him right!

DEMELZA I could *crown* him! *(then)* An' he scarcely knows I'm there.

Suddenly there's a rap on the front door. Before Demelza can intervene, Prudie has rushed off to open it.

DEMELZA *(cont'd)* Prudie! – wait! – don' open it!

CUT TO:

46: INT. NAMPARA HOUSE, HALLWAY – NIGHT 23

Before Demelza can stop her, Prudie has opened the door. Demelza rushes to intervene. But to her relief, it's someone she recognizes: Charlie Kempthorne.

DEMELZA Oh! – Charlie – I did fear 'twas th' gaugers—

CHARLIE Why should they suspect a gen'leman's house, ma'am? I come with a message for Cap'n Ross.

DEMELZA Wait there. I'll fetch him.

Demelza goes to the library. She tries to prevent Charlie coming too close to look in.

DEMELZA *(cont'd)* Ross? There's a visitor.

Charlie glances round the door into the library, but Ross comes out quickly and closes the door behind him.

ROSS What is it, Charlie?

CHARLIE Mr Trencrom say if 'ee wish to write a letter to Mark Daniel in France, do so and I'll see it gets aboard when *The One & All* sails.

Ross nods gratefully and ushers Charlie into the parlour. Demelza, feeling she might as well be invisible, returns to the kitchen.

CUT TO:

47: INT. NAMPARA HOUSE, ROSS & DEMELZA'S BEDROOM – NIGHT 23

Ross comes to bed in the early hours of the morning. He glances at the bed, assumes Demelza's asleep. But she's not. She glances at him as he undresses. As he gets into bed she wonders whether to make a move on him. Eventually she turns to him, slides her fingers lightly across his shoulders. He doesn't protest. But neither does he respond. To her dismay he's already fast asleep.

CUT TO:

48: EXT. WHEAL LEISURE – DAWN 24

Dawn breaks over Wheal Leisure. Ross stands looking down at the mine with Zacky.

ROSS Blood – and tears – and time – and money—

ZACKY Leisure served you well.

ROSS She'll serve George well. But he'll never love her as she deserves.

ZACKY You still have Grace.

ROSS For how long?

CUT TO:

49: INT. TRENWITH HOUSE, LIBRARY – DAY 24

Ross is shown in. He finds Elizabeth in turmoil.

ELIZABETH Ross! I'm so glad you're here. I want to know what I must do.

She hands him a letter.

ROSS From Pascoe?

ELIZABETH An offer has been made for Geoffrey Charles's share of Wheal Grace. *(then)* It's not the Warleggans. I've already ascertained that. Is it not astonishing?

ROSS It's a good price.

ELIZABETH But that someone should offer as much for his share as Francis first put into it? Has there been some new discovery of ore?

ROSS Far from it. Everyone knows we must close soon. *(returns to the letter)* 'The prospective buyer is a gentleman who wishes to remain nameless but who has your son's best interest at heart.' Remarkable.

ELIZABETH But what do you advise? Should I consider the offer?

ROSS Consider? You should accept it without delay.

ELIZABETH Our situation here – the money would make all the difference – but for you? Are you sure it won't compromise you? Your new partner, a stranger? I know you think it best for us, but I'd hate to think I was taking advantage of our friendship.

ROSS You must sell. It will enormously ease your situation. I'm only grateful for your hesitation – and for your loyalty all these months.

ELIZABETH Loyalty's not all on one side, Ross. Nor ever has been.

A moment of intense connection between them. Then:

ELIZABETH *(cont'd)* I regret I must decline your invitation for Christmas. I believe Francis would want me to spend it in his house.

ROSS And I regret that circumstances are such that I cannot take care of you as I might wish.

ELIZABETH We both regret that, Ross.

Another moment of intense connection. Then he kisses her hand and goes out.

CUT TO:

50: EXT. SAWLE VILLAGE – DAY 24

There are few signs of Christmas amongst the poor. Dwight can't help but notice the squalor and deprivation as he knocks at the door of Charlie's cottage. Charlie opens the door.

CHARLIE 'Tis good of 'ee to call, sur. My Lottie's some slight.

CUT TO:

51: INT. KILLEWARREN – NIGHT 24

Caroline (and Horace) and Ray eat a solitary dinner in silence. Caroline seems quiet and submissive. Ray glances at her.

RAY PENVENEN You've had time to consider your position?

CAROLINE I have.

RAY PENVENEN You must understand that though I might tolerate the young man on a professional basis, I cannot permit him to have sight of you again after his impudent pretensions to your hand.

CAROLINE I misunderstood his attentions, Uncle. Now that I apprehend them, I will know how to behave in future.

Ray squeezes her hand affectionately. She continues to eat in silence. But there is something about her expression which tells us that she has no intention of submitting to her uncle's wishes.
CUT TO:

52: EXT. OPEN COUNTRYSIDE – NIGHT 24

Dwight and Caroline go riding together again.
CUT TO:

53: INT. NAMPARA HOUSE, PARLOUR – DAY 25

Christmas Day. Demelza puts a scrawny roasted chicken on the table along with a few potatoes and other meagre garnishes. Ross is reading a newspaper and doesn't seem to notice. Defiant, Demelza takes a sprig of holly and places it on top of the chicken. Ross doesn't even look up from his newspaper.

ROSS War now seems inevitable.

DEMELZA *(ironic)* Merry Christmas, Ross!

Ross is so preoccupied he doesn't hear her and keeps on reading.

ROSS Pitt's called out the military – *(no reply)* and the French are in Antwerp.

DEMELZA *(sharp)* Gravy?

ROSS What? Oh – yes – thank you –

Now as she hands him the plate, he seems to recover his manners.

ROSS *(cont'd)* I invited Dwight to join us—

DEMELZA Oh?

ROSS He declined.

DEMELZA Just as well! 'Twould 'a meant two mouthfuls apiece instead o' three!

ROSS I expect he's meeting Caroline.

DEMELZA I expect he is.

Demelza feeds Jeremy. Of the three of them, he is by far the most vocal. Then Prudie comes in with a note. She hands it to Ross. He opens it, looks hopeful.

PRUDIE From Mr Trencrom. Brought 'ere by one Jud Paynter esquire!

DEMELZA Will he not come in and join us?

PRUDIE Oh no, not he! Jud Paynter be too busy on 'Trencrom's business' to be takin' Christmas cheer wi' the likes o' we! Too busy sluicin' 'is throat wi' Christmas rum, more like!

Ross's face has fallen. The letter has not brought good news.

ROSS Mark Daniel—

DEMELZA Yes?

ROSS Has apparently disappeared from the face of the earth.

DEMELZA Oh. *(then)* Leastways now we know.

ROSS *(grimly cheerful)* Yes. Now we know our last hope is gone!

He turns back to the newspaper and continues to eat his food. While he's immersed in the newspaper, Demelza flings the sprig of holly onto his plate and defiantly leaves the table.

CUT TO:

54: INT. TRENWITH HOUSE, LIBRARY – DAY 25

Elizabeth hands out tiny gifts to Aunt Agatha, Mrs Chynoweth and Geoffrey Charles. They are clustered round the miserable fire and don't appear very festive.

ELIZABETH *(to Geoffrey Charles)* I wish it could be more, my darling. Perhaps *next* Christmas—

Aunt Agatha has opened her present – a small bottle – sniffed it and wrinkled up her nose.

AUNT AGATHA Rose water? Do I require a fumigant?

ELIZABETH No, Aunt, but—

AUNT AGATHA Francis always knew what I liked. *(beat)* Brandywine. Port. Canary. Preferably all three.

Mrs Chynoweth unwraps a shawl – with which she's clearly struggling to be impressed.

MRS CHYNOWETH How charming. Did you make it yourself?

ELIZABETH Yes, Mama.

MRS CHYNOWETH Just the thing for guarding the fire and avoiding society!

AUNT AGATHA Then we'll all require one. Get out your needles, Elizabeth.

Mrs Tabb appears.

MRS TABB Mr George Warleggan.

George comes striding in, bows graciously. He's attractively though not ostentatiously dressed.

GEORGE My compliments of the season, dear ladies. I was passing and wondered if I might beg the favour of Elizabeth's company for a few hours? We have a small gathering at Cardew. Only if she can be spared, of course.

ELIZABETH I fear I cannot. We intend to keep Christmas quietly, just among ourselves—

MRS CHYNOWETH Elizabeth, dear, allow me to assist you in choosing a suitable gown?

Mrs Chynoweth smiles insistently at Elizabeth and gestures her out of the room. George is left alone with Geoffrey Charles and Aunt Agatha.

AUNT AGATHA *(to Geoffrey Charles)* Sit by me, child. Beware that man's pitchfork. And his tail.

She glares at George. Who smiles back politely.

CUT TO:

55: EXT. MARKET PLACE – DAY 25

George drives Elizabeth in his carriage. Impoverished villagers stare mournfully at the carriage as it passes. Then, to Elizabeth's surprise, George halts. A few scrawny children run up. George throws a handful of coins into the air and drives on.

ELIZABETH That was very generous.

GEORGE These are difficult times for the poor. One does what one can.

CUT TO:

56: EXT. WARLEGGAN HOUSE – DAY 25

George and Elizabeth drive up to Warleggan House. Footmen come out to attend them. George assists Elizabeth from the carriage and escorts her into the house.

CUT TO:

57: INT. WARLEGGAN HOUSE – DAY 25

Escorted in on George's arm, Elizabeth feels as if she's stepped into another world. No expense has been spared in decoration and hospitality. She is visibly impressed.

GEORGE May I introduce you to my friends?

He takes her over to a group of young women who are dressed in the height of fashion.

GEORGE *(cont'd)* Mistress Poldark, may I present – Miss Arabella Trevelyan – Miss Eliza Courtney-Prowse – the Honourable Miss Maria Penrose.

The women all bow to each other and look each other up and down. Elizabeth feels dowdy and old-fashioned next to these gorgeous creatures, who nevertheless seem a little in awe of Elizabeth's superior beauty. George walks Elizabeth away from the group.

GEORGE *(cont'd)* I wanted to ask your advice.

ELIZABETH Yes?

GEORGE As Geoffrey Charles's godfather, I will of course be responsible for the cost of his education until he completes university—

ELIZABETH Oh, but that's too generous – I cannot allow—

GEORGE I was not asking for your permission, Elizabeth – only your *opinion* – as to whether you favour Oxford or Cambridge?

ELIZABETH But this is beyond anything, George – I don't know what to say—

GEORGE Then may I leave you to ponder while I fulfil my obligations to Miss Trevelyan? *(leading her to a group of gentlemen)* I believe you know Sir John, Lord Devoran, Mr Alfred Barbary—

ELIZABETH Gentlemen.

They all greet each other. Then George leaves Elizabeth in their company and returns to the group of young ladies.

ON ELIZABETH: Trying to smile at the attentions of the group of gentlemen who surround her. But she can't help watching George.

ON GEORGE: Lavishing attention on Arabella Trevelyan, who is giggling and blushing and fluttering her fan. Dancing is taking place. George escorts her to join the dance.

ON ELIZABETH: Watching George dancing with Arabella Trevelyan. Thinking how well he dances, how handsome he looks. Hearing voices around her: 'I suspect it won't be long before we see a Mistress George Warleggan', 'Odds on it's the Penrose girl' and 'He won't be satisfied with anything less than an Honourable'.

CARY Nor should he be!

To her dismay, Elizabeth realizes she's actually jealous.

CUT TO:

58: EXT. NAMPARA HOUSE – DAWN 26

Dawn establisher.

CUT TO:

59: INT. NAMPARA HOUSE, PARLOUR – DAY 26

The day after Christmas. Ross, ready to leave for Truro, is sitting with Jeremy on his knee.

ROSS I've discussed it with Pascoe. We wait until late in the day to tell Cary I cannot pay. Then there's a chance they won't come to arrest me till tomorrow. So we shall have one final night at home together.

Demelza appears, dressed in her riding habit.

ROSS *(cont'd)* Where are you going?

DEMELZA *(brisk)* With you. If you think you're to play the hero an' face this alone, you're greatly mistook.

She takes Jeremy from him and hands him to Prudie.

CUT TO:

60: EXT. TRURO STREET – DAY 26

Ross and Demelza walk through the town. Ross glances sideways at Demelza – as if impressed by her no-nonsense approach.

CUT TO:

61: INT. PASCOE'S OFFICE – DAY 26

Demelza and Ross are shown into Pascoe's office. He's genuinely surprised to see Demelza.

PASCOE Mistress Poldark. This is a surprise. Something to fortify you?

DEMELZA A little port?

Pascoe serves port for all. Demelza gulps hers gratefully, then remembers her manners and tries to sip it more slowly.

PASCOE As I told you, the Warleggans declined to extend the loan. 'Tis my suspicion they care nothing for the money. What they want is the man.

ROSS And here he is.

Pascoe gives Ross an odd look – as if he's struggling to contain some great news.

PASCOE Yet I think perhaps they may be disappointed.

DEMELZA How?

Pascoe hesitates. He wants to relay this news in the least sensational way possible.

PASCOE I recently received a visit—

ROSS From?

PASCOE A person who wishes to remain nameless—

CUT TO:

62: INT. PASCOE'S OFFICE (FLASHBACK) – DAY 23 (WINTER 1792)

Pascoe is closing up for the day when a clerk's voice announces: 'A Miss Penvenen to see you, sir.' Pascoe is surprised. Caroline sweeps in majestically and holds out her hand.

CAROLINE Harris Pascoe?

PASCOE *(bows)* Miss Penvenen. I have the honour to know your uncle—

CAROLINE You are Ross Poldark's banker?

PASCOE Yes.

CAROLINE I understand he has a bill out which is shortly due for redemption.

PASCOE 'Tis not my custom to discuss a client's affairs with a third party.

CAROLINE Then let us discuss mine. I am seeking an investment.

CUT TO:

63: INT. PASCOE'S OFFICE – DAY 26

ROSS *(puzzled)* An investment?

CUT TO:

64: INT. PASCOE'S OFFICE (FLASHBACK) – DAY 23

CAROLINE I'm now of age and have money of my own. Can you assist me?

PASCOE Well, I—

CAROLINE But first I require your assurance that no one else will learn of this arrangement.

PASCOE Of course. But surely your uncle—

CAROLINE Your *absolute* assurance. Can you give it? If you cannot, I shall go elsewhere.

CUT TO:

65: INT. PASCOE'S OFFICE – DAY 26

PASCOE The proposal I'm instructed to make is this: to purchase your debt – in full – and arrange a new promissory note – at a considerably lower rate of interest.

ROSS I don't understand – how could anyone consider that an investment?

PASCOE The person concerned regards it as a mark of faith in your prospects and integrity. If you accept, the full fourteen hundred pounds will instantly be forthcoming and you may take it to the Warleggans this very hour.

DEMELZA But – who is this person? Who would do such a—?

ROSS Is it you, Harris?

PASCOE It is not. Nor am I at liberty to disclose their name. It was their express condition.

DEMELZA Is it someone we know?

ROSS Is it Trencrom?

DEMELZA Sir Hugh?

PASCOE *(ignoring this)* The money is available the moment you sign this new promissory note.

ROSS Horace Treneglos?

PASCOE I cannot tell you anything more.

DEMELZA But you, knowin' the person, do advise us to accept?

PASCOE But I, knowing the person, do advise you to accept.

Still in a daze from this shocking development, Ross picks up a quill. He hesitates. It's a time-stands-still moment. We're not convinced he will sign.

CUT TO:

66: INT. WARLEGGAN HOUSE – DAY 26

A servant brings a decanter of port and two glasses to George and Cary.

CARY Should we offer him a glass? It may be the last good port he has in a while.

GEORGE Why not? We are gentlemen after all.

They both laugh. As George gestures to the servant to bring an extra glass, another servant ushers in Ross and Demelza. They look cowed and crestfallen. George and Cary glance at each other, barely able contain their triumph.

ROSS Good day to you, gentlemen. You know my wife Demelza.

GEORGE Good day to you, ma'am. I'm delighted you could join us. May I offer you some refreshment?

DEMELZA 'Tis most kind of you, sir, but I fear 'twould not be fitting—

Ross and Demelza look at each other, as if in unbearable sorrow. Then:

ROSS Gentlemen, I regret to say – I'm unable to give you the satisfaction—

GEORGE *(smiles magnanimously)* Most unfortunate—

ROSS Of visiting me in prison. You will have to make do with this.

He puts a banker's note for £1400 on the table. Cary and George stare at it, uncomprehending.

CARY What is this foolery?

ROSS Repayment in full. Plus interest.

Cary snatches up the note, examines it as if expecting it to be some kind of fake. George is speechless.

ROSS *(cont'd)* We wish you both the compliments of the season, gentlemen.

He takes Demelza's arm and they go out. After they've gone, Cary lets out a sustained roar of fury.

CARY How? *How* has he managed it? You said he had no allies, you said he no friends—

GEORGE I was evidently wrong.

CARY We will bring him down! If it takes ten years – we will see him in the gutter – and his slut – we will make it our mission—

GEORGE Compose yourself, uncle – does half of Cornwall need to hear of this small setback?

CARY Small? You call it *small*?

GEORGE In the grand scheme of things, it *is* small. *(beat)* And there are other ways to punish him. Which do not involve money.

CUT TO:

67: INT. TRENWITH HOUSE, GREAT HALL – DAY 26

An enormous basket of sweetmeats, hothouse fruits and flowers is delivered to Elizabeth as a Christmas present. Elizabeth reads the card.

ELIZABETH From George.

Aunt Agatha scowls, but Geoffrey Charles is excited. Elizabeth smiles. She is greatly touched by the gesture.

CUT TO:

68: INT. NAMPARA HOUSE, HALLWAY – DUSK 26

Ross and Demelza come home. Both seem in a state of shock. Demelza goes straight upstairs but Ross goes into the kitchen.

CUT TO:

69: INT. NAMPARA HOUSE, KITCHEN – CONTINUOUS

Ross comes into the kitchen, puts some small packages on the table, sees the door to the larder open – and finds Prudie within, putting away preserves in the secret cache.

ROSS Prudie—?

PRUDIE Judas!

ROSS What's this? A secret cache?

He looks into the secret cache. Then questioningly at Prudie.

PRUDIE 'Twas the maid's notion, sur. She bid us not t' tell 'ee. 'Tis against 'ee goin' to prison.

ROSS What else were you not to tell me?

PRUDIE 'Ee be wantin' a list? Of *everything* she do behind yer back – to keep us all fed an' safe an' warm an' fitty?

CUT TO:

70: INT. NAMPARA HOUSE, JEREMY'S ROOM – DUSK 26

Demelza sits rocking the cradle of the sleeping Jeremy, singing softly to him:

DEMELZA *(sings)*
Kosk rag mamm –
Oh kosk mar pleg –
Kosk yn ta –
Kosk yn ta, kosk yn kres,
Hun-ro-sow hweg –
Kosk yn, kosk yn ta . . .

CUT TO:

71: INT. NAMPARA HOUSE, KITCHEN – DUSK 26

Ross sits with Prudie at the kitchen table, suitably chastened.

ROSS You're right, of course. I barely notice half of what she does. Of late I've barely noticed her at all.

He pours Prudie a glass of rum. She seems surprisingly sympathetic.

CUT TO:

72: INT. NAMPARA HOUSE, ROSS & DEMELZA'S BEDROOM – NIGHT 26

Demelza continues to sing to herself as she undresses for bed, taking off her thick woollen stockings as Ross comes in. So used is she to being ignored, she continues to hang them, and the string she uses for garters, over a chair, as if he wasn't there. He watches her in silence awhile. Then:

ROSS I bought a few things while you were at the chandler's.

DEMELZA You shouldn't have. We've so little t' spare—

ROSS You had nothing for Christmas. *(beat)* Not even my attention.

He hands her a package.

DEMELZA I need no gifts, Ross. 'Tis enough if you still care for me.

ROSS Do you doubt it?

DEMELZA I've begun to. At least – *(with difficulty)* not your liking. But mebbe – your longing—

ROSS You think I no longer love you.

DEMELZA Not in – *that* way.

ROSS Open your present.

She opens it. Inside are a pair of silk stockings. And a pair of delicate ribbon garters. They're so exquisite, Demelza actually bursts into tears. Ross is full of consternation.

ROSS *(cont'd)* What is it? Do you not like them?

DEMELZA They're too fine. When would I wear them?

ROSS Will they suit you?

DEMELZA I – cannot tell—

ROSS May I see?

DEMELZA If you like—

He leads her to the bed. Tentatively, as if expecting her at any moment to deny him, Ross pushes up her skirts till they're above her knees, till her legs are bare. She shivers involuntarily. She has not felt the touch of his hands like this for so long. Now, with infinite care, he puts on one of the stockings, gently rolling it up from her ankle until it slips just above her knee. Then, with the utmost delicacy and patience, he ties it with a garter. She is trembling. She has almost forgotten to breathe. Her face is so close to his now. She waits for him to pull back, to take the other stocking and put it on, but instead his hand begins to slide further up her thigh. He looks into her eyes, as if seeking her permission. Without a word, she consents. His mouth finds hers. They kiss hungrily. Eventually, reluctantly, they pull apart.

ROSS So you are not to be rid of me, my love.

DEMELZA So I am not to be rid of you, my love.

He pulls her towards him and they devour each other.

Episode 7

1: EXT. TRURO HARBOUR – DAY 27 (WINTER 1793)

February 1793. A ship is docked at the quayside. It's The One & All, *Trencrom's smuggling cutter. Trencrom is on the harbour giving instructions to the crew. We pull back to reveal, up on the cliffs, McNeil and Vercoe. Vercoe is watching through his binoculars. McNeil is reading a newspaper.*

VERCOE Will there be war, d'y'think?

CAPTAIN MCNEIL Inevitably. One does not send an anointed king to the guillotine and expect no consequences.

VERCOE People are nervous.

CAPTAIN MCNEIL As well they might be. Jacobin clubs close, folk dig out old weaponry. In readiness.

VERCOE For war? Or breaking the law?

They look below to where Trencrom continues to give instructions to his crew. Vercoe and McNeil make a note in their books. Clearly these preparations are of significance to them.

CUT TO:

2: EXT. WHEAL GRACE – DAY 27

Ross walks around the mine and greets the spallers and bal-maidens who are processing the newly mined ore. Ross selects a piece of rock and examines it critically as he goes into the mine.

CUT TO:

3: INT. WHEAL GRACE – DAY 27

Ross joins Zacky in the mine. He shows him the piece of rock he'd collected from the processing above.

ROSS I'd never have believed the poorness of the yield. But she's been awkward from the start.

ZACKY And never a sign o' the old Trevorgie lode – whether we come at it from Leisure or from Grace—

ROSS Yet Mark Daniel swore—

ZACKY Mark Daniel swore.

Ross tosses the rock back into the pile, picks up another and examines it.

ROSS I reckon there's more *tin* in this than copper.

ZACKY Copper lodes do often peter out that way.

ROSS What happens further down? Is there more chance of copper at greater depth?

ZACKY Some would say our *only* chance.

ROSS What do you say?

ZACKY That she's been a grievous disappointment – and if I were you, I'd not throw good money after bad. Cap'n Henshawe reckons we've enough coal for two weeks. Three, if we close the lower levels.

ROSS But going deeper is our only hope? *(Zacky nods)* Then we go deeper.

CUT TO:

4: EXT. NAMPARA HOUSE – DAY 27

Demelza is sawing logs when Garrick starts to bark. Two men approach with a mule. It's Paul and Ted. Demelza knows exactly what this means.

DEMELZA Garrick! See 'em off! Go to!

Garrick goes rushing up to them, growling. They cower away.

PAUL Nay, Mistress Poldark, we come at th' behest of Mr Trencrom—

DEMELZA I know why 'ee come. An' who sent 'ee!

She flings down her saw and starts to walk to the house, scowling.

DEMELZA *(cont'd)* Garrick, come to.

Garrick stops barking and meekly follows his mistress. Paul and Ted nervously lead the mule after her.

CUT TO:

5: INT. NAMPARA HOUSE, LIBRARY – DAY 27

Demelza watches, unimpressed, as Paul and Ted move the metal trunks and the rug covering the secret cache. Next they remove the floorboards. Inside the cache are ten five-gallon casks of Geneva rum, some tea and a roll of fancy lace. These they begin to remove.

PAUL Mr Trencrom d' send his regrets—

DEMELZA Mr Trencrom can keep his regrets and take his goods. 'Twas not the agreement to leave 'em lay nearly three weeks afore they're fetched! 'Tis takin' advantage. An' I don' like folk takin' advantage. An' neither do Ross.

CUT TO:

6: EXT. TRENWITH HOUSE – DAY 27

Establisher.

CUT TO:

7: INT. TRENWITH HOUSE, GREAT HALL – DAY 27

Elizabeth holds out her hand for Ross to kiss. Her dress is subdued though she's no longer in mourning. She looks fragile but as beautiful as ever – something to which Ross is clearly not immune.

ELIZABETH Is it true? Your promissory note was paid?

ROSS It seems we *both* have a mysterious benefactor.

ELIZABETH Could it be the same?

ROSS Who knows?

ELIZABETH But who would invest in a worthless mine?

ROSS Or a man without capital or prospects? Clearly some lunatic.

ELIZABETH But one who has the interests of the Poldarks at heart.

Ross smiles. He seems to have fooled Elizabeth about his own purchase of Francis's share in Wheal Grace.

ELIZABETH *(cont'd)* I'm glad of it. *(beat)* Though in some ways I regret the change. Now I've no further interest in Grace, you no longer have reason to call.

ROSS I will always have reason to call. If you wish it.

ELIZABETH I wish it.

A moment of connection between them.

CUT TO:

8: INT. TRENWITH HOUSE, GALLERY – DAY 27

Aunt Agatha is revealed, lurking on the gallery, having eavesdropped this entire conversation.

CUT TO:

9: EXT. TRURO STREET – DAY 27

George and Tankard stroll along the street.

GEORGE Those properties we spoke of – have they been acquired?

TANKARD The deal will shortly be concluded.

GEORGE Unwin has his uses.

TANKARD When will you demolish 'em?

GEORGE All in good time. First we increase the rents.

TANKARD The tenants will object.

GEORGE Then we evict them. Then we demolish. *Then* we build.

TANKARD The Warleggan bank!

George and Tankard walk off.

CUT TO:

10: EXT. SAWLE VILLAGE – DAY 27

Dwight is walking towards Charlie Kempthorne's cottage. Jacka Hoblyn sits outside, scowling. We go with Dwight as he approaches the door.

DWIGHT Good day t'you, Jacka.

JACKA Is it?

Now Charlie appears from the cottage.

CHARLIE Surgeon! Welcome! 'Ee could'n a' come on a better day!

DWIGHT You're in high spirits, sir.

CHARLIE So would 'ee be, an' were 'ee in my shoes!

He ushers Dwight into the cottage. Jacka follows.

CUT TO:

11: INT. KEMPTHORNE COTTAGE – DAY 27

Coming into the cottage Dwight is surprised to see Rosina.

CHARLIE Rosina's agreed t' wed me!

Dwight glances at Rosina, who flushes with embarrassment.

DWIGHT I hope you'll both be very happy.

He notices Jacka's scowl. It's clear he's not entirely happy about the match. Dwight goes to examine Lottie, who is sitting up in bed reading a book: The History of Primrose Prettyface.

DWIGHT *(cont'd)* *(to Lottie)* How are you, Lottie? Will you open your mouth so I can look at your throat?

Lottie obliges. Charlie is savouring his triumph and can barely contain himself.

CHARLIE We hope 'ee'll come to our weddin' – doesn't us, Rosina?

ROSINA 'Ais, sur. We 'ave 'ee to thank—

CHARLIE So we 'ave. Rosina's lipsy leg cured. Me 'n my consumptives. An' I now earnin' fair from sailmaking.

DWIGHT So I see—

Dwight glances round at the cottage. Unlike the other miners' cottages, this has curtains, matting on the floor, good earthenware cups, candlesticks.

DWIGHT *(cont'd)* It certainly seems to afford you a good living.

CHARLIE Hard work do that, surgeon – as you did ought t' know.

Dwight's expression tells us he feels hard work hasn't afforded him the same results.

DWIGHT And when's the wedding to be?

CHARLIE Banns called this Sunday. Nothin' to wait for now, is there? *(then)* Your turn next, surgeon!

Dwight nods politely.

CUT TO:

12: INT. NAMPARA HOUSE, LIBRARY – DAY 27

Paul and Ted put back the rug and manoeuvre the metal chests back into place.

PAUL We shan't trouble 'ee again—

DEMELZA Till the next drop? Well, see 'ee make no commotion leavin' an' bring the gaugers down upon us—

Suddenly they are interrupted by the sounds of loud barking, yelps and shrieks from the kitchen.

PAUL Oh my ivers! 'Tis they – th' gaugers—

DEMELZA Go! *Go!*

Paul and Ted run out through the front door. Demelza races through into the kitchen . . .

CUT TO:

13: INT. NAMPARA HOUSE, KITCHEN – CONTINUOUS

. . . where she is greeted by the sight of Prudie and Jud locked in mortal combat, rolling about on the kitchen floor.

PRUDIE Mincher! Lurger! So do 'ee bring 'is fizzog 'ome sometimes?

JUD I be about Trencrom's business! I be 'is man now! 'Tis on that account I mus' bide so oft in Sally Chill-off's kiddley!

PRUDIE A-what? A-studyin' th' dreg-end of a keg o' rum? I'll skat 'ee t' midjans! I'll gi' 'ee such a linsing—!

JUD Hush yer clack, woman! I didn' come 'ome to argeefy!

PRUDIE Nay, to fill thy guts an' guzzle! *(accompanying each phrase with a whack)* Lazy – lurgy – fever o' lurk – two stomachs to eat – an' neither one to work!

Jud yelps with pain. Demelza dives into the fray to try and separate them . . .

DEMELZA Leave 'im, Prudie! Leave 'im be – Jud! Enough now—

. . . but only succeeds in getting herself entangled in the struggle, along with the barking Garrick. Now Ross comes in to find Demelza, Garrick, Jud and Prudie all wrestling on the kitchen floor.

ROSS The noble art of Cornish wrestling.

Without a word they stop fighting and look up at him. Ross struggles to contain his amusement. Demelza tries to recover her dignity as she gets up and dusts herself off.

ROSS *(cont'd) (to Jud)* You have a message for me?

CUT TO:

14: INT. NAMPARA HOUSE, PARLOUR – DAY 27

Jud, cut and bruised, gratefully receives a tot of rum.

JUD Mark Daniel's been found.

ROSS Where?

JUD Cherbourg – he *was*. Then with all this kick an' sprawl, folk did start t' look him askance – so he slips away t' th' Scillies. As well he might, bein' none too bright hisself.

ROSS Can a message be got to him?

JUD 'Tis done already. *The One & All* sets sail in two days, runnin' in to St Mary's on's way to France. Mark'll meet 'ee there. Then do 'ee return th' same way.

Ross considers this. It sounds like a promising arrangement. Demelza, however, foresees problems.

DEMELZA I don' like it, Ross.

ROSS There's no other way. I must meet him.

JUD I'll tell Mr Trencrom.

PRUDIE Aye, an' when that's done, get 'is sneavy carcass back 'ere!

DEMELZA No, 'tis too risky.

PRUDIE Nay, but—

DEMELZA Trencrom's man? Let Trencrom feed 'im.

PRUDIE Aye, but—

DEMELZA There's an informer about—

JUD Tid'n I! Pick me liver, do 'ee think I be such a man?

DEMELZA O' course not! Informers be sharp an' witsy!

JUD *(too stupid to understand the implied insult)* 'Xactly.

CUT TO:

15: EXT. DWIGHT'S COTTAGE – DUSK 27

Dwight arrives home to find a horse tied up and a candle lit in the window. He smiles. He knows who his visitor is.

CUT TO:

16: INT. DWIGHT'S COTTAGE – DUSK 27

Dwight finds Caroline waiting for him.

CAROLINE I see I have a rival.

She holds up a scarf and a note.

CAROLINE *(cont'd)* 'From Rosina with love'. Is this how all your patients address you? Or just those in receipt of miracles?

She runs over and they kiss passionately. Then:

CAROLINE *(cont'd)* Uncle Ray bids me travel to London with him on the third.

DWIGHT Ah—

CAROLINE So you and I must escape on the second! *(laughing)* It will make my packing all the easier! Instead of escaping with a bundle through a window, I can have my trunks downstairs and safely stowed in the coach. *(then, seeing his worried expression)* What is it? Do you not *want* to marry me?

DWIGHT Oh Caroline – marrying you – openly – would set a seal on my happiness, which I don't deserve but would gladly take. Marrying you in *secret*, running away with you at night—

CAROLINE Yes?

DWIGHT It smacks of dishonesty – of the fortune-hunter—

CAROLINE Which we both know you are not!

DWIGHT But why can we not go to your uncle and tell him what we intend?

CAROLINE Have I not explained? *(patiently)* If we run away in secret, Uncle Ray will be furious—

DWIGHT And rightly so. He'll denounce us in the strongest possible terms—

CAROLINE But only to *himself.* In a year, he will calm down and there will be nothing to prevent a reconciliation.

DWIGHT He will accept what cannot be changed?

CAROLINE Exactly. But a direct confrontation – 'I will marry this man, with or without your blessing'? He and I will argue. His pride will not let him back down and I will never see him again.

Dwight considers her argument. Then:

DWIGHT I acknowledge the rationale but dislike the subterfuge.

CAROLINE Because you are too honourable!

DWIGHT Because my honour has been compromised before! You know this. The girl I fell in love with – she too was a patient of mine – and though her death was not at my hands, it is on my conscience.

CAROLINE That I understand, but—

DWIGHT Also on my conscience is the fact that you are giving up your fortune for me.

CAROLINE In the first place, I am not. I am only deferring it. And in the second, even if I were, it would be worth it. To be your wife – to be forced to stand on my own two feet . . . *(then, seeing his expression)* Do you doubt me?

DWIGHT Not your intent. But you may find the reality less romantic than you imagine.

CUT TO:

17: EXT. NAMPARA HOUSE – NIGHT 27

Establisher. Sounds of yelps and cursing from Jud and Prudie within.
CUT TO:

18: INT. NAMPARA HOUSE, ROSS & DEMELZA'S BEDROOM – NIGHT 27

Ross and Demelza lie in bed listening to the yelps and curses of Jud and Prudie scrapping in the kitchen below.

ROSS Conjugal bliss! A rare commodity.

DEMELZA Yes.

She doesn't elaborate – and Ross doesn't ask her to – but both are thinking the same thing: conjugal bliss is in short supply in their own marriage these days.
CUT TO:

19: EXT. TRENWITH HOUSE – DAWN 28

Dawn establisher over Trenwith.
CUT TO:

20: INT. TRENWITH HOUSE, GREAT HALL – DAY 28

Aunt Agatha is scowling from a distance as she watches Reverend Odgers, Mrs Odgers and their three children greedily tucking into food. Elizabeth appears at her shoulder.

AUNT AGATHA These gannets here again?

ELIZABETH Once a week, Aunt. You know our obligation.

AUNT AGATHA Along with repairs to the church, walls, bridges, alms for the poor . . . A fine trick – to bleed dry the foremost family in the district.

ELIZABETH The *once*-foremost family—

AUNT AGATHA *(with a scowl at the Odgers family)* A pity their appetites show no such decline. *(then)* Where's Ross? Why does he not visit so often?

ELIZABETH Ross has his own affairs to attend to. We can manage without him.

Raised eyebrows from Aunt Agatha. Elizabeth isn't fooling anyone.

CUT TO:

21: INT. NAMPARA HOUSE, LIBRARY – DAY 28

A map of the workings of Wheal Grace is spread out on the table. Ross surveys it. Demelza comes in, puts her hand on his shoulder and peers over it.

DEMELZA How long will you be gone?

ROSS Three days?

He pats her hand as if in reassurance.

ROSS *(cont'd)* Depends on the weather, and how speedily *The One & All* can load goods in France and return to collect me.

He begins to gather his things in readiness for departure.

ROSS *(cont'd)* I'll take Henshawe and Paul with me. Mark'll be glad to see his brother. And Henshawe knows Grace like the back of his hand. He'll have questions for Mark which might not occur to me.

DEMELZA Is this really our last chance?

ROSS We have two weeks of coal left. After that, the pumping engine stops and so does Grace.

He rolls up the map and packs it away for the journey.

CUT TO:

22: EXT. NAMPARA HOUSE – DAY 28

Demelza, holding Jeremy, is kissed goodbye by Ross, who mounts his horse and rides away. Prudie appears at Demelza's shoulder.

PRUDIE Don' 'ee fret, maid. Ol' Jud's on th' case.

DEMELZA *(sarcastic)* Well, that d' make all the diff'rence!

CUT TO:

23: EXT. TRURO STREET – DAY 28

Ross, Henshawe and Paul walk down the street.

ROSS Why did we not look for Mark sooner? All this time – we could've had clear direction instead of guesswork.

PAUL *(getting carried away)* And Grace could be in profit!

HENSHAWE Mebbe your luck is turnin'. First your mystery benefactor, now the findin' of Mark—

ROSS A change in our fortunes? That I could certainly drink to!

Then they spot George, walking towards them. The smallest nod of acknowledgement but no let-up in hostilities between Ross and George. George continues up the street. Ross, Henshawe and Paul continue down the street, heading for the harbour.

CUT TO:

24: INT. WARLEGGAN HOUSE, GEORGE'S DEN – DAY 28

George comes in to find Tankard waiting for him.

GEORGE You will ride to Trenwith.

TANKARD To what purpose?

GEORGE To alert the family of the latest events in France – the execution of the king, the expected response from London. Warn Mistress Poldark of potential unrest—

TANKARD Hereabouts—?

GEORGE Advise her to make secure her windows and doors.

TANKARD But will this not frighten her?

GEORGE It may well.

CUT TO:

25: INT. TRENWITH HOUSE, LIBRARY – DAY 28

Tankard has just conveyed George's message. Elizabeth is rattled.

ELIZABETH Tell Mr Warleggan I'm grateful for his concern, but – *(wondering if she dare ask this)* had he no other suggestions to make? No assistance to offer?

TANKARD I think he felt it would be impertinent to interfere with your domestic arrangements, ma'am.

ELIZABETH Of course. That's most thoughtful of him. Please convey my thanks.

Tankard bows and leaves. After he's gone:

ELIZABETH *(cont'd)* I'll ask Tabb to secure all the locks and bolts.

AUNT AGATHA Or better still, fetch me a pistol. I could stop an intruder in his tracks.

ELIZABETH I don't doubt it, Aunt. With or without a fire-arm.

She goes to a desk and gets out pen and paper. Aunt Agatha eyes her beadily. She knows exactly what Elizabeth's doing.

AUNT AGATHA To Ross?

ELIZABETH I thought I might ask him to call and advise us. I know you'd welcome that.

AUNT AGATHA *(pointedly)* Of course – 'tis only *my* comfort which concerns him here.

CUT TO:

26: EXT. TRURO HARBOUR – DAY 28

Ross, Henshawe and Paul come aboard as The One & All *prepares to leave the harbour.*

CUT TO:

27: INT. NAMPARA HOUSE, HALLWAY – DAY 28

Elizabeth's letter is delivered to Nampara – not to Ross, but into the hands of Prudie (who is looking after Jeremy).

PRUDIE Mister Ross ain't here. He'll see it when he returns.

The servant nods and departs. Prudie now notices Jeremy toddling away from her.

PRUDIE *(cont'd)* Bless 'ee, chile – Master Jeremy, come back this minute—

She stuffs the letter into her pocket and chases after Jeremy, who toddles away laughing. Prudie grabs him and gathers him up. There's a knock at the door.

PRUDIE *(cont'd)* Now what?

She opens the door to Dwight.

DWIGHT Is your master at home?

CUT TO:

28: INT. NAMPARA HOUSE, PARLOUR – DAY 28

Prudie ushers Dwight into the parlour where Demelza is practising the spinet.

DWIGHT I don't mean to disturb you. I called because Ross is usually home now.

DEMELZA He's away a few days. Is it urgent?

DWIGHT Not – in the ordinary sense—

Seeing him hesitate – and seeing Prudie still lurking:

DEMELZA *(to Prudie)* Tell Jinny to bring some tea.

Prudie goes out. Dwight seems agitated, unable to settle.

DEMELZA *(cont'd)* I know Ross won't mind me telling you this. He's gone with Trencrom's ship, droppin' off at the Scilly Isles to meet Mark Daniel –

Demelza notes the look of alarm that crosses Dwight's face.

DEMELZA *(cont'd)* Then *The One & All* will pick up Ross an' bring him home when they anchor off our cove for the drop.

Dwight is clearly troubled by the mention of Mark Daniel.

DWIGHT It seems a lifetime since that night – when you stood between me and Mark.

DEMELZA He would've killed you.

DWIGHT And I'd have welcomed it. I'd betrayed everyone and everything I held most dear. *(then)* But that's the last thing I want to remember tonight. *(hesitates, then)* I called to tell you I'm leaving.

DEMELZA To be with Caroline?

DWIGHT How did you guess?

DEMELZA You're to be married? *(Dwight nods bashfully.)* Oh, Dwight—

DWIGHT But her uncle forbids it, so we must do it in secret. We leave on Friday night.

DEMELZA Cannot you stay here?

DWIGHT Not within her uncle's reach. And besides, I owe it to Caroline to start afresh, in a new town, where my history with Keren is unknown.

DEMELZA But who'll care f'r us when you go?

DWIGHT I've been in correspondence with a colleague in London. He's a good man, older than I but with similar views. I think you'll like him.

DEMELZA Well, I'm happy for your sake, but for *ours* . . . You'll be sorely missed.

DWIGHT I want you to know – and to tell Ross – how much I owe to you both. Leaving like this – it's a great sorrow to me—

DEMELZA Marrying for love isn't a time for grievin'. Worry about us and our ailments till Friday. Then begin your new life as if we'd never been.

Dwight nods. But we can see he will struggle to put Demelza's advice into practice.

CUT TO:

29: INT. TRENWITH HOUSE, OAK ROOM – DUSK 28

Elizabeth peers out anxiously into the gathering gloom as she closes the curtains.

AUNT AGATHA Did Ross reply?

ELIZABETH He did not. It's unlike him to be so remiss. I wonder what could have detained him?

CUT TO:

30: EXT. CLIFF TOPS – DUSK 28

The sun sets. Dusk falls over Nampara Cove. Demelza looks out to sea – then down at Nampara Cove below. So many uncertainties. So much to worry about.

CUT TO:

31: EXT. SEA – DAWN 29

Dawn breaks over the sea.

CUT TO:

32: EXT. ST MARY'S – DAY 29

The One & All *is at anchor. A small longboat is being rowed towards a jetty. Ross, Henshawe and Paul are aboard.*

CUT TO:

33: INT. DWIGHT'S COTTAGE – DAY 29

Dwight begins to pack away some of his potions and bottles. He looks at the scarf Rosina has made him – and her note 'From Rosina with love'. It causes him a pang of regret. Steeling himself, he screws up the note and throws it in the fire.

CUT TO:

34: INT. NAMPARA HOUSE, PARLOUR – DAY 29

Demelza is arranging twigs and hedgerow branches in a vase when Caroline is shown in.

DEMELZA *(surprised)* Oh! Miss Penvenen!

They greet each other. This is an unexpected visit and Demelza is caught off-guard.

CAROLINE I was passing and it struck me as remiss that I've never yet paid a call.

Something in her breezy tone makes Demelza suspect this is only part of the story. Caroline seems nervous, curiously unsure of herself.

DEMELZA And soon you'll be leaving for Bath.

CAROLINE Oh! Did Dwight say so? And here am I thinking he might have changed his mind!

DEMELZA Why would he?

CAROLINE Oh, you know – men – so changeable! *(beat)* Do you not find?

DEMELZA I think Dr Enys as like as any to remain steadfast.

CAROLINE *(seemingly relieved)* Is that your experience? Of husbands, I mean? Generally to be relied upon?

An awkward moment between them. Demelza wouldn't quite go that far.

DEMELZA Some tea?

CAROLINE Why not?

Demelza rings the bell for tea and motions to Caroline to take a seat.

CAROLINE *(cont'd)* *(then, as if to change the subject)* And how fares Captain Poldark's mining venture? Is that also secure?

DEMELZA Far from it!

CAROLINE Oh dear. Well, I suppose one can't have everything!

DEMELZA No. I suppose not.

Another awkward moment between them. As if Caroline has been seeking reassurance – and Demelza has not been fully able to give it.

CUT TO:

35: INT. ST MARY'S KIDDLEY – DAY 29

The kiddley is full of locals and dodgy-looking smuggler types. The door opens and Ross, Henshawe and Paul come in, glance round to see if they can see Mark, then find a seat.

CUT TO:

36: INT. KILLEWARREN – DAY 29

Ray Penvenen is going through some paperwork as Caroline returns from her ride. She is carrying Horace.

RAY PENVENEN Ah, my dear. I've had a letter from London, requiring our attendance sooner. I don't imagine it will inconvenience you to leave on Friday rather than Saturday?

CAROLINE *(horrified but trying to remain calm)* Oh! – but it will inconvenience me a great deal! I've scarce begun to pack – and you know how Horace hates sudden changes of plan.

RAY PENVENEN I'm sure Horace will humour me if his mistress finds it in her heart to do so.

He smiles gently at Caroline – and she, having genuine affection for him, cannot bring herself to argue. Instead:

CAROLINE Come, Horace – I see we must gather your toys for our journey.

She smiles affably at Ray and goes out.

CUT TO:

37: INT. ST MARY'S KIDDLEY – DUSK 29

Ross and Paul have been drinking for some time. (Henshawe is more abstemious!) All three are in high spirits and letting their optimism run away with them.

ROSS Fifty men? I'd hope to employ twice that before next year is out! And thrice the year after!

HENSHAWE Mebbe offer to those who haven't found pitches since Grambler closed?

ROSS If I could see all Sawle and Grambler employed—

PAUL 'Twould be a fine thing—

HENSHAWE 'Twould indeed!

ROSS Here's to that—

PAUL And to Mark—

ROSS In him we trust!

Laughing, they toast and drink.

CUT TO:

38: INT. DWIGHT'S COTTAGE – NIGHT 29

Dwight is reading a letter from Caroline.

CAROLINE *(VO)* 'Dear Dwight, I must see you. There has been a complication.'

Dwight looks anxious.

CUT TO:

39: INT. ST MARY'S KIDDLEY – NIGHT 29

Ross, Henshawe and Paul have joined in with some fellow-smugglers who are singing heartily:

ALL *(sing)*

An' he was reckon'd a preacher stout
A burning, shining light.
The people all said, 'What he has in head,
Will surely turn out right.'
Oh the keenly lode, the keenly lode,
Of bals the best, me boys . . .

But Ross has already stopped singing and Paul and Henshawe have followed suit. Because the figure of Mark Daniel has appeared. He looks so ill and aged that Ross, Henshawe and Paul are temporarily speechless. Then Paul jumps to his feet and embraces Mark.

PAUL Brother! 'Tis good to see 'ee!

Now Ross greets Mark warmly. Mark seems dazed, as if he scarcely knows where – or even who – he is.

CUT TO:

40: INT. ST MARY'S KIDDLEY – NIGHT 29

Ross, Henshawe, Paul and Mark sit at a table in a quiet alcove. Paul sits beside his brother, as if to give him moral support. Ross and

Henshawe try to disguise their dismay at Mark's awful appearance. Ross brings out a bottle of brandy.

MARK *(shakes his head)* Never touch it now. Keep guard on my tongue – night an' day.

ROSS You know why we wished to meet?

MARK Like 'ee said in yer letter. 'Bout what I saw down Grace that night. Ever since I bin tryin' t' think—

PAUL 'Ee don' remember, brother?

MARK Oh, I mind what I saw. But *where* I see'd it . . . *(then)* I was fair crazed that night.

HENSHAWE Would a plan o' th' workings help?

MARK Oh it would, 't would indeed.

Henshawe gets out the map of Wheal Grace and spreads it out on the table. Mark squints at it. Ross and Henshawe exchange a glance. Now is the moment they've been waiting for – when all will be revealed. Mark studies the map, lets his finger hover over it in several places. Every time he seems to recognize something, Ross and Henshawe glance at each other. Finally Mark seems to have identified the spot. His finger hovers tantalizingly over the map. Then at the last minute he changes his mind – looks at Ross, as if struggling to summon up the memories.

MARK *(cont'd)* I went down here – I think there was water – then I walked – in the thirty level – sat down – an' thought to end it all by drownin' – then I got up – an' went bearin' east – cross a plank, half rotten— *(then)* You gave her a headstone, like I asked?

ROSS We gave her a headstone.

PAUL 'Keren Daniel, wife of Mark, aged twenty-two'. Like you asked.

MARK Twenty-two – still a child. *(then)* I'll never wed again. I d' feel I still *am* wed. *(then)* That surgeon – Enys – I reckon 'twas *he* I shoulda killed—

ROSS Try to remember, Mark. Where did you go next?

MARK Just above the gunnies, bearing right – there's an old pick down there – I took it up an' begun to cast around, like I was lookin' f'r a pitch. A fine bit of ground it looked—

HENSHAWE Where was it? *(pointing to the map)* Just here?

MARK I reckon. It ran at a steep incline – so I went on again – climbin' all the while – there was an old air shaft—

HENSHAWE *(pointing to the map)* Here?

MARK 'Twas all filled in. Reckon I was barely fifteen fathoms from grass. From there ye can turn three ways. I turned east—

ROSS *(pointing to the map)* This way?

MARK Sixty or seventy paces, then double back – an' in the turn, there's a cross-course – mostly lead and iron – so I sat and dozed – an' woke an' went on – 'twixt two narrow gunnies—

Ross and Henshawe exchange a glance. They're beginning to lose heart.

MARK *(cont'd)* Ye go down over broken ground where th' lode's been worked – but only th' bottom. Th' backs is untouch'd. There be fine quartzy rock an' gossan. 'Twas too high for me to get at, but I'd wager there's a mint o' money in that place alone!

HENSHAWE *(pointing to the map)* Just here.

MARK Just here.

Ross and Henshawe exchange another glance.

ROSS And after that you came up?

MARK After that I came up.

Mark looks pleased with himself. Paul pats him on the back. Ross and Henshawe struggle to contain the depths of their disappointment, so that Mark won't realize what is all too clear: his information has yielded absolutely nothing of use.

CUT TO:

41: EXT. CLIFF TOPS NEAR NAMPARA COVE – DAWN 30

Demelza walks along the cliff tops with Garrick and looks down into Nampara Cove as the sun rises.

DEMELZA Will it be today, Garrick? Will it be tonight?

CUT TO:

42: EXT. LONGBOAT – DAY 30

Ross, Henshawe and Paul are being rowed out to re-join The One & All.

HENSHAWE 'Twas when he mentioned quartz – I looked at ye—

ROSS And we all knew—

HENSHAWE 'Twas the first thing we'd found.

ROSS And it barely paid for the working.

They are silent a while. Then:

ROSS *(cont'd)* I blame myself—

PAUL Nay, Cap'n Ross—

ROSS To pin everything on the ramblings of a man crazed with rage and grief? What was I thinking?

PAUL It *coulda* bin true—

ROSS At the outset perhaps. But experienced miners can hardly work for months on end and not find whatever good ground is there. It's the old story. *(beat)* The drowning man and the straw.

CUT TO:

43: EXT. WOODLAND – DAY 30

Caroline and Dwight discuss the change of plan.

DWIGHT Of course I can leave tonight – if it must be—

CAROLINE It must be.

Dwight nods. He seems thoughtful.

DWIGHT I only wish—

CAROLINE Yes?

DWIGHT There were some other way – which did not require us to leave so furtively—

CAROLINE Or leave at all?

DWIGHT What d'you mean?

CAROLINE Are you sure you don't regret *more* than the manner of our leaving? Ever since we decided to go I've noticed a reluctance in you—

DWIGHT Not at all! I love you. What reluctance could I have?

CAROLINE Yet I wonder – six months from now – though I'm sharing your fireside and your bed – will you not sometimes sigh for your Cornish life and your Cornish Rosinas—?

DWIGHT I may well. They matter to me and I cannot pretend to be indifferent to their fate. But my mind is set—

CAROLINE In that case, perhaps we'd better leave at once! If Rosina is so precious to you, perhaps you'll end up jilting me for her!

DWIGHT If there's any jilting to be done, I'm sure it will be on *your* side!

Caroline laughs. They walk on, happily reconciled.

CAROLINE So tonight, then.

CUT TO:

44: INT. WARLEGGAN HOUSE, GEORGE'S DEN – DAY 30

George has summoned Tankard again.

GEORGE Enquire of Mistress Poldark if her safety measures are in place. Urge her to be vigilant—

TANKARD Is there any specific threat?

GEORGE Rumours. Word has reached me of some tinners who propose to claim their right under Stannary Law to enter private land—

TANKARD At Trenwith?

GEORGE Warn her to be on her guard.

CUT TO:

45: INT. TRENWITH HOUSE, LIBRARY – DAY 30

Tankard has carried out his instructions from George.

ELIZABETH Prospect for tin? On our land?

TANKARD These people are a law unto themselves, ma'am. And Mr Warleggan fears they may be encouraged to rise up by the example of their French counterparts.

ELIZABETH I thank Mr Warleggan for his concern.

Tankard bows and goes out.

AUNT AGATHA If Mr Warleggan was so concerned, why does he not come here himself?

ELIZABETH Or Ross. Why has he not replied to my note?

AUNT AGATHA The male of the species. Inadequate at best. Better to rely on one's own resources.

She removes a pistol from her shawl and gives an evil smile.

CUT TO:

46: EXT. NAMPARA HOUSE – DAY 30

Prudie is feeding the chickens when Demelza comes out, carrying a basket of apples and potatoes.

DEMELZA I'm away to Sawle to see if there's news. Keep Jeremy from his nap. If this be the night, I want him sound asleep all through 't.

She's about to head off when she sees a figure riding towards her. It's Elizabeth. Demelza goes over to meet her. There's a wariness and frostiness between the two women now.

ELIZABETH May I speak with Ross?

DEMELZA He's from home—

ELIZABETH Did he not receive my note?

Behind her Prudie suddenly remembers the note she had been given – which is still in her pocket. She takes it out, crumples it up behind her back.

DEMELZA Prudie? Did 'ee know of any note?

PRUDIE 'Es, mistress. I did give it Mister Ross meself – into 'is very own 'ands.

ELIZABETH Oh. Then I expect he was too busy to reply.

DEMELZA Yes. I expect he was.

A moment between them. The briefest of stand-offs. Then Elizabeth nods and rides away. Demelza watches her go, then heads off in the direction of Sawle. Prudie retrieves the screwed-up letter from behind her back – and grimaces.

CUT TO:

47: EXT. SAWLE VILLAGE – DAY 30

Walking through the village Demelza begins to notice a few tell-tale signs: people emptying sacks and saddling mules, coiling up ropes and fetching out black-tarred lanterns. She gives one man a questioning look. She gets a furtive confirmation in return. Now she knows that tonight is the night.

CUT TO:

48: EXT. KEMPTHORNE COTTAGE – DAY 30

Demelza approaches the cottage and is greeted by May and Lottie. She gives them apples and potatoes from her basket.

DEMELZA Make 'em last. I may not come again till next month.

They tuck into the apples gratefully. Now they see Rosina approaching down the street. Rosina waves excitedly and starts to run . . .

ROSINA Mistress Demelza!

. . . but in her haste she falls down and twists her knee. She screams in agony. Demelza, Lottie and May run to help her.

CUT TO:

49: INT. HOBLYN COTTAGE – DAY 30

Rosina is lying on the bed, gasping with pain.

ROSINA 'Tis like it b'long t' be 'fore Dr Enys mend it – only now 'tis worse.

DEMELZA We should send for him.

JACKA I'll set Charlie to 't.

ROSINA Nay, he be sick, 'member? Dr Enys bid him keep t' 'is bed.

DEMELZA I'll go. Keep her still an' warm. I'll return d'rectly.

ROSINA Bless 'ee, ma'am.

Demelza goes out.

CUT TO:

50: INT. DWIGHT'S COTTAGE – DAY 30

Dwight is packing away the last of his medicines into a travelling chest. As he closes the chest, a look of regret crosses his face. Nevertheless he rallies and continues the rest of his packing. There's a knock at the door. Dwight opens it . . .

DWIGHT Demelza! What brings you—?

DEMELZA Rosina Hoblyn. 'Tis her knee locked again. Can 'ee tend on her?

DWIGHT I fear – I cannot – my plans have changed – I'm due to leave with Caroline—

DEMELZA Tonight? But I thought—

DWIGHT It was tomorrow – yes – but her uncle—

DEMELZA No – no, you must go – I'll see to Rosina – or call Dr Choake—

DWIGHT Yes, that would be – no! – wait! I cannot allow that. She's my patient—

DEMELZA But Caroline expects you—

DWIGHT I think – if I leave now there'll be time—

DEMELZA Are you sure?

DWIGHT She's my patient.

He races to collect his doctor's bag.

CUT TO:

51: EXT. *THE ONE & ALL* – DAY 30

Ross, Henshawe and Paul ponder the future.

ROSS For the first time in my life, I feel old.

HENSHAWE We're none of us young as we were, Ross—

ROSS These last few years – often I've known failure, but always I've believed it a temporary setback. This time—

PAUL 'Twas a brave venture—

ROSS Was it? I begin to think it was the height of folly. To throw away a profitable investment in a mine of my own starting? And then pour everything I had – and persuade Francis to do likewise – into a played-out mine which had failed my father a quarter of a century back? Not only did I gamble with money, I gambled with the happiness and security of my workers – and most especially of my wife and child.

HENSHAWE What will 'ee do now?

ROSS Learn my lesson! *(then)* Plough my fields, harvest my crops, cherish my family. Live a quiet life.

HENSHAWE There's a lot to be said for it.

ROSS My wife would agree with you.

CUT TO:

52: EXT. OPEN COUNTRYSIDE – DUSK 30

Demelza and Dwight are galloping at break-neck speed across the moors. Far from the 'quiet life' which Ross assumes she wants, Demelza is totally fired up and loving every minute of her gallop.

CUT TO:

53: INT. HOBLYN COTTAGE – DUSK 30

Dwight comes into the cottage, followed by Demelza.

DWIGHT Tell me what happened.

He sets about examining Rosina's knee.

ROSINA I turn'd it on the cobbles, sur – an' it sudden d' go all tight—

She winces with pain as he feels for the displacement.

JACKA We thought t' send Charlie f'r 'ee but since he be sick, Mistress Poldark did kindly go—

Dwight continues to feel for the displacement.

DWIGHT What's the matter with Charlie?

JACKA Well, sur, you did oughta know that. 'Tis on account of 'ee tellin' him to stay abed that he's not helpin' with the run tonight—

Dwight is concentrating hard on manipulating Rosina's knee and he doesn't immediately take in what Jacka is saying. Suddenly he feels the knee click back into place.

DWIGHT There now—

Rosina cries out in pain. Dwight presses harder to make sure the dislocation is mended. Rosina gasps then breaks into a smile.

ROSINA What did 'ee do?

DWIGHT Can you stand up?

Rosina stands up, puts weight upon the leg.

DEMELZA 'Tis all mended?

Rosina nods, smiling, on the verge of tears.

ROSINA Oh sur, I'm *that* grateful. I was afeared 'twas gone for good—

DWIGHT I think you should wear a bandage – at least till the tendons knit together. And if it ever happens again—

JACKA Why, sur, if it do, we'd just make 'er sit quiet till we call 'ee again.

Involuntarily Dwight and Demelza exchange a glance. Meanwhile, Jacka is so impressed with Dwight, he pours him a cup of rum.

JACKA *(cont'd)* 'Ee'll take a dram, sur?

DWIGHT No, I – er— *(then, realizing it would hurt Jacka's feelings if he declined)* Thank you. That's most kind.

He drinks hastily, begins to pack up his things, keen to depart.

DWIGHT *(cont'd)* What's this about Charlie? Did he tell you I said he must go to bed?

JACKA Not I – but them as wanted his help with the run.

DWIGHT I don't understand—

JACKA 'T wasn't his turn, see? But yester eve Joe Trelask break 'is leg – an' Charlie's next on the list. So they sent round t' tell 'im be ready. But he sez he's a fever an' surgeon say he must stay abed on account of his lungs.

DWIGHT I said no such thing.

DEMELZA But why would he tell such a strammin' great tale—?

DWIGHT *(to Rosina)* Your wedding's in a fortnight?

ROSINA 'Ais—

DWIGHT He'd be anxious about the risk – and about his health. It's a thing any man would do. *(then)* I must leave you now.

JACKA *(offering his hand)* Till 'ee come agin.

DWIGHT It's been my privilege to be able to help you all.

Dwight nods and leaves. Demelza can see he's struggling. She makes her own farewells and follows him.

CUT TO:

54: EXT. SAWLE VILLAGE – SUNSET/DUSK 30

Once outside the house Dwight and Demelza take stock of the situation.

DEMELZA The informer – could it be Charlie?

They clearly both think so. Now Dwight checks his pocket-watch. Time is marching on. Demelza realizes what this means.

DEMELZA *(cont'd)* You must keep t' y'r plans—

DWIGHT No. I can go to Charlie and still have time to get to Killewarren—

DEMELZA But what will 'ee do?

DWIGHT In the first place, confirm our suspicions. We may be mistaken.

DEMELZA There mebbe no drop – or no ambush?

They look at each other – and suddenly they both know.

DEMELZA *(cont'd)* I'll come along of 'ee.

DWIGHT You must not. If you're seen out and about – and the ambush is set—

She nods in agreement.

DWIGHT *(cont'd)* Go home. I'll to Charlie—

DEMELZA Then ride like the wind – to Caroline.

CUT TO:

55: EXT. KILLEWARREN – DUSK 30

Caroline's private coach pulls up at some distance from the house, hidden from view.

CUT TO:

56: INT. KILLEWARREN – DUSK 30

Ray Penvenen is seeing to his paperwork. Caroline is pretending to read but in reality she's desperate for him to go up to his room so she can sneak off.

CAROLINE Was that a yawn, Horace? Yes, I know, my pet. We've a long journey tomorrow. And Uncle Ray is looking weary—

RAY PENVENEN Assure Horace that Uncle Ray, though undoubtedly ancient, has sufficient stamina to complete his correspondence.

CAROLINE Is it important?

RAY PENVENEN Instructions to my steward, regarding the estate while we're away.

CAROLINE How odious I should find that!

RAY PENVENEN All the more reason to marry wisely. When you come to inherit, you'll be grateful for a husband who takes such matters in hand.

Caroline looks as if she would answer back. Then thinks better of it. After a pause:

CAROLINE Well, if you will not retire, I must, for my eyes will not stay open.

RAY PENVENEN I won't be long. Goodnight, my dear.

He puts up his forehead to be kissed. Caroline does so, tenderly, though forgetting that this might be her last leave-taking for many months, perhaps for ever.

CAROLINE Goodnight, Uncle.

She goes out.

CUT TO:

57: EXT. CLIFF-TOP RIDE – DUSK 30

Demelza gallops home to Nampara. In the distance she spots a group of soldiers. She steers her horse in another direction so as to avoid them.

CUT TO:

58: EXT. KEMPTHORNE COTTAGE – DUSK 30

Dwight hammers on Charlie's door. No answer.

DWIGHT Charlie? Open the door!

Still no answer. Dwight knocks again.

DWIGHT *(cont'd)* Open the door, Charlie!

Silence. He waits. What should he do? Try again? Or leave and go to Killewarren?

CUT TO:

59: INT. KILLEWARREN, CAROLINE'S ROOM – DUSK 30

Caroline goes to her bedroom and surveys her travelling clothes all ready to leave. She sits down to write a letter: 'My dearest uncle, for most of my life you have been both father and mother to me . . .'

CUT TO:

60: EXT. KEMPTHORNE COTTAGE – DUSK 30

Dwight continues to hammer on the door. He pauses, hears a shuffling within. The door opens and Lottie stands there.

DWIGHT Lottie, I've come to visit your father.

He walks in past her.

CUT TO:

61: INT. KEMPTHORNE COTTAGE – DUSK 30

Charlie is lying in bed as Dwight comes in.

CHARLIE 'Tis kind of 'ee t' call, sur—

DWIGHT Sit up. I want to examine you.

CHARLIE Nay, but—

DWIGHT Sit up, man. You say you have a fever? Let me see what ails you.

Dwight whisks the covers off him. Charlie shrinks back nervously.

CUT TO:

62: EXT. CLIFF TOPS NEAR NAMPARA COVE – DUSK 30

Demelza rides up and spots some shadowy figures heading down to Nampara Cove. She rides on.

CUT TO:

63: INT. KEMPTHORNE COTTAGE – DUSK 30

Dwight has completed his cursory examination of Charlie.

DWIGHT You have no fever.

CHARLIE Nay, surgeon, three hours gone I was all of a shrim—

DWIGHT Why the sham? An excuse to avoid your part in the tub-carrying—

CHARLIE I swear, first it come on me like ice. Next, I be sweatin' like a weed—

DWIGHT For two years there's been an informer about—

CHARLIE Everyone d' know that. Have 'ee caught 'im?

DWIGHT I rather think I have.

For a moment neither Dwight nor Charlie can believe what's been said. Then:

CHARLIE That's a fine thing t' say!

DWIGHT How do you afford these curtains, those candlesticks? Out of sailmaking? Or selling your friends?

CHARLIE Get out now! An' take your nasty 'spicions with 'ee!

DWIGHT It's you who should get out, Charlie. Before your friends realize you've betrayed them.

CHARLIE 'Tis thee's the betrayer! Makin' eyes at Rosina – fingerin' her knee when 'ee think no one's lookin'—

DWIGHT What time is the run?

CHARLIE I don' know—

DWIGHT Is there an ambush?

CHARLIE *I don' know!*

CUT TO:

64: EXT. NAMPARA FIELDS – DUSK 30

As Demelza is entering the outskirts of Nampara land, she is shocked to encounter a soldier, Trooper Wilkins. *She pulls up her horse and tries to appear unruffled.*

DEMELZA Good even t' 'ee, sir. 'Tis a fine night.

TROOPER WILKINS Aye.

Trooper Wilkins turns away – but not before Demelza realizes he's carrying a musket. She spurs the horse on, towards Nampara, whose lighted windows can be seen in the distance.

CUT TO:

65: INT. KEMPTHORNE COTTAGE – DUSK 30

Dwight continues to challenge Charlie.

DWIGHT I think you *do* know.

CHARLIE Think what 'ee like. Ye've no proof I'm a traitor!

DWIGHT I beg to differ.

He seizes something from a table. It's the book of Primrose Prettyface which Lottie was reading (and which Hubert Vercoe was reading).

DWIGHT *(cont'd)* Where did you get this book?

CHARLIE Buyed it—

DWIGHT Where?

CHARLIE Redruth—

DWIGHT This book belonged to Hubert Vercoe, the customs officer's son. I saw it in his house—

CHARLIE That proves naught! There's many such books—

DWIGHT But none like this – with angel's wings coloured red by Hubert himself!

He takes the book and heads for the door. With a bound, Charlie leaps out of bed and bars his way.

CHARLIE What will 'ee do?

DWIGHT You'll know when I've done it.

CUT TO:

66: INT. KILLEWARREN – NIGHT 30

Caroline, now dressed for travelling, sneaks along the dark corridor, with Horace pattering behind her. She tiptoes past Ray's room – with its light still visible under the door – then along the landing. She picks up Horace and tiptoes down the stairs.

CUT TO:

67: INT. KEMPTHORNE COTTAGE – NIGHT 30

Charlie is still barring the way to the door.

CHARLIE Go home, surgeon. Forget what 'ee see'd. There's naught 'ee can do now.

CUT TO:

68: EXT. CLIFF TOPS NEAR NAMPARA COVE – DUSK 30

The soldiers and gaugers are lying in wait with McNeil and Vercoe in command.

CUT TO:

69: EXT. *THE ONE & ALL* – DUSK 30

Ross, Henshawe and Paul are ready as the ship anchors out at sea. Looking out towards the shore they see a brief flicker from a lantern. It's the signal. Without a word, they help to lower a flat-bottomed longboat from The One & All.

CUT TO:

70: INT. NAMPARA HOUSE, PARLOUR – NIGHT 30

Demelza, galvanized into action, goes round closing the curtains. Prudie comes in, looking worried and secretive.

DEMELZA There was a soldier—

PRUDIE Save us! Where?

DEMELZA By the long field. An' Ross'll walk straight into th' ambush! *(then)* Light the candles – keep 'em burning – let no one enter—

PRUDIE Why, maid, what do 'ee intend?

DEMELZA To get down to the cove – an' somehow warn 'em – 'fore the boat comes ashore—

PRUDIE *(suddenly)* Oh Judas!

Demelza realizes Prudie is staring in horror at something behind her. She turns – and sees Captain McNeil standing in the doorway. Trooper Wilkins appears behind him.

CUT TO:

71: INT. KEMPTHORNE COTTAGE – NIGHT 30

Charlie and Dwight still face each other.

DWIGHT Why would you do it, Charlie? Betray your own folk?

CHARLIE What folk? Who's my folk? No one did aught for me! Folks look only for theirselves in this life.

DWIGHT By selling their friends?

CHARLIE I done what I done. 'Ee don't 'ave t' like it – an' 'ee don't be my judge!

Suddenly he seizes a wooden chair and brings it crashing down on Dwight, who cries out in pain and collapses to the floor.

CUT TO:

72: INT. NAMPARA HOUSE, PARLOUR – NIGHT 30

Captain McNeil is pleasant but firm.

CAPTAIN MCNEIL I must ask you to remain indoors this evening. Trooper Wilkins will guard you.

DEMELZA Against what, may I ask? D' y' suppose there's an enemy about?

CAPTAIN MCNEIL Of sorts, ma'am. We have word that the smugglers intend to use your cove tonight. Where's your husband?

DEMELZA St Ives. Till tomorrow. *(trying to remain calm)* A glass of wine?

CAPTAIN MCNEIL Thank ye, no. I'm on duty.

DEMELZA What d'you want with my husband? What have we to do with this?

CAPTAIN MCNEIL Nothing, I hope. But since it's your land, I think ye can hardly be as innocent as ye look.

CUT TO:

73: INT. KEMPTHORNE COTTAGE – NIGHT 30

Dwight appears lifeless on the floor. Charlie comes over, a stick in his hand, to make sure Dwight's out cold. But just as Charlie's about to hit him again, Dwight springs to his feet and begins to defend himself.

CUT TO:

74: INT. NAMPARA HOUSE, PARLOUR – NIGHT 30

Demelza and McNeil continue their stand-off.

CAPTAIN MCNEIL Truly, ma'am, I do not lightly make war on friends, but I warned your husband once before of flying in the face of the law. If he's done it again, he must take the consequences.

CUT TO:

75: EXT. *THE ONE & ALL* – DUSK 30

Ross, Henshawe and Paul help to heave barrels into the longboat.

CUT TO:

76: INT. KEMPTHORNE COTTAGE – NIGHT 30

Dwight and Charlie are fighting tooth and nail, wrestling, grappling, rolling across the floor, scattering furniture. Now Charlie gets his hands round Dwight's throat and begins to throttle him.

CUT TO:

77: INT. NAMPARA HOUSE, PARLOUR – NIGHT 30

McNeil seems to relent.

CAPTAIN MCNEIL Believe me, ma'am, for the favour of *your* goodwill I would pay a very high price—

For a moment, Demelza feels a rush of hope. Should she take McNeil into her confidence? Is he inviting this?

CAPTAIN MCNEIL *(cont'd)* But none which involves a neglect of duty.

The moment is gone. Demelza knows that McNeil the soldier will trump McNeil the admirer.

DEMELZA What must I do?

CAPTAIN MCNEIL Make no attempt to leave. I can ill spare Wilkins, but you leave me no choice.

DEMELZA I hope this will be the last time I see you on such a mission.

CAPTAIN MCNEIL I hope so too. From now on I shall have *real* work to do. *(beat)* France declared war on England yesterday. Had they done so a week ago, we should have been spared this unhappy meeting.

He salutes and goes out.

CUT TO:

78: INT. KEMPTHORNE COTTAGE – NIGHT 30

At the point of passing out, Dwight manages to free himself from Charlie's grasp. He rolls away but Charlie lunges after him, drags Dwight back. Dwight kicks back, strikes Charlie in the chest and winds him. Now it's Charlie who's immobilized, grasping his chest and wheezing. Dwight struggles to his feet, blood on his face, his neck-cloth torn. Then suddenly Charlie leaps up, seizes a knife from the kitchen table, lunges at Dwight, who puts up his arm to fend off the blow. The knife clatters to the floor. Dwight summons all his strength and kicks Charlie in the chest again. Charlie falls backwards and crumples in a heap on the floor. Without waiting for another assault, Dwight grabs his things and runs out. Charlie lies groaning on the floor. Lottie and May appear in the doorway. They stare at the sight of their father, but don't approach him. They begin to cry.

CUT TO:

79: EXT. OPEN COUNTRYSIDE – NIGHT 30

Dwight gallops through the night along the cliff tops, heading for Nampara.

CUT TO:

80: EXT. KILLEWARREN – NIGHT 30

Caroline sneaks out of Killewarren with Horace and runs to her waiting coach.

CUT TO:

81: EXT. *THE ONE & ALL* – DUSK 30

The last of the cargo is lowered into the longboat. A lantern signal is given from The One & All. *Presently an answering signal is given from the shore.*

ROSS *(to Henshawe)* You mustn't risk coming ashore with us. Stay aboard till she docks at St Ann's.

HENSHAWE Gladly! Good luck.

They shake hands. Ross and Paul prepare to board the longboat. Henshawe remains.

CUT TO:

82: EXT. NAMPARA – NIGHT 30

Dwight rides up and sees the lights of Nampara. All around everything is still and peaceful. He can hear an owl call. The distant lowing of cattle. No one would guess what is about to unfold.

CUT TO:

83: INT. CARRIAGE – NIGHT 30

Caroline waits inside the carriage, stroking Horace to keep him from fretting. Though she herself is the more anxious.

CUT TO:

84: EXT. NAMPARA HOUSE – NIGHT 30

Dwight ties up his horse, tiptoes round to the front of the house and peers in through the window.

HIS POV: Trooper Wilkins is guarding Prudie and Demelza. Demelza seems tense but there's a look of fierce determination on her face.

Dwight realizes there's nothing he can achieve by making his presence known. He tiptoes away.

CUT TO:

85: INT. NAMPARA HOUSE, PARLOUR – NIGHT 30

Prudie sits meekly sewing but Demelza paces angrily, trying to work out a plan.

TROOPER WILKINS Take a seat, ma'am. 'Twill be a long night and you'll not wish to tire yourself.

DEMELZA I'm sure I don' wish t' be given orders in my own house!

TROOPER WILKINS Wish't or no, 'tis *my* orders we go by – so you'll kindly oblige me by keeping where I can see you.

He gestures her to sit beside Prudie. Reluctantly she does so.

CUT TO:

86: INT. NAMPARA HOUSE, KITCHEN – NIGHT 30

The kitchen door creaks open and Dwight sneaks in. Garrick lifts his head and begins to growl. Dwight shushes him. The kitchen is in darkness but he can see the light from the parlour and hear Demelza's voice.

DEMELZA'S VOICE And suppose we wish to go to sleep?

TROOPER WILKINS'S VOICE I must ask you to do so here, ma'am, so I can keep an eye on you.

Dwight casts about looking for something. Now he sees what he needs:

a small outdoor lantern and a stub of candle. He places the candle in the lantern, lights it and sneaks out again.

CUT TO:

87: EXT. LONGBOAT – NIGHT 30

Ross, Paul and two other men row the longboat away from The One & All, *in the direction of Nampara Cove.*

CUT TO:

88: EXT. PATH NEAR NAMPARA COVE – NIGHT 30

Keeping low, shielding the lantern, Dwight sneaks down towards Nampara Cove. As he approaches he sees a soldier. Then another. Then another. The ambush is set. Dwight realizes he must take a different route.

CUT TO:

89: EXT. NAMPARA COVE – NIGHT 30

Ross, Paul and the other men continue to row towards the shore.

CUT TO:

90: EXT. DAMSEL POINT – NIGHT 30

Dwight scrambles up onto Damsel Point, which overlooks Nampara Cove. In the blackness of the moonless night he can just make out the black shape of The One & All *in the darkness. The cove seems deserted. All is silent. Then, as he watches, something begins to happen. Down below on the beach Dwight can see shadowy figures beginning to move. He knows he has to think fast. He starts to gather springs of gorse, cutting off branches with a pocket knife, piling them up. The gorse rustles, dry and brittle. Once he has built a small pile, he takes the candle from the lantern and tries to set fire to the pile of dried gorse. For one terrible moment it looks as if the flames won't take hold. Then, with a sudden rush, the flames ignite and presently a fire is crackling on the headland.*

CUT TO:

91: EXT. NAMPARA BEACH – NIGHT 30

The longboat reaches the shore. Ross and Paul step onto the sand. Out of the darkness, Ted and other men come to secure the boat. Ted greets Paul.

TED Did ye find yer brother?

PAUL We did—

TED Was he well? Had he aught to tell?

ROSS To tell, yes. Of use? No.

Before Ted has time to register disappointment, something catches his eye.

TED *(suddenly)* What's that?

Gasps of shock. Everyone turns and sees the bonfire leaping and smoking up on Damsel Point. Curses from the men around. Then an unfamiliar shout and a shrill whistle. Then lanterns and figures are glimpsed, climbing down the sides of the cove. Ross runs back to the longboat.

ROSS Ambush! Relaunch! *Relaunch!*

He flings his weight against the side of the boat. Ted and Paul join him. The boat slithers back towards the sea. Two of the men in it are trying to row it away again. Paul and Ted jump in and hold out their hands for Ross to grab and be dragged along with them. Ross is about to grab them – then he changes his mind.

ROSS *(cont'd)* I'll take my chances here!

TED 'Ee'll never make it!

ROSS Row! Now! Get you gone!

He pushes the boat further into the waves. The oars catch and the boat pulls away into the darkness. All hell has now broken loose. Pandemonium on the beach. Smugglers fleeing, soldiers and gaugers chasing. Now Ross begins to run – out of the waves and up the beach. Behind him he hears a shout: 'Halt! You there!' He turns and sees a soldier pointing a musket at him. Ross veers sharply and keeps running. Another shout: 'Halt in the King's name – or I fire!' Ross ducks and switches direction. A musket explodes close to his ear. Ross turns and sees the soldier running towards him. He knocks the soldier flat and runs on.

CUT TO:

92: EXT. DAMSEL POINT – NIGHT 30

Dwight is feeding more branches onto the fire. A soldier comes up behind him and hits him on the back of the head with the butt of his musket. Dwight falls to the ground.

CUT TO:

93: EXT. CLIFF-TOP PATH – NIGHT 30

Ross keeps running. More shots are fired at him. He begins to run up a steep path at the side of the cove. Below him he can see the battle going on between soldiers, gaugers and smugglers on the beach. More shots are fired. Smugglers are falling. Others are captured without a fight. On Damsel Point the fire still blazes. Ross is out of breath now as he continues to struggle up the path. Suddenly a shape lurches out of the darkness, too quickly for Ross to avoid. It's Vercoe.

VERCOE You—!

A split second of hesitation. Then Ross punches him in the face. Vercoe falls. Ross flees.

CUT TO:

94: INT. NAMPARA HOUSE, PARLOUR – NIGHT 30

Demelza leaps up at the sound of musket fire and is halfway to the door before Trooper Wilkins intervenes.

TROOPER WILKINS None o' that, ma'am. You know the captain's orders—

DEMELZA I have a little boy upstairs! He'll be frighted! I must bring him down—

TROOPER WILKINS I can't allow that—

DEMELZA You make war on babies now? *Get out of my way!*

Trooper Wilkins bars her way. He and Demelza are face to face, eye to eye. He begins to lose his nerve.

TROOPER WILKINS *(to Prudie)* Is there a baby?

PRUDIE Course there is!

He hesitates, then:

TROOPER WILKINS Very well – but be quick about it.

He stands aside to let Demelza pass. She runs out and upstairs. Trooper Wilkins keeps guard at the foot of the stairs.

CUT TO:

95: INT. NAMPARA HOUSE, JEREMY'S ROOM – NIGHT 30

Demelza comes into the room to check on Jeremy. He is sleeping peacefully. She tiptoes over to the window, opens it and looks out. She can hear the sound of musket fire in the distance. She climbs up on the sill and begins to ease herself out of the window.

CUT TO:

96: EXT. NAMPARA HOUSE, LOW ROOF – NIGHT 30

Demelza scrambles down a low roof and drops to the ground. She starts running towards Nampara Fields and the cove.

CUT TO:

97: INT. COACH – NIGHT 30

Caroline is looking more and more despondent. Fighting back tears, she cuddles Horace.

CAROLINE Are you shivering, my precious? Perhaps we'd better go back inside before you catch a chill.

Her tears begin to fall and she makes no attempt to stop them.

CUT TO:

98: EXT. NAMPARA FIELDS – NIGHT 30

Ross is running through the fields, keeping his head down to avoid attracting attention. In the distance he can see the lights of Nampara. Then, as he scrambles across a stream, he collides with a figure who's running towards him. For a moment he's stunned – then to his immense relief:

ROSS Demelza—?

DEMELZA *Ross!* Oh thank God – I thought—

She collapses into his arms and sobs with relief.

ROSS We must get to the house—

DEMELZA There's a soldier – guardin' it—

ROSS How? Why?

DEMELZA McNeil—

ROSS Damn him—

Now she notices his hand is bleeding.

DEMELZA Are you hurt?

ROSS Just a scratch—

They're walking quickly. Suddenly they hear voices behind them.

DEMELZA They're coming—

They start to run.

CUT TO:

99: EXT. NAMPARA HOUSE, COURTYARD – NIGHT 30

Ross and Demelza run into the courtyard.

ROSS Go in through the kitchen. I must get to the cache—

DEMELZA How?

ROSS Through the side door. I have a key. Make haste—

They run and disappear into the darkness.

CUT TO:

100: INT. TRENWITH HOUSE, LIBRARY – NIGHT 30

Mrs Tabb has just brought Elizabeth and Aunt Agatha some alarming news. She bows and withdraws.

AUNT AGATHA Soldiers? At this time of night?

ELIZABETH There must be some unrest. *(then)* Why does Ross not answer my notes? Has he no care for us at all?

AUNT AGATHA He has his own family to protect.

ELIZABETH Then I must appeal for help elsewhere.

Aunt Agatha raises an eyebrow. She knows that 'elsewhere' means George.

CUT TO:

101: INT. NAMPARA HOUSE, KITCHEN/HALL – NIGHT 30

Demelza stumbles into the dark kitchen and out into the hall. There she is met by Trooper Wilkins, who is still guarding the foot of the stairs. He is puzzled by her sudden appearance.

TROOPER WILKINS Where've ye been? How did ye get down?

DEMELZA By the back stairs.

TROOPER WILKINS You never mentioned—

DEMELZA I'm here! Is that not enough?

Suddenly there's a hammering on the front door. Trooper Wilkins opens it and Vercoe bursts in. He is bleeding from a cut above the eye.

VERCOE Where's Captain Poldark?

DEMELZA St Ives, I b'lieve.

VERCOE You believe wrong. I saw him not ten minutes ago. *(to Trooper Wilkins)* Has he come in here?

TROOPER WILKINS No one's come in but you, sir.

VERCOE He was headed in this direction. He'll be somewhere about—

DEMELZA How dare you come breakin' in here – my husband will hear of it—

VERCOE And shortly, I trust! You will give us permission to search the house?

DEMELZA I most certainly will not!

Suddenly there is a further commotion and McNeil enters with more soldiers, who are dragging a dazed and bloodied Dwight, and several other smugglers. McNeil himself is wounded.

CAPTAIN MCNEIL You've searched the cellars?

TROOPER WILKINS Empty.

CAPTAIN MCNEIL No contraband?

TROOPER WILKINS None.

Demelza squares up to McNeil.

DEMELZA I told you Ross was in St Ives!

CAPTAIN MCNEIL I wish I believed you. *(to Vercoe)* Search the outhouses, the stables. I'll take the library—

DEMELZA The library? 'Tis usually locked—

CAPTAIN MCNEIL No doubt you have a key.

Demelza looks him straight in the eye, hoping against hope that the panic she now feels will not betray her to him.

CUT TO:

102: INT. NAMPARA HOUSE, LIBRARY – NIGHT 30

McNeil comes into the library, followed by Demelza and several soldiers. He seems to know exactly what he's looking for.

CAPTAIN MCNEIL Over here – bring more light!

Two soldiers bring lanterns and McNeil lights a candle. Demelza sees at once that the two chests have been moved from above the trapdoor to the cache and the rug is only half covering it. McNeil and Vercoe are searching the floor, whilst two other soldiers are rifling through chests and drawers. Demelza watches from the doorway, hardly daring to look. To her horror she sees two droplets of blood on the floor. She slides her foot over to them and tries to rub them away. McNeil now shines his light on the rug which half covers the trapdoor.

CAPTAIN MCNEIL *(cont'd) (to Vercoe)* Here it is.

He pulls away the rug and reveals the trapdoor beneath.

VERCOE Just as he said.

Demelza fails to subdue a gasp of horror. The informer – whoever he is – has done his work. McNeil finds a gap in the floorboards – pulls one up, then another, then another. Below them the trapdoor is revealed.

CAPTAIN MCNEIL Stand back, all of you. Vercoe, would ye mind?

He motions to Vercoe to pull the catch of the trapdoor. Demelza, hardly daring to, but unable to help herself, edges forward. Vercoe opens the trapdoor. Demelza closes her eyes, she sways, she could be about to faint.

CAPTAIN MCNEIL *(cont'd)* More light! Damn you!

More light is brought. Demelza edges forward, hardly daring to look. And then she does. The cache is empty.

CUT TO:

103: EXT. NAMPARA HOUSE – DAY 31

Dawn breaks over Nampara. Two soldiers are stationed by the front door. Presently it opens and Dwight comes out. He goes to retrieve his horse. Demelza comes after him.

DEMELZA They let you go—

DWIGHT Finally. Now I must go to Caroline. Pray God she'll understand.

DEMELZA O' course she will.

DWIGHT And Ross?

DEMELZA No sign of him. I cannot conceive where he'd be.

DWIGHT Not in the cache at any rate.

He mounts his horse.

DEMELZA You won't forget us?

DWIGHT Never.

A moment between them. Then he spurs on his horse and rides away. Demelza remains, worried out of her mind for Ross.

CUT TO:

104: INT. KEMPTHORNE COTTAGE – DAY 31

Zacky, Paul and Jud arrive, to find May and Lottie looking terrified – but no sign of Charlie.

JUD Where's Kempthorne? *(no answer)* Where is he?

Lottie and May shrink back from Jud. Zacky tries a gentler approach.

ZACKY Where's your father, chile? Never fear – we won't hurt 'ee.

Neither girl will answer. Lottie snatches up a book – The History of Primrose Prettyface *– and clutches it protectively as if fearing they'll take it away from her. Seeing they'll get no sense out of the girls, Jud stomps off.*

JUD *(muttering)* 'E'll have no pretty face if we get our 'ands on 'im!

Now Rosina appears.

ROSINA 'Twas Charlie. The informer.

Zacky and Paul nod sadly. Rosina seems resigned. Then she takes one look at Lottie and May and opens her arms to them. They run to her and she embraces them. They sense that Rosina won't desert the girls even if their father has.

CUT TO:

105: EXT. KILLEWARREN – DAY 31

Dwight is given a letter. He tears it open. It reads:

CAROLINE'S VOICE 'Dear Dwight, I have left for London with my uncle, a move which cannot surprise you after the fiasco of last night . . .'

CUT TO:

106: INT. COACH – DAY 31

Caroline sits with Horace and Ray in the coach on her way to London.

CAROLINE *(VO)* 'It is better this way. Ever since we agreed to elope I have known of your struggle – between your infatuation for me – and your real love: your patients. Now you need no longer worry – or give anything up – except me—'

CUT TO:

107: EXT. KILLEWARREN – DAY 31

Dwight reads Caroline's letter with mounting dismay.

CAROLINE *(VO)* 'And that you have already done. So farewell, Dwight. I shall never see you again. Your sincere friend, Caroline Penvenen.'

Dwight is almost weeping with despair.

CUT TO:

108: INT. TRENWITH HOUSE, LIBRARY – DAY 31

George has called to update Elizabeth and Aunt Agatha.

ELIZABETH George! I've been worried out of my mind—

AUNT AGATHA *I* haven't.

GEORGE There was a smuggling incident. The military were out in force.

AUNT AGATHA Pity they've nothing better to do.

GEORGE Though I'm told they had their eye on a bigger prize— *(beat)* Your nephew.

ELIZABETH Ross?

GEORGE I'm not clear as to his precise involvement. Merely that he *was* involved.

AUNT AGATHA Stuff!

GEORGE *(to Elizabeth)* It baffles me – why he considers himself above the law. Exempt from the duty we law-abiding citizens pay on *legally* imported goods—

AUNT AGATHA Piffle!

ELIZABETH Is it certain?

GEORGE As it stands – he's disappeared. On the run from justice no doubt. *(then)* I pity anyone who must depend on such a man. Oh, no doubt he'll live to fight – and offend – another day. But still—

This gives Elizabeth food for thought. And gratitude towards George. Which is exactly what George intended.

CUT TO:

109: EXT. NAMPARA HOUSE – DAY 31

Soldiers are still on guard outside the house.

CUT TO:

110: INT. NAMPARA HOUSE, KITCHEN – DAY 31

Demelza, trying to keep busy, is making rushlights with Prudie. She's beside herself with worry.

DEMELZA *(low)* He must've reached the library – the table was moved – and the rug – but if he'd no time to open the cache—

PRUDIE Where could he be?

Prudie and Demelza exchange a glance. This is baffling, and worry-ing, for both of them. Then, from outside, they hear a soldier barking out orders.

PRUDIE *(cont'd)* They soldiers—

DEMELZA *(horrified)* Have they found him?

More worried than ever, Demelza runs out into the hallway.

CUT TO:

111: EXT. NAMPARA HOUSE – DAY 31

Four soldiers march up to the gate. Demelza and Prudie come to the front door, fearing the worst. But to their surprise, the two soldiers guarding the door peel off and join the other four. Then all six march away. Demelza is relieved – but none the wiser. And no less worried for the safety of Ross.

CUT TO:

112: EXT. HENDRAWNA BEACH – DAY 31

A body is washed up on the beach. Jud and Paul are revealed, looking on.

JUD So was he kill'd? Or did he do the job hisself?

PAUL Reckon we'll never know.

CUT TO:

113: EXT. WARLEGGAN HOUSE, GEORGE'S DEN – DAY 31

George comes in to find Tankard waiting for him.

TANKARD Mistress Poldark was reassured?

GEORGE I believe so.

TANKARD I wonder she does not remarry. A husband could offer her more protection.

GEORGE He could. And he will.

Tankard eyes him curiously. Then the penny drops.

TANKARD She will surely never consent?

GEORGE How much would you care to wager?

CUT TO:

114: EXT. NAMPARA HOUSE – DUSK 31

Demelza stands in the doorway, watching the dusk gather. There's still no sign of Ross.

CUT TO:

115: INT. NAMPARA HOUSE, PARLOUR – DUSK 31

Prudie is drawing the curtains. Demelza comes in and begins to light the candles.

DEMELZA His hand was bloodied – I can't stop thinkin' of it – if 'twas worse than he thought – if he mebbe now lies somewhere, bleedin' to death—

PRUDIE Hush, maid, don' think such a thing!

CUT TO:

116: INT. NAMPARA HOUSE, LIBRARY – DUSK 31

The cache is still open and empty. Then something moves. It's a side panel. It is being pushed out from the inside. Slowly, cautiously, the panel is pushed fully out into the cache. Then, from a second cache, hidden inside the first, Ross emerges. With extreme care he climbs out. He edges towards the window to check if the coast is clear. Then he goes to listen at the door of the library. He hears footsteps approaching. He pulls back hastily as he hears Prudie going upstairs.

CUT TO:

117: INT. NAMPARA HOUSE, PARLOUR – DUSK 31

Demelza sits staring into the fire. To distract herself she begins to hum a snatch of song.

DEMELZA *(sings softly)*

I'd hold a finger to my tongue
I'd hold a finger waiting . . .
My heart is sore
Until it joins in song
With your heart mating . . .

She is unaware that she is being watched. Ross is standing in the doorway. He looks at her a long time. Then, as if sensing his eyes upon her, she looks up. She can hardly believe what she sees. Without a word she rushes to him. He holds her in his arms and crushes her to his chest in joy and relief.

Episode 8

1: EXT. NAMPARA HOUSE, COURTYARD – DAY 32 (EARLY SPRING 1793)

Demelza, carrying Jeremy, collects linens from the line. Among the items is a shirt of Ross's – threadbare and torn. As she gathers it in, she fingers the frayed cuffs and sleeves. It's too torn and frayed for Ross to keep wearing – but perhaps she can make something of it? As she glances out across the fields, she sees a figure striding towards the house. Presently Ross, soberly dressed, comes out and greets him. It's Jud. He hands Ross a note. The two men talk. There is something furtive about their conversation. Presently Jud strides away. Demelza joins Ross.

DEMELZA What did he bring?

ROSS A proposal. *(beat)* From Trencrom.

DEMELZA Judas, Ross! Will 'ee never learn?

ROSS Possibly not.

DEMELZA Tell Trencrom – till he offer to stand at court instead o' thee, he can sling his proposals – an' his guineas – an' his secret caches – off Damsel Point!

She hands Jeremy to Ross and stomps off with the linens. Ross raises an eyebrow at Jeremy – who smiles.

CUT TO:

2: EXT. DWIGHT'S COTTAGE – DAY 32

Dwight opens the door to a messenger. He is handed a package. The elegant handwriting suggests the writer is a lady. Dwight fears the worst.

CUT TO:

3: INT. WARLEGGAN HOUSE, GEORGE'S DEN – DAY 32

Rich silks and embroidery catch the light as George stands, allowing himself to be dressed. A footman holds out clothes – tasteful, expensive, beautifully made. George is calm, purposeful, full of quiet confidence. It's as if he is donning armour, preparing for battle. Which indeed he is. Cary appears.

CARY My money's on transportation.

GEORGE It's not essential. Elizabeth's already unnerved by his involvement. Any form of discredit in court today will suffice.

CARY I admire your confidence.

GEORGE When one has laid the foundations, one has every right to expect a result.

CUT TO:

4: INT. DWIGHT'S COTTAGE – DAY 32

Dwight has opened the package – to reveal a pile of letters, all addressed to 'Miss Caroline Penvenen, Hatton Garden, London'. Then there's a note from Caroline herself. He opens it. It reads: 'Dear Dwight, I am returning your letters . . .'

CUT TO:

5: INT. PENVENEN HOUSE, LONDON – DAY 32

Caroline sits at her desk writing to Dwight.

CAROLINE *(VO)* '. . . which I have fully digested and in which I find nothing to make me regret my decision. Your preference for your patients and friends is estimable . . .'

CUT TO:

6: INT. DWIGHT'S COTTAGE – DAY 32

Dwight continues to read Caroline's letter.

CAROLINE *(VO)* 'Had it not been at my expense, I would not now be requesting you never to write to me again. But it was. And I do. So adieu.'

Dwight looks resigned. It was exactly what he'd feared. He throws the package down and goes out.

CUT TO:

7: EXT. MARKET PLACE – DAY 32

Demelza walks through the market place, stopping now and then to examine some stall or the wares of some seller. She fingers some ribbons and lace, then decides they're too expensive and walks on. Presently she spots a gleaming new carriage up ahead. In it sit Elizabeth, Geoffrey Charles and Mrs Chynoweth. For a moment Demelza considers sidling off unseen – but then Elizabeth sees her. An awkward moment. It's a long time since they've met – a lot has changed – and neither are at ease with the encounter.

ELIZABETH Demelza! How are you? I've been meaning to call upon you—

Mrs Chynoweth makes the merest bow.

ELIZABETH *(cont'd)* – to thank you for your kindness these past few months—

DEMELZA Lending you my husband?

ELIZABETH In a manner of speaking—

DEMELZA Oh, you're most welcome to him! Long as you remember where he b'long and send 'im home when you're done with him!

The encounter is apparently lighthearted but in reality is anything but. Then George appears, carrying various parcels. He bows politely to Demelza.

GEORGE Mistress Poldark! Are you here for the trial? I hope you'll be well entertained.

DEMELZA Why sir, will there be jugglers and dancing bears?

Elizabeth seems keen to diffuse any potential tension.

ELIZABETH *(to Demelza)* I wish you a lenient magistrate.

DEMELZA *(smiling)* I wish us an honest one!

Demelza bows and walks off. Elizabeth is rattled by this encounter. George and Mrs Chynoweth notice but make no comment. George hands the parcels to Geoffrey Charles.

GEORGE For you, young man.

ELIZABETH George, you must stop this—

GEORGE Cannot a man spoil his godson?

George ruffles Geoffrey Charles's hair, gets into the carriage. They drive away.

CUT TO:

8: INT. MAGISTRATES' COURT, TRURO – DAY 32

Demelza makes her way into the public gallery. To her dismay, the presiding magistrate is none other than the Reverend Dr Halse. And he doesn't seem any more benign than when she last saw him. Now a court official shouts: 'Call Ross Poldark.' Demelza takes a deep breath. She's dreading, and fully expecting, Ross to treat Halse with his customary insolence.

CUT TO:

9: INT. MAGISTRATES' COURT, TRURO – DAY 32

Ross stands in the dock. He scans the court and finally finds the person he's looking for: Jud. A look passes between them. A question from Jud. Not yet answered by Ross. Now Ross turns to his nemesis – Halse – whose eyes light up at the sight of Ross standing before him.

REVEREND DR HALSE Well, well, Mr Poldark – here we are again.

Ross's face is impassive. This time it's Halse who is trying to goad Ross.

REVEREND DR HALSE *(cont'd)* There are those who seem capable of learning from their mistakes. And those who do not. Clearly you fall into the latter category.

Another glance from Ross to Jud. A decision made. A barely perceptible nod of agreement.

REVEREND DR HALSE *(cont'd)* *(getting impatient)* Mr Poldark—?

ROSS With the deepest respect, sir, I beg to differ.

Murmurs of surprise from the public. Demelza looks surprised. Ross's tone is unusually conciliatory.

REVEREND DR HALSE On what grounds?

ROSS On the grounds that on the night in question I was not at Nampara Cove, but in St Ives. *(beat)* And can produce three witnesses who will swear to the fact.

Uproar in court. This development is clearly unexpected. Especially by Demelza! Now three figures are ushered in: a farmer, his wife and their son, who stand humbly waiting to give evidence. Halse seems incensed by this turn of events.

REVEREND DR HALSE Customs Officer Vercoe alleges you were part of the smuggling operation – that you attacked him and broke his nose.

ROSS I'm sorry to hear of Mr Vercoe's injury – but as my witnesses will testify, the assailant could not possibly have been I.

The farmer, his wife and his son nod their agreement. Jud too. Halse is seething. He suspects – correctly – that this is a set-up. He consults his fellow-magistrates. He clearly doesn't like their conclusion. Eventually (and very begrudgingly) he waves Ross aside.

REVEREND DR HALSE Case dismissed.

Uproar in court. Ross stands down. Demelza is astonished. She tries to catch Ross's eye. He's looking uncharacteristically penitent. Then a court official calls, 'Call Dwight Enys.' Presently Dwight appears. In contrast to Ross, he seems irritable and determined to be combative. Reverend Dr Halse eyes him narrowly, consults with his fellow-magistrates. Then:

REVEREND DR HALSE *(cont'd)* I have perused your statement and find it singularly unconvincing.

DWIGHT In what regard, sir?

REVEREND DR HALSE No man, no educated man, can suddenly appear on a cliff edge and start building a bonfire without certain conclusions being drawn. What explanation can you offer?

DWIGHT It was a cold night – and my coat was thin.

A few muffled sniggers are heard. Reverend Dr Halse bristles.

REVEREND DR HALSE A heavy responsibility rests upon all men of reputation to help stamp out the illegal conduct of their less enlightened neighbours – not to encourage or participate in it, as, failing any other explanation, it must be assumed you were doing. What have you to say?

DWIGHT Nothing that would convince you, sir.

Halse bristles further. Thwarted in his attempt to punish Ross, he diverts his ire onto Dwight. He consults with his fellow-magistrates then smiles savagely at him.

REVEREND DR HALSE Fined fifty pounds or three months' imprisonment.

Dwight receives his sentence without comment, but with a defiant look. Ross, now a spectator, stifles a smile. This could have been him! But for once, he's learned to play the game.

CUT TO:

10: EXT. MAGISTRATES' COURT, TRURO – DAY 32

Dwight comes out of the court and sees Ross waiting for him. As he is about to make his way over, Jud intercepts him and whispers something in his ear. Dwight bristles.

DWIGHT Tell Mr Trencrom I thank him but I am perfectly capable of paying my own fine.

Jud shrugs as if to say, 'Your loss.' Dwight goes over to join Ross.

ROSS You should take his bounty. Trencrom looks after his friends.

DWIGHT Trencrom is not my friend and I did not go to all that trouble for his sake.

ROSS No, for mine. Have I told you what I feel about that?

DWIGHT Many times.

ROSS I'm under an enduring debt.

DWIGHT No—

DEMELZA'S VOICE *Enduring.*

Now they see Demelza walking towards them, smiling.

DEMELZA So now it's all over, when d'you leave for London?

DWIGHT I've no plans to do so.

DEMELZA But your wedding to Caroline—?

DWIGHT *(breezily)* Is off. *(beat)* We were incompatible. I see that now. It could never have lasted and would have led to misery on both sides.

Demelza is dismayed, Ross disappointed but not entirely surprised.

CUT TO:

11: INT. NAMPARA HOUSE, PARLOUR – DAY 32

Demelza and Ross, just returned, are having tea, Demelza sharing hers with Jeremy.

DEMELZA What made you decide? To take Trencrom's offer?

ROSS When a man's prospects are in tatters, he can ill afford to be stubborn! In four days, Wheal Grace will close. I thought you'd not care to be penniless *and* husbandless!

DEMELZA I never thought to see the day—

ROSS That I'd go to jail?

DEMELZA That you'd play the penitent to avoid it!

ROSS I played the game! Is that not what you wanted?

DEMELZA Since when do 'ee heed *my* wishes?!

They both laugh. Then:

DEMELZA *(cont'd)* Is there really no hope for Grace?

ROSS On Saturday our coal will run out, the engine will halt and so will the whole dismal venture!

DEMELZA I'm sorry for it.

ROSS I'm sorry for many things. Our workers, our coffers—

DEMELZA Our mysterious benefactor—

ROSS Whoever he is! Now he may never be repaid. But most of all, I'm sorry for you.

DEMELZA Nay, Ross.

ROSS For selling my shares in a profitable mine and sinking them into this utter folly. All I can say is, I've learned my lesson and will never again be guilty of such recklessness!

Demelza's not convinced, but she's glad to hear it nonetheless. Now Prudie comes in.

PRUDIE Cap'n Henshawe to see 'ee, sur.

Henshawe is shown in. He has a strange expression on his face – as if he's struggling to keep some excitement at bay.

HENSHAWE Cap'n Ross – ma'am – excuse the intrusion but I'd like for ye to take a look at something.

He puts down on the table a small sack.

ROSS *(amused)* What's this, the last of our coal?

HENSHAWE Young Carkeek's just come up, bringing this with him. I thought ye should see it.

Ross empties the bag onto the table. A dozen pieces of quartzose rock fall out. Henshawe watches Ross's face keenly. He doesn't want to pre-empt anything, yet he can hardly contain himself.

HENSHAWE *(cont'd)* Pick 'em up.

Ross picks one up, weighs it in his hand. It's clearly heavy.

ROSS What is it? Lead?

HENSHAWE Tin.

Ross looks surprised. This is not what he expected.

HENSHAWE *(cont'd)* It's in that main shaft we've been sinking – below the sixty fathoms. They come upon it today.

ROSS Have you been down? *(Henshawe nods)* Is there any size to the thing?

HENSHAWE Six feet or more across and we don't yet know how deep.

Demelza has been silent, all the while watching Ross like a hawk. She can tell that all his senses are suddenly on alert – though he's refusing to let himself get too excited.

ROSS You know I'm in the process of closing the books. On Saturday the venturers at Wheal Radiant will make me an offer for our head gear and Grace will close.

HENSHAWE And this? *(the quartzose rock)*

ROSS We've spent eighteen months seeking copper. You expect me to get excited over a small parcel of tin?

Demelza and Henshawe exchange a glance. There's always been an understanding between these two – and Henshawe's look at Demelza now is to ascertain whether she thinks he should persist. She raises an eyebrow to suggest he should.

DEMELZA Who found it?

HENSHAWE Ted Carkeek and Paul Daniel.

ROSS And they think they've discovered El Dorado?

HENSHAWE *(calm but firm)* I'd like for you to come and see it for yourself.

Ross and Demelza exchange a glance. Demelza's look says, 'It can't hurt, can it?' Ross gets up, nods to Henshawe. As they go out, Demelza picks up a piece of rock and weighs it in her hand. It's heavy. Could Henshawe be right? She follows them out.

CUT TO:

12: EXT. WHEAL GRACE – DAY 32

The slow, measured swing of the balance bob of the huge pumping engine dominates the scene. Henshawe, Ross and Demelza approach Wheal Grace together. Demelza is carrying a basket.

HENSHAWE Trevithick reckons his engine should last fifty years—

ROSS No doubt he's right—

HENSHAWE *(pointedly)* Given the opportunity.

Ross glances at him keenly. He can tell that Henshawe is quietly excited about this potential discovery. Now, as they near the mine, they – and we – are struck by its bustle of activity: men, women and children all hard at work. They look up expectantly as Ross passes, as if willing him to find a way – any way – to keep the mine going. As they approach the mine entrance, Ted and Paul are waiting, trying to suppress their excitement.

PAUL 'Tis worth a look, Cap'n.

TED You'll not be disappointed!

HENSHAWE *(to Demelza, as a joke)* Will 'ee be joinin' us below, ma'am?

DEMELZA I d' think not, sir. But do 'ee take my assistant an' let 'im report back to me?

A smile of amusement between them. Henshawe salutes. Demelza gives Ross a look of amused defiance and heads off.

CUT TO:

13: EXT. SAWLE COTTAGES – DAY 32

Demelza is singing to herself as she approaches Sawle Cottages where Rosina, Lottie and May Kempthorne are embroiled in animated conversation. Seeing her, Lottie and May run towards her to see what she has in her basket for them. Demelza hands them some apples and some bread, then goes into the cottage.

CUT TO:

14: INT. SAWLE COTTAGES, BETTY'S COTTAGE – DAY 32

Demelza comes in to find the heavily pregnant Betty. Rosina follows her in.

BETTY Is't true? A keenly lode found – an' the mine saved?

DEMELZA Oh, I wish, Betty – as much as you!

ROSINA But wishin' don't make it true?

BETTY I'll save *my* wishes for an easy birthin'.

DEMELZA Now that is wishful thinkin'!

Everyone laughs. Dwight appears with Lottie and May.

DWIGHT Good day to you, ladies.

ROSINA Don' 'ee fear, Betty – if anyone can make it right, 'tis Dr Enys!

One thing is certain: Caroline may not want him, but he's still very popular amongst his patients – especially Rosina. They all clamour round him. He catches Demelza's eye and they exchange a smile.

DEMELZA What 'tis to be a miracle worker!

CUT TO:

15: INT. WHEAL GRACE, TUNNEL – DAY 32

Ted holds up a lantern for Ross to inspect the seam of tin. Ross peers at it closely. Paul and Henshawe also cluster round. Paul and Ted exchange hopeful looks. Henshawe tries to remain impassive. Ross hacks away at it a while, peers more closely still. A hush. Everyone's waiting for his verdict. Eventually:

ROSS I agree. It's not unimpressive.

HENSHAWE You said all along you'd a feeling to go deeper.

ROSS Yes, but for copper, not for tin. Anyway, it may be just the merest pocket. *(then, seeing Ted and Paul look disheartened)* Bring up as much as you can before we close. It will make a difference to your final earnings.

PAUL We'd've give up more easily without this find.

ROSS I know that, Paul. But it's come too late to save us.

He gives them a look of commiseration, then heads back along the tunnel. Henshawe follows him. When they're away from the men:

HENSHAWE 'Tis a queer one, though. Copper under tin, you'd expect—

ROSS But not tin under copper?

HENSHAWE T' my mind, what's needed is breathin' space – to see if this'll amount to anything—

ROSS I'd agree, but how's it to happen? I tell you, I haven't twenty pounds in the world.

HENSHAWE Well, there's the rub—

ROSS There's four days before we close. They'd be advised to work hard till Saturday.

He heads off up the tunnel. Henshawe follows, thoughtful.

CUT TO:

16: EXT. SAWLE COTTAGES – DAY 32

Dwight and Demelza emerge from Betty's cottage.

DEMELZA Betty seems fair?

DWIGHT I wish she were stronger. But all these people are half-starved—

DEMELZA She's braver than she looks. We all are!

DWIGHT She wants me at the birthing – though in truth, she's as well off with you and Mrs Zacky—

DEMELZA It'd make her easier, knowing she be tended by a man of learning!

DWIGHT *(laughs)* With little *practical* experience!

DEMELZA Not so! What 'ee done for Rosina – was that not practical?

Rosina has been waiting for them. Clearly she's smitten with Dwight.

ROSINA Was indeed!

DWIGHT Has your knee given you any trouble since the night of the ambush?

ROSINA No, sur. An' I'm that grateful. What would've 'appened if 'ee hadn't come to help me?

DEMELZA You'd be wed to Charlie—

ROSINA An' never known'd he was th' informer. 'Tis better this way.

Dwight and Demelza walk on. Dwight is thoughtful.

DEMELZA Is it? If you hadn't helped Rosina—

DWIGHT I'd be married, in a new town, tending new patients, living a new life.

DEMELZA Rosina's knee do 'ave much to answer for!

DWIGHT It has saved me from myself at any rate!

They both laugh, but she can see Dwight's heart is not in it.

CUT TO:

17: INT. NAMPARA HOUSE, PARLOUR – DUSK 32

Ross, with Jeremy on his knee, is examining some pieces of ore which contain samples of tin from the latest find. The tin catches the light. Demelza is laying out the pieces of a bodice which she is making out of Ross's frayed shirt. She glances up at Ross and sees he is unexpectedly preoccupied by the samples.

DEMELZA This new find – what do it mean?

ROSS In a word – nothing. *(then)* Oh, perhaps if we'd struck a massive bed of tin, requiring minimum outlay and promising quick returns—

DEMELZA But tin d' fetch less than copper—

ROSS Considerably less—

DEMELZA An' I never heard tell of any *sizeable* find hereabouts—

ROSS Which is what makes me think this will all peter out. Besides, what good would it do? The tin industry's much depressed. And no one would be willing to finance an exhausted copper mine on the strength of a few samples of rock.

DEMELZA A pity.

ROSS There it is.

Ross lets Jeremy down to play on the floor. They go back to their separate tasks. Then:

DEMELZA Did I tell you I met Horace Treneglos at the market?

ROSS Was he well?

DEMELZA He sent his compliments – and said 'twas a pity you'd sold *all* your shares in Wheal Leisure.

Ross halts. She waits for him to reply or deny it.

DEMELZA *(cont'd)* I said he was mistaken – for if you had, you'd surely have told me.

Ross hesitates. He's always known he would have to tell Demelza some time. Unfortunately this is not the ideal moment.

ROSS I've been meaning to mention this for some time but not quite known how to begin.

Demelza waits – sensing Ross's unease and correctly guessing the cause.

ROSS *(cont'd)* As you know, Francis sunk his last six hundred pounds into Wheal Grace.

DEMELZA Yes—

ROSS When he died he left Elizabeth with considerable debts. To relieve her poverty, I bought his Wheal Grace shares through a third party, knowing Elizabeth would not accept the money as a gift.

DEMELZA But why should you—?

ROSS I felt myself under a burden of obligation – to Francis – and his family – which is now discharged.

Demelza is silent. She's not sure if Ross expects her to be understanding or angry.

ROSS *(cont'd)* Of course, when I did it, we had Trencrom's money coming in. Since the ambush—

Demelza says nothing, continues to pin together the bodice.

ROSS *(cont'd)* Are you angry?

DEMELZA That you help Elizabeth—

ROSS And Geoffrey Charles—

DEMELZA And leave Jeremy and me to fend for ourselves?

ROSS You have *me* to fend for you. They have no one.

DEMELZA Are you sure?

Ross looks at her in surprise. What can she mean?

DEMELZA *(cont'd)* I did hear that George is being very obliging—

ROSS Oh, doubtless he *would* be if Elizabeth would let him. But she will not.

Demelza nods, a kind of 'You know best, Ross' nod. For some reason, her lack of a challenge makes him feel he has to justify himself all the more.

ROSS *(cont'd)* One of George's ambitions, before Francis died, was to drive a wedge between our two families – and the easiest way was by befriending theirs. In offering to help Elizabeth now, he's simply continuing the same tactics.

DEMELZA Yes, Ross.

ROSS Though it wasn't my aim in arranging this money for her, it does have the effect of strengthening her hand against him.

DEMELZA Yes, Ross.

She continues to lay out and pin the bodice. For reasons he can't explain, Ross is uneasy about her lack of further argument. He's considering whether to try and justify himself further. In the end he decides against it.

CUT TO:

18: EXT. NAMPARA HOUSE – DAY 33

Early morning. Demelza comes to the front door with Jeremy in her arms and looks out over the fields. Presently she sees Prudie rushing across the meadow towards the house.

PRUDIE Betty Carkeek! – 'Tis 'er time – an' Dr Enys can't be found—

DEMELZA *(shouting back into the house)* Ross? Fetch me the brandywine!

Prudie runs up, wheezing and gasping for breath. Ross appears behind Demelza with a bottle of brandy. Demelza takes it and deposits Jeremy in Ross's arms. Then she turns Prudie round and points her in the direction of Sawle. As they head off, Ross has barely time to wrangle Jeremy when Jud bustles up.

JUD Cap'n – 'oo's'it – Wheal – Henshawe – askin' f'r 'ee – mine – yourn – whatever—

Ross hands Jeremy to Jud and walks off. Jud looks at Jeremy as if to say 'What the hell do I do with this?' Jeremy lets out a wail of dismay.

CUT TO:

19: EXT. SAWLE COTTAGES – DAY 33

Demelza and Prudie rush up to the cottages.

CUT TO:

20: INT. SAWLE COTTAGES – DAY 33

Demelza and Prudie rush in to find Betty is in labour.

DEMELZA Where's Dr Enys?

BETTY Rosina's gone f'r 'im—

A roar of pain from Betty. Demelza gets out the bottle of brandy.

DEMELZA Don' 'ee fret, Betty – I've fetched 'ee something f' the pain!

At that moment Rosina runs in, followed by Dwight.

ROSINA I found 'im, Betty! Dr Enys be 'ere!

CUT TO:

21: INT. WHEAL GRACE – DAY 33

Henshawe is showing Ross the latest samples which have been brought to the surface. Paul, Ted and Zacky wait excitedly as Ross examines the rocks. They can hardly contain themselves.

PAUL We've open'd her up a tidy bit these past days—

TED This last we brought up – 'tis as rich as ever I see'd—

ZACKY More 'n more it look like a lode of value – not just a freak bunch—

Ross nods, takes on board all they're saying but won't allow himself to get carried away. Now Henshawe beckons him aside.

HENSHAWE *(low)* More 'nit go against the grain t' let 'er fill up with water – knowin' what's down there—

ROSS It goes against the grain at *any* time – but without coal to keep the pump working—

HENSHAWE Well, that's what I bin thinking. *(beat)* If I'm eagerer than you, then I'm also abler to back my judgement. Wheal Leisure's done well for me and I've made savings. I could put down a hundred pounds – 'twould see us through another month—

ROSS *(amazed)* You'd be willing to do that? After all our failures?

HENSHAWE In a day or so we'll know better. If nothing comes of it, we can close and I'll have lost twenty pounds. If it go on as I think it may, I'll back it a month longer.

Ross can hardly believe what he's hearing.

HENSHAWE *(cont'd)* But we must move now. With your permission I thought to send out for more coal.

ROSS By all means – send out.

Ross's face struggles not to betray the smallest sign of a feeling to which he has for some time been a stranger: hope.

CUT TO:

22: INT. SAWLE COTTAGES, BETTY'S COTTAGE – DUSK 33

Gasps of pain. Betty's face is contorted with agony. Demelza is holding her hand. Prudie, looking on, is nodding wisely.

PRUDIE 'E'll be a boy, tha's sure! They'm trouble e'n *afore* they born!

Then Betty gives an almighty roar. Dwight delivers the baby with calm efficiency. The baby cries. Dwight cuts the cord then hands baby Carkeek to Demelza to swaddle. Presently Ted's voice is heard.

TED'S VOICE Betty? 'Ee'll never guess! There's news o' Grace—

He comes in – to see Demelza with his newborn son in her arms.

DEMELZA An' a fine new Carkeek boy!

Ted seems more taken aback at all these people in his humble cottage than at the news of his new baby.

DEMELZA *(cont'd)* What news o' Grace?

TED She's to stay ope another month!

BETTY 'Tis a blessing we never look'd for.

TED God willin' the lode should hold – an' I'll be able to feed my family!

Everyone laughs. Demelza offers Dwight a swig of brandy. He declines, but Prudie fetches cups and pours for the rest of them.

PRUDIE To young Master Carkeek!

TED And tin!

CUT TO:

23: EXT. WHEAL GRACE – DAY 34

Early morning. Mine workers applaud as fresh coal supplies arrive at the mine. Everywhere there is a sense of optimism and hope. Ross and Henshawe look on with satisfaction. Ted comes up to them.

TED *(to Ross)* God bless 'ee, sur.

ROSS Bless Captain Henshawe. He's our saviour!

Ted knuckles his forehead to Henshawe and heads to the mine.

CUT TO:

24: INT. WARLEGGAN HOUSE, GEORGE'S DEN – DAY 34

George is practising his sparring, alone. Cary wanders in.

CARY This is becoming an obsession. Are you planning to join the army?

GEORGE Why would I do that? When I have battle fronts of my own at home.

He practises a few more moves. Then:

GEORGE *(cont'd)* Which reminds me – have those forces been deployed yet?

CUT TO:

25: EXT. TRENWITH HOUSE – DAY 34

A bedraggled and surly bunch of militant tinners arrive and begin to set up their dig in full view of Trenwith. Almost as if they've been sent – and told where to dig.

CUT TO:

26: INT. TRENWITH HOUSE, LIBRARY – DAY 34

Elizabeth comes in to find Aunt Agatha and Mrs Chynoweth enthroned on either side of the fire, Aunt Agatha asleep and snoring. Elizabeth seems upset.

MRS CHYNOWETH Don't scowl, dear. A wrinkled brow is not becoming.

ELIZABETH I'm at my wits' end with Tabb. He contradicts everything I say – as if he thinks *he* is master here now.

MRS CHYNOWETH Dismiss him.

ELIZABETH But then Mrs Tabb will go – and I will have to engage new servants – and they will never learn our ways. *(then)* And now these letters have come – all these questions which apparently only I can answer: a tithe of one pound, six shillings on the seines of certain fishing boats in Sawle. Should the fishermen be pressed for money? I don't know! Should they? Can I afford *not* to press them? Whose need is greater?

Now she looks out of the window and to her horror sees the militant tinners starting to dig.

ELIZABETH *(cont'd)* Dear God, is there no end to it?

MRS CHYNOWETH What is it?

She gets up and comes over to the window.

MRS CHYNOWETH *(cont'd)* Who are these people?

ELIZABETH Tinners. Exercising their rights under Stannary Law to prospect for tin—

MRS CHYNOWETH On your land? But this is outrageous! Vulgars permitted by law to violate the purlieu of a gentleman's estate! How can such a thing be lawful? It's monstrous! *Monstrous!*

She begins to go red in the face – then to choke – then her features begin to convulse. Outrage has turned to apoplexy.

CUT TO:

27: EXT. SAWLE COTTAGES – DAY 34

Demelza brings more food for Lottie and May, who are being looked after by Rosina.

DEMELZA 'Tis a blessing the girls have 'ee t' care f'r 'em.

ROSINA Who else is there, now their father's gone?

Now Dwight emerges from Ted and Betty's cottage.

DWIGHT The child seems lusty – and Betty shows no sign of childbed fever. I hope they'll both survive.

Then a Trenwith servant comes up and gives him a note. He opens it and glances at it briefly.

DWIGHT *(cont'd)* From Mistress Poldark at Trenwith. Her mother's been taken ill. *(to the Trenwith servant)* Tell your mistress I'll be there directly.

CUT TO:

28: INT. WHEAL GRACE, TUNNEL – DAY 34

Ross watches as Paul, Ted and Zacky work an underhand stope of tin. Henshawe joins him.

ROSS No sign of it petering out?

HENSHAWE Far from it. *(then)* You know I'm not one to raise hopes, but it could be significant.

Ross takes his own pickaxe and joins Zacky, Ted and Paul at the rock face.

CUT TO:

29: INT. TRENWITH HOUSE, BEDROOM – DAY 34

Mrs Chynoweth lies in bed, paralysed, her face horribly contorted. Dwight has just examined her.

DWIGHT The damage is considerable. She'll need constant care for the foreseeable future. Possibly the rest of her life.

ELIZABETH But – we cannot afford a nurse – who is to provide—? *(then, realizing the implications)* Me. I must be the one to take care of her.

AUNT AGATHA Who's to take care of *me*? I was here first!

Elizabeth turns and looks from Aunt Agatha to her mother and back again. She sees her future stretching ahead in poverty and misery with her at the beck and call of two invalids.

ELIZABETH I must speak to Ross.

AUNT AGATHA You'll get no sympathy from that quarter! He was never a fan of your mother.

Dwight gives her a look of sympathy. He can see she's in an impossible situation.

DWIGHT Is there no one else you can turn to?

CUT TO:

30: EXT. TRENWITH HOUSE, DRIVE – DAY 34

George rides through the gates. He looks purposeful and majestic. (He will ride in the direction of the militant tinners.)

CUT TO:

31: INT. TRENWITH HOUSE, BEDROOM – DAY 34

An anguished Elizabeth is standing by the window looking out at the militant tinners. In the bed Mrs Chynoweth lies paralysed and drooling. Elizabeth glances at her in despair, then back to the window.

HER POV: George gallops up. How has Elizabeth never before noticed how well he rides, how handsome he looks? He slows down as he nears the tinners. He speaks to them, he appears to remonstrate with them. Then, to Elizabeth's amazement, they begin to pack up their gear. George rides towards the house.

CUT TO:

32: INT. TRENWITH HOUSE, LIBRARY – DAY 34

George is waiting in the Library as Elizabeth comes in.

GEORGE I came as soon as I heard. How is she?

ELIZABETH Very bad. Dr Enys fears she may never recover.

GEORGE You must know how that grieves me.

ELIZABETH I know how fond you are of her.

GEORGE *(as if it's just occurred)* Do you know what I wish?

ELIZABETH No.

GEORGE That you would allow me to make all the necessary arrangements. Engage a separate establishment for her, here at Trenwith, so that no further burden need fall on you.

ELIZABETH I couldn't let you do that—

GEORGE You're so frail, Elizabeth. You try to be strong but now it is you who need care. Let me provide it.

ELIZABETH You're very kind, George – but I'm stronger than I look. I will *have* to be. One must take what life sends.

GEORGE But not what *I* send?

ELIZABETH You've already given so much—

GEORGE For my godson – a few trifles. For yourself? Nothing. At least let me help your dear mother.

ELIZABETH Your generosity makes me ashamed to refuse you *anything*.

GEORGE If there was one thing you did not refuse me, it would solve everything.

ELIZABETH What's that?

GEORGE Yourself?

Suddenly Elizabeth feels faint. She opens her mouth to speak but finds the words won't come out. She wants to pretend not to understand his meaning but they both know she does. George sees her wavering – and seizes his moment.

GEORGE *(cont'd)* Before you speak, let me add one thing. You must be aware how long I've loved you. Serving you only as I could – paying back Francis's card debts, waiving the interest on his loans, allowing no thought of retaliation when he persistently insulted me. Since his death I've served you in any way you would allow. And will continue to do so, whether or not I stand to gain by it.

ELIZABETH And I'm more than grateful—

GEORGE But now I ask you to marry me. I say that I love you. I don't flatter myself that you love me. I think you might like and respect me. And I hope in time that liking might become something more.

ELIZABETH But—

GEORGE I can't bring you breeding. But I can bring a kind of gentility which is all the more punctilious for being only a generation deep. As for material considerations—

ELIZABETH George, please—

GEORGE Oh, I know you would never marry for money. If you did, you would not be the person I know you to be. But at the risk of offending, let me be clear about what I can offer.

Elizabeth looks out of the window and sees the tinners, now packed up, beginning to move away.

GEORGE *(cont'd)* My house is four times the size of Trenwith. I have twenty servants. A park of five hundred acres. My own carriage. A phaeton. You could have one too. Or three or four. I would take you to London or Bath. You would wear the finest clothes, the rarest jewels, mix with the best in society. As my adopted son, Geoffrey Charles would be my heir. There's very little you and I could not achieve if we put our minds to it. For so long you've lived in a cage. Will you not allow me to give you the key?

ELIZABETH Oh George – I don't know what to say—

And in that moment George sees hope where before he had hardly dared imagine it. He is at her side in an instant, taking her hand, kissing it respectfully.

GEORGE Say nothing, my dear. I don't ask for an answer now. I only ask permission to *give*.

ELIZABETH It's just that I feel – so alone—

GEORGE Loneliness is not one-sided, Elizabeth. A man may feel it too. Especially when he has loved as long and as devotedly as I have.

He lets go of her hand, bows respectfully and goes out. Elizabeth can hardly believe what she has heard – or allowed to go unchallenged. She is so overcome, she sinks into a chair as if she's about to faint. After a moment Aunt Agatha comes in.

AUNT AGATHA 'And the devil taketh him up into an exceeding high mountain and showeth him all the kingdoms of the world; and saith: "All these things will I give thee . . ."'

Elizabeth is irritated by this intervention and determined not to be bullied by Aunt Agatha.

ELIZABETH Yes, Aunt. All these things and more besides. A fortune for my boy – to make up for the one his father lost.

AUNT AGATHA And what is he expecting in return? A heart? Is he aware that you have none to give? *(beat)* Having long ago bestowed it elsewhere?

Elizabeth glares at Aunt Agatha. At this moment she hates her. But she doesn't deny the truth of what she's said.

CUT TO:

33: INT. WHEAL GRACE, TUNNEL – DAY 34

Close on Ross as he takes a lantern and shines it into the worked-out open space above where he, Paul, Zacky and Ted have been working. A great cavernous space is revealed. A look of concern crosses his face. He knows what this means.

ROSS How soon till we need timbers?

HENSHAWE Timbers cost.

ROSS And without them?

HENSHAWE You know as well as I do—

ROSS Is it a risk we're willing to take?

HENSHAWE It's a risk we've been taking for some time.

Ross considers this, not without concern.

ZACKY We've shored it up as best we can.

ROSS So you think it'll hold?

HENSHAWE I've seen gunnies like this last for twenty years.

PAUL We're willin' to chance it.

TED We'd sooner 'ee spent money on coal t' keep the pump going.

Ross looks at Henshawe as if to say, 'Are we sure about this?'

HENSHAWE There's not a mine in existence wouldn't take the same chance.

Paul, Ted and Zacky are nodding their agreement. Henshawe too. Ross bows to their better judgement.

CUT TO:

34: EXT. NAMPARA HOUSE – DAY 35

Dawn establisher.

CUT TO:

35: INT. NAMPARA HOUSE – DAY 35

Demelza is proud of the bodice she has made out of Ross's frayed shirt. She holds it against herself as Prudie comes in.

PRUDIE A pretty little piece!

DEMELZA I shall wear it today. There be visitors expected.

PRUDIE Do I know 'em?

DEMELZA One of 'em you even *like*!

CUT TO:

36: EXT. TRENWITH HOUSE, TURRET ROOM – DAY 35

Elizabeth is seen at the window of the Turret Room, looking out. She's expecting visitors. As we go closer we see she's on edge, as if she's not completely looking forward to receiving them. Now a carriage arrives and presently James Blamey – in his midshipman's uniform – alights and ceremoniously assists his stepmother Verity to do likewise.

CUT TO:

37: INT. TRENWITH HOUSE, GREAT HALL – DAY 35

Verity leads the way in, James bouncing eagerly behind her like a boisterous puppy, looking around him in amazement.

JAMES You grew up here? 'Tis a veritable galleon compared to my father's humble sloop. Aye aye, Captain! *(He salutes the portrait of Charles.)* Or should I say Admiral?

VERITY *(laughing)* My father! Charles William Poldark.

JAMES Then he's my grandfather-by-proxy since you're my commanding officer, Step-mama!

Verity and James laugh. Their relationship is delightful to see – relaxed and familiar. Then Elizabeth comes in. She seems slightly hesitant. Verity rushes forward to greet her.

VERITY My dear! How are you? May I introduce my stepson. Midshipman James Blamey. My sister-in-law Elizabeth Poldark.

JAMES *(open-mouthed at Elizabeth's beauty)* Your servant, ma'am.

Amused, Verity tips James's chin so that his mouth snaps shut.

VERITY *(affectionate)* Close the hatch, dear. We don't want to be catching flies, do we? *(to Elizabeth)* Well, Elizabeth—

ELIZABETH Well, cousin. How good of you to come.

Elizabeth seems almost embarrassed, as if she's hiding something. Then Aunt Agatha's voice is heard, booming from the Oak Room.

AUNT AGATHA'S VOICE Is that little Verity? Bring her to me this minute.

Verity and James exchange a glance. James does a mock-grimace. Clearly Verity has told him all about Aunt Agatha.

JAMES *(low, to Verity)* Cutlass at the ready?

Verity giggles and escorts James towards the Oak Room. Elizabeth, feeling slightly left out, follows.

CUT TO:

38 INT. TRENWITH HOUSE, LIBRARY – DAY 35

Elizabeth and Verity take tea. Geoffrey Charles looks on as Aunt Agatha and James play a hard-fought game of cards (which Aunt Agatha has no intention of losing).

VERITY *(low)* Had I known of your mother's condition, we'd not have dreamed of intruding. How difficult it must be for you.

ELIZABETH It was – at first – but now she has a nurse and a maid—

VERITY *(surprised)* Is that not expensive?

ELIZABETH *(to change the subject)* How strange it must be for you here – without Francis.

VERITY No more than for you.

ELIZABETH I've had to grow used to it – for Geoffrey Charles's sake.

VERITY And can you?

ELIZABETH For my son I must do whatever's necessary.

Before Verity has a chance to digest the implications of this, there is a roar of triumph from Aunt Agatha. She has won the game.

AUNT AGATHA Haaaa! *(to Geoffrey Charles)* And *that*, boy, is how you put the navy in its place!

JAMES *(to Verity and Elizabeth)* Your great-aunt is a fiend at French ruff. *(low, to Verity)* Obviously I let her win!

VERITY *(low)* Obviously!

They exchange a smile.

VERITY *(cont'd) (to Elizabeth)* We're expected at Nampara. You'll go with us?

ELIZABETH Oh – I—

AUNT AGATHA Yes, Elizabeth?

ELIZABETH I have a headache.

Aunt Agatha eyes Elizabeth beadily. Verity notices. Something's puzzling her. What's going on?

CUT TO:

39: INT. NAMPARA HOUSE, HALLWAY – DAY 35

Verity and James are given a hearty welcome by Ross and Demelza and shown into the house.

ROSS Did Elizabeth not wish to join you?

CUT TO:

40: INT. NAMPARA HOUSE, PARLOUR – DAY 35

Ross and Demelza escort Verity and James into the parlour.

VERITY She's much distressed over her mother's illness. She sends her apologies and her love.

JAMES *(to Ross)* Mistress Poldark is a thing of beauty, d'you not think? Were I five years older, I'd throw myself at her feet!

VERITY She would very likely trample you underfoot!

They all laugh.

VERITY *(cont'd)* On our way over, I noticed the engine chimney of the mine still smoking.

ROSS Oh, we continue to limp on – existing on a shoe-string, everything against us—

DEMELZA Not entirely, Ross! *(to Verity)* Tin has been found. We don't know how far or how deep it goes, but—

ROSS The quality of the ore is promising – I admit it!

VERITY I'm very glad for you. A change in your fortunes is long deserved.

JAMES *(glancing round)* You keep a very fine ship, Captain! D'you have your own cabin?

ROSS *(laughing)* Naturally, sir. Would you care to inspect it?

JAMES Ha! So I should! Lead on, sir!

Ross, knowing Demelza is itching to speak to Verity, escorts James out.

CUT TO:

41: EXT. WOODLAND – DAY 35

Dwight, on horseback, has halted in the place where he and Caroline used to meet. He's thinking of her. He returns to the present. He knows it is folly to dwell on what he has lost. He spurs his horse and rides on.

CUT TO:

42: INT. NAMPARA HOUSE, LIBRARY – DAY 35

Ross and James Blamey are relaxing in the library. Ross hands James a glass of rum.

ROSS Your ship is *The Thunderer*?

JAMES The frigate *Hunter*, under Admiral Gell. We're in Plymouth Sound at present but under sailing orders next week. I'm monstrous glad of it. I'd not want the war to end before I've had the chance to pepper the Frenchies!

ROSS *(laughing)* Oh, I'm sure there'll be opportunities for glory before the war's over!

Now there's a knock on the door and Dwight comes in.

DWIGHT Oh! – my apologies—

ROSS No, come in, Dwight – join us. May I introduce Midshipman James Blamey. My good friend Dr Dwight Enys.

JAMES Your servant, sir.

DWIGHT And yours, sir.

JAMES If ever you tire of life ashore, consider us poor souls in the fleet! We're in dire need of good surgeons.

DWIGHT Is that so?

JAMES Honour and glory beckon – as well as blood and gore!

DWIGHT Honour and glory I can do without! But a mission – somewhere useful to direct my energies—

JAMES We can surely provide *that*!

ROSS And a good skirmish is a fine distraction!

DWIGHT The point is, to *do* something—

ROSS I agree. Idleness allows us too much time to *think*!

They all laugh. But the look which passes between Ross and Dwight tells us they understand each other very well.

CUT TO:

43: INT. NAMPARA HOUSE, PARLOUR – DAY 35

Demelza and Verity sit by the fire. Verity is holding Jeremy. She's wondering how to broach a delicate subject.

VERITY D'you see much of Elizabeth?

DEMELZA She don' seem inclined to visit us now – though she's happy enough to admit Ross. Or was. Why d'you ask?

VERITY I don't know – there's something – I cannot put my finger on it – she seems a little on edge – as if innerly excited. *(beat)* And I got the impression—

DEMELZA Yes?

VERITY That she thinks her circumstances are about to change.

DEMELZA Oh.

Demelza's face falls. A horrible thought has occurred to her.

VERITY Do you know why that might be?

DEMELZA P'raps you should ask Ross.

VERITY That sounds a little bitter.

DEMELZA Do it? I only meant, he sees more of her than I. *(then)* I know he did love her – so when he goes to see her I'd not be human if I didn't wonder what they say to each other. Or if they still have feelings—

VERITY You think they do?

DEMELZA They were each other's first love. As Ross is mine and Andrew is yours. I think such a love cannot easily be put aside.

VERITY But you've no reason to think—

DEMELZA No reason. Just— *(then)* Ross'd never mean to hurt me – but if it came to a choice between me an' Elizabeth – *(beat)* an' Elizabeth now free—

VERITY You cannot believe that?

But it's clear that a part of Demelza does indeed believe it.

DEMELZA *(to change the subject)* But what a treasure is James! He's like the west wind – all gusty and clean and kind. An' he adores you.

VERITY And I him. As if he were my own son.

DEMELZA Oh, Verity, I'm that glad. It d' make up for—

She hesitates, not wanting to state the obvious.

VERITY For what? My not having a child of my own? *(Demelza nods.)* Oh, but that's the most wonderful thing, my dear. There is nothing to make up for.

Demelza looks at her quizzically. Does Verity mean what Demelza thinks she means? Verity, suddenly close to tears, nods excitedly.

DEMELZA Oh, Verity! When?

VERITY About October.

Demelza and Verity fall into each other's arms and hug each other.

CUT TO:

44: INT. NAMPARA HOUSE, ROSS & DEMELZA'S BEDROOM – NIGHT 35

Ross and Demelza are in bed. Ross seems to be asleep but Demelza is tossing and turning. Eventually Ross reveals himself to be awake too.

ROSS Is it Verity's news which keeps you awake?

DEMELZA I think so.

ROSS I can't imagine what else it could be.

DEMELZA No. I don't suppose you can.

Unaware of the barb in her retort, Ross turns over and goes back to sleep. Demelza lies on her back and stares at the ceiling. As her eyelids begin to close, she can hear Verity's voice saying:

VERITY'S VOICE I got the impression – that she thinks her circumstances are about to change.

Demelza closes her eyes.

DISSOLVE TO:

45: EXT. NAMPARA HOUSE (DEMELZA'S FANTASY) – DAY 36

Ross rides away from Nampara with Elizabeth on his horse, sitting where Demelza usually sits. Elizabeth turns back and smiles triumphantly at Demelza, who is standing in the doorway of Nampara, watching them leave.

ELIZABETH Goodbye, my dear. Be brave. You've always known this day would come.

DISSOLVE TO:

46: EXT. NAMPARA HOUSE – DAY 36

Demelza comes back to the present. It's early morning. She is standing in the doorway of Nampara as she was in her dream. She is still preoccupied with thoughts of Ross and Elizabeth. She is about to go back inside when she sees an actual horseman approaching. As he gets nearer, she realizes it's Captain McNeil. He is riding one-handed, his arm in a sling.

CUT TO:

47: INT. NAMPARA HOUSE, PARLOUR – DAY 36

Demelza serves tea to Captain McNeil.

DEMELZA Is it not dangerous, Captain? Riding when you're not recovered?

CAPTAIN MCNEIL You leave me no choice! I was hoping you'd visit me, as I convalesce. Or else, that I'd receive an invitation to visit *you*.

DEMELZA Last time you came without an invitation.

CAPTAIN MCNEIL That was in the course of duty. This is in the pursuit of pleasure.

DEMELZA As you see, my husband is not here.

CAPTAIN MCNEIL Are you sure of that? *(smiles knowingly)* On my previous visit, you told me he was from home. Yet we both know he was somewhere about the house.

DEMELZA Do we?

CAPTAIN MCNEIL Indeed, I thought it probable that if I posted a watch long enough, we'd discover where he was hiding.

DEMELZA And did you post such a watch?

CAPTAIN MCNEIL I did not.

DEMELZA Why?

CAPTAIN MCNEIL I have too great a regard for you, ma'am.

Demelza raises an eyebrow to suggest she thinks this is mere gallantry.

CAPTAIN MCNEIL *(cont'd)* In truth, had I conceived it my

duty, I would have done so – but my heart was not in it. I'm a soldier not a spy. I hold nothing against Captain Poldark except that he married so charming a wife. So I trust you hold nothing against me for what I did.

DEMELZA Indeed, I'm obliged to you for what you did not do.

A brief moment between them. Light flirtatiousness at this point – though it's clear that both McNeil and Demelza acknowledge that she is in his debt. Then:

CAPTAIN MCNEIL So now I'm forced to venture out for company and gossip. What can you tell me? What news of your cousin-in-law, Mistress Elizabeth?

DEMELZA I'm sure I've heard nothing.

CAPTAIN MCNEIL Truly? I'd've thought you of all people would know—

DEMELZA *(hardly daring to ask)* What do you hear?

CAPTAIN MCNEIL Only that Sir Hugh Bodrugan – who shares a tailor with a certain person – tells me that certain person has just ordered his wedding clothes!

DEMELZA Judas! Who's that?

CAPTAIN MCNEIL Can you not guess?

All kinds of awful thoughts flash through her head. For one wild, irrational moment she's about to name Ross.

CAPTAIN MCNEIL *(cont'd)* Why, George Warleggan! Had you no idea?

DEMELZA Oh! No! – That is, yes – I did somewhat suspicion—

CAPTAIN MCNEIL No doubt you'll be able to ask him yourself at the ball.

DEMELZA The ball—?

CAPTAIN MCNEIL Sir Hugh is to give a ball in a fortnight's time. I hope you'll favour me with the ecossaise?

DEMELZA *(distracted)* Oh! – yes – o' course – I— *(gets abruptly to her feet)* Thank you for calling, Captain McNeil.

McNeil also gets to his feet.

DEMELZA *(cont'd)* I must see to Jeremy. Pray excuse me.

She hurries out, leaving McNeil rather bemused about her abrupt and rather flustered departure.

CUT TO:

48: INT. NAMPARA HOUSE, KITCHEN – DAY 36

Demelza comes into the kitchen in a daze. She can't believe what she's heard – and she doesn't know whether she's relieved or appalled. Prudie looks at her in amazement.

PRUDIE What ails 'ee, maid?

DEMELZA George Warleggan— *(beat)* Is to marry Elizabeth—?

PRUDIE Mr Ross'll be surprised.

DEMELZA Mr Ross mustn't be told. *(then)* Oh, he'll hear soon enough. But it won't be from *me*!

CUT TO:

49: EXT. WHEAL GRACE – DAY 36

Ross comes up from working in the mine to find Dwight has just finished tending his mining patients.

ROSS Phthisis and scurvy? No wonder you've had your fill.

DWIGHT I confess, a new challenge would suit me.

ROSS A war would certainly supply that.

DWIGHT Are you not tempted yourself?

ROSS If duty calls, I won't ignore it. But I know enough of combat not to relish it.

DWIGHT Whereas I – can almost hear the cannons as we speak!

And indeed an ominous rumbling does make itself heard. For a moment Ross and Dwight are confused. It seems to be coming from underground. Ross and Dwight look at each other in alarm.

CUT TO:

50: INT. WHEAL GRACE, TUNNEL – DAY 36

Paul, Zacky, Ted and various others working at the lode hear a rumbling above them and realize something is wrong. Then chunks of rock and boulders begin to fall.

ZACKY She's comin' down. Run! *Run!*

They start to run.

CUT TO:

51: INT. NAMPARA HOUSE – DAY 36

Demelza and Prudie hear the rumbling. They look at each other in horror. They know what it means. Demelza runs for the door. Prudie snatches up Jeremy as if to protect him.

CUT TO:

52: INT. WHEAL GRACE, TUNNEL – DAY 36

Boulders are raining down. Ted, Paul and Zacky are running along the tunnel, trying to protect themselves from falling rocks. But to no avail. The roof of the tunnel caves in. Ted and Paul are buried beneath an avalanche of rock.

CUT TO:

53: INT. WHEAL GRACE, SHAFT – DAY 36

Ross and Dwight rush down the ladder, followed by Henshawe.

CUT TO:

54: INT. WHEAL GRACE, TUNNEL – DAY 36

The rockfall has ceased and great clouds of dust make it almost impossible to see anything. There's an ominous silence. Then, out of the dust and darkness, a single candle appears and begins to shed some light. It belongs to Zacky – who has escaped the rockfall and who now starts to manhandle some of the boulders away.

ZACKY Paul? Ted? Are 'ee there? Can 'ee hear me?

There's no answer and no sign of movement. Now Ross appears, followed by Dwight and Henshawe.

ROSS How many?

ZACKY Paul – Ted – young Ellery – Joe Nanfan—

ROSS Where are they?

ZACKY Couldn' tell – hereabouts, I reckon—

Ross dives in and starts manhandling the boulders, helped by Henshawe and Zacky. Presently a low groan and some feeble coughing is heard. They scramble to remove more boulders. A body is revealed.

ROSS It's Paul! Make haste! Dwight, over here!

Dwight rushes over and begins to tend Paul, while Ross, Henshawe and Zacky continue to move the boulders.

CUT TO:

55: EXT. WHEAL GRACE – DAY 36

A scene of chaos and panic. People are rushing up to the mine, having just heard the news. Injured men, bloodied and bruised, are being brought out, lain down to be tended by their wives and mothers. Prudie is handing out brandy. Paul is brought out, apparently dead, being attended by Dwight. Beth Daniel rushes up. Another miner – Joe – also apparently lifeless, is brought up and laid down. Demelza rushes to help him. His mother rushes up. Women and children are weeping. Families wait by the entrance for men still unaccounted for. Now Ross appears. Demelza catches his eye. His expression is deathly.

ROSS Who's unaccounted for?

HENSHAWE Dan Curnow, Ted Carkeek.

ROSS We don't stop till they're found.

He heads for the mine entrance again, followed by Henshawe.

CUT TO:

56: INT. TRENWITH HOUSE, LIBRARY – DAY 36

Elizabeth is mending a threadbare dress, surrounded by a drooling Mrs Chynoweth and an Aunt Agatha who is muttering to herself as she does her tarot cards. George is shown in.

GEORGE Forgive my intrusion. I thought to bring you the news before you heard it elsewhere. There's been an accident at Wheal Grace. Your cousin-in-law—

ELIZABETH *(hardly daring to ask)* Is dead—?

GEORGE Is very much alive. Only the poor souls who labour for him have paid the ultimate price.

ELIZABETH What happened?

GEORGE What inevitably happens when corners are cut and safety is abandoned in favour of profit.

ELIZABETH I can scarce believe it. Ross of all people—

GEORGE Is a desperate man – grown increasingly desperate. But this will surely be the death knell? One can only feel for his wife and child – innocent casualties of his overwhelming hubris – now condemned to a life of penury—? *(then, realizing he's had the desired effect)* Oh, but forgive me for keeping you from your dear relations. Give my regards to them both.

And before she can invite him to stay, he goes out. Elizabeth hesitates. Aunt Agatha looks up at her. And in that moment she knows – and Elizabeth knows – what is going to happen next. And so Elizabeth calmly gets up and follows George out. Aunt Agatha watches her go. She turns up a card: it's the devil. After a moment, she herself gets up and goes into the Great Hall.

CUT TO:

57: INT. TRENWITH HOUSE, GREAT HALL – DAY 36

Aunt Agatha approaches the window.

HER POV: George is about to mount his horse when Elizabeth comes out. She goes over to George. He turns to her. They converse a while. What they're saying, we can't hear. Then George makes an expression of gratitude, takes Elizabeth's hand and kisses it.

Aunt Agatha knows what this means. Presently Elizabeth returns. After a pause:

AUNT AGATHA I hope you know what you're doing.

The two women face each other, defiant, in no doubt of each other's feelings about what has just happened.

CUT TO:

58: EXT. WHEAL GRACE – DUSK 36

As dusk falls the full scale of the disaster is clear. It looks like a war zone. Injured men lie all over the area outside Wheal Grace, their families beside them, some standing and staring in despair, others trying to take care of them while they wait for Dwight to come and tend them. Demelza is kneeling beside Beth Daniel, helping her to clean up Paul – who miraculously has survived. Ross is comforting Joe's grandmother, as Joe's mother and sisters help to tend his wounds. Miraculously, he too is alive. Now Ross goes over to where Dwight is giving mouth-to-mouth resuscitation to Ted Carkeek. He's performing it with great calm and commitment but his increasing desperation is showing through. His efforts are not working. Ted shows no signs of life. Ross kneels down beside him.

ROSS What can I do?

Dwight shakes his head.

DWIGHT He was buried too long. I can't bring him back.

Ross looks at Dwight in horror. Both of them are close to tears.

DWIGHT *(cont'd)* There's nothing you can do here, Ross. Help the others.

Ross gets up and walks over to where Henshawe is surveying the scene. They both look down at the full extent of the carnage.

HENSHAWE One dead.

ROSS Two.

HENSHAWE And five badly injured.

ROSS I'm to blame.

HENSHAWE Nay, Ross—

ROSS I should have ordered timbers.

HENSHAWE We're all to blame. We knew the risk—

ROSS Grace is mine. I should have insisted.

Now, as they watch, they see Betty Carkeek approach, anxious, fearful. Now Demelza has seen her too. Time seems to slow down as Demelza rushes to intercept her, to be beside her when the awful truth dawns. Now Betty has realized, has seen who it is that Dwight kneels beside. Demelza is at her side – has her arm round her shoulder – is helping to steady her as her legs buckle beneath her – is guiding her over till she falls to her knees beside the outstretched body of Ted and weeps on his chest.

Ross and Henshawe watch this unfold from afar – helpless to intervene – sick to the heart at this disaster which both know could have been prevented.

HENSHAWE Twenty fathoms of pumping gear gone. Six weeks or more to clear the debris. Two hundred pounds won't do it – even if either of us had the capital.

ROSS Even then, I wouldn't attempt it. *(then)* This mine has cost two lives. It was an ill-conceived venture from the start. It will never open again.

Henshawe nods, resigned, pats Ross on the back as if in consolation, then walks away, leaving Ross to contemplate the ruins of his mine and his future. Surely things can't get any worse than this?

CUT TO:

59: INT. TRENWITH HOUSE, ELIZABETH'S ROOM – NIGHT 36

Elizabeth begins to write a letter.

ELIZABETH *(VO)* 'My dear Ross, I do not know how to write this letter or to tell you what I have to say . . .'

CUT TO:

60: INT. WARLEGGAN HOUSE – NIGHT 36

George is boxing with his instructor as Cary comes in. He is unusually buoyant and the instructor is having to work especially hard. Cary is impressed.

CARY Are you ahead?

GEORGE I've already won.

For a moment Cary doesn't compute what he's being told.

GEORGE *(cont'd) (still boxing)* I've secured the hand – of the woman I love—

Then an equally pleasant thought occurs.

GEORGE *(cont'd) (still boxing)* And in so doing – will deal the deadliest blow – to my bitterest enemy.

CARY I congratulate you.

GEORGE I congratulate myself. It's not given to many – to achieve so much – at a single stroke.

And without thinking, almost on instinct, he lashes out a killer punch and knocks the instructor out cold. George can't help laughing.

GEORGE *(cont'd)* Sometimes I don't know my own strength!

CUT TO:

61: INT. NAMPARA HOUSE, HALLWAY – NIGHT 36

Demelza and Ross return home. On a table in the hallway is a letter. Demelza sees it first, suspects what it might be, and scuttles away hurriedly, not wanting to be there when Ross opens it. He picks it up. Demelza heads into the parlour.

CUT TO:

62: INT. NAMPARA HOUSE, PARLOUR – NIGHT 36

Demelza hardly dares to look at Ross as he comes into the room. He tosses the letter down onto the table.

ROSS After such a day, the very last thing I need.

DEMELZA *(hardly daring to ask)* What is it—?

ROSS Sir Hugh Bodrugan – inviting us to a ball.

DEMELZA *(shocked and relieved)* Oh!

ROSS Obviously we'll decline.

DEMELZA Of course.

Normally we know she'd argue, but tonight she's just relieved it isn't the letter she'd feared it was. Ross goes to the cupboard and gets out the brandy. Presently Prudie appears.

PRUDIE *(with a glance at Demelza)* Letter jus' come from Trenwith.

ROSS Thank you, Prudie.

He takes the letter. Glances at it idly. Puts it down. Pours himself a drink. All the while Demelza is staring at the letter as if expecting it to explode. Prudie – suspecting what the letter contains – makes a swift exit. Eventually – and evidently not expecting anything of importance – Ross opens the letter.

DISSOLVE TO:

63: INT. TRENWITH HOUSE, ELIZABETH'S ROOM – NIGHT 36

Elizabeth paces, as if thinking aloud what she wants to write to Ross.

ELIZABETH I know what I have to say will distress you – and I, who gave you so much pain once before, would do almost anything than hurt you again and in the same way. Yet it seems I must. Oh Ross, my life has been a very frustrating one. And since Francis died, a lonely and an empty one. Perhaps I am the wrong sort of person to be left alone. I seem to need the strength and protection only a man can give. *(beat)* I have agreed to marry George Warleggan.

The room seems to go dark.

DISSOLVE TO:

64: INT. NAMPARA HOUSE, PARLOUR – NIGHT 36

Ross is staring at the letter with absolute incomprehension. Demelza watches him, hardly daring to breathe, knowing without being told the rage which is beginning to build in his expression and his body. It's as if it's surging through his veins now, taking possession of him before her very eyes. Suddenly:

ROSS I'm going to Trenwith.

DEMELZA No, Ross. Not tonight—

ROSS I must speak with Elizabeth—

DEMELZA Ross, you cannot—

ROSS Do you know what this is?

DEMELZA Is it about George?

ROSS You knew?

DEMELZA I heard rumours—

ROSS And you didn't think to tell me?

DEMELZA An' get my head snapped off?

ROSS This – *thing* – must be stopped.

DEMELZA How can it be stopped? It cannot be stopped—

ROSS You think so?

DEMELZA How will you stop it? You cannot stop it—

ROSS Perhaps you don't *want* me to stop it!

DEMELZA P'raps I don't! An' especially not like this—

ROSS Like what?

DEMELZA Whatever way you intend!

ROSS How do you know what I intend?

DEMELZA How do I know anything, Ross? How do I know *you*? And yet I think I do!

She's standing in the doorway now, as if to block his way. He makes to leave. She stands firm.

ROSS Please get out of my way.

DEMELZA Don't go there tonight, Ross. Wait till tomorrow—

ROSS Please – get out of – my way.

They face each other. Not once has he raised his voice or been aggressive, yet she knows he is in the grip of a passion and a rage which neither he nor she can stop. She steps out of his way. He leaves without looking at her.

CUT TO:

65: EXT. CLIFF TOPS – NIGHT 36

Ross gallops at break-neck speed to Trenwith.

CUT TO:

66: EXT. TRENWITH HOUSE – NIGHT 36

The house is in darkness as Ross gallops up the drive, dismounts and ties up his horse. He hammers on the door. The sound echoes in the stillness of the evening air, but no one answers. He hammers again. Still no answer. He looks up at the house. No sign of life anywhere. What to do next? Should he take Demelza's advice and come back tomorrow? He considers a moment. But the very idea enrages him. He's a man possessed now. He begins to prowl round the side of the house. He makes no attempt to be quiet or secretive. We go with him as he scans the windows for signs of light. Nothing. Silence. Now he begins to try the doors and windows. All locked. His impatience grow-ing, he rattles a couple of windows. To no avail. Finally his fury gets the better of him. He kicks at a flimsy-looking back door. It gives way. He lets himself into the house.

CUT TO:

67: EXT. TRENWITH HOUSE, ELIZABETH'S ROOM – NIGHT 36

Elizabeth is preparing for bed. She hears a noise below. Instinctively, she knows who it is. She moves to bolt her bedroom door. And then she hesitates.

CUT TO:

68: INT. TRENWITH HOUSE, UPSTAIRS PASSAGE – NIGHT 36

Ross moves quietly along the passage. Inside the house he's quieter now, not wishing to alarm any of the inhabitants. At the far end he can see a glimmer of light coming from beneath a door. He moves towards it. He's almost there when the door opens. Elizabeth comes out.

ELIZABETH Ross—

Ross's expression is impassive, his voice calm. But Elizabeth knows him too well to be taken in by his even voice.

ROSS I came to pay my respects—

ELIZABETH For what?

ROSS And to thank you for your letter.

ELIZABETH There's no need—

ROSS Oh, but there is.

ELIZABETH Perhaps tomorrow would be—

ROSS Not tomorrow. Now.

ELIZABETH Downstairs, then. I'll get a candle—

She goes back into her room. Ross follows her.
CUT TO:

69: INT. TRENWITH HOUSE, ELIZABETH'S ROOM – CONTINUOUS

Elizabeth, fetching the candle from beside her bed, turns and sees that Ross has followed her inside.

ELIZABETH Ross, I don't think—

ROSS I should be in here? There's no one to consider but you and I.

He closes the door firmly behind him. They face each other across the room. Elizabeth assesses him, his mood, the likelihood of him exploding. She decides to try and placate him.

ELIZABETH Ross, I so hated having to send you that letter – but really, I've said all there is to be said—

ROSS I disagree.

He contemplates her a moment, wanting to choose his words carefully. Then:

ROSS *(cont'd)* Perhaps you could clarify something for me? George Warleggan—

ELIZABETH Yes?

ROSS A man I consider my greatest enemy. You – I've long considered my greatest friend. In which particular am I most adrift?

ELIZABETH It's not as simple as that, Ross – you must understand my position – of course I'm happy and proud to think of you as my greatest friend—

ROSS Well, it was *more* than that, as I recall. Did you not tell me, barely twelve months ago, that you'd made a mistake in marrying Francis? That you realized quite soon? That it was always *I* you had loved?

ELIZABETH And do you think I would ever have said those words if I'd known what would happen to Francis?

ROSS And yet they cannot be *un*said.

ELIZABETH I felt you needed to know – that if you were unhappy in those early days, then so was I. That the mistake was not yours, but mine—

ROSS That 'mistake', as you call it, has cost many people dear. Francis – yourself – myself. What mistake are you making now?

ELIZABETH I don't expect you to understand—

ROSS Try me.

ELIZABETH George has been so good to me since Francis died – so kind—

ROSS Do you marry a man out of gratitude?

ELIZABETH No, not just that. Oh Ross, you're wrong to think of him as your greatest enemy—

ROSS The man who tried to get me hanged—

ELIZABETH I don't believe that's what he intended. And now – I think I can help mend the breach between you—

ROSS Are you marrying him for his money?

ELIZABETH *(a flash of anger)* How dare you! *(then, realizing she must keep things calm and measured)* God knows I've made mistakes in my life, Ross – but I've tried to be loyal to the people I care for. What seems like disloyalty now – to you – is actually loyalty to my son. I must think of him now. What do you suggest for me? Thirty years of widowhood and loneliness? Can you offer me anything else? *(no reply)* Do you?

A huge moment between them. Can he – will he – offer her anything more?

ROSS Do you love George?

They face each other – and in that moment Elizabeth knows Ross is not going to offer her anything more.

ELIZABETH Yes.

Ross looks at her in disbelief – which quickly gives way to disdain.

ROSS Why do I not believe you? Why does this remind me of when you said you loved Francis? I was simpler then and believed you. I don't believe you now.

He's closer to her now, his face close to hers.

ROSS *(cont'd)* You ask me would I condemn you to thirty years of widowhood? Why would I need to? You could have your pick of *thirty* men! But I will not see you condemned to George.

ELIZABETH Please leave now, Ross. I'm my own mistress and will not be instructed. I'm sorry you feel like this but I cannot help it—

ROSS Oh, you've never been able to help *anything*, have you? It's all been beyond your control. Full of good intentions, leaving a trail of havoc in your wake! Perhaps you can't help this either—

He seizes her and kisses her. For a moment she's too stunned to resist. Then she pushes him away.

ELIZABETH This is contemptible – to insult me like this when I have no one to turn to—

ROSS I oppose this marriage, Elizabeth. I'd be glad of your assurance that you'll not go through with it.

ELIZABETH When you've just called me a liar? Why would you believe me now if you didn't believe me a minute ago?

ROSS Both of us know you do not love George!

ELIZABETH I love him to distraction and will marry him next month!

He grabs her again and begins to kiss her – this time with more force and passion. She tries to push him away but he refuses to release her.

ELIZABETH *(cont'd)* Let me go! Ross! Let me go!

She hits him in the face. But to no avail. He continues to devour her. She manages to push him away again.

ELIZABETH *(cont'd)* Stop this! Ross! I'll scream—

ROSS Do so—

ELIZABETH You're hateful – horrible—

ROSS Scream—

ELIZABETH I detest you—

ROSS Whatever you say – I don't think I can believe *anything* you tell me now—

ELIZABETH I hate you—

ROSS No, you don't. You never have! And you never will.

He pushes her towards the bed. She glances at it, already knowing what will follow.

ELIZABETH Ross! You would not dare! You would not *dare*—

ROSS Oh, I would, Elizabeth. I would – and so would you.

He throws her onto the bed, sprawls on top of her and continues to kiss her voraciously. Momentarily she struggles, but soon the taste of his mouth on hers, the desire for him which has never been satisfied, asserts itself. She pulls his face towards her. His hand slides beneath her nightgown.

CUT TO:

70: INT. NAMPARA HOUSE, ROSS & DEMELZA'S BEDROOM – NIGHT 36

Demelza walks up and down with a restless Jeremy in her arms, trying to soothe him back to sleep.

CUT TO:

71: INT. NAMPARA HOUSE, KITCHEN – NIGHT 36

Jud and Prudie sit at the table in the darkness, listening to Demelza's footsteps up above. They know something momentous has happened – that it's to do with Ross – and Elizabeth – that Demelza is the casualty – and that it could have catastrophic consequences for all.

JUD Ted'n right.

PRUDIE Ted'n fit.

JUD Ted'n fair.

PRUDIE Ted'n.

Prudie consoles herself with another tot of rum.

CUT TO:

72: INT. TRENWITH HOUSE, AUNT AGATHA'S ROOM – NIGHT 36

Aunt Agatha lies wide awake, straining to hear what's going on. Of course she can't hear a thing, but that doesn't stop her from trying.

CUT TO:

73: INT. NAMPARA HOUSE, ROSS & DEMELZA'S BEDROOM – DAWN 37

Dawn light steals into the room. Demelza lies wide awake with the sleeping Jeremy in bed beside her. She looks numb, incapable of feeling. Which is probably just as well.

CUT TO:

74: INT. TRENWITH HOUSE, ELIZABETH'S ROOM – DAWN 37

Dawn is breaking. Elizabeth is sleeping. The place beside her in bed is empty. Now Ross is revealed, already up and almost dressed. He's trying not to wake her – but we can't be sure whether this is out of consideration or an eagerness to depart unseen. As he's about to leave, Elizabeth stirs, awakens, looks at him expectantly.

ROSS I must go – before the household wakes—

ELIZABETH What should we—?

ROSS I must think—

ELIZABETH When will you—?

ROSS Soon—

A moment between them. And in that moment we know Elizabeth expects him to return – and that Ross is completely conflicted. A final look between them. Then he leaves.

CUT TO:

75: EXT. TRENWITH HOUSE – DAWN 37

Ross gallops away from Trenwith. Elizabeth is revealed in the Turret Room window, watching him depart. Hopeful of his return.

CUT TO:

76: EXT. NAMPARA HOUSE, COURTYARD – DAWN 37

Demelza is hanging out linens to dry. All of them hers, including the new bodice – none of them Ross's. Her face is open but impassive. It's impossible to know what she's thinking. She hears the sound of approaching hoof beats. Imperceptibly she stiffens. Presently Ross rides into the courtyard. His face is suffused with guilt. He dismounts. He walks over to Demelza. She looks him in the eye – and in that moment she knows – and he knows she knows – what has happened between him and Elizabeth. He's struggling now. Faced with this woman who has loved him unequivocally and unconditionally for so long, the enormity of what he's done begins to dawn on him.

ROSS Demelza – what can I say? It was something – I cannot explain – it had to be done – you must see I had no choice—

DEMELZA *(calmly)* Nor I.

Suddenly, and without warning, she socks him in the face, so violently that he is knocked off balance and staggers backwards. With the merest flicker of satisfaction, she walks off without another word.

Episode 9

1: EXT. WHEAL GRACE – DAY 37 (SPRING 1793)

GV: Wheal Grace. The day after the mining disaster and the mine is silent.

CUT TO:

2: INT. NAMPARA HOUSE, ROSS & DEMELZA'S BEDROOM – DAY 37

Demelza sits in bed singing to Jeremy.

DEMELZA *(sings)*
How the tide rushes in
And covers footprints in the sand
As my hope erased and carried
Out of my hands

How the tides ebb and flow
As driftwood toss'd upon the shore
And my heart is cast aside
And lost evermore

CUT TO:

3: INT. WHEAL GRACE, CHANGING HUT – DAY 37

Ross sits, head in hands, recalling the horror of the mine disaster. As he closes his eyes, scenes from the disaster flash before his eyes: the rockfall, the injured miners, the panic and chaos. He recalls the cries of pain and the rumble of falling debris. Presently a cough announces the arrival of Henshawe. Ross looks up. He's sporting a black eye (from where Demelza hit him).

HENSHAWE We've had visitors, Cap'n. From Wheal Radiant. *(beat)* Do we wish to sell our head gear?

ROSS They didn't waste much time! *(then)* What have they offered?

HENSHAWE A fair price. They're decent men. *(then)* They know it could happen to the best of us.

ROSS The best of us would have bought timbers.

A moment between them. Henshawe acknowledges their joint culpability.

HENSHAWE The men knew the risks.

ROSS Did their wives? Their children?

HENSHAWE 'Tis the business, Ross.

ROSS No longer, it seems.

It's said with a half-smile, without a shred of self-pity or bitterness. But we're in no doubt about how gutted Ross is that it's come to this. They look down the hatch, then close it shut. Now, as Ross gets up to go outside, Henshawe notices his bruised eye.

HENSHAWE Was that from the mine?

ROSS What? *(realizing Henshawe means his bruise)* Oh – no – my wife took exception to something I said!

Henshawe roars with laughter, assuming Ross is joking. And Ross doesn't disabuse him.

CUT TO:

4: INT. NAMPARA HOUSE, ROSS & DEMELZA'S BEDROOM – DAY 37

Demelza sits in bed, continuing to sing to Jeremy.

DEMELZA *(sings)*

Yet though the ocean
with waves unending
Covers the earth,
Yet is there loss after all?

For what e'er drifts from one place
Is with the tide to another brought
And there's naught lost
beyond recall
Which cannot be found, if sought.

There's a tentative knock at the door. She ignores it. The knock comes again. She doesn't respond. Eventually the door opens and a bewildered Prudie comes in.

PRUDIE 'Ee be comin' down for breakfast?

DEMELZA Thank 'ee, Prudie. Master Jeremy and I will be takin' our breakfasts here from now on.

PRUDIE But—

DEMELZA 'Tis a more genteel way of doin', I think. An' Master Jeremy an' I is gentlefolks after all.

PRUDIE Nay, but the chores—? They be pilin' up downstairs—

DEMELZA You're mistook, Prudie. 'Tisn't fitty for I to be mendin' an' cookin'. I see that now and shall mend my ways accordingly.

Prudie shrugs. 'Fair enough'. In truth she can't blame Demelza for taking this stance. It does, however, have implications for her.

CUT TO:

5: EXT. OPEN COUNTRYSIDE – DAY 37

Ross is riding home when he sees someone riding towards him. As the rider gets nearer we realize it's George – whose eyes light up when he sees Ross.

GEORGE Ah, Ross, this is well met! I was just debating whether to write and offer my commiserations.

ROSS On what?

GEORGE Your recent loss. Or should I say losses?

No reply. George senses he has the upper hand.

GEORGE *(cont'd)* Of which the list seems endless! Your earlier loss of Wheal Leisure? The recent closure of Wheal Grace? Oh, and perhaps you have not heard. Elizabeth and I are engaged.

Ross is aware that George is goading him – which makes him all the more determined not to rise to the bait.

GEORGE *(cont'd)* So in the grand scheme of things, you appear to be in disarray. And I appear to have won.

Ross is on the verge of exploding. He could so easily get the upper hand by telling George about his night with Elizabeth. Except, of course, it's the last thing he would ever do. He reins himself in and smiles politely.

ROSS As you say, George. You appear to have won.

So for once it's Ross who rides off, apparently vanquished, leaving George apparently triumphant.

CUT TO:

6: INT. TRENWITH HOUSE, ELIZABETH'S ROOM – DAY 37

Elizabeth is lying in bed – wide-eyed, wondering – 'What will happen next?'

CUT TO:

7: EXT. NAMPARA HOUSE – DAY 37

Thoughtful, Ross rides home. As he approaches the house, he slows down, as if knowing what his reception will be.

CUT TO:

8: INT. NAMPARA HOUSE, KITCHEN – DAY 37

Prudie is fumbling with the churn, trying to make butter. Jud is watching, unimpressed. Jeremy is playing with Garrick.

PRUDIE Churn? I? An't churned since—

JUD The maid first come an' show'd 'ee what a dog's gizzards 'ee ever made of it?

PRUDIE Smirk all 'ee like. She'll give 'ee no aid wi' the calves now – or the seedin'—

JUD Tid'n right.

Now Ross comes in.

ROSS Where's your mistress?

PRUDIE Abed.

ROSS She's unwell?

PRUDIE Mus' be.

Ross looks from Jud to Prudie. It's clear what they're thinking: Demelza is not ill and Ross has brought this situation wholly on himself. Now Prudie sets a hideous-looking pie before him.

ROSS What's this?

PRUDIE *(offended)* What do it look like?

ROSS I can't decide. Hence the enquiry.

PRUDIE 'Tis that long since mistress let me bake, I've mislaid all my skillage.

ROSS So it appears. Perhaps you could mislay this and bring me something edible.

He gets up and goes out.

CUT TO:

9: INT. NAMPARA HOUSE, ROSS & DEMELZA'S BEDROOM – DAY 37

Demelza is finishing breakfast when there's a knock at the door and Ross comes in.

DEMELZA *(pleasantly)* Oh, you're still here? Is Trenwith not yet in readiness? But surely Elizabeth's anxious to have you there? Would you like for me to help you pack?

Ross grits his teeth and ignores her taunts.

ROSS I thought you should know that we're selling the head gear of Grace. The venturers at Wheal Radiant have offered a fair price—

DEMELZA *(ignoring this)* D'you suppose she ever seriously meant to marry George? Surely it was just a trick – to get you to declare your hand?

ROSS I've no idea what her intention was.

DEMELZA Still, it worked, did it not? She got what she wanted.

ROSS You would have to ask *her* what she wanted.

DEMELZA Did she not make it perfectly clear? Did not *you?*

ROSS Demelza – I have never claimed to be perfect—

DEMELZA Perfect? Have I ever asked for that? Not as I recall. But p'raps my memory serves me ill, for I seem to remember we promised to 'forsake all others'. But mebbe such vows apply only to common folks an' not to gentry.

ROSS I realize I've betrayed your trust—

DEMELZA Forfeit—

ROSS And that your pride is wounded—

DEMELZA My *pride?* My – pride? *(determined to retain her composure)* To think, I did always look up to you – respect you – revere you as my master long before you were my husband—

ROSS I see that, but—

DEMELZA *(laughing at the very idea)* For it seemed to me, unschooled as I was, that you were not like other men. That you had a kind of nobility – not of birth, but of character. And I was proud to think a man like you had married me. So now to discover that you are so much *less* than other men. Are fallen so low because so far. 'Tis not my pride that's wounded, Ross. 'Tis my pride in *you.*

She resumes her breakfast. Defeated, Ross leaves.

CUT TO:

10: INT. TRENWITH HOUSE, TURRET ROOM – DAY 37

A restless Elizabeth paces the room, looking out as if expecting to see someone. Frustrated, she leaves the room.

CUT TO:

11: INT. TRENWITH HOUSE, GREAT HALL – DAY 37

Elizabeth comes in. Aunt Agatha, playing solitaire, glances at her keenly.

AUNT AGATHA When do you expect him?

ELIZABETH Who?

Aunt Agatha raises an eyebrow which says, 'We both know who I mean.'

AUNT AGATHA My nephew is not always the most subtle of men. Nor the most discreet.

ELIZABETH I'm sure I don't know what you—

AUNT AGATHA Don't be coy, Elizabeth. There is no one here but ourselves. *(then, seeing her continued reticence)* You will note that I have never married. Perhaps you think that was an accident.

ELIZABETH Well, I—

AUNT AGATHA Perhaps I think so too sometimes. And then I remind myself that I've yet to meet the man who could better me. *(then)* It is the better man we long for, is it not? Sometimes he is not the most convenient man.

Elizabeth is stunned. Is Aunt Agatha really giving her approval?

AUNT AGATHA *(cont'd)* Come, let us not pretend we would prefer a Warleggan under this roof to a Poldark.

Elizabeth stares at Aunt Agatha in astonishment.

AUNT AGATHA *(cont'd)* Of course I'm sorry for his kitchen maid. We have much to thank her for. But one has to acknowledge the prior claim.

Elizabeth is reeling from Aunt Agatha's unabashed frankness. But crucially she doesn't argue with it.

AUNT AGATHA *(cont'd)* So we can assume he will return to this house as soon as he has put his own in order?

Elizabeth doesn't reply, but the fact that she doesn't contradict Aunt Agatha suggests this is exactly what she wishes and expects.

CUT TO:

12: INT. WARLEGGAN HOUSE, GEORGE'S DEN – DAY 37

George sits with Tankard, who is taking notes as George dictates a list of names.

GEORGE Lord and Lady Devoran – Sir John Trevaunance – Unwin Trevaunance. Lady Whitworth—

TANKARD Her son Osbert?

GEORGE The Honourable Maria Agar – Sir Hugh Bodrugan—

TANKARD His brother Robert—

GEORGE William Hick – Mr and Mrs Alfred Barbary – Ray Penvenen and his niece Caroline—

CUT TO:

13: INT. LONDON HOUSE – DAY 37

Caroline, playing cards with a friend, has just been given the news of the forthcoming nuptials.

CAROLINE George Warleggan to marry Elizabeth Poldark? I was never more astonished in my life. *(then)* I could have sworn her interest lay elsewhere. *(then)* But plainly a lady may not always have what her heart desires!

They both laugh.

CUT TO:

14: INT. DWIGHT'S COTTAGE – DAY 37

Dwight is dissecting a human heart, examining it closely and making notes. His monastic existence and loneliness are matched only by his fanatical devotion to his research.

CUT TO:

15: INT. TRENWITH HOUSE, LIBRARY – DAY 37

Elizabeth is embroidering. We get the impression she's doing something – anything – to keep her mind off waiting for Ross. Aunt Agatha watches her beadily. Elizabeth puts aside her embroidery, gets up, goes to a desk and takes out pen, ink and paper. Then she hesitates. Should she write to Ross? She is conscious of Aunt Agatha's eyes boring into her. She's in turmoil. What should she do? Aunt Agatha is itching to comment. Wisely she refrains. But Elizabeth can't help herself. She begins to write a letter.

CUT TO:

16: INT. NAMPARA HOUSE, PARLOUR – DAY 37

Demelza is giving Jeremy his lunch as Ross comes in.

ROSS Demelza – we cannot continue like this— *(no reply)* If you could try to see this from *my* perspective—

DEMELZA *(laughs in disbelief)* Soon you'll be askin' me to see it from *Elizabeth's!*

ROSS Hardly—

DEMELZA O' course 'tis no mystery. She cannot wait to install you in her house – or her bed—

ROSS Demelza—

DEMELZA Indeed, I do suspicion her letter say exactly that!

ROSS Letter?

DEMELZA Came an hour since. No doubt she's wondering what's keeping you. Truly we d' wonder that ourselves, don' we, Jeremy?

ROSS May I see it?

DEMELZA I put it on your pillow. *(beat)* In the library.

Ross looks at her, uncomprehending. Then he goes out.

CUT TO:

17: INT. NAMPARA HOUSE, LIBRARY – DAY 37

Ross comes into the library and sees that a small camp bed has been set up. The message is clear: this is where he'll be sleeping from now on. Now he picks up the letter, which is on the pillow of his camp bed. The handwriting is neat – there is nothing to give away the identity of the sender – but it is clear Ross assumes it's from Elizabeth. His hand is almost shaking now. What will she say? He still hasn't made up his mind what he thinks about the events of the other night. He takes a deep breath and opens it. We are close on his face now. His brow furrows. He looks nervous. Then confused. Then disbelieving.

CUT TO:

18: INT. NAMPARA HOUSE, PARLOUR – DAY 37

Ross comes back into the parlour with the letter. Prudie takes one look at him, picks up Jeremy and takes him out. After she's gone:

ROSS I may be away tomorrow night.

Demelza steels herself. So finally, he's leaving her.

ROSS *(cont'd)* I am going to Truro and might not be back till the day after.

Demelza gives a small smile of contempt. 'As if!'

ROSS *(cont'd)* What?

DEMELZA Why not say it, Ross? 'I am going to Elizabeth.'

ROSS The letter was not from her.

DEMELZA Course not.

ROSS Read it if you wish.

He puts the letter on the table. She's dying to pick it up but her pride makes her leave it untouched.

ROSS *(cont'd)* Richard Tonkin has been released from debtors' prison and wishes to see me.

She looks at him narrowly. It's obvious she still doubts him.

ROSS *(cont'd)* No doubt to ask if I can assist him the way I did Harry Blewitt when Carnmore collapsed. But as you know, I've no money to spare.

DEMELZA *(false cheeriness)* A pity. You'll miss the Bodrugan party.

ROSS That's the least of my regrets.

He looks her in the eye, willing her to understand what he means. She wilfully misunderstands his meaning.

ROSS *(cont'd)* Demelza, I would never deliberately hurt you – you of all people must know that—

DEMELZA Must I, Ross? So I'm to assume you inflict pain by accident? Without a second thought?

ROSS In the moment – I admit – there was no thought – of you – of the pain I might cause – *(then)* It was as if I was – possessed—

DEMELZA O' course. No fault of yours. A greater power – and you and she helpless to resist—

ROSS In a way – yes!

Demelza explodes with derision.

ROSS *(cont'd)* Perhaps I might have hoped for some understanding – knowing you as I do—

DEMELZA Knowing me to be kind and simple and giving? Would you like for me to leap off Hendrawna cliffs – so you may bury me at your convenience and marry again at leisure?!

ROSS I don't blame you for your anger – but how does it serve us now?

DEMELZA Serve us, Ross? How did you serve us? How does *this* serve us?

Suddenly, without warning, she sweeps the crockery off the table towards him. Then she marches out of the room. Ross begins to pick up the shattered pieces of crockery. Presently Prudie comes running in.

PRUDIE Judas, what 'appened? The pots is all scat t' jowds!

ROSS I caught my sleeve on the cloth.

A look on Prudie's face which says 'As if!'

ROSS *(cont'd)* Clear this away.

Ross walks out, crunching his feet on the broken crockery. Prudie, on her knees clearing up, gives him a glare as he passes.

CUT TO:

19: INT. WARLEGGAN HOUSE, GEORGE'S DEN – DAY 37

George continues to dictate notes to Tankard.

GEORGE Lavish, of course! No expense spared. After all, how often does a man get married?

A footman brings a letter to George. He glances at the handwriting and smiles.

TANKARD From the lady herself?

GEORGE No doubt anxious about some detail of trimming or confectionery. Will you excuse me?

Tankard gets up and goes out. George opens the letter. His expression changes to one of disbelief.

ELIZABETH'S VOICE 'My dear George, I am writing to request the smallest of favours. A postponement of our wedding . . .'

As he reads, disbelief gives way to rage. We think he's about to explode – but by an almighty effort of will, he subdues his rage by crushing the letter in his fist.

CUT TO:

20: INT. TRENWITH HOUSE, TURRET ROOM – DAY 37

Elizabeth sees George ride up to the gates but slow down and become more sedate as he rides up the drive. His face is stern. She's not looking forward to this encounter.

CUT TO:

21: INT. TRENWITH HOUSE, GREAT HALL – DAY 37

George sits waiting for Elizabeth. He's still seething – but when Elizabeth comes in, his expression changes and is all smiles and affability.

GEORGE My dear, I cannot make head nor tail of your letter. What can you mean by it?

ELIZABETH George – I beg you – try to understand my position. These past few days – it has dawned on me how rash I've been – plunging into this marriage. Such haste does not look seemly.

GEORGE And you tell me this a week before the wedding? When all the guests are invited?

ELIZABETH *(shocked)* But did we not agree this was to be an entirely private wedding?

GEORGE A few of my closest friends would be hurt to be excluded. I am proud of my bride. I want to show her off to the world!

ELIZABETH George, I have promised to marry you – but I feel it would not be fair – to either of us – to marry in haste.

George contemplates her a moment – and a suspicion arises.

GEORGE Is this anything to do with Ross?

ELIZABETH Why would you think so?

But her flushed face has already given her away.

GEORGE Is it?

ELIZABETH No! That is – obviously he does not favour the arrangement—

GEORGE Has he been here?

ELIZABETH He called—

GEORGE And he is behind this change of heart! I knew it!

ELIZABETH No! It is my own delicacy – seeing him – reminded me how soon it is since Francis died— *(then)* I beg you not to be angry with me.

With a supreme effort George quells the rage he feels. Elizabeth looks unbearably fragile and tearful. He walks away, to calm himself down, then returns, smiling, to Elizabeth. He takes her hand.

GEORGE I want to be indulgent, both before and after our wedding. It's a bitter disappointment to me – but I will try to agree to your wishes if you will promise me one thing.

ELIZABETH Yes?

GEORGE That you name another date – tonight.

ELIZABETH Oh – no – I cannot—

GEORGE Come, my dear, let us compromise so that *both* of us may get something from the arrangement. Grant me the consolation of being able to fix a date – a month from today.

ELIZABETH *(panicking)* So soon?

GEORGE What is there to wait for? What do you imagine will happen in the meantime?

ELIZABETH I – do not know. It is just – a fancy I have—

GEORGE Can I rely on you, Elizabeth?

Elizabeth turns away so that George can't see the torment of indecision on her face. She feels trapped, cornered. Why the hell hasn't Ross come? How long can she stall George? Now George comes up behind her and lightly rests his fingers on her shoulder.

ELIZABETH Very well. A month from today.

Elizabeth closes her eyes and remembers who else had kissed her only hours before.

CUT TO:

22: INT. TRENWITH HOUSE, ELIZABETH'S ROOM (FLASHBACK) – NIGHT 37

Ross and Elizabeth in bed, kissing passionately.
DISSOLVE TO:

23: INT. TRENWITH HOUSE, ELIZABETH'S ROOM – NIGHT 37

Elizabeth lies awake. Fretful. Bewildered. Why hasn't Ross returned?

CUT TO:

24: INT. NAMPARA HOUSE, LIBRARY – NIGHT 37

Ross is wide awake on the camp bed. He's restless, the bed is small and uncomfortable. But that's not why he can't get to sleep.
DISSOLVE TO:

25: INT. NAMPARA HOUSE, ROSS & DEMELZA'S BEDROOM (FLASHBACK – SERIES 1 8/77)

Demelza lying in bed, just awakened from her fever, sees Elizabeth in the doorway.
DEMELZA Has she come to take you?
ROSS No, my love. She will never take me.
DISSOLVE TO:

26: INT. NAMPARA HOUSE, ROSS & DEMELZA'S BEDROOM – NIGHT 37

Demelza lies wide awake.
CUT TO:

27: EXT. NAMPARA HOUSE – DAWN 38

A stormy dawn breaks over Nampara.
CUT TO:

28: INT. NAMPARA HOUSE, LIBRARY/HALLWAY/ KITCHEN – DAY 38

Ross is tidying away his camp bed and gathering his things ready to depart for his trip to Truro. He looks up and sees Demelza standing in the doorway, watching him, her expression almost amused. Not wishing to get into further argument, Ross walks out past her into the hallway. Demelza follows him.

DEMELZA Give my best to Elizabeth.

ROSS Was I not clear? I'm not going to Trenwith.

DEMELZA *(sarcastic)* No, Ross. To 'Truro'. I remember now.

Ross walks off, angry. Demelza, seething, heads into the kitchen – where Prudie greets her.

PRUDIE Servant come from Werry House. Sir Hugh d' beg to know will 'ee attend the party?

DEMELZA Judas! I forgot to reply to his invitation! Do 'ee tell the servant we most sincerely regret that Captain Poldark has been called away. *(Then a thought occurs.)* But Mistress Demelza would be delighted to attend.

Prudie gives her a beady look. This doesn't bode well.

CUT TO:

29: INT. TRENWITH HOUSE, LIBRARY – DAY 38

Aunt Agatha is shuffling cards. Elizabeth is sewing. Presently they hear the sound of a horse's hooves on the gravel outside. Elizabeth jumps up.

ELIZABETH Finally!

AUNT AGATHA Compose yourself, Elizabeth—

ELIZABETH What shall I say? How should I proceed—?

AUNT AGATHA With resolve, girl. 'Tis no easy thing you contemplate—

ELIZABETH But – what will he propose?

AUNT AGATHA 'Tis for you to dictate terms, Elizabeth. You have more to lose.

They wait on tenterhooks as Mrs Tabb goes to open the front door. Then, to their surprise, Verity comes in.

VERITY *(to Elizabeth)* Oh my dear, I had to come. When I heard you'd postponed the wedding, I knew at once what was behind it.

A glance between Aunt Agatha and Elizabeth. Elizabeth, appalled, is so panic-stricken, she promptly faints.

CUT TO:

30: EXT. OPEN COUNTRYSIDE – DAY 38

Ross, riding to Truro, encounters Dwight, who is on his rounds. Dwight looks quizzically at Ross's bruised face.

DWIGHT I don't recall seeing that. Was it got in the rockfall?

ROSS It must have been. Where are you headed?

DWIGHT I've been summoned to Trenwith. I imagine to treat Mrs Chynoweth. *(then)* How's Demelza bearing up?

Ross looks self-conscious. Does Dwight know something?

DWIGHT *(cont'd)* After the disaster? She was a godsend that day. I know I'm preaching to the converted, but you've married a remarkable woman.

ROSS Indeed.

Dwight doesn't notice Ross's struggle.

DWIGHT And where are *you* bound?

ROSS Truro. To meet my old friend Tonkin.

DWIGHT Was he not sent to debtors' prison? After Carn-more—?

ROSS Yes. And now he's out, I fear he wants to tap me for a loan. And since I haven't two shillings in the world— *(then)* But anything's better than sitting at home and watching my mine get dismantled.

DWIGHT Shall we meet later? Take supper? Or would you prefer to dine with Demelza?

ROSS Let's sup together.

Ross and Dwight part.

CUT TO:

31: INT. NAMPARA HOUSE, ROSS & DEMELZA'S BEDROOM – DAY 38

Demelza gets out her best gown ready to take to Werry House. She looks up to see Prudie standing in the doorway, watching her.

PRUDIE I know what 'ee be thinkin'—

Demelza gives her an 'oh really?' look.

PRUDIE *(cont'd)* What's good for the gander—?

Demelza doesn't argue with her.

PRUDIE *(cont'd)* Don't blame 'ee, maid. But no good'll come of it.

DEMELZA 'Twill make *me* feel better.

Demelza continues to pack. Prudie continues to fret.

CUT TO:

32: INT. TRENWITH HOUSE, ELIZABETH'S ROOM/ CORRIDOR – DAY 38

Elizabeth is lying in bed, having been attended by Dwight. Now he comes out of the room and speaks to Verity, who is waiting outside.

DWIGHT There's no cause for alarm. Mrs Poldark has a fragile disposition – and doubtless she's been under some strain of late—

VERITY Did she tell you she's postponed her wedding to George Warleggan?

DWIGHT Indefinitely?

VERITY For a month.

DWIGHT Give her these powders. I'll call again tomorrow.

Dwight goes. Verity goes back into Elizabeth's room.

VERITY My dear, what a fright you gave us.

ELIZABETH Oh, Verity – I'm in such turmoil—

VERITY Of course you are! And you think I cannot guess the reason?

Elizabeth is so horrified she can barely speak. Has Verity guessed her secret?

VERITY *(cont'd)* Let us not speak of it now. You must rest. I will bring you your medicine.

She goes out. Elizabeth remains, horrified.

CUT TO:

33: EXT. RED LION INN – DAY 38

Establisher.

CUT TO:

34: INT. RED LION INN – DAY 38

Ross comes in to find Tonkin waiting for him. Tonkin leaps to his feet and greets Ross enthusiastically.

ROSS It's good to see you at liberty.

TONKIN I'll not forget your kindness. When hard times come, many friends fall away. You did not. *(then)* But your own affairs—

ROSS Do not prosper—

TONKIN So I hear. *(noticing Ross's bruise)* You still bear the scars!

They both sit down. Tonkin calls for ale.

TONKIN *(cont'd)* You'll be wondering why I asked to see you.

Ross nods affably. But he can feel a plea for money coming up.

CUT TO:

35: EXT. WERRY HOUSE – DAY 38

A footman, carrying Demelza's travelling bag, leads Demelza towards the house. A few guests are already gathered, among them George and Tankard, who are talking to Sir Hugh. George is stony-faced (he has a lot on his mind). Then Sir Hugh notices Demelza. He breaks away from George and Tankard and comes to greet her.

SIR HUGH So, Mistress Demelza, you've ventured to trust yourself to my care and left your husband by the fireside.

DEMELZA Yes, sir, I decided 'twas not the weather for firesides. Or husbands!

Sir Hugh roars with laughter.

SIR HUGH Now where have they put you? The Red Room, I believe. 'Tis most convenient—

DEMELZA For what, sir?

SIR HUGH Ease of access, ma'am. As I recall, the catch is broken!

DEMELZA I'd need to be drunken indeed to welcome such a fault!

SIR HUGH That can be arranged!

He roars with laughter at his own wit, gives her a slavering kiss on the hand and orders the servants to show her to her room. We go with her.

DEMELZA *(to herself)* Very drunken indeed.

CUT TO:

36: INT. RED LION INN – DAY 38

Ross and Tonkin continue their discussion.

TONKIN Two years ago you advanced Harry Blewitt the sum of two hundred and fifty pounds.

ROSS And believe me, I regret I was unable to do the same for you.

TONKIN It saved him from debtors' prison. He was able to rearrange his finances and start a small boat-building venture.

ROSS He's had his fill of mining? I don't blame him!

TONKIN When I left prison, he invited me to become his partner in the business.

ROSS I'm delighted for you, sir. I, on the other hand, am considering re-joining my regiment.

TONKIN Can I persuade you to delay a while?

CUT TO:

37: INT. WERRY HOUSE, GUEST BEDROOM – DAY 38

Demelza comes into the room and finds a dressing table where a decanter of port and a glass are waiting for her. On the table is a box containing patches, white powder, rouge, burnt cork, carmine . . . From the open window she hears the sound of male laughter in the garden below. She goes to the window and looks out. Below she sees Sir Hugh laughing and joking with Captain McNeil. She now knows who her target for the night is. She pours herself a glass of port and begins to prepare her face for the party.

CUT TO:

38: INT. RED LION INN – DAY 38

TONKIN Our venture at present is small – but we have high hopes. Of course, if we had more capital, our progress would be swifter.

ROSS Forgive me, sir, I must stop you there. If you're looking for investment, you've come to the wrong man.

Tonkin looks at Ross and roars with laughter.

TONKIN Investment? Dear me, no, sir. That isn't it at all.

He hands Ross the boatyard accounts. Ross examines them.

ROSS You've tripled your income in six months?

TONKIN 'Twas a moderate investment when we set out – but with the war, demand has gone sky high – and now—

ROSS You've the makings of a first-rate business.

TONKIN And you too, sir, if you choose.

CUT TO:

39: INT. WERRY HOUSE, STAIRCASE – DUSK 38

From above we see Demelza descending the staircase, towards the party.

CUT TO:

40: INT. WERRY HOUSE – DUSK 38

Music is playing. Sir Hugh is chatting to Margaret, who is gaudily dressed and clearly on the lookout for her next step up the social ladder. George is chatting to Tankard. He's not in a great mood (since the delay to his wedding) and doesn't decline when Tankard tops up his glass with port. We've rarely seen him so on edge. He seems to be looking for something on which to vent his frustration. Now a hush seems to fall. There are a few raised eyebrows, surprised expressions. Demelza has entered the party. She looks unsteady (from nerves and from the quantity of port she's consumed), her dress is low-cut, her make-up is gaudy and she's all alone. Sir Hugh's face lights up. He breaks away from Margaret (who looks very put out) and hastens to greet her.

SIR HUGH Mistress Demelza! This is a sight for sore eyes!

He kisses her hand. Demelza smiles flirtatiously.

DEMELZA Perhaps you'll introduce me to your friends?

SIR HUGH By all means!

He leads her over to a couple of male guests, who look her up and down appreciatively. Meanwhile an idea has occurred to George. He whispers in Tankard's ear. Tankard looks confused. Then affronted.

TANKARD Surely you jest?

GEORGE On the contrary.

TANKARD She was a scullery maid!

GEORGE Then you should find her all the more eager to *serve*! *(seeing Tankard hesitate)* Come, man, I'm in sore need of entertainment!

TANKARD So you wish me to heap further ignominy on Poldark . . .

GEORGE By debauching his wife! Precisely! Come, I'll introduce you.

George strolls over to where Sir Hugh and his guests are chatting to Demelza. Tankard follows.

GEORGE *(cont'd)* Mistress Demelza. Is Ross not here?

DEMELZA He's been called away on business. Where is Elizabeth?

GEORGE She has family matters to attend to.

DEMELZA I can imagine.

She is so tempted to tell George about Ross's night with Elizabeth. And for a moment George is unnerved. But as Demelza doesn't elaborate, he reasserts himself.

GEORGE May I introduce Mr Tankard?

TANKARD Your servant, ma'am.

GEORGE He's a little shy and barely knows a soul. Perhaps you'll take pity on him.

DEMELZA *(determined to flirt with anyone and everyone)* P'raps I will! D'you dance, sir?

TANKARD I could be persuaded.

Now they are accosted by Margaret, who is still bristling from her snub by Sir Hugh. She looks Demelza up and down and decides she needs putting in her place.

GEORGE Mistress Demelza, d'you know our friend Margaret Vosper? Mistress Ross Poldark. I believe you ladies have something in common.

MARGARET *(with a smirk)* I believe we do!

DEMELZA An' what would that be?

SIR HUGH Both devilish pretty women who have only to crook a finger and the men come running?

Demelza, knowing exactly what George was insinuating (that both she and Margaret have had sex with Ross!), ignores him and decides to flirt with Sir Hugh.

DEMELZA I'd no idea there were so many handsome men in Cornwall, Sir Hugh. 'Tis fortunate you need not fear the competition.

Sir Hugh ogles Demelza appreciatively and cosies up to her. Piqued, Margaret goes on the offensive.

MARGARET I've buried several husbands and serviced countless more – and I never see the point in beating about the bush. If you've a fancy for someone, go up and ask 'em!

GEORGE That all sounds very *businesslike.*

TANKARD And honest. A gentleman knows where he stands and so does a lady.

DEMELZA *(to Tankard, flirtatious)* Myself, I prefer to take time in makin' up my mind. Even if it do seem like beatin' about the bush— *(to Margaret)* I should rather do that than get scratched and worn on every bush I see!

MARGARET And does your husband share your delicacy?

She smiles insolently and leads Sir Hugh away triumphantly. Demelza forces a smile, but inside she's seething. Margaret's suggestion of Ross's promiscuity has not gone down well. She could happily wipe the smirk off George's face too. She turns her attention to Tankard.

DEMELZA Shall we dance, sir?

She's about to give her hand to Tankard when she is accosted by Captain McNeil.

CAPTAIN MCNEIL Mistress Poldark! What a happy coincidence. May I escort you to supper?

DEMELZA Now you mention it, I do have something of an appetite!

CAPTAIN MCNEIL And I'm a great believer in indulging such a thing!

DEMELZA *(to Tankard)* Pray excuse me, sir. You may reclaim me presently.

She's so suggestive, even McNeil is surprised. Not caring now where these flirtations might lead, Demelza takes his offered arm and they go in to supper. George and Tankard exchange a glance. Clearly Demelza is 'up' for something tonight. And George could not be more delighted.

CUT TO:

41: INT. TRENWITH HOUSE, ELIZABETH'S ROOM – DUSK 38

Elizabeth is sitting up in bed when Verity comes in, bringing her medicine, and sits beside her.

VERITY My dear, I would speak with you—

ELIZABETH *(terrified)* I – I do not feel strong enough to—

VERITY Elizabeth, don't be afraid. I understand your feelings. They're quite natural. After all that has happened—

ELIZABETH What can you mean?

VERITY I sympathize more than you think. You wonder how you can give your hand to George – when your heart is committed elsewhere.

ELIZABETH Yes – but – more than that—

VERITY There can be no more than that, my dear. You must let him go. You must move forward. He would want you to.

ELIZABETH I do not think so—

VERITY But I know that he would. And who can say better than I? As his sister—

Elizabeth looks suddenly confused. Are they talking about the same person?

VERITY *(cont'd)* He is dearer to me than almost anyone. And I know he and George were enemies at the end. But Francis would want you to be happy. And if George is your choice, I believe you would have his blessing.

Elizabeth is reeling. She realizes her mistake and knows how close she came to revealing her secret (about her night with Ross). But she's still in turmoil about her feelings for Ross. And Verity's kindness has exacerbated, not relieved her anguish.

ELIZABETH And yours?

VERITY And mine.

CUT TO:

42: INT. WERRY HOUSE – NIGHT 38

Demelza is dancing with McNeil. It's a boisterous, energetic dance and Demelza is getting hot and giddy. She and McNeil continue to exchange looks and smiles, although from time to time she flashes a smile at Tankard too. George watches, intrigued. He whispers something to Tankard. They both laugh. As the dance comes to an end, Demelza is breathless and perspiring. McNeil escorts her away from the throng.

DEMELZA Dear life, I'm so hot I could faint!

CAPTAIN MCNEIL Then 'tis fortunate you have someone to catch you!

Demelza laughs – far more enthusiastically than the joke warrants.

CAPTAIN MCNEIL *(cont'd)* And now I have some sad news. Tomorrow I leave to re-join my regiment.

DEMELZA I think I shall weep!

CAPTAIN MCNEIL So I wonder, as a special favour tonight, would you consider calling me – Malcolm?

DEMELZA And in turn, you'll be wishing to call me Demelza?

CAPTAIN MCNEIL 'Tis a very pretty name. What does it mean?

DEMELZA My mother once told me that in the true Cornish tongue it means 'thy sweetness'.

CAPTAIN MCNEIL I would rather it meant 'my sweetness'.

Demelza smiles at him. So far she's felt in command of the situation. Now for the first time she feels she's heading into dangerous territory.

DEMELZA *(fanning herself)* 'Tis very close in here.

CAPTAIN MCNEIL Shall we take a breath of air in the garden?

He offers her his arm. She hesitates – then takes it.

CUT TO:

43: INT. DWIGHT'S COTTAGE – NIGHT 38

Dwight opens the door to Ross.

DWIGHT Well? Did they fleece you like footpads?

ROSS No. They showered me with blessings! *(beat)* The debt repaid – in full – or a share in a profitable business.

DWIGHT That's excellent! What will you do?

ROSS Truth be told, I'm half-tempted to follow your lead and enlist!

DWIGHT What, now? When things are looking up? Surely you've too much to keep you here?

ROSS Yes. You would think so.

DWIGHT But?

ROSS When are our choices ever straightforward?

CUT TO:

44: EXT. WERRY HOUSE, GARDENS – NIGHT 38

McNeil and Demelza stroll together. They are not the only ones strolling in the garden but McNeil steers Demelza away from the others. Now they are standing very close together. Demelza shivers.

CAPTAIN MCNEIL Are you cold? May I fetch your wrap?

DEMELZA I have none.

CAPTAIN MCNEIL I'm glad of it. For I know a better way to warm you.

He puts his arm round her shoulders. She remains absolutely still and he does not encroach further, as if hoping that if he keeps his arm there long enough, she won't notice.

DEMELZA You're most attentive, Malcolm.

CAPTAIN MCNEIL You cannot be short of attention, surely? Everywhere I look, men are snarling over you. But I fancy they don't suit you as well as—

He hesitates. Inviting her to supply the word.

DEMELZA As well as—?

That's it. She knows she's issuing an invitation. McNeil leans towards her and kisses her. Since Demelza keeps her eyes open, we can tell that she's in two minds about this kiss, about McNeil and about what she's getting into. Finally McNeil releases her.

CAPTAIN MCNEIL Since the moment I met you, I've wanted to do that.

DEMELZA I hope you were not disappointed.

CAPTAIN MCNEIL On the contrary, you have given me an appetite for more.

He leans towards her for another kiss. She pulls back slightly.

DEMELZA I think we should return to the party.

CAPTAIN MCNEIL Will you not give me a word of encouragement before we go?

DEMELZA Surely you've had more 'n enough already.

CAPTAIN MCNEIL But will you not give me something to hope for? Later? Tonight? *(whispering)* Which is your room?

Demelza hesitates. Now is the moment to decide. Is she going to go all the way?

DEMELZA I'm not well acquainted with this house. I think Sir Hugh called it – the Red Room?

CAPTAIN MCNEIL I know it. *(whispers in her ear)* Thank you, my sweetness. Thank you.

He kisses her ear, then leads her back towards the house.

CUT TO:

45: INT. DWIGHT'S COTTAGE – NIGHT 38

Ross and Dwight have finished supper and are now drinking port. Ross seems thoughtful. Dwight notices.

DWIGHT You seem distracted—

ROSS Do I?

DWIGHT Despite your good fortune. Is all well at home?

ROSS Yes – and no. Demelza and I . . . *(hesitates, then)* Let us just say that attachments – are complicated. As you well know.

DWIGHT Your cousin-in-law might agree!

ROSS Elizabeth?

DWIGHT It was she I was called to attend at Trenwith. A fainting fit. She's postponed her wedding—

ROSS She has? Are you certain?

DWIGHT Clearly the thought of marrying George Warleggan was more than she could stand!

Ross is so shocked he is unable to speak. What did he expect? A postponement? A cancellation? And what did he want? To his surprise, he realizes he's still not sure.

CUT TO:

46: EXT. WERRY HOUSE – NIGHT 38

The last few guests (those who are not staying the night) are departing from the party.

CUT TO:

47: INT. WERRY HOUSE, GUEST BEDROOM – NIGHT 38

Demelza comes into her room and shuts the door. There's a catch on the door. She tests it to see if it fastens. It doesn't. She sits down on the bed and tries to decide what to do. Horribly sober now, she pours herself a glass of port and knocks it back. She shivers with cold. She warms her hands at a candle. She pours herself another glass of port. The decanter is now empty and she has nothing left to bolster her courage. She sits down on the bed then jumps up again. She's had second thoughts. Before she can act on them there's a soft knock at the door. McNeil appears, closes the door behind him.

DEMELZA Did anyone see you?

CAPTAIN MCNEIL I hope I know how to conduct an ambush, my darling!

He comes up to her and without any preliminaries, takes her in his arms and begins to kiss her. Again her eyes are open. Again she's not exactly sure she likes this. To play for time, she pulls back from him.

DEMELZA So you leave tomorrow?

CAPTAIN MCNEIL At noon—

DEMELZA And I shall not see you again—

CAPTAIN MCNEIL You shall if you wish. You may write to me at Winchester—

He continues to devour her with kisses. Though she's trying to be a willing participant, she's less and less convinced that this is what she wants. Her eyes are wide open. She closes them and tries to re-engage with McNeil, to get into the mood. But it's no use. His moustache is tickling her, his kisses don't excite her. She opens her eyes, breaks free from his mouth and tries to push him away.

DEMELZA Malcolm—

CAPTAIN MCNEIL My angel?

DEMELZA Are you kind?

CAPTAIN MCNEIL Immensely.

DEMELZA Then I want you to bear with me – to understand – why I led you to believe – *(then)* 'Tis on account of my husband—

CAPTAIN MCNEIL Don't think of him—

DEMELZA He's betrayed me with another—

CAPTAIN MCNEIL Is he insane?

DEMELZA And because of that, I thought – I should do the same—

CAPTAIN MCNEIL Most assuredly—

DEMELZA And of all the men I could have chosen, you seemed the most kind. But now I begin to wonder—

CAPTAIN MCNEIL Set your mind at rest – I'm the soul of discretion—

DEMELZA No – please – hear me out—

CAPTAIN MCNEIL Have I told you how beautiful you are?

DEMELZA I begin to realize something – about myself – call it weakness, if you will, but – I cannot give myself—

CAPTAIN MCNEIL You can—

DEMELZA To any man except my husband. I am bound to him. I wish it were not so but—

CAPTAIN MCNEIL My angel, it does you credit to be so delicate – but think for a moment of *me* – who's been looking forward to this encounter as to a mortal's taste of heaven—

DEMELZA Sir—

CAPTAIN MCNEIL Your duty now is not to your husband, but to *me*.

He begins to kiss her again, this time more assertively. Demelza begins to struggle.

DEMELZA Malcolm, please—

He continues to force himself upon her. She struggles even harder – eventually kneeing him in the groin. She breaks away from him. Now they're facing each other across the room. Both are breathing heavily, locking eyes as if preparing for battle – one to assault, the other to resist. But now McNeil sees something in Demelza's eyes which tells him she will never surrender to him. His expression goes cold.

CAPTAIN MCNEIL I like a woman who knows her own mind. I thought you were such a one. My mistake.

He goes out. Demelza is still shaking. Her face is red hot. She buries her face in her hands as if overcome with shame.

DEMELZA *(under her breath)* I hate you, Ross – I *hate* you!

CUT TO:

48: INT. SAWLE KIDDLEY – NIGHT 38

Ross comes into the kiddley and sees Zacky and various other miners drinking together. They're surprised but pleased to see him.

ZACKY Brings 'ee here, Ross?

ROSS A disinclination to go home early!

ZACKY Join us, then! As we drown our sorrows! Eke out the last of our earnin's!

ROSS Don't remind me.

ZACKY Nay, Ross, don't take it hard. We all were willin' to work without timbers. *(beat)* An' were it to do again, we'd none of us think twice.

ROSS You cannot mean that. After we lost Ted?

ZACKY Risky work's better than none. *(seeing Ross look unconvinced)* Grace put food on our table. *(genuine)* An' more' n that – she give us hope – the means to make our own way. The harder we work'd, the more we prosper'd. 'Tis not many can say that.

ROSS No, I see that.

ZACKY I tell 'ee, were it not that the lode's buried 'neath thirty fathom of rock, we'd be back down there like a shot.

ROSS You would?

ZACKY With Ted's blessing!

The other miners all smile and nod their agreement. This gives Ross pause for thought.

CUT TO:

49: INT. WERRY HOUSE, CORRIDOR – NIGHT 38

Sir Hugh Bodrugan appears at the end of the corridor and begins to move, with exaggerated stealth, towards the door of Demelza's room. Almost salivating as he tiptoes his way down the corridor, he is stopped in his tracks by the appearance of another man who emerges from the shadows of the corridor and is about to try the door handle to Demelza's room.

SIR HUGH Damn, blast and set fire to it!

The man leaps away from the door. It's Tankard.

TANKARD What the blazes—!

CUT TO:

50: INT. WERRY HOUSE, GUEST BEDROOM – NIGHT 38

Demelza, sitting on the bed in absolute despair, hears voices outside the door and starts to panic.

CUT TO:

51: INT. WERRY HOUSE, CORRIDOR – NIGHT 38

Tankard and Sir Hugh confront each other.

SIR HUGH I believe you're lost, sir. Your room is on the east side.

TANKARD Thank you, sir. I know very well where my room is. And who *this* one belongs to.

CUT TO:

52: INT. WERRY HOUSE, GUEST BEDROOM – NIGHT 38

Demelza is horrified at the thought of having to face anyone – least of all someone she's flirted with and encouraged – after her humiliating encounter with McNeil.

CUT TO:

53: INT. WERRY HOUSE, CORRIDOR – NIGHT 38

TANKARD Dammit, sir, she as good as invited me. Now why don't you scuttle off and turn a blind eye?

SIR HUGH Blind eye? I was going in there myself!

TANKARD What? Don't tell me she invited *you?*

SIR HUGH Not in so many words – but a nod's as good as a wink—

TANKARD She was being polite—

SIR HUGH Polite, be beggared! What did she say to you?

TANKARD It was more a question of her *manner*—

SIR HUGH Blast it, man, you've had no invitation! You thought to try your luck!

TANKARD Blast *yourself*, sir! *I* was here first!

SIR HUGH But I'm the host – 'tis only right I should have first pick!

TANKARD A host should yield to a guest, as you very well know! 'Tis the proper etiquette—

SIR HUGH Etiquette be damned! If you go into that room, I go with you!

They both halt, realizing things have got out of hand.

TANKARD I don't fancy we'll win her *that* way! *(then)* Suppose we toss a coin?

SIR HUGH Humph! I still believe I have the stronger claim, but no one shall say I'm not a sportsman.

Tankard gets out a coin.

TANKARD Call.

SIR HUGH Heads.

TANKARD Tails! Stand aside, sir.

With seething resentment, Sir Hugh watches Tankard go into Demelza's room. Admitting defeat, he's about to leave when he hears:

TANKARD *(cont'd)* What the devil—?

Sir Hugh goes rushing into the bedroom.

CUT TO:

54: INT. WERRY HOUSE, GUEST BEDROOM – NIGHT 38

Sir Hugh comes in to find Tankard looking puzzled and the room empty. Then Tankard draws Sir Hugh's attention to the window, which is wide open. They both go over to it, look out of it, then at each other.

SIR HUGH Stap me, I never knew a woman who promised so much and delivered so little!

United in frustration and disappointment, they go out.

CUT TO:

55: EXT. WHEAL GRACE – DAY 39

Sunrise over the mine. The mine is still deserted and silent.

CU: Ross, contemplating it from afar.

CUT TO:

56: INT. WHEAL GRACE, CHANGING HUT – DAY 39

Ross and Henshawe come into the office. They brush dust and debris from a desk and set two chairs beside it. They sit down and look each other in the eye.

ROSS So these are my choices. A new business. A fresh start. Almost a *guarantee* of profit if the war continues. *(beat)* Or the money.

HENSHAWE What would you do with it?

ROSS Put it aside to pay off my debts? Use it for more immediate needs at home? Or throw it down a bottomless shaft where fifteen hundred of mine has gone already.

Henshawe nods but declines to comment.

ROSS *(cont'd)* What do you think I should do?

HENSHAWE I think we both know what you should do. *(beat)* Or else why are we sitting here now?

Ross and Henshawe look at each other. Henshawe raises an eyebrow.

HENSHAWE *(cont'd)* Shall I inform the Wheal Radiant venturers—?

ROSS That our head gear is no longer for sale?

Ross permits himself a smile. They both know what he's going to do with the £250.

CUT TO:

57: EXT. TRENWITH HOUSE, GARDENS – DAY 39

Elizabeth is pacing restlessly. She's approaching the end of her tether. What can be keeping Ross? She can't keep George at bay for ever.

CUT TO:

58: EXT. FIELDS NEAR TRENWITH – DAY 39

Returning home, Ross sees Trenwith in the distance. He hesitates, knowing now he can delay no longer – he really must go and see Elizabeth.

CUT TO:

59: INT. TRENWITH HOUSE, GARDENS – DAY 39

Elizabeth sees Ross's horse in the distance. Her hopes rise.

CUT TO:

60: EXT. FIELD NEAR TRENWITH – DAY 39

Ross hesitates – and hesitates some more. The implications of what he is considering are too enormous to contemplate. He hesitates – then decides to ride on.

CUT TO:

61: INT. TRENWITH HOUSE, GARDENS – DAY 39

Elizabeth is appalled to see Ross ride away.

CUT TO:

62: INT. NAMPARA HOUSE, KITCHEN – DAY 39

Jud is scrubbing a cooking pot and Prudie is chopping vegetables as Ross arrives home. They scowl at him. Unimpressed by his behaviour, they hold him entirely to blame for the fact that they no longer have Demelza to do their chores.

ROSS Where's Demelza?

PRUDIE Out.

ROSS Since when?

JUD *(to Prudie)* Since she went t' Bodrugan's party?

ROSS Did she say she would stay the night?

PRUDIE *(to Jud)* Did she?

JUD *(to Prudie)* Don' recall—

PRUDIE *(to Jud)* P'raps she be 'avin too good a time to come 'ome!

ROSS So you've no idea where she is.

Jud shrugs and Prudie shakes her head.

PRUDIE *(to Jud)* Reckon she's as much right as any to stay out all night?

JUD *(to Prudie)* Reckon she do.

In no mood to engage with this unhelpfulness, Ross goes out, before his temper gets the better of him.

CUT TO:

63: EXT. HENDRAWNA BEACH – DAY 39

Demelza is walking along the beach, trailing her gown through the surf. Her make-up still smeared, her hair dishevelled, her expression cold. She doesn't care that she's ruining her dress.

CUT TO:

64: EXT. CLIFF-TOP PATH – DAY 39

Ross, on his way to Werry House, looks down to the cove below and sees Demelza walking along the beach. He watches her a while. She seems utterly desolate. He dismounts, ties up his horse and goes down to meet her.

CUT TO:

65: EXT. HENDRAWNA BEACH – DAY 39

Demelza continues to walk through the surf. She feels numb, cold. Now, as she looks up, she sees Ross coming towards her. Her expression changes from coldness to brittle brightness.

DEMELZA Ross! How kind of you to come and meet me! Did you have a pleasant time at Trenwith?

ROSS I told you – I went to Truro to meet Richard Tonkin. I don't lie to you, Demelza. When I go to Elizabeth, I will tell you.

DEMELZA Oh, but does that not unfairly constrain you? To have to inform your wife every time you go to see your mistress?

ROSS Tell me when you've done, then we can speak.

DEMELZA No, Ross, you tell me when *you* have done!

They face each other, Demelza with blazing hostility, Ross with frustration that she's wilfully misunderstanding him.

ROSS It was never my intention to go to Trenwith.

DEMELZA Whatever you say, Ross. Do what you will. Go and live with her if you wish.

She begins to walk on, through the surf. Ross follows her.

ROSS It's quite possible that her marriage will still go ahead.

DEMELZA No doubt you did your best to prevent it.

ROSS No doubt I did.

DEMELZA Does she love George, then?

ROSS No, she does not.

She steals a glance at him – and in that moment she realizes that she is not the only one in torment. But ultimately it gives her scant consolation.

ROSS *(cont'd)* Demelza, I cannot blame you for your anger. But if you could bide a while – have a little patience.

DEMELZA Patience?

ROSS This thing will play itself out – sooner or later—

DEMELZA Will it? Oh, I see. So you wish me to sit an' twiddle my thumbs till you decide whether or not you want me?

ROSS It's not a question of wanting you. It's a question of not – wanting *her*.

DEMELZA *Do* you want her?

ROSS No! – I don't know – that is – yes, sometimes – but—

DEMELZA I'm not content to be second best.

ROSS Have I asked you to be?

DEMELZA Have you not made me so?

ROSS Why am I still here, Demelza? Why d'you suppose I'm still here?

DEMELZA I don't know, Ross. Why *are* you still here? Because Elizabeth can't make up her mind?

ROSS No!

DEMELZA Because Elizabeth won't have you? Because she knows George is the better bet?

Ross is seething now. So is Demelza. Again they stand and face each other, both implacable. Then:

ROSS I came here with good news! To tell you that Blewitt can repay the money I lent him.

He waits for her to comment. She doesn't.

ROSS *(cont'd)* We can reopen Grace.

Demelza keeps walking and doesn't answer.

ROSS *(cont'd)* You're spoiling your dress, Demelza!

But Demelza keeps on walking. Ross follows her. He knows he's handled things badly. Again. If only he knew how to put them right.

CUT TO:

66: INT. TRENWITH HOUSE, LIBRARY – DAY 39

Elizabeth comes in to find Aunt Agatha playing solitaire. Elizabeth sits down and takes up her embroidery, trying to occupy herself. Aunt Agatha eyes her beadily. She can see Elizabeth is in turmoil. Should she say something? Finally:

AUNT AGATHA You must take the decision alone.

ELIZABETH Aunt?

AUNT AGATHA You cannot wait for him to help you.

For a moment Elizabeth is tempted to pretend she doesn't know what Aunt Agatha's talking about. But one look at Aunt Agatha tells her pretence would be futile.

ELIZABETH I don't understand. How can he treat me so? How can he leave things so – up in the air?

AUNT AGATHA And not for the first time.

ELIZABETH Exactly! Once before I waited for him – to come and see me – and when he did not—

AUNT AGATHA You married Francis. *(then)* And now?

ELIZABETH I do not know!

Finally the enormity of her situation begins to dawn on her. And once it does, the floodgates open.

ELIZABETH *(cont'd)* He's deserted me. He tried to stop this marriage but offered nothing in return. He has taken what was not rightly his and walked away from the consequences. Why did he have to come? I hate him for it! He's left me with only one possible choice!

CUT TO:

67: EXT. CHURCH – DAY 40

Bells ring out as newlyweds George and Elizabeth exit the church, surrounded by guests. Elizabeth looks radiant but fragile. George looks triumphant.

CUT TO:

68: INT. WHEAL GRACE – DAY 40

A hatch opens. Ross, Henshawe and Zacky peer down the shaft. They are armed with mining tools, keen to begin the work of clearing the debris.

HENSHAWE I estimate it will take two weeks to clear the rubble.

ZACKY Then we'll have her up and running again?

ROSS What are we waiting for?

Ross leads the way.

HENSHAWE I see Ross be not at his cousin's wedding?

Zacky gives Henshawe a look which says: 'I think we all know why!'
CUT TO:

69: INT. TRENWITH HOUSE, LIBRARY – DAY 40

Newly returned from the wedding, Geoffrey Charles is gazing wistfully at the portrait of Francis. Verity escorts Aunt Agatha in. She is struggling to remain bright and cheerful.

VERITY Such a pity that relations with George are so strained that Ross could not attend the wedding.

AUNT AGATHA If you say so.

Verity glances at Aunt Agatha suspiciously. What does Aunt Agatha know that she's not telling? Verity hands her a glass of port. Aunt Agatha notes how lost Geoffrey Charles now seems.

AUNT AGATHA *(cont'd)* Come and sit with me, child.

He does. She takes his hand affectionately. They make a poignant sight, old and young sitting together.

VERITY So now you are all that remains of the Trenwith Poldarks.

AUNT AGATHA No doubt Warleggan would dispense with us if he could.

VERITY You'll hardly see him, Aunt. His own home Cardew is so much grander than this – why would he even *visit*? Elizabeth may come to see her mother. But to all intents and purposes, you are mistress now.

AUNT AGATHA And you'll visit me often?

VERITY Like old times.

A moment between them.

VERITY *(cont'd)* If we close our eyes, it will seem like twenty years ago – Francis and Father still alive – and Ross riding over every day!

Even Aunt Agatha goes misty-eyed at the thought.

AUNT AGATHA Ross. Yes. How different might it all have been.

She doesn't elaborate and Verity doesn't ask her to. Even though Verity has no inkling of the truth, she recognizes that some things are better left unspoken.

CUT TO:

70: INT. INN, BEDROOM – NIGHT 40

Elizabeth prepares for her wedding night. George comes up behind her and kisses the back of her neck. Elizabeth doesn't flinch as we might have expected her to. It's clear her resentment against Ross has made her determined to forget him. She lets her robe slip from her shoulders. The message is clear: it is George who is in possession now.

CUT TO:

71: INT. NAMPARA HOUSE, LIBRARY – NIGHT 40

Ross is preparing for bed. He sits on his camp bed, examining a sample of rock. He looks up and sees Demelza standing in the doorway. She puts Jeremy down so that he can run to kiss Ross goodnight.

ROSS He must wonder why I sleep here now.

DEMELZA P'raps you should tell him.

ROSS Because you don't wish to have me near you?

DEMELZA Or because you find me distasteful after the delicate charms of Elizabeth?

ROSS Demelza—

She picks up Jeremy and goes out. Defeated, Ross takes solace in the one thing he can exert a modicum of control over: the mine. The tin sample he's holding glistens in the candlelight.

CUT TO:

72: EXT. COAST – DAY 41

Waves crashing on rocks. Various coast GVs.

CUT TO:

73: INT. WHEAL GRACE, CHANGING ROOM – DAY 41

Two weeks later. The noise of the pumping engine tells us it's working again. Dwight stands watching as Ross, Henshawe, Zacky and two other miners get changed, ready to start work in the reopened Wheal Grace.

DWIGHT You'd never think you almost lost your lives down there.

ZACKY We've all got to go sometime!

Zacky goes down the hatch.

DWIGHT I wish Ted could've lived to see the day.

ROSS You did all you could.

DWIGHT It wasn't enough. *(then)* I wonder if the navy's so desperate as to need a second-rate surgeon?

ROSS The navy will need every man it can get if the war continues.

But Dwight seems unconvinced.

HENSHAWE *(to Ross)* An auspicious day! Mistress Poldark should be here! She've always took an interest in our ventures before.

ROSS *(tight-lipped)* Demelza has business elsewhere.

CUT TO:

74: INT. NAMPARA HOUSE, PARLOUR – DAY 41

Demelza is taking tea with Verity. She is as dressed up as we've ever seen her – something which doesn't escape Verity's notice – and she seems unusually animated.

VERITY I'm amazed you could find time to meet. With the mine opening and the farm needing attention?

DEMELZA A lady does not farm.

VERITY *(laughing)* Of course not, but you've never—

DEMELZA Been a true and proper lady? *(before Verity can argue)* Now I shall be. For why should I spend my time skivvying, mending and baking? When, as I recall, Elizabeth never lifted a finger for Ross an' he was still besotted with her.

VERITY But no longer. And not for many a year.

DEMELZA Oh, 'tis of no concern t' me where his affections d' lie.

VERITY You cannot mean that?

Demelza hesitates. She is so tempted to tell Verity what Ross has done. But in the end she restrains herself.

DEMELZA When Elizabeth agreed to marry George, Ross showed that his attachment to her was by no means past.

VERITY *(surprised)* Yet it *will* pass.

DEMELZA Perhaps. *(then, breezily, to change the subject)* So what do you hear of the bride and groom? Will they stay away long, d'you think?

CUT TO:

75: EXT. PENVENEN LONDON HOUSE – DAY 41

Elizabeth and George walk up the steps to the house.
CUT TO:

76: INT. PENVENEN LONDON HOUSE – DAY 41

Elizabeth and George, both lavishly dressed, stand in a spacious entrance hall. Elizabeth looks around, impressed. George contemplates his wife with proprietorial satisfaction.

GEORGE You were born for this life, my dear.

ELIZABETH *(with a smile)* I like to think so.

GEORGE London is full of beauties, but you will outshine them all.

A footman comes to lead them away.
CUT TO:

77: INT. PENVENEN HOUSE, DRAWING ROOM – DAY 41

Caroline sits with George and Elizabeth at a tea table.

CAROLINE Such a privilege to have Lord and Lady Warleggan to tea! *(then)* Oh, have I ennobled you prematurely? I'm sure the honour will soon be forthcoming!

George smiles his approbation at the thought and acknowledges Caroline for the compliment.

CAROLINE *(cont'd) (to Elizabeth)* Are you pleased with London?

ELIZABETH Very much.

GEORGE And intend to visit often.

CAROLINE And how is Cornwall? Do you see anything of Dr Enys?

ELIZABETH He attends my mother.

CAROLINE So he's finally moving in more exalted circles!

ELIZABETH I fear not, ma'am. I think my mother is his only fee-paying patient.

GEORGE And you're settled in London?

CAROLINE I have been. But now that I'm overshadowed by the new Mrs Warleggan, I may have to move elsewhere!

ELIZABETH You're very kind, ma'am.

CAROLINE But how secretive you've been! Your wedding was announced so late, my uncle and I could not attend.

GEORGE My wife kept me waiting a while till she gave her answer.

CAROLINE Quite right. Marriage lasts a lifetime. A lady must be sure she's making the right choice!

Everyone laughs. But as we go closer on Elizabeth, we can tell that someone else has just flitted into her thoughts.

CUT TO:

78: INT. WHEAL GRACE, TUNNEL – DAY 42

Ross, stripped to the waist, is working alongside his men. It's hot, backbreaking work but Ross welcomes it, finding it both distracting and therapeutic. Finally, exhausted, he wipes the sweat away, picks up his discarded shirt and begins to make his way back along the tunnel to the ladder. Then he hears a voice behind him:

ZACKY Ross! Captain Henshawe be callin' f'r 'ee—

ROSS Can it wait?

ZACKY There's something he need 'ee t' see.

Ross heads back down the tunnel.

CUT TO:

79: INT. CARRIAGE – DAY 42

Elizabeth and George are returning home from their honeymoon. They are beautifully and stylishly dressed and seem very well pleased with themselves.

GEORGE I've been thinking about our domestic arrangements—

ELIZABETH You'll be glad to return home to Cardew.

GEORGE I had thought so. But now I believe I've a fancy to live somewhere else.

CUT TO:

80: INT. WHEAL GRACE, TUNNEL – DAY 42

Ross makes his way down the tunnel and finds Henshawe – who stands looking at something (the lode – but we don't see it). Ross joins him. His jaw drops. Henshawe and Ross stand staring at the sight in absolute disbelief.

CUT TO:

81: INT. TRENWITH HOUSE, GREAT HALL – DAY 42

Dwight is on his way out, having attended Mrs Chynoweth. He is met by Aunt Agatha.

AUNT AGATHA How fares your patient?

DWIGHT Mrs Chynoweth is a little improved, ma'am – but it will be a long road to recovery.

AUNT AGATHA And not one on which you'll be accompanying her.

DWIGHT I beg your pardon?

AUNT AGATHA Oh, not through any choice of mine. That idiot Choake will be tending her from now on. That should finish her off!

DWIGHT I'm sorry – may I ask? – What has happened?

CUT TO:

82: INT. WHEAL GRACE, CHANGING HUT – DAY 42

A hand takes the top off a bottle of rum. The bottle is passed from Ross to Henshawe.

ROSS I can scarce believe it.

HENSHAWE Nor I. When first I saw it – I thought my eyes deceived me.

ROSS What does it mean?

HENSHAWE It means I'm breaking the habit of a lifetime and taking a drink!

He takes a swig from the bottle of rum. Ross laughs and shakes his head. Clearly something momentous has happened.

CUT TO:

83: INT. NAMPARA HOUSE, HALLWAY – DAY 42

Dwight has called to tell Demelza the news. Demelza is pacing, restless.

DEMELZA It cannot be—

DWIGHT There's no doubt. As of tomorrow everything will change.

DEMELZA But Ross—

DWIGHT I know. It will be the bitterest blow.

And as she considers this news, a feeling stirs in Demelza's heart. Finally she feels a tiny spark of compassion for Ross.

CUT TO:

84: EXT. OPEN COUNTRYSIDE – DAY 42

Ross rides home from the mine.

CUT TO:

85: INT. NAMPARA HOUSE, PARLOUR – DAY 42

Ross comes home to find Demelza repairing her damaged gown.

ROSS I have something to tell you.

She seems tight-lipped, looks up briefly but doesn't speak and goes on with her mending.

ROSS *(cont'd)* We reached the tin lode that was buried. We've been working it for some days now. Today the lode split. One half is twice the size of the old lode. Henshawe says he's never seen richer ground.

He waits for her to get enthusiastic. She merely nods her approval and goes on with her mending.

ROSS *(cont'd)* Demelza, d'you understand what this means? I'll be able to pay back the interest on our loan. More than that, soon we'll be in a position to repay our mysterious benefactor *in full*!

DEMELZA I'm very glad for you, Ross.

ROSS And for *us*? D'you not see how this changes things? It will mean not just survival – not even a good living – but wealth!

Demelza gives a sad little smile.

DEMELZA After so long. The very thing we hoped for. And now it's here.

ROSS Has it come too late? Have we found riches and lost the thing that really counts?

A moment between them. She can see how hard he's trying now. Her feelings of compassion grow. She can barely bring herself to tell him her news.

DEMELZA I have something to tell you.

ROSS Yes?

DEMELZA I heard it today – and would not wish you to hear from another – knowing it will grieve you.

Something in the tone of her voice alarms Ross. He looks at her closely.

ROSS Tell me?

CUT TO:

86: EXT. TRENWITH HOUSE – DAY 43

The carriage drives up to Trenwith. Liveried servants stand to attention, ready to greet George and Elizabeth as they return in triumph. Aunt Agatha is there, holding Geoffrey Charles's hand. As the carriage door is opened, she releases him to run and greet his mother. Elizabeth sweeps her son into her arms. But something has subtly changed in George's expression. He no longer feigns affection for Geoffrey Charles. In fact, he seems to view Elizabeth's undisguised affection for her child as a kind of weakness. Now he and Aunt Agatha eyeball each other. Neither bothers to disguise their hostility.

Outside the gates Ross rides up and halts at a distance.

His POV: George, triumphant, talking to Elizabeth, giving instructions to his servants. As Elizabeth glances up she sees Ross. Their eyes meet. The coldness of the look she gives him tells him, not only is she lost to him for ever, but that she will never be able to forgive him. She doesn't draw George's attention to him but instead threads her arm through George's and allows him to lead her away into the house. Before she disappears she gives a final glance at Ross over her shoulder. The message is clear: George Warleggan is now in full possession.

Episode 10

1: EXT. TRENWITH HOUSE – DAY 44 (AUTUMN 1793)

On the horizon, two distant figures walk towards each other. Though not immediately recognizable, we presently realize that one is Elizabeth, the other is George. At first we are too far away to hear their conversation, but when they meet, Elizabeth says something to George which makes him seize her hand and kiss it with joy and gratitude.

GEORGE My dear Elizabeth, you have made me the happiest of men.

CUT TO:

2: EXT. CLIFF TOPS – DAY 44

Demelza stares out to sea. What is she to do with her life?
CUT TO:

3: EXT. WHEAL GRACE – DAY 44

GVs of busy, bustling Wheal Grace.
CUT TO:

4: INT. WHEAL GRACE – DAY 44

Three miners are enthusiastically going about their work.

CUT TO:

5: INT. WHEAL GRACE, CHANGING HUT – DAY 44

Ross sits at the desk. Paul, Zacky and the last few miners queue up to be paid by Ross, who notes each entry in the book. As Paul is paid:

PAUL Can scarce sleep at night – for dreamin' o' the lode an' wantin' to get back to her!

They all laugh. As Paul leaves, Zacky is paid.

ZACKY 'Tis a miracle. A mine that do actually pay?

ROSS Not just pay! Yield riches!

ZACKY Your gamble has paid off.

ROSS Our gamble.

ZACKY Your capital, Ross. Your faith. Take the credit. You've earned it.

Now Henshawe comes in.

HENSHAWE There's soldiers in the village.

ZACKY On Warleggan business?

ROSS I'd put money on it!

HENSHAWE Or looking for men to enlist?

Ross, Zacky and Henshawe exchange a glance.

ZACKY An' we thought war couldn't touch us here.

CUT TO:

6: INT. TRENWITH HOUSE, LIBRARY – DAY 44

Toy soldiers are lined up. Geoffrey Charles is revealed, playing with them. We reveal George and Elizabeth watching.

ELIZABETH He plays beautifully by himself.

GEORGE Yet it's a lonely thing, to be an only child.

Suddenly we get a brief glimpse into the loneliness of George's childhood. Now, as they watch, a servant comes in and removes the portrait of Francis.

ELIZABETH Oh! Must it go? I think Geoffrey Charles will miss it.

Geoffrey Charles glances up, sees the portrait being removed but says nothing.

GEORGE But my dear, this is where I'd hoped that my gift to you—

ELIZABETH Which?

GEORGE A portrait of us both – painted by the celebrated John Opie?

ELIZABETH You spoil me.

George kisses her hand. Then he sees Tankard in the doorway.

GEORGE Would you excuse me, my dear?

George goes off to meet Tankard. Only when he's gone does Geoffrey Charles speak . . .

GEOFFREY CHARLES How long will Uncle George stay, Mama?

ELIZABETH Oh, sweetheart, Uncle George lives here now. You must think of him as your new papa.

But it's obvious that Geoffrey Charles is not enamoured of the idea.

CUT TO:

7: INT. TRENWITH HOUSE, CORRIDOR – DAY 44

George leads Tankard from the library.

TANKARD I came just now from Wheal Agnes—

GEORGE Any – difficulties?

TANKARD The usual – objections—

GEORGE Which were dealt with—?

Tankard gives a sinister nod.

GEORGE *(cont'd)* So the thing is done?

TANKARD *(nods)* Wheal Agnes is now closed.

George nods his satisfaction. Then:

GEORGE And the other matter we discussed?

CUT TO:

8: EXT. TRENWITH LAND – DAY 44

Tom Harry and another servant are erecting a fence at the point where Nampara land meets Trenwith land. Some bal-maidens and miners, including Paul, are passing along the usual path. They come up against the newly erected fence.

TOM HARRY *(shouting at them)* Hop it now! This be private land!

PAUL Since when?

TOM HARRY Since Mr Warleggan be master 'ere!

PAUL He can't do that! This is open land!

TOM HARRY No longer. An' Mr Warleggan'll 'ave 'ee hang if he catch 'ee 'ere again!

The alarmed miners hesitate – till Tom Harry marches at them, a rifle over his shoulder. The women scream, turn and flee. Tom whacks Paul across the head as they go. He yelps in pain and has to be helped away by his fellow-miners. As Tom turns back he sees George approaching with Tankard.

TANKARD Is that – wise?

GEORGE A man who owns land has a right to enclose it – to prevent those with no rights from trespassing.

TANKARD But to use force – needlessly – is to court enemies—

GEORGE *(amused)* Are you becoming squeamish?

TANKARD I merely question the virtue of provoking one's neighbours. *(beat)* Great or small.

CUT TO:

9: INT. NAMPARA HOUSE, LIBRARY – DAY 44

Ross sits at his desk, counting out coins. He picks up a handful, feels the weight of them in his hand, as if he can't quite believe they're real. Now he sees Demelza pass the door. She is about to walk past without coming in.

ROSS *(calling out)* Demelza?

Demelza reappears, comes into the room.

ROSS *(cont'd)* Wheal Agnes is closed.

DEMELZA On whose orders?

A look between them. They both know.

DEMELZA *(cont'd)* Now Grace'll have every man, dog and mule in the county beggin' for work!

Ross raises an eyebrow. He can see she's spoiling for a fight. She's about to go out. He's about to let her. Then:

ROSS Demelza—

She halts.

ROSS *(cont'd)* Give me your hand.

She does, reluctantly. He pours coins into her hand.

ROSS *(cont'd)* Cast your mind back a twelvemonth. How many times did we think all was lost?

Demelza raises her eyebrows. She knows he wants her to be glad for them both, but she withholds her approval.

ROSS *(cont'd)* You'd surely not wish to be back there again?

DEMELZA Would I not, Ross?

It's said without malice or resentment. The simple, painful truth. She walks out again. Ross is left clinking coins.

CUT TO:

10: INT. SAWLE KIDDLEY – DAY 44

Dwight is tending a cut on Paul's head while two other wounded miners (Jory and Dan) wait for treatment – and Jud, Zacky and other disgruntled villagers look on.

DWIGHT You're sure it was on Warleggan orders?

PAUL Looka Jory – looka Dan. Do 'ee not recognize th' handi-work?

DWIGHT *(to Jory and Dan)* You were at Wheal Agnes?

The two men nod miserably.

JUD I tell 'ee, Warleggan d' think he can do as 'ee please.

PAUL He needs reinin' in.

ZACKY Who's to do it? The man owns half the county!

JUD Them Frenchies 'ave the right idea! Eh, Dr Enys?

DWIGHT I used to think so. But what began as a just cause has since become a bloodbath.

JUD 'Twill 'appen 'ere soon enough! *(brandishing his drink)* To liberty! – 'quality! – an' fraternizication – or some such!

Everyone laughs. Except Dwight. Who knows enough of war and bloodletting to know it's no joke.

CUT TO:

11: INT. DWIGHT'S COTTAGE – DAY 44

Dwight comes in, weary from treating his patients. As he puts down his bags, he sees a letter which has been left on his tray. He opens it, reads it, explodes with anger and disbelief, screws up the letter and throws it on the floor. He walks off. The letter remains on the floor. Presently a hand (Dwight's) retrieves it.

CUT TO:

12: INT. KILLEWARREN, PARLOUR – DAY 44

Dwight is peering into the open mouth of Ray Penvenen, who is wrapped in a blanket, looking grey-faced and gaunt.

DWIGHT Drink?

RAY PENVENEN Regularly.

DWIGHT Wine?

RAY PENVENEN Canary.

DWIGHT Appetite?

RAY PENVENEN Voracious.

DWIGHT Urine?

RAY PENVENEN Unusually sweet – so Dr Choake informs me.

DWIGHT And his diagnosis?

RAY PENVENEN A fever. Then gout. Then a wasting condition. Then a tuberculous infection. Have you anything to add?

DWIGHT Only that I believe him to be utterly mistaken. *(beat)* It is the sugar sickness. The symptoms are unmistakable.

RAY PENVENEN What must I do?

DWIGHT Give up most of the things you eat and drink. Wine especially.

RAY PENVENEN And that will cure me?

DWIGHT No. But it may prolong your life.

RAY PENVENEN But will my life be worth living? It hardly sounds like it!

Dwight begins to pack up his things.

RAY PENVENEN *(cont'd)* You and I did not part as friends, so I'm all the more obliged to you for coming.

Dwight nods stiffly but doesn't reply.

RAY PENVENEN *(cont'd)* I hope you understand that I would have been failing in my duty had I not prevented the attachment between you and my niece. It was no reflection on your personal capabilities.

DWIGHT Only my lack of fortune.

Ray has the goodness to look embarrassed. Now he knows he must break some difficult news.

RAY PENVENEN I feel it only fair to tell you that Caroline will shortly be engaged to Lord Coniston, eldest son of Earl Windermere.

Though he feels as if he has been punched in the gut, Dwight's voice remains even.

DWIGHT I congratulate Miss Penvenen.

He continues to pack away his things.

RAY PENVENEN I hope the information will not now distress you.

DWIGHT Not in the least, sir. I bid you good day.

*He walks out, determined now to take crucial – and irrevocable –
action.*

CUT TO:

13: INT. NAVY OFFICES – DAY 44

*Dwight sits in front of a panel of three senior navy officers as one of
them asks: 'You are quite clear, Dr Enys, what you are signing up for?'*

DWIGHT The duration of the war? Which you assure me will
be long, desperate and bloody. I may not return to these
shores for years. Or indeed at all. *(then)* Where do I sign?

*The officers glance at each other. Clearly Dwight is determined. The
senior navy officer pushes a document towards Dwight. He takes a
pen and signs without hesitation.*

CUT TO:

14: EXT. TRENWITH HOUSE, GROUNDS – DAY 45

*A fence post is hammered into the ground. Tom Harry supervises as
the fence is erected.*

CUT TO:

15: INT. TRENWITH HOUSE, LIBRARY – DAY 45

*George is poring eagerly over a document, watched by Tankard who
seems increasingly uneasy.*

TANKARD I wonder – is it wise to seek *more* confrontation?

GEORGE Is there, or is there not, some doubt over the legal-
ity of this arrangement?

Elizabeth comes in.

GEORGE *(cont'd)* Ah my dear, the sale of Geoffrey Charles's shares in Wheal Grace. We fear it may have been fraudulent. D'you recall Ross mentioning any new shareholders?

ELIZABETH You must know I've had no dealings with Ross since before our marriage.

George eyes Elizabeth keenly. He can see that the mention of Ross has disturbed her (though he does not guess at the real reasons for this).

GEORGE Of course, my dear. Do not distress yourself. Leave me to deal with the matter.

CUT TO:

16: INT. TRENWITH HOUSE, LIBRARY – DAY 45

George is dictating a letter to Tankard.

GEORGE 'Dear Poldark, as you are a trustee of Francis's estate perhaps you can shed light on certain recent transactions which appear troubling . . .'

CUT TO:

17: INT. NAMPARA HOUSE, PARLOUR – DAY 45

George's letter is open on the table. Ross is composing a letter in return.

ROSS *(VO)* 'Dear Warleggan, as you are *not* a trustee of Francis's estate, I do not consider the business in any way concerns you . . .'

CUT TO:

18: INT. TRENWITH HOUSE, LIBRARY – DAY 45

George struts up and down, irritated, dictating a letter to Tankard.

GEORGE 'Dear Poldark, it may have escaped your notice that Elizabeth and I are now married. In attending to Francis's estate I am merely trying to take the burden off her. She has been unwell and would prefer to meet you at Trenwith – if you could trouble yourself to attend.'

CUT TO:

19: EXT. TRENWITH HOUSE – DAY 45

Ross hammers irritably on the door of Trenwith.

CUT TO:

20: INT. TRENWITH HOUSE, TURRET ROOM – DAY 45

Elizabeth hears the sound of the door below. She is tense and tight-lipped.

CUT TO:

21: INT. TRENWITH HOUSE, GREAT HALL – DAY 45

Ross is shown into the hall. Aunt Agatha is on her way out. Both are unaware that Elizabeth is watching from the gallery above.

AUNT AGATHA These are pleasant times, nephew! No mine or peasant safe from assault? Or is that just in our house?

ROSS You need not remain here, Aunt. Come and live at Nampara.

AUNT AGATHA And let that upstart win?

She walks out, crossing with George who arrives with Tankard. (Elizabeth immediately pulls back out of sight.) Immediate friction. George and Ross contemplate each other with hostility.

GEORGE We need not take much of your time – provided you can supply sufficient explanation.

ROSS Where is Elizabeth?

GEORGE Resting. We can complete the business without her.

ROSS I think not. She is co-trustee in Francis's estate. I shall do nothing without her presence.

GEORGE *(smiling)* She has signed a power of attorney so that I may act on her behalf.

He shows Ross a document. Ross glances at the power-of-attorney document, as if suspecting a forgery.

GEORGE *(cont'd)* At her request – since she wants nothing more to do with you.

ROSS Shall we get on?

George, stifling a smirk, leads the way towards the library.

Up on the gallery Elizabeth leans forward to listen.

CUT TO:

22: INT. TRENWITH HOUSE, LIBRARY – DAY 45

Ross declines George's offer of a seat. George signals to Tankard to open proceedings.

TANKARD The half-share in Wheal Grace, held on behalf of Mrs Warleggan's son Geoffrey Charles, disposed of at the beginning of the year—

ROSS What of it?

GEORGE We are not satisfied that the transaction was legal.

ROSS It was legal.

A look between George and Tankard. Clearly Ross is going to be diffi-cult.

ROSS *(cont'd)* Mrs Poldark – Mrs *Warleggan* – received six hundred pounds on behalf of her son for a half-share in a worthless mine.

GEORGE Who was so foolish as to pay her that sum?

ROSS I was.

CUT TO:

23: INT. TRENWITH HOUSE, CORRIDOR – DAY 45

Elizabeth is listening, just outside the entrance to the library. She is shocked by this news.

CUT TO:

24: INT. TRENWITH HOUSE, LIBRARY – DAY 45

A look between George and Tankard. Ross knows immediately what they're thinking. He endeavours to remain calm.

ROSS In January Elizabeth was in dire straits. Having per-suaded Francis to sink his last six hundred pounds into the mine, I felt duty bound to give Elizabeth the money back. Knowing she would not accept it as a gift, I devised a strategy to do so without her knowing. Now if you'll excuse me—

GEORGE One moment—

Ross halts.

GEORGE *(cont'd)* You claim you acted with good intent. But circumstances have since changed. What you took from Elizabeth and her son—

ROSS *Purchased*—

GEORGE Is now worth more than what you gave for it. Should you now not return the half-share of this *successful* mine into the custody of the child's trustees?

ROSS In other words, you.

GEORGE As his adoptive father, naturally I would manage his affairs—

ROSS Last January, had the Wheal Grace stock come onto the market, it would not have fetched *ten pounds*! The mine was finished. We kept her going through the winter. With our bare hands we reopened her after a catastrophic rockfall. We risked all we had – and against all odds, we struck tin. So now I deem the profit *mine*. Not Elizabeth's, not Geoffrey Charles's and most especially not yours. So unless you have anything to add—

GEORGE Only that you may wish to consider how poorly this reflects on you. A man who cheats his young ward?

Ross contemplates George with amused contempt.

ROSS Up to now I've offered no violence. But if you persist—

GEORGE You would not dare lay a finger on me—

ROSS Because your army of servants will protect you?

GEORGE Go back to your scullery maid!

Ross's face hardens.

CUT TO:

25: INT. TRENWITH HOUSE, CORRIDOR – DAY 45

Elizabeth is transfixed in horror. Knowing Ross as she does, she knows there can only be one response to George's jibe.
CUT TO:

26: INT. TRENWITH HOUSE, LIBRARY – DAY 45

For a moment Ross grapples silently to contain his rage. Then suddenly it overcomes him and with a terrifying release of pent-up fury, he launches himself at George.
CUT TO:

27: INT. TRENWITH HOUSE, CORRIDOR – DAY 45

Elizabeth runs off, horrified.
CUT TO:

28: INT. TRENWITH HOUSE, LIBRARY – DAY 45

Ross lands a punch but George gives back as good as he gets. Now the two of them are slugging it out, each inflicting damage on the other. Tankard is dithering in the corner, not daring to intervene. The battle continues. Initially they are well matched, but gradually Ross begins to get the upper hand, due mainly to the blind rage which makes him more dangerous and out of control than we've ever seen him before. Sensing this, Tankard runs out.

TANKARD Kemp! Harry! Triggs! In here!

As Ross continues to attack George, Tom Harry and two footmen burst in. Two go to attack Ross while the other comes to help George. George is furious at his own humiliation.

GEORGE Get this man out of my house!

ROSS Your house, George? I think you'll find it's Geoffrey Charles's.

Tom Harry and Triggs bundle Ross out of the room.

CUT TO:

29: INT. TRENWITH HOUSE, GREAT HALL – DAY 45

Ross is bundled through the hall towards the front door. Elizabeth – now on the gallery above – watches as the battered and bleeding Ross is ejected from the house.

CUT TO:

30: INT. NAMPARA HOUSE, PARLOUR – DAY 45

Demelza is holding Jeremy for Dwight to examine.

DWIGHT A mild colic. I'll mix him a sedative.

DEMELZA You'll stay till Ross returns?

DWIGHT Of course. I've some news.

Something in the tone of his voice alarms Demelza.

DWIGHT *(cont'd)* I've applied for a post as surgeon in the navy. I expect to leave any day.

DEMELZA Oh, but Dwight—

DWIGHT I must gain more experience – and the war will surely supply that. And besides – I've had news of Caroline.

DEMELZA *(guessing)* She's to be married.

DWIGHT To a Lord Coniston.

DEMELZA I'm that sorry.

DWIGHT I am not. It was the spur I needed to put her behind me.

DEMELZA But you did love her—

DWIGHT We would never have been happy. We're too dissimilar.

DEMELZA Ross and I are not alike.

DWIGHT And are you always content? Is there never a moment's discord or doubt?

Demelza hesitates. She's about to open up, to share some of her woes. And Dwight senses it. But as she's about to speak, the door opens and Ross comes in. He's in an appalling state. His coat is badly torn, his shirt is shredded, he is bleeding badly from a wound above his eye and his face is bruised. Demelza screams in alarm.

DEMELZA Judas! What happened?

CUT TO:

31: INT. TRENWITH HOUSE, LIBRARY – NIGHT 45

George is dabbing at his cut face, watched by Elizabeth. He winces as he touches one of the cuts. Elizabeth moves to help but he waves her away.

GEORGE It's a scratch. *(unable to resist the lie)* And nothing compared to what I gave Ross!

ELIZABETH I hope he will have learned his lesson.

GEORGE It's high time he learned to pick his battles.

He returns to dabbing at his face. Elizabeth takes the cloth and this time he allows her to minister to his wounds.

CUT TO:

32: INT. NAMPARA HOUSE, ROSS & DEMELZA'S BEDROOM – NIGHT 45

Demelza is getting ready for bed. As she turns she is aware of Ross – his cuts and bruises now cleaned up – standing in the doorway. He hesitates to come further into the room.

ROSS Are you angry?

DEMELZA Little boys fighting?

ROSS He was offensive— *(beat)* About someone other than myself.

She realizes from his tone that he means her. She feels slightly mollified. Then:

DEMELZA I can scarce believe we're losing Dwight.

ROSS Nor I. Indeed, it makes me wonder – if *I* should go?

DEMELZA What? Because your dearest friend is running away, so must you?

ROSS Because I'm a soldier – and if my regiment requires me— *(then)* Obviously the thought of leaving you and Jeremy—

DEMELZA It wouldn't be the first time you'd considered such a thing!

There. She's alluded to it. Ross and Elizabeth.

DEMELZA *(cont'd)* And how *was* Elizabeth?

ROSS She avoided me.

DEMELZA As you've avoided her.

ROSS What would you have me do?

DEMELZA I would have you be honest, Ross! To her. To me. To yourself!

ROSS Am I not honest? Where am I not honest now?

DEMELZA Go to war, Ross. Play at soldiers. Or stay home and save all Cornwall! What it is to be married to such a great man!

Ross opens his mouth to speak. He wants to argue with her. But he knows he hasn't a leg to stand on. Resigned, he goes out.

CUT TO:

33: INT. NAMPARA HOUSE, LIBRARY – NIGHT 45

Ross prepares for bed. He sits on his camp bed and looks thoughtful. Then he gets up and goes to one of the oak chests. He opens it. Inside is his army captain's uniform. He takes it out and considers it thoughtfully.

CUT TO:

34: EXT. NAMPARA HOUSE – DAY 46

Early morning. Ross gallops away from Nampara.

CUT TO:

35: INT. NAMPARA HOUSE, ROSS & DEMELZA'S BEDROOM – DAY 46

Demelza is having breakfast in bed with Jeremy when Prudie comes in.

PRUDIE Letter come. *(She hands it over.)* An' Mister Ross d' go to Truro.

Demelza nods, apparently disinterested. Then she opens her letter. And smiles.

VERITY *(VO)* 'My dear Demelza, as my time draws near, I'm both excited and afeared in equal measure—'

CUT TO:

36: INT. VERITY & ANDREW'S COTTAGE – DAY 46

A heavily pregnant Verity is writing to Demelza.

VERITY *(VO)* '– and with Andrew away at sea, I begin to miss my Nampara cousins most dreadfully. How I wish I had your strength to see me through. How fortunate are you to have Ross always at your side—'

CUT TO:

37: INT. NAMPARA HOUSE – DAY 46

Demelza smiles wryly as she reads Verity's letter.

DEMELZA *(to herself)* Yes, how fortunate!

CUT TO:

38: EXT. TRURO STREET – DAY 46

Ross walks towards Pascoe's office. He passes two soldiers – and brushes shoulders with them. As they walk on, he glances back at them.

CUT TO:

39: INT. PASCOE'S OFFICE – DAY 46

Pascoe shows Ross into his office.

PASCOE Re-join your regiment? Just as your mine begins to prosper and your family's secure?

ROSS It's *because* we're secure that I'd consider going. But obviously I'd need to put my affairs in order first. Beginning with George. He's contesting the sale of my nephew's shares in Wheal Grace.

PASCOE The deal was entirely legal. But that may not deter him. He has the funds to finance a lawsuit – and to drag it out for years—

ROSS *(laughter)* All the more reason to escape! I've had my fill of court!

PASCOE Though what could be his purpose—

ROSS To get his hands on Grace the way he did Leisure? Especially now she prospers. Which reminds me: my mystery benefactor—

PASCOE Yes—

ROSS I wish to repay him. *(beat)* So tell me his name.

PASCOE You recall that the loan was given in confidence—

ROSS Come, Harris, I cannot go away to war without thanking him in person. Who is he?

PASCOE Well – as to that – I don't recall ever mentioning a 'he' at all—

CUT TO:

40: INT. NAMPARA HOUSE, PARLOUR – NIGHT 46

Ross, having returned from Truro, has just told Demelza the news.

DEMELZA Caroline Penvenen?

ROSS Our mystery benefactor! Dwight must have told her of our difficulties. But is it not astonishing?

Demelza, who is mending a dress, merely shrugs.

DEMELZA *(pleasantly)* I dare say she's taken a fancy to you.

ROSS I'm a married man.

DEMELZA An' that would make *all* the difference?

She goes on with her mending. Ross decides to bite the bullet.

ROSS Demelza – it was one *night*. A single encounter. How long will it take you to forgive me?

DEMELZA I don't know, Ross. How long would it take you to forgive *me*?

ROSS That's hardly the same. You would never do a thing which *required* my forgiveness.

DEMELZA *(amused at his arrogance)* Are you sure?

She eyeballs him defiantly. Suddenly he hesitates – returns her stare – doubts begin to creep in. Demelza continues to smile defiantly. And then the penny drops.

ROSS When?

DEMELZA Werry House? After the ball? *(beat)* Captain McNeil came to my room.

ROSS How could he *dare*?

DEMELZA Because I invited him.

Ross is speechless. Demelza's almost enjoying herself.

DEMELZA *(cont'd)* After your antics with Elizabeth, I thought I deserved a turn myself—

ROSS A turn? How far did—?

DEMELZA Kisses – caresses – then I sent him away—

ROSS *(exploding)* Good God, Demelza – was that not enough? I tell you, I don't admire you for this. It does you no credit. Nor me neither!

DEMELZA And what 'credit' did your night with Elizabeth do *me*?

ROSS That's entirely different!

DEMELZA How is it different?

ROSS I take no pride in my visit to her – but it was the out-come of a devotion which on my side had lasted ten years! Not some tawdry little passion worked up over a glass of port with an opportunist soldier who took what was on offer—

DEMELZA That was precisely what was not on offer! I did not permit him—

ROSS How am I to know *what* you permitted him?

DEMELZA You're right, Ross! How *are* you to know? If you trust me not – and I trust you not – what is the point of our marriage at all?

ROSS I entirely agree. What *is* the point?

A moment's stand-off between them, then Ross walks out. Furious. Determined. His mind is made up.

CUT TO:

41: EXT. NAMPARA HOUSE – NIGHT 46

Establisher.

CUT TO:

42: INT. NAMPARA HOUSE, LIBRARY (MONTAGE) – NIGHT 46

Ross takes a cloth to clean the brass buttons of his army uniform; Ross lays out his sash; Ross lays out his epaulettes; Ross cleans his sword. Presently he hears the front door slam. He pauses. Oh well, if that's Demelza gone he's not surprised. He resumes cleaning his sword.

CUT TO:

43: EXT. NAMPARA FIELDS – DAWN 47

Dawn establisher. Sunrise. Mist across the fields.

CUT TO:

44: INT. NAMPARA HOUSE, KITCHEN/PARLOUR – DAWN 47

Prudie is bringing food to the table. She's in a bad mood, muttering to herself.

PRUDIE . . . bangin' an' clatterin' all hours o' the night – an' a person d' need 'er beauty sleep if she's t' rise 'fore dawn an' cook vittles fer . . .

She's come into the empty parlour.

PRUDIE *(cont'd)* Mistress?

CUT TO:

45: INT. VERITY & ANDREW'S COTTAGE – DAY 47

Esther Blamey opens the door to Demelza and Jeremy, and Jud (who has escorted them, with the luggage).

ESTHER Welcome, ma'am. My father's at sea, so has asked me to be here in his stead.

Demelza is astonished at the change in Esther. Not that her reserve has entirely disappeared but her sullenness has.

ESTHER *(cont'd)* We expect the confinement any day.

Now Verity, heavily pregnant, comes to welcome Demelza with open arms.

DEMELZA Oh, Verity!

Verity and Demelza embrace. Verity is glowing with happiness.

DEMELZA *(cont'd) (low)* This is a turn-about!

VERITY Andrew insisted I was not left unattended. But that *she* should be the one to come?

Demelza is astonished. But gratified. Such a contrast to her own household.

CUT TO:

46: INT. NAMPARA HOUSE, LIBRARY – DAY 47

Dwight comes through into the library.

DWIGHT Ross, I came to tell you that—

He walks into the room and to his astonishment is met by the sight of Ross in his army uniform.

DWIGHT *(cont'd)* Ross? You surely don't intend—

ROSS Am I not a soldier?

DWIGHT With a family, a prosperous mine, a settled life – *(then, laughing)* but perhaps that's the problem. You're so blest you have nothing to fight for! *(then)* What does Demelza say? *(then)* Does she even know?

ROSS She will soon enough.

Dwight considers the implications of this. He decides it would be unwise to challenge Ross at this point.

ROSS *(cont'd)* Dwight – I must tell you – my mysterious bene-factor – is Caroline.

DWIGHT *(incredulous)* But – how—? Why would she—? *(then)*

Her heart is so generous – it's not unlike her to do such a— *(then)* How could she know? Who told her? *(then, realizing)* I can only apologize if I spoke too freely of your business affairs.

ROSS I can only express my gratitude that you did! *(then)* I owe you both more than I can say. Together you've saved me! And in return—

DWIGHT I assure you, I've no regrets. And nor, it appears, has Caroline. *(then)* And now we may be brothers-in-arms! *(beat)* My posting is through. *HMS Travail.* I leave for Plymouth tomorrow.

A big moment between them. They shake hands.

ROSS God speed!

DWIGHT And good luck!

CUT TO:

47: INT. NAMPARA HOUSE, LIBRARY – DAY 47

Items – including the uniform – are thrown into a travelling bag. Ross is packing to leave. Presently he becomes aware of Prudie scowling in the doorway.

PRUDIE Why would 'ee go?

ROSS Because – though my own household is clearly in disarray! – there is something I can mend.

PRUDIE Without tellin' mistress?

ROSS Demelza has chosen to be elsewhere. She can hardly complain if I do the same.

CUT TO:

48: INT. VERITY & ANDREW'S COTTAGE – DAY 47

Demelza sits with Verity, who looks increasingly uncomfortable as the birth approaches! Esther entertains Jeremy.

VERITY *(low)* She's growing used to me. *(then)* Am I not the luckiest of women?

DEMELZA The most deserving!

VERITY And you?

DEMELZA *(laughs)* Lord knows what I deserve!

Verity looks at her closely.

VERITY How is Ross?

DEMELZA *(hesitates, then)* At war with himself – and the idea of George – at Trenwith—

Verity nods. She knows Demelza also means Elizabeth.

VERITY I too struggle with the idea of my family home in the hands of a Warleggan. But Elizabeth has made her choice and—

Suddenly she gives a little intake of breath. Demelza looks at her keenly. Verity forces a smile.

VERITY *(cont'd)* It's nothing. A slight cramp. It's been happening since last night.

DEMELZA *(with a smile)* Then it may not be 'nothing'!

CUT TO:

49: EXT. OPEN COUNTRYSIDE – DAY 47

A coach rattles across open countryside.
CUT TO:

50: INT. COACH – DAY 47

CU: Ross, travelling. Determined. On a mission.

CUT TO:

51: EXT. TRENWITH LAND – DUSK 47

Prudie is hurrying home with a basket of provisions. It's getting dark. To convince herself she's not nervous, she's singing to herself under her breath.

PRUDIE *(sings under her breath)*

Some say the devil's dead . . .
an' buried in Fowey harbour
Some say he'm alive agin
an' wedded to a barber . . .

She comes round a corner to find herself face to face with Tom Harry, pointing his gun at her.

TOM HARRY Stand and deliver!

Prudie screams, drops her basket and runs off, screeching. Tom Harry roars with laughter. He picks up an apple which has rolled away out of the basket, takes a bite, swaggers off, confidence growing, beginning to think himself invincible.

CUT TO:

52: EXT. LONDON STREET – DAY 48

Boots (belonging to a figure as yet unidentified) step down from a carriage. We follow them as they walk through puddles, through mud, grime and dollops of manure on a London street. Past passing carts and feet. They go up to a front door. A footman standing outside opens the door. The feet – now muddy – pass inside . . .

CUT TO:

53: INT. PENVENEN HOUSE, LONDON – DAY 48

. . . and into an impressive hallway. The footman closes the door behind him. Ross is revealed. He glances down at his boots. Muddy on the marble floor. The footman now beckons him: 'This way, sir.' Ross follows.

CUT TO:

54: INT. PENVENEN HOUSE, LONDON – DAY 48

Ross is shown into a room where Caroline greets him.

CAROLINE Captain Poldark, what a treat! Yet I've seen no flags out for your visit!

ROSS They put the flags out when I *leave!*

She offers her hand. He kisses it. Caroline is wearing the latest high-waisted London fashion. She motions him to sit.

CAROLINE Tell me all the news of Cornwall.

SOUND OVER: *The cry of a baby.*

CUT TO:

55: INT. VERITY & ANDREW'S COTTAGE – DAY 48

A swaddled baby boy – ANDREW BLAMEY II, who is now a few

hours old – is handed back to his adoring mother Verity. Demelza and Esther crowd round to admire the new arrival.

CUT TO:

56: INT. PENVENEN HOUSE, LONDON – DAY 48

CAROLINE So what brings you to London?

ROSS A need to see justice done. *(beat)* My mine has begun to prosper. It was your loan which enabled me to keep it open till we struck tin.

CAROLINE *(amused)* My loan—?

ROSS Oh, there's no point denying it. So now you stand accused of wilfully saving three people from the worst disaster bankruptcy can bring.

CAROLINE And what is my sentence?

ROSS To bear the brunt of my eternal gratitude. And to shortly take receipt of repayment – in full.

CAROLINE So instead of thanking me you should be congratulating me on my shrewd business sense!

ROSS I believe congratulations of another sort are due. Your engagement to Lord Coniston?

CAROLINE *(laughing)* Arthur has made me several offers of marriage. Which I've so far declined.

ROSS May I ask why?

CAROLINE Oh, the usual capriciousness of my sex!

ROSS And presumably you do not love him.

CAROLINE As you say, I do not love him.

ROSS In fact, it's probable you still love Dwight Enys.

Caroline helps herself to biscuits and sherry, so as to avoid having to answer.

ROSS *(cont'd)* Since you left he's been unable to settle. Oh, he's no idea I'm here and would certainly have forbidden me had he known. But I thought you should know that he's joined the navy.

Caroline's mask slips. She's aghast at this news.

CUT TO:

57: INT. VERITY & ANDREW'S COTTAGE – DAY 48

Verity cradles her sleeping baby. She observes Demelza who is lost in thought. Verity watches her a while until Demelza, suddenly aware that she's being watched, makes an effort to appear cheerful.

VERITY What has he done? *(beat)* Or not done?

Demelza doesn't reply – and Verity can see she's hit the nail on the head. She hesitates to intervene. But eventually she knows she must.

VERITY *(cont'd)* Perhaps you think it's unforgiveable. Perhaps it is. *(no reply)* Andrew killed his wife. There was no intent to harm – but harm was most grievously done. Andrew served his sentence – yet many felt he should never be forgiven. For many years he believed it himself.

DEMELZA Then he met you.

VERITY Perhaps I was foolish – desperate – but I wanted to believe he had learned his lesson. I granted him a second chance. *(beat)* I've never for one moment regretted it. And least of all today. *(looking at her baby)*

DEMELZA Andrew regretted what he did. I'm not sure Ross does. *(then)* You will not ask me what he did.

VERITY You would not tell me – for fear I should think badly of him.

Demelza realizes, to her surprise, that Verity is right.

VERITY *(cont'd)* Nothing is beyond repair – if you have the will to mend it.

DEMELZA But why should *I* be the one to mend it?

CUT TO:

58: EXT. TRENWITH HOUSE, GROUNDS – DAY 48

Tom Harry is patrolling the finished fence with his gun.
CUT TO:

59: INT. PENVENEN HOUSE, LONDON – DAY 48

Ross and Caroline continue their discussion. Caroline begins to sense that Ross has a hidden agenda.

CAROLINE Why have you come here?

ROSS To ask why you left Cornwall? Why you refused Dwight a second chance – after he'd explained what happened on the night of the ambush?

CAROLINE Did you not see him? – in the weeks before we were due to elope? He behaved as if he were contemplating something shameful. Deserting his beloved patients – in the middle of the night? – for the fleshpots of Bath! You may think me a shallow creature, but in truth I could see what a miserable life we'd have if he spent his days regretting all he'd left behind.

ROSS But could you not have returned to Cornwall? Defied your uncle?

CAROLINE Lived in a cottage and dined off sprats? Can you picture it? Nor could I. In asking Dwight to leave Cornwall, I was expecting too much of him. Since I left Cornwall, I've realized I was asking too much of myself.

ROSS So in effect, your love could not surmount the obstacles.

CAROLINE In effect, it could not.

ROSS *(a pause, then)* Why do I not believe you?

CUT TO:

60: INT. VERITY & ANDREW'S COTTAGE – DAY 49

Verity holds her baby as Demelza prepares to leave. She's summoning up her courage to speak to Demelza. Finally:

VERITY What is it that most troubles you? The thing itself? Or something more?

DEMELZA The thing itself! *(then)* No, 'tis more. 'Tis the running away! The hiding from what has passed! The refusal to look it in the face and stand the consequence.

VERITY But – isn't that what you are doing? Even now?

DEMELZA What would you have me do?

VERITY Oh, Demelza, I cannot instruct you. I do not even know the deed. But reason cannot guide you. Only the heart. And sometimes what the heart dictates makes no sense at all. Yet it must be followed.

A huge moment between them. Demelza silently acknowledges the truth of what Verity's saying. She now knows what she must do. She and Verity embrace. Then Esther brings Jeremy and Demelza leaves, accompanied by Jeremy and Jud. Verity remains, holding baby Andrew, Esther beside her.

CUT TO:

61: EXT. HEADLAND OUTSIDE PLYMOUTH – DAY 49

Dwight, now in naval uniform, stands beside a milestone which points to Plymouth. Looking out across the bay he sees a distant fleet of ships, ready to depart for war.

CUT TO:

62: INT. RISING SUN INN, PLYMOUTH – DAY 49

The inn is full of military and navy types, soldiers and sailors. In a corner, men are queuing up to enlist with a recruiting officer. Dwight comes into the inn. He looks an impressive figure – and seems to have a new lease of life now that his decision is made. He is greeted by some other navy officers who shake his hand and make further introductions.

CUT TO:

63: EXT. NAMPARA HOUSE – DAY 49

Establisher.

CUT TO:

64: INT. NAMPARA HOUSE, HALLWAY – DAY 49

Jud opens the front door and struggles in with Jeremy and the luggage. Prudie comes running out of the kitchen but stops short at the sight of Jud. He purses his lips, expecting a kiss.

JUD Did 'ee miss I?

PRUDIE Miss 'ee? Aye, y' black worm! Leavin' I alone t' fend off villains an' footpads! Fat lot o' use 'ee be! Lizzardy louse! *(then)* Where's the maid?

JUD Left us at Bargus Crossroads.

PRUDIE Bound for where?

JUD Nowhere that'll do 'er any good.

CUT TO:

65: EXT. HEADLAND – DAY 49

Demelza walks briskly along the headland. Her expression is determined and her walk is purposeful. She is heading for Trenwith. One way or another, she's determined to seize back control of her life.

CUT TO:

66: INT. RISING SUN INN, PLYMOUTH – DAY 49

Dwight is conversing with some of his fellow-officers when the door opens and Ross, in travelling clothes, comes in. Dwight can hardly believe his eyes.

DWIGHT Ross? Are you a figment of my imagination?

ROSS *(laughing)* I hope not! I'm in Plymouth to see my colonel and thought I would look you up.

DWIGHT How did you find me?

ROSS I went to your ship, enquired of the crew and they told me you were staying here till your quarters are ready.

DWIGHT I'm astonished!

ROSS I'm ravenous! When do we dine?

CUT TO:

67: EXT. TRENWITH LAND – DAY 49

Demelza is approaching the enclosed Trenwith land. She stops, surprised at the new fence, then thinking nothing of it, clambers over it and continues on her way.

CUT TO:

68: INT. RISING SUN INN, PLYMOUTH – DAY 49

Food is placed on the table and Ross and Dwight tuck in.

DWIGHT Is Demelza well?

ROSS I couldn't say. I've been in London.

DWIGHT What on earth took you there?

ROSS Caroline?

For a moment Dwight is speechless.

ROSS *(cont'd)* I went to thank her for the loan. And to congratulate her on her engagement. Which I was unable to do. Since it turns out there's no such event.

DWIGHT I – don't understand—

ROSS I also made mention of her uncle's ill health. Which may account for her decision to visit him. Whether she has another purpose—

DWIGHT What? – So Caroline is—? *Where* is she?

ROSS Standing just behind you.

Dwight wheels round and sees Caroline standing there. He leaps to his feet. Caroline looks tense and uncomfortable. Neither knows what to say.

CUT TO:

69: EXT. TRENWITH LAND – DAY 49

Demelza stands looking at the distant Trenwith House. She knows what she wants to do, but now she's here her courage fails her. She turns to walk away. And then she sees Elizabeth come out of the house, walking towards the woods. Demelza begins to walk back towards Trenwith.

CUT TO:

70: INT. RISING SUN INN, PLYMOUTH – DAY 49

Ross, Dwight and Caroline are now sitting in a quiet booth. Dwight and Caroline continue to look tense and uncomfortable. Ross realizes he will have to take charge.

ROSS Believe me, I do not lightly meddle in other people's affairs. That's been Demelza's way and I've often chided her for it. But lately I've been coming round to her way of thinking.

Dwight and Caroline glance up at Ross, then at each other. Encouraged, Ross continues.

ROSS *(cont'd)* Demelza would say that if two people love each other – then the obstacles which keep them apart *must* be substantial, else they lack the courage of their convictions.

Dwight and Caroline continue to look at each other. In each other's presence, all their resistance is melting away. But something is happening for Ross too. It's as if by repeating Demelza's words, he's reminding himself of how precious she is to him, how much he loves her, what a mistake he could be on the verge of making.

ROSS *(cont'd)* I think she would also say that life holds very few things that are genuinely worth having. And if you possess them, then nothing else matters. And if you don't possess them, then everything else is worthless.

CAROLINE And yet – to gamble on the unknown?

DWIGHT Is not all life a gamble? And does the gambler always come off worst? *(then, to Ross)* I suspect that those who suffer most are the ones who ignore their heart's desire – and spend the rest of their lives regretting it.

The effect on Ross is profound. Very calmly he gathers his things and goes out. Dwight and Caroline barely register his departure. A long moment between them. Then:

CAROLINE And now no doubt you hate me.

DWIGHT And now no doubt I hate you.

Suddenly Dwight takes Caroline's face in his hands and kisses her passionately.

CUT TO:

71: EXT. TRENWITH HOUSE, FOLLY – DAY 49

Elizabeth is walking in the woods by the folly when she hears a noise behind her. She turns – and sees Demelza. For a moment Elizabeth is too stunned to speak. Demelza, too, is silent. So many things that could be said. So many things flashing through Elizabeth's mind. Anger. Shock. Fear. Eventually:

ELIZABETH Does Ross know you're here?

DEMELZA Is Ross my keeper?

ELIZABETH Why have you come?

DEMELZA I thought 'twas to tell you that I hate you. That you've marred my faith and broke my marriage. That I envy you. For the passion you roused which Ross could not withstand. That I pity you. Because you could never make up your mind. But now I wonder, what do any of it matter? What you did – what Ross did – cannot be undone. And you both must live with that. But I need not.

ELIZABETH What will you do?

DEMELZA Take my child and go back to my father's house.

ELIZABETH You would leave Ross?

DEMELZA I will no longer be ruled by what he did. *(beat)* So you're welcome to him.

She walks away. Elizabeth remains. Her expression hardens.

CUT TO:

72: INT. ARMY OFFICES – DAY 49

A panel of three officers is in session. Ross sits, in his uniform, before them.

ROSS Captain Ross Poldark, of His Majesty's Sixty-Second Regiment of Foot.

One of the officers pushes forward a document. Ross takes it, reads it, picks up the pen to sign. And then he pauses.

CUT TO:

73: EXT. TRENWITH LAND – DAY 49

Demelza is clambering over the fence which encloses Trenwith land. As her hand grabs the fence, a gunshot whistles through the air and shatters the fence, grazing her wrist as it does so. She screams, falls to the ground. Presently she hears footsteps. She gets to her feet. Tom Harry appears, carrying a gun. Demelza looks at him in astonishment.

DEMELZA Did you fire that gun? *(exploding)* Y' might've *killed* me! What d' y' mean by firing without checkin' there's folk about?

TOM HARRY Orders, Mrs. Shoot all folks a-strayin'—

DEMELZA No one's *strayin'*! I'm Mrs Warleggan's cousin—

TOM HARRY Oh, I've tell of *'ee*, Mrs! Bit of a mixed breed, 'tis said!

Suddenly Demelza becomes aware that her wrist is bleeding.

DEMELZA Now see what 'ee 've done!

TOM HARRY 'Ee won't die of it. Now be off before I fire again!

He points the rifle at her, advances towards her. She backs away, terrified. Suddenly she sees George strolling towards them, a sarcastic smile on his face.

GEORGE Mistress Poldark! Are you lost?

DEMELZA Do I look it?

GEORGE You look as if you might be intending to trespass on private property.

DEMELZA This is open land – an' has been since ever I came here—

GEORGE It is Trenwith land – and incursions from the rabble will not be tolerated.

DEMELZA On pain of death?

She holds up her bleeding arm for him to see.

GEORGE My man is under orders to caution, not maim. I trust you'll recover. It will teach you not to stray in future.

DEMELZA And who'll teach you to be a *gentleman?*

George bristles. This is hitting him where it hurts. A moment's stand-off between them. Then Demelza turns and walks away.

CUT TO:

74: INT. RISING SUN INN, PLYMOUTH – DAY 49

Dwight and Caroline sit in a corner of the inn. All around them are naval officers and soldiers. But they are in a world of their own and are not aware of them. Now Dwight places a makeshift ring – made of twine – on her engagement finger.

CAROLINE Have you really captured me, Dr Enys?

DWIGHT You understand – this changes nothing—

CAROLINE It changes everything!

DWIGHT I've signed away my liberty—

CAROLINE And so shall I!

DWIGHT To the navy. For the duration of the war—

CAROLINE But we can still be married?

DWIGHT On my very first shore leave – whenever that may be—

CAROLINE I will go home to my uncle. I will nurse him – and wait there till you return—

DWIGHT And I will write to Ross and Demelza – asking them to take care of you—

CAROLINE I need no taking care of!

DWIGHT Caroline, I'm going to war. It would be foolish to pretend there's no risk. If the worst should happen – if I should not return—

CAROLINE Why would you speak of such things?

DWIGHT Because I must. Because you are enlisting in a venture every bit as fraught as my own. And you must know what you are putting your name to.

CAROLINE I am putting my name *aside* – and taking that of the man I love. *(then)* How long do we have?

DWIGHT I sail on the evening tide.

CAROLINE Then these are our last few hours?

DWIGHT They are.

She looks him long and hard in the eyes. Then:

CAROLINE Where is your room?

He hesitates. Does she really mean what he thinks she means? He struggles with his sense of propriety, of honour. And then he sees her beautiful face, beseeching him, offering what days ago was beyond his wildest dreams. He stands up and offers his hand. She takes it.

CUT TO:

75: INT. NAMPARA HOUSE, PARLOUR – DAY 49

Jud and Prudie are having supper. Prudie is giving Jeremy his.

PRUDIE Fences, my ivers! Niver needed 'em in *my* day—

JUD World's gone to pot! 'Tis a cryin' disgrace—

Suddenly Prudie screams. Demelza has just walked in – and her arm is bleeding. Prudie rushes to help her.

PRUDIE What 'appened?

DEMELZA 'Tis a scratch – 'tis all. That luggard Tom Harry—

PRUDIE He niver shot at thee?

DEMELZA On the path by Trenwith—

PRUDIE On Warleggan orders?

JUD I'll give 'im orders!

DEMELZA Nay, Jud, I want no more feudin' between our families. Tell no one of this – least of all Ross.

PRUDIE Let me bind it f'r 'ee, maid.

DEMELZA I can manage. *(to Jud and Prudie, firm)* Say nothin'.

She goes out. Jud and Prudie exchange a glance.

CUT TO:

76: EXT. HEADLAND – DUSK 49

Caroline stands watching as, in the distance, the fleet puts out to sea.

CUT TO:

77: EXT. SHIP DECK (*HMS TRAVAIL*) – DUSK 49

Dwight looks out to sea.

CUT TO:

78: INT. NAMPARA HOUSE, PARLOUR – NIGHT 49

Demelza comes into the parlour, her arm now bandaged. Prudie glances nervously at Demelza. Demelza eyes her suspiciously.

DEMELZA Where's Jud? *(no answer)* Prudie?

PRUDIE Nay, I know not.

But something in her expression makes Demelza suspicious.

DEMELZA Tell me?

PRUDIE He went to the village—

DEMELZA For what? *(no answer)* Prudie? To do what?

CUT TO:

79: INT. SAWLE KIDDLEY – NIGHT 49

Jud is rallying Paul and various other villagers who are roaring their approval and agreement.

JUD He've closed Agnes!—

PAUL Laid off half o' Leisure!—

JUD Give'd thee a twaggin'!—

PAUL *An'* old Prudie!—

JUD Try'd to murder I!—

PAUL 'Ave Cap'n Ross hang!—

JUD An' now he's gone an' shot the mistress!

Roars of horror and disgust.

PAUL She's not dead?

JUD Nay, she's fitty – but *he* won't be when I'm done with him! Who's with me?

Paul and the other villagers jump to their feet, uttering shouts of 'I, I'm with 'ee!', 'Count me in', etc.

JUD *(cont'd)* We'll set a ring round Trenwith – an' burn it t' th' ground!

CUT TO:

80: INT. NAMPARA HOUSE, PARLOUR – NIGHT 49

Demelza is horrified to learn of Jud's mission.

DEMELZA But why didn' 'ee stop him?

PRUDIE *(outraged)* Stop 'im? Why, 'twas I *tell'd* 'im t' go! George Warleggan d' think he can throw's weight around an' tramp common folk b'neath 'is boot. But to fire at *thee*? 'Tis too much!

DEMELZA Oh, Prudie – what've 'ee done?

Demelza rushes out.

CUT TO:

81: EXT. COUNTRYSIDE – NIGHT 49

Villagers are rushing about, grabbing pitchforks, mining pickaxes, burning torches, etc., and running to join Jud and Paul, who are marching in the direction of Trenwith.

CUT TO:

82: INT. TRENWITH HOUSE, GREAT HALL – NIGHT 49

George and Elizabeth are dining alone. George, as ever, is meticulously well mannered and very frugal in his food and wine.

GEORGE I think, in January, we will settle in town. At least until after the event. Trenwith is so out of the way. And I must be on hand to keep an eye on the new building—

ELIZABETH The Warleggan bank?

GEORGE We start demolishing those unsightly hovels next month. Of course my prime concern is for you—

Elizabeth smiles gratefully. Then the door opens and Demelza walks in. George jumps to his feet. Elizabeth's initial shocked expression swiftly turns to one of hostility.

GEORGE *(cont'd)* What d'you want?

DEMELZA To tell you to bar your doors. There's unrest in the village. They may march on Trenwith—

Elizabeth jumps to her feet and looks panic-stricken.

GEORGE You expect me to believe this?

DEMELZA I've no love for you, George – nor you, Elizabeth – but for the sake of Geoffrey Charles and Agatha, I urge you—

GEORGE A mob would be ill-advised to trespass here. They

would be breaking the law and I would see to it that they hang.

DEMELZA If they didn' string you up first!

ELIZABETH Is that a threat?

DEMELZA It's a plea – f'r 'im to come to his senses.

ELIZABETH Ross sent you?

GEORGE How could he? He'll be on his way to France now. *(seeing Demelza's look of surprise)* My informers tell me he's re-joined his regiment. *(seeing Demelza's look of shock)* Oh, surely he hasn't snuck away without telling you? But perhaps, having tasted defeat at home, he's gone to vent his rage on a different enemy.

DEMELZA Defeat?

GEORGE As you see. His foe is in possession of the field. Of his ancestral home. Of the woman he loved. And in March the rout will be complete. When Elizabeth gives birth to a Warleggan heir.

Absolute shock from Demelza.

GEORGE *(cont'd)* I look forward to Ross's congratulations. If he ever returns. For now, let it stick in his craw that the Warleggan line is set to continue – that it will rise and eclipse anything the Poldarks have achieved or ever will achieve.

A huge moment between Demelza and George. George goes and stands behind Elizabeth's chair, takes her hand proprietorially and smiles in triumph. It's a defining moment.

GEORGE *(cont'd)* But don't let me keep you from your scullery.

DEMELZA Perhaps you should barricade yourself in yours.

GEORGE To what purpose?

DEMELZA To save yourself from bein' lynched?

She indicates the window behind George – where blazing torches can be seen in the distance. Elizabeth looks panic-stricken – and George looks horrified. For a moment he seems paralysed with fear. Then:

GEORGE *(shouting out)* Tankard? Harry? Triggs? Kemp?

Demelza walks out as Elizabeth and George run around in panic and Tankard, Tom, Kemp and Triggs come running in.

CUT TO:

83: EXT. TRENWITH HOUSE, DRIVE – NIGHT 49

Angry villagers set fire to the fence, then, carrying burning torches, pitchforks, pickaxes, etc., march towards the gates of Trenwith. Jud and Paul are at the forefront.

CUT TO:

84: INT. TRENWITH HOUSE, TURRET ROOM – NIGHT 49

Elizabeth, clutching Geoffrey Charles, and Aunt Agatha look through the window as the burning torches approach the gates and begin to make their way up the drive. As the mob marches closer, Elizabeth is close to fainting with terror. Suddenly the front door opens and Demelza walks out.

CUT TO:

85: EXT. TRENWITH HOUSE – NIGHT 49

Demelza walks out – to face the angry mob.

DEMELZA Paul – Jud – don't do this! – not for my sake. Lead 'em home, I beg 'ee. There's women and children inside.

PAUL If Warleggan have no care for ours, why should we care f'r 'is?

More shouts of agreement from the mob.

DEMELZA Go home. Save yourselves. They 'ave weapons—

JUD So 'ave we!

PAUL An' 'tis time to see 'im taste 'is own medicine!

Angry shouts of agreement from the other villagers. Now George comes out with Tom, Tankard, Kemp and Triggs. They're all armed.

GEORGE Be advised – we have firearms – and won't hesitate to use them!

JUD Coom on, then – coom on!

GEORGE Don't tempt me, Mr Paynter. I'd dearly love to send you to the devil!

JUD As 'ee tried once before? An' see how well *that* worked!

TOM HARRY There'll be no second coming f'r 'ee this time!

GEORGE Take aim!

Tom Harry and George point their weapons at the mob. Demelza rushes forward and throws herself between them.

DEMELZA These people are your neighbours! Why do you treat them so?

GEORGE They are threatening my family – and must take the consequences.

A shot is fired. Screams. Shouts. A gasp from Demelza. Is she hit? She can find no sign of blood. But the shot didn't come from George or Tom. It came from behind. Now the sound of a horse's hooves approaching. The mob scatters. Ross rides up. He doesn't look at Demelza or any of the mob. Instead he eyeballs George.

ROSS Put up your weapons.

GEORGE You will not command me—

ROSS *Put up your weapons!*

He points his own pistol directly at George. George hesitates, is about to put up his weapon. Then, daring George to do the same, Ross empties his pistol. George does not. Nor do any of the others. And yet we know that it's Ross who's in command, not George.

GEORGE Lost our nerve, have we? Didn't fancy the battle-fields of France?

ROSS My servant informed me of one closer to home.

GEORGE And on which side will you fight, Ross? For the civilized world? Or the revolution?

ROSS On the side which stands for humanity. Which would seem to preclude yours.

GEORGE So what do you intend? To incite a riot? Quite your speciality!

ROSS These people need no inciting. They would happily tear you limb from limb. And with good cause. *(beat)* But they would pay for it.

JUD What do us care?

PAUL 'Twould be worth every penny!

Now Ross turns to the mob.

ROSS I urge you to go home. Do not give this man an excuse to see you hang.

The mob hesitates, shifts uneasily, looks as if they may not heed Ross's words.

ROSS *(cont'd)* You have families, wives, children. Look after them. They're worth ten of this sorry excuse for a man! *(then)* Go home.

Paul and Jud glance at each other. Then they and the rest of the villagers begin to withdraw. George's bravado begins to rise again.

GEORGE Should you not join your comrades? *(i.e. the villagers)*

ROSS Have a care, George. Do you really want to provoke

me? You know I could call them back in an instant. At any time.

GEORGE And this is what you came back for?

ROSS No. I came back for someone I love.

In the Turret Room, Elizabeth gasps with shock.

GEORGE She no longer wants you.

ROSS I realize that. But I'll fight for her nonetheless. If she will give me the chance.

George thinks Ross is speaking of Elizabeth (so does Elizabeth). But instead he holds out his hand to Demelza. A huge moment between them. She hesitates. Then she takes his hand. He pulls her up onto the horse. As they ride away – through the retreating villagers, through the burning torches – Ross turns, looks over his shoulder. He sees Elizabeth, through the open window of the Turret Room. Their eyes meet. Then he turns away and rides with Demelza into the night.

Seeing the mob withdraw, Tom Harry is all for blasting them in the back with his gun. Knowing this really would cause Ross to wreak havoc, George restrains him.

CUT TO:

86: INT. NAMPARA HOUSE, ROSS & DEMELZA'S BEDROOM – NIGHT 49

Demelza comes in and begins to gather her belongings together. Presently Ross appears. He stands in the doorway, hesitating to come further into the room. He watches her without registering what she's doing.

ROSS So she's with child. *(no reply)* George must be exultant. *(no reply)* To be in my family's home – in full possession of—

DEMELZA Everything you hold dear.

ROSS Not everything. But yes – many things I hold dear.

She turns to face him. A huge moment between them. Ross is clearly very shaken. It's all Demelza needs to know. Her expression is cold and without sympathy.

DEMELZA You'll get over it.

She goes out, taking her bag. Ross is nonplussed. He has no idea what's happening.

ROSS Demelza—?

CUT TO:

87: INT. TRENWITH HOUSE, LIBRARY – NIGHT 49

Geoffrey Charles lies asleep with his head on Elizabeth's lap. She strokes it tenderly. George is working at his desk.

GEORGE I trust you know we were never in any actual danger. Ross thought to scare us, but in the end he was forced to back down.

Elizabeth nods. She seems unconvinced. For some reason this riles George. And so, though he knows it's a stupid thing to do, he just can't resist punishing Elizabeth for her lack of faith in him:

GEORGE *(cont'd)* I've been thinking of Harrow. *(beat)* For Geoffrey Charles. *(beat)* He's still overly attached to his mama. We must toughen him up.

ELIZABETH You mean – send him away?

GEORGE To one of the best schools in the country.

ELIZABETH But he's so young – he will miss it here. And I—

GEORGE Will have *our* child to attend to. Geoffrey Charles has had you all to himself. Now he must learn to be a man.

George gets up and goes out. Elizabeth sits, frozen in horror. She's already beginning to question her choice of husband.

CUT TO:

88: INT. NAMPARA HOUSE, HALLWAY/PARLOUR – NIGHT 49

Rain is falling outside as Demelza stands by the open front door, looking out. She's dressed for travelling and has a travelling bag beside her. Ross comes out of the library and halts, amazed.

ROSS What are you doing?

DEMELZA I'm taking Jeremy – to my father's house – an' from there – who knows?

ROSS *(bewildered)* You're leaving me? But I came back for you. I chose to return.

DEMELZA 'Tis not my concern what you choose. Only what *I* choose. And why would I choose a man whose heart b'long to another?

ROSS Demelza – you are my wife—

DEMELZA Raised from the gutter to be a great lady? But I'll never be such a one – an' what do I care? For I'm fierce and proud and steadfast and true. An' I'll not settle for second best.

ROSS Why *would* you be?

DEMELZA Because you love Elizabeth! Because you will always love Elizabeth. Because you cannot conceal your pain that George now possesses her body an' soul! Do you deny it?

A massive moment between them. Suddenly Ross realizes he has yet to communicate to Demelza the realization which has been dawning on him for some time. He knows he must do it carefully. So he begins, knowing he's walking a minefield, that at any moment she could get the wrong end of the stick and simply walk away.

ROSS I do not deny that I loved her. Long before I set eyes on you, she was my – perfect – untouchable love – beside which no one else could compare. *(then)* When a man has wanted something for so long – has dreamed of it – but never possessed it – it seems to him as a Holy Grail – and he may spend his whole life yearning for it.

DEMELZA Whereas I – am dull – imperfect – ordinary—

ROSS Not ordinary! But yes – imperfect. Human! *Real!* And what that night with Elizabeth taught me— *(then)* God knows, had there been any other way for me to come to my senses— *(then)* But my arrogance – my idiocy – has been spectacular and I will not seek to justify it. *(then)* All I can say is that after that night – *because* of it – I came to see that if you bring an idealized love down to the level of an imperfect one, it isn't the imperfect one that suffers. *(then)* My true, real and abiding love – is not for her – but for you.

A huge moment between them. A massive dawning realization from Demelza that something has changed for Ross. That he truly has turned a corner. They look at each other a long time.

CUT TO:

89: INT. KILLEWARREN, PARLOUR – NIGHT 49

Caroline walks in – and almost gives Ray a heart attack!

RAY PENVENEN Caroline! Oh, my dear niece, to see you here – I'm all amazement!

She embraces him tenderly.

RAY PENVENEN *(cont'd)* But what of Lord Coniston? What will he think?

CAROLINE That he has lost me to a better man? I am come back to care for you, Uncle. Now tell me what Dr Enys prescribes?

RAY PENVENEN Here is his list of instructions.

Caroline takes it and reads it eagerly.

RAY PENVENEN *(cont'd)* I'm beginning to think I misjudged that young man. Of course you do not waste a moment's thought on him?

CAROLINE Not a single one, Uncle.

She embraces him tenderly, all the while smiling to herself as she looks at the ring Dwight has given her.

CUT TO:

90: INT. NAMPARA HOUSE, ROSS & DEMELZA'S BEDROOM – NIGHT 49

Demelza, wearing a nightgown, is standing in front of the fire. There is a knock at the door and Ross comes in. He seems diffident, unsure of his reception.

ROSS I have something for you.

He shows her a small box.

DEMELZA A bribe?

ROSS A token. Of my love. And devotion.

Ross gives her the gift. She unwraps it. It's the ruby choker they had to sell.

DEMELZA *(amazed)* My necklace? The one we sold? How did you find it again?

ROSS By searching. And refusing to give up.

Demelza considers a while. Then:

DEMELZA Will you still go to war?

ROSS Some day. Not now. I have something better to fight for.

Another moment of consideration. Then:

DEMELZA What did you think – when you saw Elizabeth tonight?

ROSS That she was a stranger to me. An enemy, even. *(then)* That part of my life is over. She will never come between us again.

CUT TO:

91: INT. TRENWITH HOUSE, LIBRARY – NIGHT 49

Elizabeth, tearful, sits stroking the hair of the sleeping Geoffrey Charles. Aunt Agatha comes in.

AUNT AGATHA What did you expect – when you made a pact with the devil?

ELIZABETH I hoped – still hope – that George may be more accommodating – once his child is born.

AUNT AGATHA He may. *(beat)* But are you willing to wait that long?

ELIZABETH March is not so far away.

AUNT AGATHA Unless it comes sooner.

ELIZABETH *(confused)* What?

AUNT AGATHA The child?

ELIZABETH Why should it?

Aunt Agatha raises an eyebrow. Suddenly the penny drops for Elizabeth. Her eyes widen in horror. There are no words to describe the enormity of this realization. Or its implications.

CUT TO:

92: EXT. HENDRAWNA BEACH – DAWN 50

Demelza stands looking out to sea as the day breaks. Presently Ross comes and stands beside her. Their reconciliation – though tentatively begun – is far from complete – and Ross is almost afraid to move in case the spell is broken. Then she turns to him. He moves closer. She doesn't recoil. He kisses her tentatively. She closes her eyes and allows herself to feel the first stirrings of warmth and happiness again. We pull back and up, soaring above until Ross and Demelza are two tiny figures in a vast expanse of beach, watching the sun rise on a new day.